Fay Weldon

was born in England and raised in New Zealand. She took degrees in Economics and Psychology at the University of St Andrews in Scotland and after a decade of odd jobs and hard times began writing fiction. She is now well known as novelist, screenwriter and cultural journalist. Her novels include *The Life and Loves of a She-Devil*, *Puffball*, *The Cloning of Joanna May*, *Affliction*, *Worst Fears*, *Big Women* and *The Bulgari Connection*. She has several collections of short stories to her name: her latest being *A Hard Time To Be a Father* and she has also written a collection of essays, *Godless in Eden*. Fay Weldon lives in London.

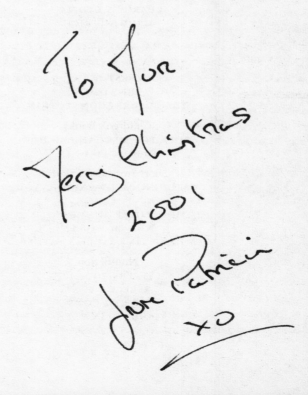

FAY WELDON

Rhode Island Blues

Flamingo

An Imprint of HarperCollins*Publishers*

Flamingo
An Imprint of HarperCollins*Publishers*
77–85 Fulham Palace Road,
Hammersmith, London W6 8JB

Flamingo® is a registered trademark of
HarperCollins*Publishers* Ltd

www.fireandwater.com

Published by Flamingo 2001
9 8 7 6 5 4 3 2 1

First published in Great Britain by
Flamingo 2000

This novel is entirely a work of fiction.
The names, characters and incidents portrayed in it are
the work of the author's imagination. Any resemblance
to actual persons, living or dead, events or localities is
entirely coincidental.

Author photograph © Nigel Sutton

ISBN 0 00 655162 9

Set in Sabon

Printed and bound in Great Britain by
Clays Ltd, St Ives plc

1

'I'm old enough to speak the truth,' said my grandmother, her voice bouncing over the Atlantic waves, ridiculously girlish. 'Nothing stops me now, Sophia, not prudence, or kindness, or fear of the consequences. I am eighty-five. What I think I say. It is my privilege. If people don't like what they hear they can always dismiss it as dementia.'

My grandmother Felicity had seldom refrained from speaking the truth out of compassion for others, but I was too tired and guilty to argue, let alone murmur that actually she was only eighty-three, not eighty-five. Felicity spoke from her white clapboard house on a hillside outside Norwich, Connecticut, with its under-floor music system and giant well-stocked fridge, full of uneatable doughy products in bright ugly bags, Lite this and Lite that, and I listened to her reproaches in a cramped brick apartment in London's Soho. Her voice echoed through an expensive, languid, graceful, lonely, spacious, carpetless house: she kept the doors unlocked and the windows undraped, squares of dark looking out into even blacker night, where for all anyone knew axe murderers lurked. My voice in reply lacked echo: here in central London the rooms were small and cluttered and the windows were barred, and thick drapes kept out the worst of the late-night surge of noise as the gay pubs below emptied out and the gay clubs began to fill. I felt safer here than I ever did when visiting Felicity on her grassy hillside. A prostitute worked on the storey below mine, sopping up any sexual fury which might feel inclined to stray up

1

the stairs, and a graphic designer worked above me, all fastidious control and expertise, which I liked to think seeped downwards to me.

Mine was a fashionable, expensive and desirable address for London. I could walk to work, which I valued, though it meant pushing my way through crowds both celebratory and perverse: the tight butts of the sexually motivated and the spreading butts of gawking tourists an equal nonsense. Was there no way of averaging them out, turning them all into everyday non-loitering citizens? But then you might as well be living in a suburb, and for my kind of person that meant the end.

I was tired because I had just got back from work, and it was late at night. I was guilty because it was two weeks since my grandmother's noisy friend and neighbour Joy – neighbour in the sense that their two great lonely houses were just about within hailing distance – had called me to shout down the line that Felicity, who lived alone, had had a stroke and was in hospital in Hartford. I had a deadline to meet. I am a film editor. There comes a certain point in a film production when the editor ceases to be dispensable: when you just can't afford to be ill, go insane, have a sick grandmother. Joy's call came at just such a moment. You have to be there in the editing suite and that's that. There are things in your head which are in nobody else's. *Tomorrow* was a feature film, a US/UK co-production with pretensions, a big budget, a big-time director (Harry Krassner), and a host of marketing people now hovering and arranging PR and previews, while I still struggled under pressure of time to make something erotic out of not-enough footage of teenage copulation which neither party had seemed to go to with much pleasure. I did not fly to my grandmother's side. I simply forgot her until I could afford to remember her. Now here she was again, her suppertime my bedtime, not that she ever acknowledged a difference in time zones if she could help it.

I gritted my teeth. Sometimes the ghost of my mad mother stands between myself and Felicity, damming up the flow of family feeling; a sepulchral figure, like one of those school-crossing ladies

2

who step out unexpectedly into the road to let the children through, making the traffic squeal to an unwilling halt.

I had a recurring dream when I was small in which my mother did exactly that, only the sign in her hand read not '*Children crossing*' but '*Your fault, Felicity*'. Except I knew that if she ever turned the sign, the other side would have my name on it. It would read, '*You're to blame, Sophia*'. I always managed to wake myself up before I had to face the terror of the other side. I could do that as a child – control my dreams. I think that's why I'm reckoned to be a good film editor: what is this job of mine but the controlling of other people's fantasies? I take sleeping pills, most nights: they stop my own dreams. I have enough of them by day to keep anyone sane.

As it happened Felicity had been let out of hospital within the day, having suffered nothing more than a slight speech impediment, which had by now cleared. But I wasn't to know that at the time.

'Sophia,' she was saying, 'I want to sell this house. The truth is I'm bored to hell. I keep waiting for something to happen but happenings seem to have run out. Is it my age?' Well, come the eighth decade I daresay 'happenings', by which most women mean love striking out of a clear sky, would indeed run out. Everything must come to an end. She said she was thinking of moving into assisted housing: some kind of old-persons' community. I said I was not sure this was a recipe for a lively life. She said just because people were old didn't mean they weren't still alive. She was going to hold her nose and jump: the house was already on the market, she was already selling bits and pieces in the local flea markets, there were some family things I might want to have, and if so I had better come over and claim them.

I felt the tug of duty and the goad of guilt and the weight of my ambivalence: all the emotions, in fact, commonly associated with dealing with family. She being my only relative, I felt the burden more acutely. I loved her. I just wanted her far away and somewhere else. And if I were to read my own behaviour finely, it was worse than this.

*   *   *

As I'd callously worked on after Joy's first phone call, resisting the notion that in the face of death all things to do with life should pause, I knew that if Felicity would only just die the issue of fault would be set to rest, forever unresolved. I could just be me, sprung out of nowhere, product of my generation, with the past irrelevant, family history forgotten, left to freely enjoy the numerous satisfactions of here and now, part of the New London Ciabatta Culture, as the great Harry Krassner was accustomed to describing it.

Myself, Sophia King, film editor, living day-by-day in some windowless room with bad air conditioning and the soothing hum of computerized technology, but free of the past. Easier by far to make sense of Harry Krassner's uneven footage than of real life, to let images on film provide beginnings, middles, ends and morals. Real life is all subtext, never with a decent explanation, no day of judgement to make things clear, God nothing more than a long-departed editor, too idle to make sense of the reels. Off to his grandmother's funeral mid-plot, no doubt.

Go into therapy, peel off the onion layers, turn the dreams into narrative, still the irritating haphazardness of everyday real life remains. Film seems more honest to me: actuality filtered through a camera. Felicity must not be allowed to interfere with my life, in death any more than she had in life. Bored she might be, but she had her comforts, money from dead husbands, a Utrillo on her wall, a neighbour called Joy, who shouted energetically down the telephone. I remembered how, when I was ten years old and Felicity was my only source of good cheer, she had cut herself off from me, left her daughter Angel, my mother, to die without her, fled back home to the States and not even come back for the funeral. I had forgotten how angry I was with her: how little I was prepared to forgive her. What had been her own emergency, her own internal editing, so desperately required that she abandoned us? Once, when I was small, ordinary simple family love had flowed from me to Felicity only to be fed back by her, through this act, as unspoken condemnation.

My mother had done even worse by the pair of us, of course, and returned love with hate, as insane people will to their nearest and dearest, be they parent or child, and there can be nothing worse in the world. But at least my mother Angel had the excuse of being mad. Felicity was reckoned sane.

'You didn't come over and visit me in hospital when for all you knew I might have been dying,' said Felicity now, at my sleeping time, suppertime for her. What did she care about my convenience? What was the point of reminding her of the past?
'You were only in hospital for a night,' I protested.
'It might have been my last night,' she said. 'I was fairly frightened, I can tell you.'

Oh, brutal! And I was so tired. I had only just returned from the cutting room when the phone call came. Harry Krassner would be in at ten the next morning, with the producer, for what I hoped against hope would be an acceptance of the fine cut. I was not sure which seemed the more fictional – Felicity's phone call or the hours I'd just lived through. My eyes were tired and itching. All I wanted to do was sleep. This voice out of the past: still with the actressy lilt, just a little croakier than last time she'd phoned, a few months back, might have been coming out of some late-night film on TV for all it was impinging upon my consciousness. Yet she and I were each other's only relative. My mother's death was decades back. We both had new skins. I had to pay attention. 'You'd have been back home even before I'd got to the hospital,' I pointed out.
'You weren't to know that,' she remarked, acutely. 'But then you never thought family was very important.'
'That isn't true,' I snivelled. 'It's you who chose to live somewhere else. This is home.'
This was ridiculous: it was like the first time you go to visit a therapist: all they have to do is say something sympathetic and look at you kindly: whereupon self-pity overwhelms you and you weep and weep and weep, believe you must really be in a mess and sign up for two years. I put my weakness down to exhaustion: some feeling that I wasn't me at all, just one of the cast of some bad late-night TV film, providing the formulaic reaction.

'It was that or go under myself,' she said, snivelling a little herself. 'All I ever got from family was reproaches.' (A splendid case of projection, but Felicity, like so many of her generation, was a pre-Freudian. Hopeless to start wrangling, let alone say she'd started it.) She pulled herself together magnificently. 'It was a moment of weakness in me to want you to be present while I died. If someone is not there while you live why should you want them there when you die? Just because they share a quarter of your genetic make-up. It isn't rational. Do you have any views as to what death actually is?'

'No,' I said. If I had I wasn't going to tell Felicity and certainly not while I was so tearful and tired.

'You wouldn't,' said my grandmother Felicity. 'You have been permanently depressed since Angel died. You won't allow yourself a minute's free time in case you catch yourself contemplating the nature of the universe. I don't blame you, it's fairly rotten.' The stroke must have had some effect on Felicity for since my mother Angel's death she had scarcely mentioned her name in my presence. My deranged mother died when she was thirty-five: my father hung around to do a desultory job of bringing me up, before dying himself when I was eighteen, of lung cancer. He didn't smoke, either, or only marihuana.

'The fact is,' said Felicity, who had deserted my mother and me at the time of our worst tribulations, and I could not forget it, 'I'm not fit to live on my own any more. I spilt a pint of boiling milk over my arm yesterday and it's hurting like hell.'

'What did you want boiling milk for?' I asked. This is the trouble with being a film editor. It's the little motivations, the little events, you have to make sense of before you can approach the bigger issues.

There was a silence from the other end. I thought longingly of bed. I had not made it that morning; that is to say I had not even shaken out the duvet and replaced it with some thought for the future. It's like that towards the end of a film gig. Afterwards, you can clean and tidy and housewife to your heart's content, put in marble bathrooms with the vast wages you've had no time or inclination to spend: in the meantime home's just somewhere you lay your head on a sweaty pillow until it's time to get up and go to work again.

*   *   *

6

'I hope you're not taking after your mother,' said Felicity. 'Off at a tangent, all the time.' That was, I supposed, one way of describing the effects of paranoid schizophrenia, or manic depression or whatever she was said to have.

'Look,' I said, 'don't try to frighten me.' The great thing about being brought up around the deranged is that you know you're sane. 'And you haven't answered my question.'

'I was heating the milk to put in my coffee,' said Felicity. 'Eighty-six I may be, standards I still have.'

She was growing older by the minute, as if she was wishing away her life. I couldn't bear it. I kept forgetting how angry I was with her, how badly she had behaved, how reasonable my resentment of her. I loved her. Before my mother died, after my father had disappeared, I'd come home one day to find her darning my school socks. No-one else had ever done that for me, and I was hopeless at it, and there was no money to buy new. I'd been going round with holes in my heels, visible above my shoes. I still have a problem bothering about ladders in tights. I just can't care.

'Oh, Grandma,' I found myself wailing, 'I'm so glad you're okay. I'm so sorry I didn't come over.'

'I'm not okay,' she said. 'I told you. I have a nasty burn on my forearm. The skin is bright red, wrinkled and puckered. I know it is normally wrinkled and puckered, and you have no idea how little I like my body these days, but it's not normally bright red and oozing. You just wait 'til you're my age. And you will be. We just take turns at being young.'

'Can't you call Joy?' I asked.

'She's too deaf to hear the phone,' said Felicity. 'She's hopeless. It has to be faced. I'm too old to live alone. I may even be too old for community living. Don't worry' – for my heart had turned cold with fear and self-interest and my tears were already drying on my cheeks, and she seemed to know it – 'I'm not suggesting we two live together. Just because we're both on our own doesn't mean that we're not both better off like that. It's just that I need help with some decisions here.'

I refrained from saying that I did not live on my own, but surrounded by tides of human noise which rose and fell at predictable

7

times likes the surges of the sea; that I had good friends and an enviable career, and a social life between gigs; and it was the life I chose, much peopled by the visible and the invisible, the real and the fantastic, and extraordinarily busy. Felicity was sufficiently of her generation to see *on your own* as being without husband and children, which indeed, at thirty-two, I was. We know how to defend ourselves, we the survivors of the likes of Felicity and Angel, against the shocks and tribulations that accompany commitment to a man, or a child, or a cause.

'Can we talk about this tomorrow, please?' I said. 'Can't you call out a doctor to look at your arm?'

'He'd only think I was making a fuss,' she said, as if this went without saying, and I remembered that for all her years in America she was still English at heart. 'You really aren't being very helpful, Sophia.' She put the phone down. I called her back. There was no reply. She was sulking. I gave up, lay fully clothed on the bed and went to sleep, and in the morning thought that perhaps I had imagined the whole conversation. There was to be little time to think about it.

2

It was a hideous morning in the cutting room: Harry Krassner was there, of course – a large, hairy, noisy, charismatic man. Powerful men in film tend to fall into two types – the passionate endomorphs, who control you by rushing at you, physically or psychically, and charming and overwhelming you, and the blood-less ectomorphs, who do it by a mild sneer in your presence and a stab in the back as soon as you turn. Krassner was very much the former type. Clive the Producer, small and gay and treacher-ous, the latter.

As we tried to concentrate on the screen, and resolve our differ-ences, the room filled up with people in one state of crisis or another. The tabloids had discovered Leo Fox, our handsome young lead, was gay: Olivia, his fictional girlfriend, had declared mid-interview in one of the broadsheets that she was a lesbian. Harry was good enough to remark that in the circumstances I had done a good job with the sex scenes. I refrained from retorting that had he supplied me with twenty per cent more footage I could have made a better job of it still: Clive failed to refrain from remarking that perhaps the casting director and the PR people should be sacked: the dotty woman from wardrobe insisted on being present though obviously there was absolutely nothing she could do about anything at this stage. Harry's stubbly chin brushed against my bare shoulder rather frequently. The shoulder was not meant to be enticing: the air conditioning had broken down, naturally, and the temperature was way above normal. I was down to my camisole, and wore no bra. I don't have breasts of any great weight or size.

'You've got beautiful skin,' he said, at one juncture, while we were rewinding. I could feel the idiot lady from wardrobe bristle. Sexual harassment! But it wasn't like that. He had just noticed I had beautiful skin – I do: very pale, like Angel's – and remarked upon it: it was a statement of fact, not a come-on. I simply do not rate in the love lives of these people: they are married to women to die for, in the 99.9 percentile when it comes to brains, beauty and style, and for their lovers they have the most beautiful creatures in the world to choose from. That the girl- or boyfriends are very often pains in the butt, shaped by cosmetic surgery, drug-addicted or compulsive kleptomaniacs, or solipsistic to a degree, or could hardly string two words together or work the microwave – forget an editing deck – is neither here nor there. Hollywood lovers have legs long enough to wrap around the likes of Harry's neck: brains are the opposite of what is required, which is rough trade of any gender, though with the edges smoothed over, to serve as a trophy to success. The brave deserve the fair. I might have a good skin and Harry might notice it but I was still just part of the production team talent.

The trouble is that if you mix with people like this, share space with them and common purpose, the men you meet in the club or the pub or in the lending library just don't seem up to much. Even Clive, coming into a room, slight and gay and bad-tempered-looking as he is, and the boring end of the business, seems to suck all the vitality out of the space and take it for himself, leaving everyone else feeling and looking vapid.

If I went home alone from parties it was from lack of interest in any man present – there was a whole new race about of slender, shaven-headed, just-about-non-gay men in dark clothing, all laying tentative hands upon one's arm, with liquid, suggestive, cocaine-driven eyes – but who cared? They were as likely to be as interested in a free breakfast as in free sex: a dildo would be as provocative, and less given to complaint.

*   *   *

The day proceeded: there was no lunch break: at one stage Harry threw coffee across the room, complaining about its quality. Clive was in danger of rubbing Danish pastry into the sound deck, and I pointed it out to him, and from his expression got the feeling I would never be employed again by him – not that I cared, I hated the film by this stage, a load of pretentious rubbish, and anything he ever made would have the same loathsome quality, so why should I ever want any job he had to offer? Harry laughed when I said as much: I tossed my head and my hair (red and crinkly) fell out of its tough restraining ponytail and Harry said 'Wow!'; the scriptwriter banged upon the door and was refused entry, the wardrobe woman pointed out that she had spent $100,000 dollars unnecessarily, since I had abandoned the entire Versace sequence, and I asked her to leave, since obviously she had only been hanging around using up our valuable oxygen in order to make this stupid point – in a $30,000,000 film what was $100,000 dollars – and she slammed out.

The credits and titles people became hysterical and complained we had left them no time, which we hadn't: while we were mid-provisional-dub the composer – they always take things literally – who was rumoured to have OD'd turned up and wept at what he heard, so we wished openly he had been left to die.

The PR debacle was at least turned around: young Leo announced to the media mid-morning that he was bisexual – people are always reassured by classifications – and Olivia mid-afternoon that her lesbianism wasn't a permanent state: she'd just once been seduced by her English teacher at school, and everyone who watched the sex scenes would see for themselves just how much she truly, erotically, madly fancied Leo. A crisis about a double booking in the preview theatre was narrowly averted, and by midnight Clive admitted the fine cut was ninety-five per cent right and no-one would notice the missing five per cent except he himself, the only one with any taste, and declared the picture locked.

I emerged gasping into the fetid Soho air with Harry, who asked if I had a bed he could sleep upon. He did not want to face the glitter of his hotel. I thought this was a feeble reason but said okay. He trailed after me to my peculiar residence, climbed my many flights of stairs with a kind of dazed, dogged persistence, looked around my place, said, 'Very central,' demanded whisky which I refused him, put his head upon my unshaken pillow, pulled my matted duvet over him and fell sound asleep. The phone rang. It was Felicity. She said she had tripped and sprained her ankle and it would be her hip next. I said I would come over on the next available flight. I lay on the sofa and slept. I did not attempt to join Harry in the bed. There would be no end of trouble if I did. Women should not venture out of their league or their hearts get broken. And I was just production team talent who happened to have a bed which the director didn't need a taxi to get to. And Clive was too mean to provide a limo.

3

Not far from Mystic, not far from Wakefield, well protected from any traffic noise by woods and hills, just out of Connecticut and into Rhode Island, stood the Golden Bowl Complex for Creative Retirement. Rhode Island is a small dotted oblong on a map, one of the six states that compose New England, the smallest, prettiest, most crowded and (they say) most corrupt state of them all, though who's to judge a thing like that? It is the indigenous home of a breed of russet feathered hens, the Rhode Island Red, now much appreciated by fanciers the world over. It is crowded in upon, squashed, by Connecticut, Massachusetts and the Atlantic Ocean; it is lush with foliage: birches, poplars and ginkos that turn gold in autumn, and mountain maples and ash, and hickories that turn orange, and red oak and red maple, sassafras and dogwood that turn scarlet. It is sprinkled with wild flowers in spring: ornithological rarities and their watchers spend their summers here. It has sheltered beaches and rocky coves, faded grandeurs, and a brooding, violent history of which an agreeable present makes light. It is the home of the brave, *the better dead than red state*. In November, of course, it is much like anywhere else, dripping and damp and anonymous. Better to turn the attention inward, not out. So thought Nurse Dawn, executive nursing officer of the Golden Bowl Complex.

The Golden Bowl is constructed much in the fashion of the former Getty Museum outside Los Angeles; that is to say it is an inspired version of a Roman villa, pillared and pooled, lilied and creepered, long and low, and faced with a brilliant white stone which in California looks just fine but under soft Rhode Island skies can startle. The young and unkind might say it glared rather than glowed: the elderly however valued its brightness, and marvelled at the splendour in which they could finish their days, and for this reason the local heritage groups had bitten back protest and allowed its existence.

Even as Sophia travelled to Boston on her sadly delayed visit to her grandmother, Nurse Dawn, together with Dr Joseph Grepalli, specialist in the medical arts and Director of the Golden Bowl, contemplated a bed rendered empty by the sudden death of its previous occupant, Dr Geoffrey Rosebloom. The windows were open, for the decorators were already at work; new white paint was being applied throughout the suite – Dr Rosebloom had been a secret smoker, and the ceilings were uncomfortably yellowed – and an agreeable classic pink-striped wallpaper pasted up over the former mauve and cream flowers. So long as wallpapers are pale they can be put up fresh layer upon old layer, without ever having to strip off the original. The difficulty with strong colours is that if there's any damp around they tend to seep through to discolour the new. Only after about six layers will the surface begin to bubble and the wall have to be stripped down to its plaster, but that will happen on average only every five years or so. The pink and white was only the second layer since the Golden Bowl had been opened twenty-two years back. The occupant before Dr Rosebloom had been one hundred and two years old, in good health and spirits to the end, and had also died suddenly in the same bed. The mattress had been in good condition and management had not considered it necessary to replace it at the time.

'Two sudden deaths in the same bed,' said Dr Grepalli, 'is too much.' He was a genial and generous man. 'This time round the mattress at least must be replaced.'
'You can hardly blame the bed for the deaths,' said Nurse Dawn, who pretended to be genial and generous but was not. 'Dr Rosebloom smoked – look at the state of the ceiling: if he'd had more self-control we wouldn't be having to repaint – I daresay some respiratory trouble or other triggered the infarction.'

'Ah, Nurse Dawn,' said Dr Grepalli, affectionately, 'you would like everyone to live for ever in perfect health, behaving properly.' 'So I would,' she said. 'Why would God let some of us live longer than others, if he didn't want us to learn more in the extra time?' In her book self-improvement must be continuous, and no respite offered even to the elderly.

The Golden Bowl housed some sixty guests, known to themselves and others as Golden Bowlers. All had had to be over seventy-five at the time they joined the community, and still capable of congregate living. If you were, this augured well for your longevity. The weak had been carried off by now; only the vital and strong remained. The average age of death among Golden Bowlers was a ripe ninety-six, thanks to the particular nature and character of the guests as selected by Nurse Dawn. She had no actuarial training: she worked by instinct. One look was enough. This one would last. *Welcome.* That one wouldn't. *We are so sorry, we have no spaces.*

Death was far from an everyday occurrence at the Golden Bowl, albeit one that was inevitable. Guests moved, within the same building complex, from Congregate Living (when you just didn't want to be alone) to Assisted Living (when you needed help with your stockings) to Continuing Care (when you needed help with your eating) to Nursing Care (when you took to your bed) to, if you were unlucky, Intensive Care (when you wanted to die but they didn't let you). Families were encouraged to hand over complete responsibility. Over-loving relatives could be more damaging to an old person's morale, more detrimental to the Longevity Index, than those who were neglectful. One of Dr Grepalli's most successful lectures was on this particular subject. Just as a teacher tends to dislike parents, and hold them responsible for the plight of the children, so did Dr Grepalli mistrust relatives and their motives. The doctor was a leading light in the field of senior care administration, appeared on TV from time to time, and wrote articles in *The Senior Citizen Monthly* which would be syndicated worldwide. Golden Bowlers admired him greatly, and were proud of him. Or so Nurse Dawn assured him.

*   *   *

The longest stay of any Golden Bowler had been twenty-two years: the shortest five days, but that latter was a statistical anomaly, and therefore not used in any averaging out. In its twenty-two years of existence only eight patients had ever moved out before, as it were, moving on. The degree of life satisfaction at the Golden Bowl was high, just inevitably short, though a great deal less short than in similar institutions charging similar prices. Not that there were many around like the Golden Bowl, where you could stay in one place through the increasing stages of your decrepitude. It was customary for the elderly to be wrenched out of familiar places and be moved on to more 'suitable' establishments, as the degree of their physical or mental incompetence lurched from one stage to the next, and in the move lost friends, and often possessions, as space itself closed in around them. At the Golden Bowl, whatever your condition, you watched the seasons change in familiar trees and skies, and made your peace with your maker in your own time.

Joseph Grepalli and Nurse Dawn shivered a little in the chilly morning air that dispersed the smell of paint, but were satisfied in their souls. Dr Rosebloom had died suddenly in his sleep at the age of ninety-seven, not a centenarian, but every year over ninety-seven helped ease the average up. He had not done badly, even though he smoked.

The mattress and armchair of the deceased – being perfectly clean – were to be taken to be sold at the used furniture depository: it was remarkable, as Joseph Grepalli remarked, how though a bed could escape the personality of the one who slept in it, an armchair seemed to soak up personality and when its user died, became limp and dismal.

'Such a romantic,' said Nurse Dawn. 'I do so love that about you, Joseph.' The armchair looked perfectly good to her: it was in her interests to keep spending to a minimum but Joseph had to be kept happy, strong in the knowledge of his own sensitivity and goodness. New furniture, she agreed, would be bought at a discount store that very day.

*　　*　　*

The Golden Bowl had at its practised fingertips the art of providing Instant Renewal of mind and artifacts to maximize peace of mind and profits too. To this end policy was that no single room, suite, or full apartment should be allowed to stay empty for longer than three days at most. But no sooner, either: it took three days, and even Nurse Dawn agreed on this point, for the spirit of the departed to stop hanging around, keeping the air shivery, bringing bad judgement and bad luck. The waiting list was long; it might take guests a month or so to wind up their affairs and move in, but they would pay from the moment their accommodation fell available, ready and waiting. That way the aura of death, the sense of absence caused by death, would be less likely to endure. As with psychoanalysis, the fact of payment had a healing, restoring function. It reduced the ineffable to the everyday.

The bathroom cabinets had to be replaced; as well: Joseph had a superstition about mirrors: supposing the new occupant looked in the mirror and saw the former occupant looking out? Mirrors could be like that, maintained Joseph Grepalli. They retained memory; they had their own point of view. Aged faces tended to look alike in the end: one tough grey whisker much like another, but their owners did not necessarily see it like this. Joseph allowed himself to be fanciful: he himself was a Doctor of Literature; his father Dr Homer Grepalli, the noted geriatric physician and psychoanalyst, had bequeathed him the place and he had made himself an expert. Nurse Dawn was qualified in geriatric psychiatry, which was all that the authorities required.

'We have twenty-five people on the waiting list,' said Nurse Dawn, 'but none of them truly satisfactory. Drop-down-deaders: overweight or sociopathic: there is a Pulitzer winner, which is always good for business, but she's a smoker.'

Nurse Dawn slipped between Joseph's covers of a night: she was a sturdy, strong-jawed woman of forty-two, with a big bosom and a dull-skinned face and small dark bright button eyes. She looked better with clothes off than on. She clip-clopped down the corridors by day on sensible heels, her broad beam closely encased in blue or white linen, exhorting Golden Bowlers to further and deeper self-knowledge.

'I trust your judgement, Nurse Dawn,' said Dr Grepalli. For some reason he felt uneasy, as if standing in front of the lobster tank at a fish restaurant, choosing the one to die for his delight.

'In fact the whole lot of them sound troublesome and unprincipled. Not one's as easy as they used to be. Even the old have developed an overweening sense of their own importance. They've caught it from the young.' By troublesome she meant picky about their food, or given to criticism of the staff, or arguing about medication, or averse to group therapy, or lacking in get-up-and-go, or worse, having too many relatives who'd died young. All prospective Golden Bowlers had to provide, as well as good credit references and a CV, a family history and personality profile built on a questionnaire devised by Nurse Dawn herself.

Joseph Grepalli was a bearish, amiable, charismatic man, not unlike, as Sophia King was later to discover, Director Krassner. Inside the first Nurse Dawn was the second, a truly skinny woman not even trying to get out, preferring a cup of sweet coffee and a Danish any day.

'We must spread the net,' said Joseph Grepalli. 'We must trawl deeper.' The guests called him Stéphane, after Stéphane Grappelli: those who feel helpless always nickname those in charge: even the mildest of mockery helps.

4

I arrived at Felicity's house, Passmore, 1006 Divine Road, just past midnight. The United Airlines Heathrow–Boston flight left at 12.15 – I was on standby so had the *will-I-fly, won't-I-fly?* insecurity to endure for more than an hour. I never like that. I am not phobic about flying. I just prefer to know where I'm going to be in the near future. I'd left the Great Director still asleep in my bed, and a note saying I'd gone to look after my sick grandmother, and I'd be back after the weekend. They didn't need me for the dub. Any old editor would do now the picture was locked and no-one could interfere with what was important. I'd have enough eventual control of the music to keep me happy when I got back. I know a good tune but nothing about music proper and am prepared (just about) to let those more knowledgeable than me have the first if not the last say on a film to which I am to give my imprimatur.

I was upgraded to Business Class, which was fine. The travel agent had passed on the info that I was involved with the new Krassner film *Tomorrow Forever* (ridiculous title: it had started out as a sultry novel called *Forbidden Tide*, stayed as a simple *Tomorrow* for almost a year of pre-production, which was okay, since it was a kind of time travel film backwards and forwards through Leo and Olivia's relationship: the *Forever* had crept in towards the end of filming and suited the posters, so it had stayed) and showbiz gets all privileges going. Do you see how difficult it is to get these fictional exercises out of my mind? Now I'm giving you the plot of *Tomorrow Forever*, which I have stopped myself doing so far.

It was an easy flight: I can never sleep on aircraft, and so watched a video or so on the little personal TV provided with every expensive seat. I miss the general screen now available only at the cheap back of the plane, where you share your viewing pleasure with others, but I would, wouldn't I? Films are meant to be watched with other people: compared to the big screen videos are poor pathetic things, solitary vice.

Boston is one of the easiest airports through which to enter the US as an alien. Immigration's fast. I took a short internal flight to Hartford, the Yankee city, these days national home of the insurance business. So far so good. But at Hartford, alas, I was met by Felicity's friend and neighbour Joy, determined to drive me the fifteen miles to Passmore, at 1006 Divine Road. Joy lived in Windspit, number 1004. If flying doesn't make me nervous, other people's driving does, especially when the driver is both near-sighted and deaf, and shouts very loud as if to make sure the world is very sure of her, even though she is not very sure of it.

'I'm seventy-nine, you wouldn't think it, would you,' Joy shrieked at me, summoning a porter to take my bag to her Volvo. Her face was gaunt and white, her hair was wild, blonde and curly, her mouth opened wide in a gummy smile. She was dressed more like a Florida golfing wife, in emerald green velvet jump suit, than the decorous widow my grandmother had described. She was wonderfully good-hearted, or believed she was, just noisy. The Volvo was dented here and there and the wing mirror hung at an angle.

'Not for a moment,' I said. I did not want to worry or upset her. There was no way of getting to my destination without her help. The wooded roads were gathering dusk. Joy would put her foot on the brake instead of the accelerator, or vice versa, or both together, and when the Volvo stopped with a shudder she'd decide she had run over some dumb creature and we'd stop and get out and search for the victim with a torch she kept handy for the purpose. She did not pull the car over to the side of the road before doing so, either. Luckily at this time of night the back roads were more or less deserted. No Indian tracker she: she made so much noise any wounded animal with the strength to flee would have left long ago.

'I'm not like you English, I don't beat about the bush. I'm an upfront kind of person,' she shouted as we climbed back into the car after vain pursuit of a non-existent limping skunk. 'I can't be left to be responsible for your grandmother any more. It isn't fair on me. She must go into a congregate community, with others her own age.' I agreed that she should, though the term was unfamiliar to me.

'It would be okay if Felicity would do as she's told, but she won't,' roared Joy later, by way of explanation. I agreed that it was difficult to get Felicity to do as she was told.

'Now that that bullying bastard of a husband has died and left her in peace poor Felicity deserves something for herself.'

I had met Exon (like the oil disaster, minus the extra 'x') and he had never struck me as a bullying bastard, just a rather dull nice pompous man, a Professor of Law at the University of Connecticut, who had died four years back, and who had had a lot to put up with from Felicity. I said as much to Joy. It was unwise. She slammed her feet down on both brake and accelerator together and when the bump and stop came – Volvos can do a lot but cannot mind read – insisted on turning off the headlights to save the battery and going right into the forest with her torch, clambering up banks and down gullies in search of a deer she was convinced she had winged. This time I refused to go with her. I had remembered Lyme's disease, the nasty lingering flu-like illness which you could catch from the deer tick, a creature the size of a pin's head which jumps around in these particular woods. They leap on to human flesh, dig themselves in and bite. All is well if you bother to do a body search and your eyesight is good and you pluck them off with tweezers within twenty-four hours: but overlook just one and they bed in and you can be off work for months. I was safer in the Volvo with the doors and windows closed. I did not know how high the ticks could jump. The next thing would be – if this were a comedy film – Joy would break her ankle, and the volume of her distress would be awesome. Even as I thought these uncharitable thoughts there was a rumble and a rising roar and an eighteen-wheel truck swerved past us, the breath of its passing shadowing the windows, missing me and the Volvo by inches. It went blazing and blaring off into the dark. I simply blanked my mind, as I do during the commercials on TV, waiting for real life to start again. I was in shock.

'These truck drivers should be prosecuted,' she yelled when she got back into the driving seat seconds later. 'They should remember there might be cars parked out here, with their lights off to save the batteries.'

'Of course they should,' I said. 'Though we weren't exactly parked.' Her veined hands tightened on the wheel.

'I can see you have a lot of Felicity in you,' she said. She'd quieted considerably. 'You English can be so sarcastic. This car could have been a write-off and you're so cool about it.'

I refrained from comment. We drove the rest of the way in silence. She seemed chastened. There were no more animal stops and she peered ahead into the dappled dark and tried to pay attention. There was something very sweet about her.

One way and another, what with travel, terror, amazement, and the effort of not saying what I thought, by the time I got to Felicity's I was exhausted. Felicity had waited up, playing Sibelius very loud, the privilege of those who live a fair distance from their neighbours. Lights were low and seductive, the furniture minimalist. She reclined on a sofa, wrapped in a Chinese silk gown of exquisite beauty, which fell aside to show her long graceful legs. Not a sign of a varicose vein, but she was, I noticed, wearing opaque tights, where once she would have been proud to show the smooth whiteness of bare unblemished skin. The central heating was turned up so high she could not have been feeling the cold. She looked frailer than when I last saw her, which disconcerted me. She had always been light and thin and pale, and fine-featured, but now she looked as if someone should slap a red fragile sticker on her. Her hair, so like mine in colour and texture, had faded and thinned, but there was still enough of it to make a show. Her eyes were bright enough, and her mind sharp as ever. She looked younger, in fact, than her friend Joy. She had one arm in a sling and a bandaged ankle, which she kept prominently on display, just in case I decided she could look after herself. I was family, and she was claiming me.

'How was Joy's driving?' Felicity was kind enough to ask me, having been the one to inflict her on me. 'I hope she wasn't too noisy.'

Crazed by weariness I replied by singing *A Tombstone Every Mile* at the top of my voice, a trucker's song about the notorious stretch of wooded road which had claimed more truckers' lives than any-where else in the entire US and had been the title song of a pale *Convoy* imitation I'd once worked on. I could see that if someone like Joy had been travelling the road by night for the last fifty years a myth of haunting might well arise. I tried to explain my thinking to Felicity but my head fell in sleep into my hot choles-terol-lowered, pasteurized, fat-free, sugar-free Milk and Choco Lite Drink.

Oddly enough, what most exhausted me was the recurring vision of Director Krassner's locks of unkempt hair creeping out between my duvet and my pillow back home. I was in flight, I could see that. Perhaps I had come not so much to rescue Felicity as to escape emotional entanglement. Felicity woke me up sufficiently to lead me to the spare room, where she took off my coat and my boots and stretched me out with a pillow under my head. She seemed to have become more maternal with the passing of the years. I felt I was at home. She could claim me if she wanted me.

The minute proper sleep was possible it eluded me. I wondered whether to call the cutting room in the morning and decided not. Just as social workers have to harden their hearts against empathy with their clients, and nurses must learn not to grieve when patients die, so film editors must steel themselves against too much involvement with their projects. A gig is a gig. You must forget and move on. But this was a big film. It was hard. The PR budget was about three-quarters again on top of the actual shooting budget: the studio had put a lot behind it. It would move into the group consciousness of nations. It would take up oceans of column inches. The editor, that is to say me, the one on whom the success or otherwise of the film depended – forget script, forget stars, everything depends upon the cut – would of course hardly get a mention. Writers complain of being overlooked, but their fate is as nothing compared to that of the editor. The sense of martyrdom is quite pleasant, though, and feeling sorry for yourself nurturing through the lonely nights.

The bed creaked. Like so much else it was wooden. Everything echoes in these new-old houses: the wood forever shifts and complains: the timber is twenty years old, not the two hundred it pretends to be. Raccoons and squirrels scamper in the lofts. Sexual activity between humans could not happen without everyone else in the house knowing. Giant freezers and massive washing machines, enviable to British minds, root the house in one place, where it seems determined to dance free in another. In the morning I looked out over a damp November landscape which seemed determined to keep nature at bay. The land had been cleared of native trees and laid down in grass; low stone walls separated well-maintained properties: there were no fences or hedges to provide privacy, as there would have been in England: distance alone was enough. Lots of space for everyone for those with nothing to hide and a good income. How could Felicity have lived alone here for four years? I asked her over breakfast the next morning – Waffles-Go-Liteley and sugar-free maple syrup and caffeine-rich coffee, thank God.

'I was trying to oblige time to pass slowly,' she said. 'Someone has to do it. Time is divided out amongst the human race: the more of them there are the less of it there is to go round.' I wondered what poor dead Exon would have made of this statement. Taken her to task and demanded a fuller explanation, probably. He had always been part charmed, part infuriated by what he called Felicity's Fancies. During the twelve-year course of her marriage to him, at least in my presence, the fancies had dwindled away to almost nothing. Now it seemed the wayward imaginative tendency was reasserting itself, bouncing back. This is what I had always objected to about marriage: the way partners whittle themselves down to the level of the other without even noticing.

It is all dumbing down and lowest common denominator stuff and not annoying the other. It has to be if you want to get on. And lying stretched out nightly alongside another human being, comforting though it may be, is as likely to drain the essential psyche as to top it up.

'It was very annoying of Exon to die on me,' she said. 'I was much fonder of him than I thought. I never loved him, of course. I never loved anyone I was married to. I tried but I couldn't.' And she looked so wretched as she said this that I forgot London, I forgot films, I forgot floppy-haired, sweaty, exhausted Director Krassner and everything but Felicity. I put my hand on hers, old and withered as it was compared to mine, and to my horror tears rolled out of her eyes. She was like me, offer me a word of sympathy and I am overwhelmed with self-pity.

'It's the painkillers,' she apologized. 'They make me tearful. Take no notice. I bullied you into coming. It was bad of me. The fall made me feel older than usual and in need of advice. But I'm okay. I can manage. You can go home now if you like. I won't object.'

'Oh, charming,' I thought, and said, 'But I don't know anything about life in these parts. I know nothing about gated living, or congregate living, or any of the things you have this side of the Atlantic. We just have dismal old people's homes. Why can't you just stay where you are in this house and have someone live in?'

'It would be worse than being married,' she said. 'There wouldn't be any sex to make up for being so overlooked.'

I said I supposed she'd just have to ask around and do whatever it was her friends did in similar situations. She looked scornful. I could see how she got up their noses. 'They're not friends,' she said. 'They're people I happen to know. I tried to stop Joy meeting you at the airport, but she will have her way. I worried every moment.'

She wanted me to go for a walk with her after breakfast but I declined. I did not trust the Lyme tick to keep to the woods. There didn't seem much to see, either. Just this long wide Divine Road with curiously spaced new-old houses every now and then at more than decent intervals. Here, Felicity said, lived interchangeable people of infinite respectability. She explained that the greater the separation, the bigger the lot, the more prestigious the life. Money in the US was spent keeping others at a distance, which was strange, since there was so much space, but she supposed the point was to avoid any sense of *huddling*, which the poor of Europe, in their flight to the Promised Land, had so wanted to escape. Strung out along these roads lived men who'd done well in the insurance business or in computers, and mostly taken early retirement, with wives who had part-time jobs in real estate, or in alternative health clinics, or did good works: and a slightly younger but no wilder lot from the university – but no-one of her *kind*. She hadn't lived with her own kind, said Miss Felicity (Exon had liked to call her this and it had stuck) for forty-five years. What had happened to Miss Felicity, I wondered, when she was in her late thirties? That would have been around the time of her second and most sensible American marriage, to a wealthy homosexual in Savannah. The end of that marriage had brought her the Utrillo – white period, Parisian scene with branch of tree: very pretty – which now hung in state in the bleak, high Passmore lounge which no-one used, to the right of the gracious hall with its curving staircase and unlocked front door. The second night of my stay – the first night I was too exhausted to care – I crept out after Felicity had gone to bed and locked it.

'It's a bit late to go looking for people of your own kind,' I said. 'Even if you'd recognize them when you came across them. Couldn't you just put up with being comfortable?' She said I always had been a wet blanket and I apologized, though I had never been accused of such a thing before. There was no shortage of money. Exon, who had died of a stroke, she told me, the day after handing in a naval history of Providence to his publishers, had left her well provided for. He had died very well insured, as people who live anywhere near Hartford tend to be. She could go anywhere, do anything. It seemed to me that she had stayed where she was, four months widowhood for every year of wifehood – a very high interest rate of thirty-three per cent as if paying back with her own boredom, day by day, the debt she owed sweet, tedious Exon. Now, recovering from whatever it was had to be recovered from, she was preparing for her next dash into the unknown: only at eighty-five, or -three, or however old she really was (she was always vague, but had now reached the point where vanity requires more years, not fewer) the dash must be cautious: the solid brick wall of expected death standing somewhere in the mist, not so far away. She was sensible enough to know it, and wanted my approval, as if paying off another debt, this one owed to the future. I was touched. It was almost enough to make me want children, descendants of my own, but not quite.

5

By the afternoon Miss Felicity's plunge into a new life had taken on a certain urgency: Vanessa, one of the part-time real estate wives, called on her mobile phone to say that she had a client she was sure would just adore the house, and who was prepared to take it, furniture and all, and had $900,000 to spend but would want to move in within the month. Miss Felicity, faced with the reality of a situation she had brought upon herself, and too proud to draw back, and moved by my advice (I had woken in the night with a mean and manic fear that now we were getting on so well she would change her mind and want to come and live in London, to be near me) had calmed down and decided she would like to stay in the neighbourhood, and, what was more, had settled in to the idea of 'congregate living'. She would start looking this very day.

Joy, summoned for coffee, and today dressed in yellow velour and with a pink ribbon in her hair, was alarmed at so much haste. Felicity might make more from her house if she hung on, she shrieked. Joy's brother-in-law might want to move back into the neighbourhood, and maybe would be interested in the property: these major life decisions should not be taken in a hurry. But Felicity, meantime, unheeding, was unwinding the bandage round her ankle.

'What are you doing?' demanded Joy.

'Rendering myself fit for congregate living,' said Felicity. 'I don't want to give the impression that I need to be assisted. Let's see what there is around Mystic.'

'Mystic!' screamed Joy, teeth bared. Every one of them a dream of the dentist's art, but you can never do anything about the gums. 'You can't possibly want to be anywhere near Mystic. Too many tourists.'

'I've always just loved the name,' said Felicity. Joy raised her plucked eyebrows to heaven. What few hairs she allowed to remain, the better to reinforce the pencilled line, were white and spiky and tough.

'I thought the whole point,' yelled Joy, 'was that you wanted assistance. Assisted care. Someone to help you take a shower in the mornings.'

'That is definitely going too far,' said Felicity and left the room, giving a little flirtatious kick backward with one of her heels, while Joy forgot to smile and ground her white teeth. 'There's nothing whatsoever the matter with that ankle,' yelled Joy. 'She just wanted you over here and she got her own way.'

The seaside town of Mystic (population 3,216) lies a little to the north of where the Quinebourg River splits and meets the Atlantic just before Connecticut turns into Rhode Island. In the summer the place is full of holiday-makers and gawpers: it is less fashionable and expensive than Cape Cod further up, or the tail of Long Island opposite, but it has some good houses, some good wild stretches of beach, and attracts admirers of the old 1860 wooden bridge, which still rises and falls to let the shipping traffic through. Or so the brochures said and so it proved to be. Joy insisted on coming with us on our tour of the area: so we went in her new and so far undented Mercedes – obtained for her by her brother-in-law Jack, a retired car dealer – and I was allowed to drive.

Old people do indeed seem to congregate around the town: the Mystic Office of Commerce handed out brochures a-plenty. I could understand the charm of the name, *Mystic*, tempting in the hope, so needed as life draws to its inevitable end, that there is more to it than meets the eye. A place close enough to nature to make sunsets and stormy weather a matter of reflection, in which to develop a sense of oneness with the universe, in which to lose, if only temporarily, the pressing consideration of the shortness of our existence here on earth. A more benign and tranquil version

29

of nature than in most other places in the US. No hurricanes, no earthquakes, no wild fluctuations of heat and cold to disturb old bones, only the Lyme tick which no-one took any notice of, in spite of the fact that the illness is serious enough to carry off the aged and delicate. Maybe Mystic's convenient distance from New York, not so near as to make popping in to see the old relative an everyday affair, not so far as to make a fortnightly visit too difficult, was the greater attraction. Or perhaps homes for the elderly were just these days a fine growth market: this is trading country, as a British admiral once observed, seeing the New England settlers trading with his fleet during the War of Independence. For whatever reason there were more residential homes for the aged up and down these ponds, these woods, these beaches, and these back roads, than I'd have thought possible.

When I asked what exactly we were looking for, Felicity said, 'Somewhere with good vibes', at which Joy snorted and said she thought cleanliness, efficiency, good food and a good deal was more to the point.

Good vibes! I thought Felicity would be lucky to find them anywhere in New England. Although a landscape may look stunningly pleasant and tranquil, the ferocious energies of its past – and few landscapes are innocent – are never quite over. The impulse to exterminate the enemy, to loot and plunder, to gain confidence with false smiles before stabbing in the back, is hard to overcome: if it's not with us in the present it seeps through from the past. And these are dangerous parts: the first coast of the New World to be colonized, three and a half hundred years back. Bad things have been able to happen here for a long, long time. A massacre here, death by hunger there; an early settlement vanished altogether over winter: no trace left at all when the ships come creeping up the coast with the spring. And who in the world to say what happened? We all await the great debriefing when everything will be made known, the Day of Judgement which will never come.

Later the plantation owners of the South made this coast their summering place: later still the mob leaders from Chicago: then the Mafia. Of course they did. Like calls to like. The strong colour of old wallpaper had ample time to show through to the new, and they liked it. The edginess of something about to happen, something just happened. Vacations can be so dull.

Good vibes! Maybe it was in Felicity's nature forever to be moving on, in search of a landscape innocent of earlier crimes. If so she would be better advised to go West than East, where there wasn't so much history. Joy was by nature a stayer in one place, Felicity a mover on. Felicity would always listen and learn and be enriched, Joy would shut her mind to new truths. Felicity was inquisitive and never averse to a little trouble and discomfiture, Joy never wanted to stir anything up. Therein lay the difference between them, though God knows both ended up in much the same condition in life, living in the same kind of clapboard house, in the same kind of widowhood, albeit Joy today in startling yellow velour, and Miss Felicity in a floating cream and green dress bought at great expense at Bergdorf Goodman, and an embroidered jacket of vaguely ethnic but tasteful origin, cut so as to hide any thickening of the waist or stooping of the shoulders. She held herself erect. From the back she could have been any age: except perhaps her ankles were too thin to belong to a truly youthful person.

We took the coast road out of Mystic to historic Stonington, the Rhode Island side of the river from Mystic, where there's a statue of a Pequot Indian with a large stone fish under each arm. Old people tottered around it, relatives holding dependent arms: a group whizzed about it in mechanized wheelchairs, never too old to be a danger to others. They came, in whatever state, to contemplate the past, since there was so little future to contemplate: they invaded the nearby souvenir shops by the busload, while old limbs still had the strength. We all want to think of our nation's past as wondrous and charming, as we would want to think of our own. But Joy declined to get out of the car.

'I'm no tourist,' she said. 'I live round here. As for those Red Indians, they take everything and give nothing back. If China invaded they wouldn't object to being defended, I can tell you that.'

Felicity slammed the door as she got out of the car. But Joy lowered the window.

'Scarcely a pureblooded Pequot left,' she shouted after us. 'They've all intermarried with the blacks anyway. Now they run their casinos tax-free on Reservation land. They rake in millions and are let off taxes, just because their ancestors had a hard time. Poor Mr Trump, they say he's having a real bad time in Atlantic City, because of Indians.'

'Hush!' begged Felicity.

'You're so English, Felicity! If the old can't speak the truth who can?' Calm, quiet people turned to stare at Joy. Her white-powdered, hollow-eyed face stared out of the darkness of the car, her chin resting on the ledge of the lowered window, which I thought was rather dangerous. Supposing it suddenly shot up? I couldn't think who she reminded me of and then I realized it was Boris Karloff in *The Mummy*. Some people, as they get older, simply lose their gender.

'I've nothing against them personally,' she shrieked. 'But if I was one of them I wouldn't want to be called a Native American. The way I was brought up, a native is a savage.' Felicity and I, realizing there was no other way of silencing her, simply gave up our exploration of the town and got back into the car. Joy smiled in triumph.

We saw a couple of what were called congregated communities, but they were built around golf courses. Those who lived there looked as if they had stepped straight out of the advertisements: the strong, well-polished, smiling elderly, their hair wet-combed if they still had any – and there were some amazing heads of hair, not necessarily natural, to be seen, in both sexes. The men wore bright polo shirts, the women shell suits. They made Felicity feel frail. By mistake we saw an assisted living home where the old sat together with their zimmer frames, backs to the wall, glaring at anyone who dared to come into their space. The sense of quiet depression was such I could have been back in my own country. The smell of cheap air freshener got into my lungs. Felicity looked shocked. Joy wouldn't step inside the room they showed us, so proudly.

* * *

'I'd rather die,' she shrieked. 'Why don't they just polish themselves off?' If the inhabitants heard they did not stir. Management did, and showed us hastily out, but not before giving us their list of charges.

I relented. Nothing we saw looked at all suitable for my grandmother's dash into the future. I told Felicity if she wanted to come back to London I'd do what I could for her: find her somewhere near me, even with me. I declared myself prepared to move house to live somewhere without stairs, into the one-floor living that seemed to be a requisite for anyone over sixty. I spoke coolly and my reluctance by-passed my brain and settled itself in my stomach in the form of a bad pain: appendix, maybe.
'She'll drive you crazy,' shouted Joy. 'You'll regret it.'
Felicity persisted that she did not want to return to London, even to be near me. (The pain at once subsided.) I was too busy, too taken up with my own life. She would just feel the lonelier because she'd never get to see me, and I would just feel the guiltier for the same reason. Besides, she was used to the US.

Life in England was too cramped, too divorced from its own history, the young had no interest in the old, the IRA left bombs around, the plumbing was dreadful and she was too old to make new friends. And we certainly could not live together. Joy was right, I would kill her, or she me. I did not argue. We went home in depressed silence.

'You just have to be patient,' said Joy, softer again. 'Don't sell to this stupid client of Vanessa's. Anyone who wants to move in within the month is bound to be a bad neighbour. You do owe a little consideration to the rest of us.'
She took the wheel of the car and bumped off in a way that never happened when I drove. It was scarcely more than a year old, and fitted with every possible kind of gadget to ensure a smooth ride. I don't know how she managed it.

When we got back to the serenity of Passmore we found that a brochure had been pushed through the letterbox. It was from an establishment called The Golden Bowl Complex for Creative

Retirement. Felicity examined it over toasted cinnamon bagels spread with Cream Cheese Favorite Lite. 'This Golden Bowl place,' said Felicity, 'doesn't sound too bad at all. They have a Nobel Prize winner in residence, and a Doctor of Philosophy. Fancy being able to have a conversation with someone other than Joy. And what synchronicity that it should arrive today!'

It would have been even more synchronicitous if it had arrived in the morning rather than the afternoon, so we could have visited it when in the area, but I held my tongue. The Golden Bowl charged at least double the fees of any other institution we'd seen, and they went up ten per cent each year. Which when you worked it out meant that in ten years' time you would be paying double. But by then Miss Felicity would be well into her nineties. It might not be so bad a deal. It was a gamble who would end up making money out of whom.

I hoped her liking for the place wasn't because it was the most expensive on offer. Reared in penury as she had been, Felicity now had an almost innocent faith in the power of money: she believed that the more you spent the better value you would get. She always bought the most expensive bottle of wine on the menu. She'd choose caviar not because she liked it but because of what it cost.

The Golden Bowl, according to its brochure, was an establishment run on therapeutic lines. Golden Bowlers (ouch! but never mind) were encouraged to live life to the full. Age need not be a barrier to the exploration of the self, or the exercise of the mind. Golden Bowlers were not offered the consolations of religious belief, which came with difficulty to the highly educated: but rather in some vague, Jungian notion of 'adjustment to the archetype' in which all staff were trained, and could bring joy and relief through the concluding years. Reading between the lines, those who ran the Golden Bowl held no truck with reincarnation; death was death, and that was that. What they were after was reconciliation with what had gone before since nothing much was to come. And they mentioned the word death, which nobody else had done.

*　　*　　*

34

It was persuasive, and Felicity and I were persuaded. I should have spoken out more firmly against a Residential Home for the Aged where the residents were known as Golden Bowlers. I should have realized that the connection with Ecclesiastes, which I assumed, was minimal. It wasn't mentioned in the brochure.

> *Remember now thy Creator in the days of thy youth,*
> *while the evil days come not,*
> *nor the years draw nigh,*
> *when thou shalt say,*
> *I have no pleasure in them;*
> *While the sun,*
> *or the light,*
> *or the moon,*
> *or the stars,*
> *be not darkened,*
> *nor the clouds return after the rain:*

How did it go after that? My mother Angel would teach me chunks of the Bible. It was her lasting gift to me, along with life itself, of course.

> *. . . and desire shall fail:*
> *because man goeth to his long home,*
> *and the mourners go about the streets:*
> *or ever the silver cord be loosed,*
> *or the golden bowl be broken at the fountain,*
> *. . . then shall the dust return to the earth as it was:*
> *and the spirit shall return unto God who gave it.*

Felicity would never acknowledge that the Golden Bowl, whatever that was meant to represent, was cracked. A day would never dawn when she took no pleasure at all in it. There was bound to be trouble. *'Vanity of vanities,' saith the preacher, 'all is vanity.'* But we were blithe: we put our trust in synchronicity.

The next morning Felicity consulted the *I Ching*, the Chinese Book of Oracles with the Foreword by Jung himself, to see what that had to say about the Golden Bowl. She had been in her fifties in the mid-sixties, when I was born, when the *I Ching* was all the rage.

*　　*　　*

She had just found her pencil and got round to throwing the coins when Joy appeared shouting in through the French windows, a vision in orange velvet with a crimson headband, determined that this day she would really make her mark upon the world. Felicity had the grace to hastily hide the coins under a sheet of paper. And then we all set off in high spirits to inspect the Golden Bowl, Felicity, Joy and me, in Joy's Mercedes. Once again I drove. It was fun, all of a sudden.

'This place is going to be just as terrible as the others,' Joy assured us, quite softly. She was wearing her hearing aid and it was a bright morning so no doubt the world was less misty than usual. 'But it's nice to be driven.' This morning she had a flask of vodka with her and lifted it to her lips from time to time as she sat in the back seat. I could see her in the mirror. She had apparently decided I was to be trusted.

'I didn't have time to read the coins,' Felicity confided in me on the way. 'But I threw *Duration* leading to *Biting Through*. Thirty-two leading to twenty-one: lots of changing lines, which means we're in a volatile situation.' I hadn't heard talk like this since I was a little girl, when my mother would scarcely buy groceries without consulting the *Chinese Book of Wisdom*.
'Oh yes,' I remarked. 'Is that good or bad?'
'*Duration*.' She quoted from memory. 'Success. No blame. Perseverance furthers. It furthers one to have somewhere to go.'
'Like the Golden Bowl?'
'I should think that's what it meant, wouldn't you?' I concentrated on the road. Over the hills I could catch a glimpse of the sea, a thin edge of blue melting into a hazy sky. It was a good day for November: there had been a sharp, hard wind during the night but it had dropped, and the sky was left watery bright. Maybe on just such a day the sails of the Viking longships had caught the sun as they approached the coast. On such a day perhaps the captain of an English privateer had stumbled on deck and said, 'Beautiful morning for November,' while wondering if he would live to see the evening. To wonder about death was more common-place once than it is now, and the present must have seemed the

more glorious. Inland the trees, heretofore muzzy with wet leaves, had become stark and bare and beautiful overnight.

'Poor Joy,' said Felicity loudly, to anyone who cared to hear. 'She has such a drink problem.' Joy had turned off her hearing aid.

6

Nurse Dawn looked out of the French windows of the Atlantic Suite which Dr Rosebloom had so recently and suddenly vacated, and averted her eyes. She did not like the woods, which were allowed to creep so near to the portals of the property. It was too gentle and crowded and coy a landscape for her. She felt circumscribed and somehow on hold, as if her life had not properly begun.

The sky seemed too small. It was too quiet. If you listened you could hear the tiresome swish of ocean as a background to birdsong. There was somewhere to go and everyone else knew where except her.

A group of guests passed in the corridor on the other side of the door, their voices drifting. They were chanting, which was gratifying, but not gratifying enough, on their way from an Ascension meeting in the Library, still brimming with cheerful animation, summoned up somehow from within their feeble beings.

> *'What do Golden Bowlers do?*
> *We live life to the full.'*

Self-hypnosis could do so much: in the end, whatever Dr Grepalli had to say on the subject, *joie de vivre* failed in the face of bad knees, and dimming eyes. Silence fell again. There seemed today some dulling barrier between Nurse Dawn and the enjoyment of life. Everything became a source of irritation. People raved about the wondrous colours of the trees in these parts after the first few sharp frosts of autumn, but to her the trees in their autumn dress looked garish, like colours from a child's painting set. And now in November there was no splendour in their absence of dress, their dank nakedness. She wanted to be back home to the wheat plains and a great expanse of sky, where the roads were straight and dusty and yellow, and dry, even at this time of year; and the sound of wind, not sea, was the background to everyday life; and twisters came like the sudden vengeance of God, reminding one of sin, and with sin, salvation. But it could not be. This was where the money was, where she had managed to carve her niche. There were as many old people back there as here, of course, and as much work to be done for them, but they were a grittier, suspicious lot. They would be embarrassed rather than charmed by Dr Grepalli's methods, and far less easy about parting with their money. They thought more about their relatives and what good their small savings could do when they were gone than about their own comfort and state of mind. And coming out of a rural community as they did, they tended to lose heart as they reached their gnarled and wrinkled end: what was the point of you if your back was bad or your legs wouldn't work. Here at the prosperous edges of the sea, oldsters seemed to keep going longer and in better shape. Certainly they'd acquired more money in their lifetimes, doing less.

Nurse Dawn had a profit-share in the Golden Bowl: she had persuaded Dr Grepalli that this was only just and fair. She hadn't exactly asked him to marry her and he hadn't exactly declined: she hadn't exactly threatened to inform the Golden Years Welfare Board (originally appointed by Dr Homer Grepalli, Joseph's father) that she and he enjoyed a sexual relationship, and he hadn't exactly asked her not to.

'Dawn,' he'd remarked once, as her head nuzzled beneath the bedclothes, 'I hope you're doing this because you want to, not because you think it will help you control me. You are something of a control-freak, as you must realize. Which suits me: and suits our guests; as we get older we feel relieved if there is someone around telling us what to do, even if we don't care to do it. But I do want you to be aware I'm not open to blackmail.'

'The Board wouldn't like it,' she had surfaced to say, shocked.
'The Board wouldn't mind in the least,' Dr Grepalli said. 'They're all free-love civil libertarians: pre-Aids thinkers, existentialists, older than we are – not a single one below sixty, and far less censorious than our generation. Nevertheless I can see the justice of giving you a twenty per cent share of my own annual profit-related bonus, since you do so much for my morale and the wellbeing of the guests, who all adore you. As I do.'

Dr Grepalli was too self-aware and ironically minded ever to do as he really wanted – or rather have done to him – which would be to be tied up by a ferocious woman in a nurse's uniform, who would insult him and walk all over him in high-heeled shoes, and brandish a whip, but Nurse Dawn seemed a heaven-sent compromise, and it suited him to pay her, and added an agreeable complexity to their relationship. It was part of the unspoken deal. Both knew it.

Nurse Dawn had worked the twenty per cent share out as a good $700 a week on top of her existing salary, and rising. Guests paid not a decreasing but an increasing sum – year by year – for their stay. This was only reasonable. They needed more care. More trays of food had to be fetched and carried, more medication provided and more eccentricities and forgetfulness coped with. Relatives and lawyers sometimes protested at the Golden Bowl's charging arrangements, seeing, annually, an exponential loss of expected family inheritance, but soon came to see the sense of it. The older anyone's relatives were, after all, the less likely was anyone to want to take them home again.

> *'The longer you Stay,*
> *The more you Pay,*
> *Lucky Golden Bowler!'*

The unspoken benefit, of course, was that guests were conscious that management had an incentive to keep them alive as long as possible. Let your room fall empty, as Dr Rosebloom had, and the newcomer entered at the lower rate. Golden Bowlers were encouraged to see the Golden Bowl as home, and their fellow guests as family: it was hoped that little by little they would loosen close ties with their birth families. It was easier for everyone that way, as it was seen to be for nuns and monks. And after eighty that was more or less what guests amounted to: sex being hardly a motivating force in their lives any longer, they could focus on their spirituality. Family and friends were of course allowed to visit, but were never quite welcomed. News from outside too often upset. Relatives would turn up merely to pass on bad news that the resident was helpless to do anything about. Someone had died, someone else gone to prison, been divorced, great-great-grandchildren were on Ritalin.

By and large, or so it was concluded at the Golden Bowl, the relatives you ended up with were a disappointment: not at all what one had dreamed of when young. They were usually a great deal plainer than one had hoped: the good genes were so easily diluted, while the bad ran riot. The bride's handsome husband turned out to be an anomaly in a family as plain as the back of a bus, and it was only apparent at the wedding. Took only one son to marry a dim girl with big teeth in a small jaw and you'd produce a whole race of descendants in need of orthodontics but not the wit or will to afford them. If the boy hadn't gone to that particular party on that particular night – and fallen for an ambitious girl with small teeth in a big jaw – how different the room full of descendants would look: how much greater the sum of their income. The old easily grew sulky, seeing how much of life was chance, how little due to intent. Unfair, unfair! It's the familiar cry of the small child, too; only between the extremes of age do we have the impression there's anything we can do about anything.

The decorators were packing up in Dr Rosebloom's suite. Nurse Dawn was pleased with the work they had done, but did not tell them so. Rather she chose to find flaws in a section of the pink striped wallpaper where the edges were admittedly slightly mismatched. The decorators were duly apologetic and agreed, after a short brisk discussion, to accept a lesser fee. Nurse Dawn also got a percentage of any savings she could make on the annual maintenance budget, in the management of which she had lately found serious shortcomings.

In Nurse Dawn's opinion praise should be used sparingly, since it only served to make those who received it complacent. Her children, had she had any, would have grown up to be neurotic high-achievers: come home proudly with news of a silver medal, and be scolded for not getting the gold. The decorators slunk away, disgraced. Nurse Dawn strolled around the suite, observing detail, trying to envisage its next occupant. That was how she made her choices: in much the same way as she chose numbers for the lottery, willing good fortune to come her way, envisaging the numbers as they shot up on the screen.

The bathroom had been pleasingly redone with marble veneer tiles that could have passed for the real thing, and gold stucco angels surrounded the new bathroom cabinet. Nurse Dawn's fallback position, she decided, would be the eighty-year-old female applicant, the Pulitzer Prize winner, who smoked. She would be given the suite on condition she gave up smoking. This she would promise to do: this she would fail to do: and Nurse Dawn would be at a psychological advantage from the outset. There wasn't actually much to be feared from lung cancer: if you were a smoker and it hadn't got you by eighty it was unlikely to do so at all: nor would other forms of cancer be likely to surface. Death would be by stroke or heart attack or simply the incompetence of being which afflicted the individual as the hundredth year approached. The Pulitzer winner was of the lean hard-bitten hard-drinking kind: they tended to last well. The Golden Bowl could, she supposed, do worse.

Nurse Dawn's attention was drawn to a Mercedes sweeping through the opening of the gold-and-metal appliqué gates, copies of the ones at the entrance to London's Hyde Park, put up in honour of the Queen Mother, aged a good ninety-eight at the time of their erecting. The Mercedes did not proceed to the front of the house where regular parking was obviously to be found, but drew up outside the French windows of the Rosebloom Suite, which everyone much got out of the habit of calling it, only a few feet from where Nurse Dawn stood, lamenting the view. Three women got out. A skinny young person in sweater and jeans, with Botticelli hair and a high forehead, and two women in their later years. One, in her mid-seventies, Nurse Dawn supposed, was hideously attired in an orange velvet tracksuit and crimson headband, and had a bulky waist – which did not augur well for a long life span – but the other one, dressed in strange and impractical gauze and gossamer floating drapes, looked slight but promising. Early eighties, passing at first glance for ten years younger. A one-time actress or dancer, maybe. Her movements were both energetic and graceful: her back was scarcely bowed – HRT from early middle age, Nurse Dawn surmised, always a plus – a graceful head poised on a long neck, tactfully scarved to hide the creases.

'Parking's round the front, in the space designated,' called Nurse Dawn, as the party disembarked, but they took no notice, though they had heard perfectly well.

'There's lots of room,' the young woman said. 'And we're here now.' She had an English accent. If the relatives were English and far away so much the better. 'Can we talk to whoever's in charge?'

'I'm in charge,' said Nurse Dawn, and seeing it was more or less true, felt much better. She might have reached her forties without husband, children, or home of her own, which was the fate of many, God alone knew, but at least she was accumulating money in her bank account, very fast indeed, and would not, as her mother had always promised her, end up with nothing.

She saw how Felicity lingered in the Rosebloom Suite, with its pretty pink and white paper, admired the view, laughed with pleasure at the absurdities of the bathroom cabinet, and heard her say, 'I could live in a place like this. It seems more *me* than that great creaky house ever did.'

She heard Joy reply, shocked, at the top of her voice, 'That's your home you're talking about, Miss Felicity.'

Nurse Dawn was pleased to understand it was the quiet one, not the noisy one, who was looking for a home. If she made so much noise now what would she be doing in ten years' time? The vocal cords were often the last to go. And Felicity's reply, 'I was never happy with my own taste. I don't think we need look further than here,' came almost as a relief.

The English girl said, 'Come on now, this is the first place we've seen. You can't make up your mind just like that.'

'I can,' said Felicity. 'And I have. What was I told this morning? *It furthers one to have somewhere to go?* This is the somewhere.'

Nurse Dawn led the party through to the front reception area, where they should have been in the first place, imbuing a proper sense of reverence, where busts of Roman Caesars stood on marble plinths, and said, 'You must understand we have a long waiting list, and all applicants must first be vetted, and then voted for. We're very much a family here.' This deflated the spirit of the group considerably, as Nurse Dawn had intended. She preferred supplicants to pickers and choosers.

Being a woman of quick decision she had already decided to accept Felicity for the Atlantic Suite, but it was wise to let her fret a little. She would be quite an asset: she moved and spoke gracefully, and was of good appearance, and though no kind of intellectual, unlike the Pulitzer Prize winner, would not annoy the other guests by smoking. Moreover, she quoted from the *I Ching* – 'it furthers one to have somewhere to go' could only come from this source – which meant Dr Grepalli would put up no objection. Jungians clung to one another in their absurdities.

7

You can run, but you can't hide. When we got back to Passmore there was a black limo waiting, with New York plates. I was needed back in the Soho editing suite, urgently. I was to take the nine p.m. Concorde flight out of Kennedy. *Tomorrow Forever* was, as I say, a big-budget film. The percentage cost of Concorde tickets for a deviant editor was minuscule, compared even to leaving the Versace sequences on the cutting room floor. I told the driver to wait while I thought about it, but Felicity asked him in and gave him coffee and cookies. Joy made a hasty exit: the driver was some kind of bearded mountain tribesman and made her nervous. He rose to his feet when she left the room, and bowed with exquisite courtesy, but that only made her the more nervous.

I could not work out at first how anyone knew where to find me. Air travel slows my mind. True, I'd told my friend Annie where I was going. But she wouldn't have told anyone: and the designer upstairs had my key to let out the cat but I'd just told him vaguely I was off to visit a sick relative: I then remembered that some of my conversation with Felicity had been through the answering machine. The bastard Krassner must have listened to what we said, and then put his people on to it. Film folk can do anything if they put their mind to it. They bribe phone operators and computer hackers and dig dirt on anyone they want. They are ruthless in defence of the people's entertainment and their own profit, which comes to the same thing. Perhaps Krassner had stayed in my apartment for some time after he woke – how many days ago was it now, four? I had not envisaged that until now: I had simply assumed that being at the best of times in such a hurry, he would have woken, perhaps found some coffee, to which he was welcome, and left at once, back to work. If he had time to spare he would surely have more glamorous and rewarding women than me to pursue and persecute. I felt the less inclined to return and fish the team out of whatever trouble they were now in. I called the editing suite but no-one replied. No doubt they were too busy to so much as pick up the phone for a call they had not initiated.

I had woken up a little. I liked the clear air and the woods and the deer ticks kept at a safe distance from the house, and Felicity was cheerful and Joy was funny and we'd spent a good morning at the Golden Bowl, and the world of downtown Soho seemed a long way away and not a place anyone would gladly return to, not even by way of Concorde and free gifts in best-quality leather which nobody ever wanted. Felicity had been enchanted by the Golden Bowl: we had been shown over its gracious Library, its sparkling clean kitchens, where only the best and freshest food was prepared, and not a sign of a Lite packet anywhere; its Refectory, where guests could sit and eat by themselves at little round one-person tables – though Nurse Dawn did not approve of this: the digestive processes apparently function better if eating is a social affair – its elegant community rooms, its nursing wing, empty of patients: we met Nurse Dawn's team of nurse-attendants, all bright, cheerful and friendly: we met the Professor of Philosophy, though his eyes were dull and all he wanted to talk about was the state of the golf course. We were told that Felicity could bring her own furniture in if she required though most Golden Bowlers chose to abandon the material trophies of the past, the better to live in the present. She should live very much as she lived at home. Various amiable and reasonably intelligent persons passed us in the corridors, of whom only a small percentage had walking frames, and one or two of the elderly gentlemen gave Felicity a second look. That really pleased her. In the country of the blind the one-eyed man is king, and in a nation-state such as the Golden Bowl Felicity would have more people at hand to admire her than she would if she kept the company of those younger than herself. We looked in at a Psychic Nourishment session in the Conservatory – the soul needs nourishment as much as does the body, according to Dr Joseph Grepalli, whom we were privileged to actually meet in his very grand offices. He had the rooms above the Portico: the only suite to which stairs were required. His wide windows looked out over the long rectangle of the lily pool. There were learned books in his bookcase.

'We are blessed by synchronicity, dear lady,' said Dr Grepalli to Felicity. 'Our brochure comes through your letter box the very day your granddaughter arrives from London: you make the decision to remake your life amongst others of like mind, and our new Atlantic Suite, now converted from one of the libraries to personal use, is ready for occupation. All these things are a good sign. As Nurse Dawn will have told you there is already a long list of people waiting to join our community, but if you would be good enough to fill in the questionnaire, we'll see what we can do, and we will let you know within the next couple of weeks.'

He was, even to me, an attractive man, broad-chinned, bright-eyed, on the jowly side. I like men a little fleshy, Kubricky. In fact, Dr Grepalli reminded me of the abominable Krassner. Thinking back, it seemed strange to me now that I had not joined the latter in my bed. My last sexual relationship had been over six months previously, and that had been fleeting. My grandmother Felicity was obviously impressed by Dr Grepalli. Her wrinkled eyelids drooped over her still large, clear eyes. She actually fluttered her lashes, and moistened her lips with her tongue and sat with her hands clasped behind her neck. She had not read as many books on body language as I had, or heard so many directors expound on it, or she would have desisted. She was in her mid-eighties, for God's sake, and forty years older than he.

To be seen from Dr Grepalli's side window, at a little distance from the main villa, was a long, low building. Of this particular place we had not had a guided tour. As I looked an ambulance drew up and a couple of men went inside with a trolley, and a couple of nurses came out: the bleached, hard, noisy kind you tend to find in places other than the Golden Bowl. Dr Grepalli decided the sun was getting in our eyes and drew the net curtains between my eyeline and the building. I didn't ask him what went on in there. But obviously some old people get Alzheimer's: in the end some fall ill, some die. It can get depressing for others. There would be some form of segregation: there would have to be, to keep the fit in good cheer.

I fought back my doubts. All this was too good to be true.

Dr Grepalli and my grandmother were having a conversation about the *I Ching*. Let the living and lively respond to the living and lively, while they can. Joy gaped open-mouthed. I don't think she really understood what was going on, perhaps because she was wearing her hearing aid again and unaccustomed sound came to her undifferentiated.

'But some of those people were chanting,' she protested on the way home. 'They were all out of their minds. And did you see the potatoes in the kitchen? All different shapes and sizes with dirt on them.'

'Potatoes come from the ground, Joy,' said Felicity. 'They are not born in the supermarket. That's what vegetables look like in real life. I loved that place. All such a hoot. Now all I have to do is wait and see and pray.'

'Oh they want you all right,' shouted Joy. 'They want your money.'

But here was the limo come especially for me, here in my hand was the Concorde ticket, there was the thought of Kubricky-Krassner back home. There was the driver whose name was Charlie, and who looked like a mountain tribesman in *The Three Feathers*, dangerous and glittery-eyed, glancing with meaning at his watch. It would not do to cross him. 'You go on back to London, Sophia,' said Felicity. 'There's nothing more you can do here. I'm going to become a Golden Bowler. If I don't do something I shall just fade away.'

'I think you're crazy,' roared Joy. 'And you're selling this place far too cheap. I'm going to ask my deceased sister's husband, Jack Epstein. He's in car dealership in Boston.'

I thought I could safely leave them to it. I had done what I had been summoned to do: endorse Felicity's decisions. She seemed well and positive. She could look after herself okay without me. I decided not to thwart the mountain tribesman but simply to go home. Joy was not best pleased, but didn't set up too many difficulties, impressed as she was to discover I was the kind of person for whom limos were sent from New York. She had assumed, I suppose, that I was someone's PA. Or the make-up girl.

Felicity finished asking advice of the *I Ching* while Joy helped me get my few things together. That is to say she banged and crashed about, and tripped over chairs and the edges of carpets and got in the way.

'I'd have gone on looking after your grandmother if I could,' she shouted. 'But I'm too old for the responsibility.'

'Don't worry about it,' I said. 'I'm family. It's up to me.'

'The only family I have left is Jack,' she said. 'That's my deceased sister Francine's husband.' Jack and the sister Francine came into her conversation rather frequently, I noticed. Something beyond her betrayal of my grandmother was bothering her.

'You young things and your careers!' she said. 'I'll help her pack up the house, of course. Someone's got to. A lot can go in storage, I daresay.'

'I don't know how sensible that is,' I said. 'When and where is everything ever going to come out of it? Better sell up and use the money.'

I felt brutal saying it, but it was true. The storage space of the Western world is full to overflowing with the belongings of deceased persons, which no-one quite knows what to do with, let alone who's the legal owner. I cut a prize-winning documentary about this once. *You Can't Take It with You.*

'I'll get Jack to help her sell the antiques,' said Joy. 'There are so many villains around, just waiting to take advantage of old women alone.'

I said that the only thing she had of any real value was the Utrillo, and presumably Felicity would take that with her to the Golden Bowl. Joy asked what a Utrillo was and I explained it was a painting, and described it. Joy doubted that it was worth anything, being so dull, but had always quite liked the frame.

'It's not as if Felicity is going far,' Joy consoled herself. 'Only just over the state line to Rhode Island. It's a much rougher place than here, of course, all has-beens and losers, artists and poets, yard sales and discount stores. Everyone rich and poor trying to pick up a bargain, and still they think well of themselves. They'll have to wake up when the new Boston to Providence Interstate cuts through. Forget all those woods and falling-down grand houses, it'll be just another commuting suburb. Property prices will soar: the Golden Bowl will sell up and what will Felicity do then?'

> 'She'll go to the barn,
> And keep herself warm,
> And hide her head under her wing.
> Poor thing,'

I murmured, and then was sorry because she had no idea what I was talking about. How could she? When I was small my mother Angel would say the rhyme if I ever worried about the future, and really it was no consolation at all.

> 'The north wind doth blow,
> And we shall have snow.
> And what will poor robin do then?
> Poor thing.'

'Things looked kind of permanent, at the Golden Bowl,' I corrected myself. 'And they seemed very responsible. They won't just dump her.'

'That's what they want you to feel,' said Joy. 'But the marble is only veneer and that terrible white stone is so cheap they can hardly give it away. Why can't she go somewhere more ordinary? Why does she have to be so special?'

'The *Ching* was very positive about the Golden Bowl,' said Felicity, when I came down with my bag, closing the book and rewrapping it in the piece of dark-red silk kept for the purpose. I felt such affectation to be annoying. 'Though it seemed to see some kind of lawsuit in the future. *Thus the kings of former times made firm the laws through the clearly defined penalties.* What do you think that means?'

'I have no idea,' I said, briskly. 'I do not see how throwing three coins in the air six times can affect anything.'

'Darling,' said Felicity, 'it isn't a question of affecting, but reflecting. It's Jung's theory of Synchronicity. But I know how you hate all this imaginative stuff.'

I said I'd rather not talk about it. My mother Angel had kept a copy of the *I Ching* on her kitchen shelf. She had no truck with silk wrappings or respect. The black-and-red book, with its white Chinese ideograms, was battered and marked by put-down coffee cups. 'What's the big deal,' she would say, 'it is only like consulting a favourite uncle, some wise old man who knows how the world works. You don't have to take any notice of what he says.' She would quote from Jung's Foreword. '*As to the thousands of questions, doubts, and criticisms that this singular book stirs up – I cannot answer these. The* I Ching *does not offer itself with proofs and results, it does not vaunt itself, nor is it easy to approach. Like a part of nature, it waits to be discovered.*'

One day when Angel had brought home bacon and sardines from the shop, rather than the milk we needed, because she'd thrown the coins before leaving the house and come up with something disparaging about pigs and fishes, I'd lost my cool and protested. 'Why do you have to throw those stupid coins, why can't you make up your own mind, then at least I could have some cereal! You are a terrible mother!' She'd slapped my face. I kicked her ankles. She seldom resorted to violence. When she did I forgave her: she'd get us confused: it was hard for her to tell the difference between her and me. To rebuke me was to rebuke herself. The sudden violence meant, all the same, that the downward slide into unreason was beginning again, and I knew it, and dreaded the weeks to come. My violence, in retaliation, was childish, but that was okay inasmuch as I was a child; I must have been about ten. Her white skin bruised easily. The blue marks were apparent for days. I felt terrible. I think that was at a time before my father left me alone with her: he simply didn't understand mental illness. He felt she was wilful and difficult and was doing everything she could to upset and destroy him, while doting on me. I tried to tell him she was crazy but he didn't believe me. I expect believing it meant he would have to take responsibility for me, and he wasn't the kind of man to do that. He was an artist of the old school. Children were the mother's business. Anyway he left, sending money for a time. I was alone with her for six months before Felicity turned up to look after us. I'd found her phone number in my mother's address book and called her. We'd run out of money and there was no food in the cupboard and my mother wasn't doing anything about it. My grandmother stayed until my mother was hospitalized, and I was in a boarding school, and then went back to her rich old husband in Savannah, the one who left her the Utrillo. She couldn't stand any of it. Well, it was hard to stand. Visit my mother in her hospital ward, in a spirit of love, and find her white-faced with wild glazed eyes, tied down, shrieking hate at you. They didn't have the drugs then they do now, and made no effort to keep the children away. I told them at school I was visiting my mother in hospital, but I didn't tell them what kind of hospital. In those days to have an insane relative was a shame and a disgrace and a terrible secret thing in a family. No sooner had Felicity flown out than my mother simply died. I like to think she knew what she was doing, that it was the only way out for all of us. She managed to suffocate herself in a straitjacket.

'Throw the coins and throw the pattern of the times,' Angel would say cheerfully, in the good times, and she'd quote Jung's Foreword, which she knew by heart, relieving me of the duty of believing what she believed.

'To one person the spirit of the I Ching appears as clear as day, to another, shadowy as twilight, to a third, dark as night. He who is not pleased by it does not have to use it, and he who is against it does not have to find it true.'

As if that settled everything. I try to keep my mind on the good times, but you can see why I like to live in films rather than in reality, if it can possibly be done. I wondered what Krassner's hang-up was. I thought I probably didn't want to know, it was an impertinence to inquire. Art is art, forget what motivates it. What business of anyone else's is why?

Felicity walked with me to the limo, her step still light, her head held high: age sat on her uncomfortably: it didn't belong to her: I wanted to cry.

'Thank you for coming all this way,' she said. 'I do appreciate it. It's made things easier. That place is okay, isn't it? Of course I'd rather live with family, but one doesn't want to be a burden.'

'That place is a hoot,' I said. 'I'd give it a go. If you don't like it I'll come over and we'll try again.'

I sank into the squashy real-leather seat.

'Of course you're not my only family,' said Felicity. 'There was Alison. Though I daresay they changed her name.'

Charlie was looking at his watch. But I was truly startled. I kept the limo door open. We couldn't leave until I shut it.

'Alison?'

'I had Alison before I had your mother,' said my grandmother. 'On my fifteenth birthday. That was in London, back in the thirties. I wasn't married. That made me a bad girl. They made me keep the baby for six weeks, and breastfeed, then they took her away, put her out for adoption.'

'How could they be so cruel?' I stood there with the car door open, in the middle of Connecticut, and the past came up and slammed me. And it wasn't even mine, it was hers.

'In the name of goodness,' she said. 'Most cruelties are. It was in case we changed our mind, but how could we, we unmarried mothers? We had nowhere to live, nowhere to go.'

'Who took the baby?'

'I don't know. They didn't tell you. It wasn't allowed. They said so you could put the past behind you and the baby could live without the stigma of its birth. They said it was for everyone's good but really it was for our punishment. It was a long time ago. Don't worry about it. She'd be in her late sixties now, if she made it to that.'

'An aunt,' I said, jubilant.

'Always thinking about yourself,' said Felicity, wryly, and there was nothing for it. I had to go. Other people took more than three hours to drive to New York, but Charlie the mountain man got to Kennedy in two and a half.

8

Alison! A long lost aunt! So long as she could be traced: so long as she had survived. But sixty something years was not so long a time in a Western society; the probability was that she would be still in this world. Chances were that she would have married, had children, grandchildren; that she could provide me with a host of cousins and little relatives, all only a half step away. As ready a family as one of the cake mixes in my grandmother's refrigerator: just add water and stir: pop in the oven and there you are, evidence of the continuity of family affection. Go for the pleasure, the ready-made, not the pain and boredom of finding the bowl, the wooden spoon, beating the sugar into the butter until the wrist tired. Just hang around, and lo, a family turns up.

Leaning against Concorde's flimsy hull on the way back to London (I had a window seat but there was nothing to see outside but navy-blue), sipping orange juice, I wondered from whence these domestic images came. When I was small, in the patches when she was sane, which grew fewer and fewer as the years went by, my mother Angel would bake cakes and I would help. Then I was truly happy: we both were. I would scrape the bowl of the creamy mixture: lick the wooden spoon. The taste of damp wood would come through with the vanilla essence.

So much of the time, at least when I was working, I rejoiced in my lack of family. I was not burdened as others were, by the guilt and obligations that seemed to go along with having parents, of whom one should be seeing more, or doing more for, desire and duty forever conflicting: the problems of children, ditto.

'Just a grandmother in Connecticut' seemed more than enough to me: far enough away, and of her own volition, to be out of the dreaded Christmas equation which afflicts so many these days: who goes where: which step-child to which step-house, which natural child to which parent, who is to take in the reproachful aged. 'Oh, now she's moved to Rhode Island,' sounded as if she were not an invention, and static, but a living, moving in-touch person. And only a fraction nearer.

I had noticed, mind you, that if I were out of the editing suite for more than a couple of days I would begin to feel a little uneasy, a little unbolstered up, as it were, by my comparative aloneness in the world. Others had parents and aunts and children: their Easters and Passovers were well peopled: their Christmas lists were full of duty items, and duty, I had come to observe, can feel less onerous than freedom: the need to enjoy oneself can become oppressive. As my due to Christmas festivities I would visit my mother's headstone at Golders Green crematorium, and consider the meaning of life and death for half an hour or so, until cold seeped through the soles of my boots. Not, I came to the conclusion fairly early on, that there were any conclusions to come to. There was the pleasure one got in getting things right, and a disappointment that one day one could no longer do so, it would be too late. I hoped nobody noticed this lack of affect in me. I put on a brave face. And if someone were needed to work on Christmas Day, I would always volunteer.

Between jobs, the cracks showed. They were beginning to yawn wide enough to fall into. Colleagues were all very well: they adored you until the show ended, and then failed to recognize you in the street the following week; there were drinks and jokes in the pub with proper friends, and dancing and sexual overtures in the club, and films to go to, and plays, and theatre, and books. Girlfriends were fine until they got married or solidly partnered and drifted off into their *folies à deux* or, with-children, *à trois* or *quatre*, when you, little by little, turned into the baby-sitter, and a haze of domestic triviality drooped like a dull cloud over the old association, and the friendship faded away to Christmas card level: and others you thought were permanent in your life you quarrelled with or they quarrelled with you, over ridiculous things, over borrowed clothes or hurt pride or imagined insults, and that was always upsetting, and there was no sex by which to re-register and consolidate former affections. As if female friendship wasn't made to endure, was a false conceit: as if sexual relationships plus children was all that really kept people together, and God knew even that didn't seem to be enough. Some tried lesbian togetherness but I never really fancied it: it was either too possessive or too bent on variance for comfort, and you'd still find yourself jumping when the phone rang. Is it him, is it her, what's the difference? Oddly, the young gay men now around town in such numbers seemed to make more reliable and lasting friends than anyone else: true, their partners changed more frequently and the splits were accompanied by the most dreadful tantrums, but their laughs and their lamentations mixed agreeably: they created more of a noisy family feel than the females managed.

My usual answer to the unease about whither and whence, alone, was simply to begin another job. Directors waited for my services. I was as busy as I needed to be. Get back to the cutting room and the dissection of fantasy, and the possibility of an award, an Oscar even, if not this year, then next, and the comfort of one's prestige in the film business, the working end of it at any rate, if not the Oscar Versace summit, and I'd be just fine again. But I could see I could do with an aunt. One sprung ready-made into my life, without the complications of a shared past. Alison!

If there was an aunt maybe there would be an uncle to go with her? But maybe not. The men in my family tended to fade out of sight in the bright glare of the female personalities with which they were confronted. Mind you, there was fresh blood in there somewhere: this Alison would have had a father. Who fathered an illegitimate baby back in the nineteen-thirties and then scarpered? Not anyone nice. But I assumed Felicity wanted me to go in search of her long-lost daughter, otherwise she wouldn't have mentioned her. Would she?

*   *   *

The elderly woman in the Hermès scarf and sensible shoes in the seat next to me called the steward. He arrived, obsequious, resentful and rubbing damp palms together. It is as difficult for Concorde to provide a more luxurious service than First Class on a regular flight as it is for First Class Regular to do much better than Club Class subsonic. There must be an end to the distinction between one grade of smoked salmon and the rest, the taste and texture of one rare globule of caviar and the next. The battle to justify the extra thousands spent by customers cannot be left to speed and convenience alone. There must be luxury enough to shame the opposition. Catering feels it too must do its best, but imagination fails. The staff just has to learn to bow yet lower, and it hurts, and it shows.

'Last time I was on this blasted machine,' said my neighbour, 'there were shreds of real orange in the juice. I'll swear this is condensed.'

The steward went forward and came back with the cardboard container to reassure her. 'Nothing but the best of freshly squeezed real oranges,' claimed the box. She refused to be reassured.

'I have no proof the juice came out of that particular box,' she said. The steward offered to provide witnesses. She declined the offer. The cast, as she called them, would only stick together and lie. 'Why didn't you just squeeze fresh oranges?' she demanded. He said there was a space problem on Concorde. She said oranges, properly packed, wouldn't necessarily take up more room than boxes. He said they would: oranges were round and boxes were square. So they wrangled on. The human race, even on Concorde, is in search of an occupation. The Mach meter showed 2.2. More than twice the speed of sound. The metal against which my arm rested became uncomfortably hot. I thought maybe the whole machine would melt. I expressed my worry to the steward. He felt the wall of the plane, and studying his once handsome face, grown soft from the habit of an unfelt politeness, and petulant from the obligation to justify, justify, justify, I thought I saw alarm writ there. As one does.

'Oh it does that sometimes,' he said. 'If we overheat the pilot will cut back.' Even as we spoke the Mach meter fell rapidly to 1.5 and the metal cooled almost instantaneously.

'There you see,' he said, triumphantly. The woman beside me snorted and fell asleep. I slept too and dreamed of Aunt Alison, who looked like one of the motherly types you see on packets of cake mixes. She folded me in her arms and said, 'There, there.' That was all but when I woke up there were tears on my cheeks.

9

The film had been unlocked, that was what had happened, why I had been sent for. A rare event. Young Olivia's female live-in lover Georgia, slighted by Olivia's claim that she was no lesbian but the mere victim of child-abuse at the hands of a female teacher, had made an unsuccessful bid to end her life, first e-mailing the news desks with her suicide note: she had been stomach-pumped in time. Georgia's parents had not helped, joining in the media fray, accusing Olivia, our film's gentle heroine, of seduction of their daughter, who had been all set to marry a parson. The PR panic was sufficient to infect the studio back in Hollywood. They flew over to sort things out, which only happened in real emergencies. Had they been able, they would have cut off my head and had my brain pickled and turned into some sort of memory bank unit, always accessible, but they couldn't do that, so they had to pay the price of a Concorde ticket and have my body as well as my brain in the editing suite. They breathed down my neck and shuddered when Harry smoked, which he did more than usual for their benefit. 'The Studio' consisted of a sharp young man and a sharper young woman with big hair and a narrow tiny face. She had LA hips, which are wider than those you see skittering about in New York. Californians are built bigger, spreading into available space. Texas is not so far away, in perceptual reality.

The decision finally reached was that I was to recut the love scenes between Leo and Olivia to show an absence of passion rather than a surfeit, as both young people struggled to define their gender identity. This was no great problem for me, since it reflected the actuality of what went on between them on camera. The end was to be changed, which fortunately there was sufficient random footage around to do: a conventional happy ending became one rather less conventional but more convincing. Olivia went off into the sunset with her best friend: Leo with his. The suggestion that the same-sex friends were shortly to be lovers I was able gently and delicately to imply. The film could now be described as brave and edgy, pushing back the frontiers of contemporary experience, it no longer had to be a heart-warming story of young love. It would not please the overseas Islamic markets, but would do fine in the non-Catholic West. 'The Studio' were thrilled by their own decision, seeing it as, I quote, 'seminal to a new generation of gender cinema'. We went into a London pub (their idea) to celebrate and they drank gassy water and managed to score some coke – the supply side in LA had recently run into some trouble, apparently – and got the last flight home.

Nearly everyone was happy about this new turn of events, except by all accounts Krassner, who bit my neck as I did what I was paid to do, and handsomely paid at that. Krassner's artistic integrity was acknowledged to be under threat, though I had the feeling he would be laughing like the rest of us if he didn't have a reputation to preserve. The writer was not particularly happy, either, but then writers never are, and Clive our producer, whose film was now going to come in way over budget, was white and exhausted, and in a state of shock, but this is what producers are paid to be.

'Please do not bite my neck,' I said to Krassner. But I had come to almost like the slightly sweaty, anxious, obsessive smell of his breath as he craned alongside me towards the screen, and it mingled with mine. Stray strands of black hair interwove with my red tendrils, which by sheer bulk and energy won any encounter. If I tossed my hair out of my eyes, as I did from time to time, a few strands of his would leave his scalp and end up in mine. There seemed an intimacy between us, the greater because we had failed to spend the night together. Matters were still all promise, no disappointment. My bed had held a companionable waft of

Krassner as I snatched a couple of hours' sleep before getting to the cutting room, and to my surprise I hadn't minded one bit. He'd left a note saying he had wormed the cat: a homey touch, though he had not shaken out the duvet. But then, neither had I before he got under it.

'I'm not biting,' he said, now. 'I'm neurotically gnawing.' It was true, his teeth – all his, and perfectly capped or veneered or implanted or whatever they did with the teeth of the older man nowadays – slipped gently over the surface of my skin, his full lips following. You don't get anywhere in film by claiming sexual harassment: that's for people about to get out of the business anyway. You can get a handsome award but you never work again. For some it's worth it. Not me. And I liked him gnawing me.

We were three hours into editing when Krassner got a personal phone call from LA. His turn to disentangle his hair from mine, leaving a few more of his strands behind. He took the call. 'Why hello, darling,' he said. 'Yuh, the rumours are correct, we're up shit creek again. I'm stuck here. Why don't you fly over to me instead of me going over to you?'

I stopped listening: how stupid I had nearly been: I cut off all reaction. Any shoulder in a storm, that was all my shoulder was to Krassner. Someone nudged me and said that's Holly Fern on the line – I'd heard of her, who hadn't: she being the new talent on the block, singing and dancing, according to her people, just like a reborn Ginger Rogers – I thought that was pretty stupid because whoever these days had heard of Ginger Rogers – and with a degree in philosophy which publicity also foolishly did to death. It was from a crap college. 'Against stupidity,' my mother Angel once said to me, 'the Gods themselves strive in vain.'

Nobody had hair as good as mine, but hair isn't everything, and just because I got up ordinarily with mine in the morning, didn't mean others couldn't get the same effect out of a hair salon, if they were prepared to spend half a day achieving it. I wiped Krassner out of my mind, moved my shoulder out of his line. Back at the console he dug me in the ribs and said, 'Whatzamatter with you?' but I didn't deign to reply. It doesn't do to aim too high, the fall's too hurtful.

10

That night I called Felicity. I tried to get her to tell me more about Aunt Alison but she wouldn't.

'I shouldn't have brought it up,' she said. 'What's the point?' She quoted from Tennyson's The Lotos-Eaters.

'*We have had enough of action, and of motion, we,*
Roll'd to starboard, Roll'd to larboard, when the surge was
  seething free,
Where the wallowing monster spouted his foam-fountains in
  the sea.'

No, she hadn't heard yet from the Golden Bowl but if they wouldn't have her she would sell up anyway and go round the corner to the nearest residential house. Joy's brother-in-law Jack had turned up and made an offer on the house and she had had to disappoint Vanessa.

'How much?' I asked.

'$750,000,' she said.

'But that's lower!' I was shocked.

'It's all he can afford, I won't have to pay agent fees and I don't want to disappoint Joy.'

'How do you know he can't afford it?' I asked. 'Because Joy said so?'

'I don't know what you've got against Joy. She's a better friend than you ever were a granddaughter. Just because she's a bad driver doesn't mean she's a bad person.'

'No,' I said bitterly, 'she just prefers animals to people. Big deal. Is Joy's sister moving in too?'

'She died a year ago: Joy hated her, loved him.' I asked if this meant there was romance in the air and Felicity told me not to be absurd. Joy hated sex but liked to have a man about the place to shout at.

Felicity was not moved by my anxiety that the house was sold, and the Golden Bowl had not yet confirmed her apartment. She said one room was much like another when you got older: one steak as hard on your teeth as the next. The *I Ching* had given her *Biting Through, Chen Chi*. She must bite resolutely through obstacles: then she would be rewarded with supreme success. I could tell these were mere delaying tactics: she would talk about anything at all except my lost aunt. I cut her short and asked her directly who the father of her first baby was. I pointed out that these days there is no family decision which can be made without consultation: if you gave away a family member you were giving away relatives for future generations, too, and you had to be answerable to them.

To which she replied tartly that I was a fine one to talk, since I was slipping out from under and having no children at all.

I said no, that's why I wouldn't be answerable to anyone, lucky old me. But she had, and so she was. You had to know your genetic background if only to keep the Insurance Companies happy.

She said don't teach your grandmother to suck eggs: she lived in Norwich, Connecticut. There were only two things to bear in mind. Death Only Insurance Policies meant they bet you you'd live longer than you thought you would, and annuities meant you bet them you'd outlive what they predicted. And they had whole departments working on it and you didn't, and they normally won.

I said, though diverted, don't change the subject, and repeated the question. 'Who was the father of your adopted child?'

'That is simply not the kind of thing you ask in proper circles,' said Felicity, hoity toity, 'and it is not your bloodline so what has it got to do with you anyway?'

'I hope he stayed long enough to take off his boots,' I said, 'and give his name.' Felicity, provoked as I had hoped, spoke haughtily. 'He was not unknown to me, but it is not something I am prepared to talk about. I gave birth on my fifteenth birthday. Honestly, Sophia, would you want to remember such a thing? I know fifteen is nothing these days, but back in the thirties, certainly in the circles in which I moved, it was really something. I gave birth in a Catholic Home for unwed mothers and bad girls didn't get given chloroform, which was the only anaesthetic available in childbirth at the time. That was to help teach us the wisdom of not doing it again.'

'It didn't work. Later on you had Angel.'

'I took care to be married, and by that time there was gas-and-air. You really must not pry. So far as I am concerned my life began when I married a chicken farmer from Savannah. Anything that happened before that I have sensibly wiped out of my memory. It is all nothing to do with me.'

I wondered how she would get on at the Golden Bowl, where the old wisdom of not thinking about unpleasant things was hardly encouraged. But Felicity could always invent a life story for herself, and go with that, if she so preferred. Or did the spirit of invention, as with the emotions, as with the body, get tired with age? There was a quaver in her voice: a frisson of self-pity I had never heard before. The telephone conversation ended unsatisfactorily, with me anxious for her welfare and her ordering me to not stir up the past. But I had what I wanted. Two further clues. Her fifteenth birthday and a Catholic Home for unwed mothers.

The *Tomorrow Forever* team, I know, employed the services of a detective agency. The next day I put them on to the job of finding Alison. They offered to lose the cost in the general film expenses, but I said no, this was private work, I would foot the bill. There was now some talk of changing the title to *Forever Tomorrow*. I couldn't see that it made much difference. Felicity's birthday was 6 October. A Libran, fair and square and in the middle of the sign, better at being a mistress than a wife, not that I held any truck with astrology. There can't have been a great number of babies born to fifteen-year-olds in London on 6 October 1930, in a Catholic Home for unwed mothers, and presumably some records of adoptions would have been kept. And with any luck the right ones would have survived the blitz, and I had always seen myself as a lucky person, though I knew enough from working on a film called *Fire over England* that great chunks of the national archive went up in flames in 1941.

If I couldn't have Krassner I wanted a family. I wanted to be bolstered up, I wanted to be enclosed, I wanted someone to be around if I were ill, I wanted someone to look at my calendar and notice that the cat was due for his second worm pill. You could write yourself notices and pin them on a board as much as you liked, but how did you make yourself look at them? You had to have a back-up system.

11

'What do Golden Bowlers do?
They live life to the full!'

By the end of November Felicity was settled into the Atlantic
Suite of the Golden Bowl Complex. Her house had been sold to
Joy's brother-in-law Jack, at a knockdown price. At the last
moment he had had second thoughts about purchasing and she
had brought the price down a further $50,000. It scarcely mat-
tered. She had $5,000,000 in the bank: the interest on which was
sufficient to pay all costs at the Golden Bowl, though if she lived
to ninety-six or more, and rates continued to rise exponentially
by ten per cent a year, she would have to begin to dip into capital.
She could afford to buy a small gift here, give a little to charity
there, though she had never been the kind to dress up and go to
functions and give publicly. Too vulgar for Miss Felicity: too much
gold and diamond jewellery on necklines cut too low to flatter
old skin.

Felicity's lawyer Bert Heller, Exon's old friend, was satisfied that
he had done his best by the old lady, as she had once alarmingly
overheard him referring to her. Her will was in order and left
everything to her granddaughter Sophia in England. Joy was
pleased her friend was near enough to visit but that instead of
having the responsibility of an elderly widow living alone
next door, prone to falls and strokes, she now had the comfort
of a brother-in-law as a neighbour, one who would look after,

rather than need to be looked after. The move had suited everyone.

All Felicity had to do now, in fact, in the judgement of the outside world, was settle down, not make trouble, and live the rest of her days in peace.

And why not? The Atlantic Suite was composed of three large rooms, a tiny kitchen, a bathroom embossed with plated gold fittings and more than enough closet space: the view was pleasant: the rooms spacious. The world came to her through CNN, if she cared to take an interest in it, though few at the Golden Bowl did. Most preferred to look inwards and wait their turn to get a word in at group therapy. The decor and furnishings were pleasing and she had never been sentimental about her belongings: most had gone to auction. Sometimes Miss Felicity would remember a dress she had particularly liked and wonder what became of it: or a charming plate she'd owned, or a scrapbook she'd once compiled. Did people steal things, had she lost them, had she given them away? Why try to remember? It hardly mattered. She had a photograph of her granddaughter in a silver frame on her bedside table, but that was to keep Nurse Dawn quiet. Nurse Dawn, helping her unpack, had found it and stood it there when first Felicity arrived, and Felicity did not feel inclined to take on Nurse Dawn at the moment: she would wait until something more significant was at stake. To have family photographs on the bedside table suggested that life – by which she supposed she meant sex – was in the past.

Besides, Sophia had inherited Angel's Botticelli hair: Felicity was not sure she wanted to be presented with the sight of it night and day. So she simply put the photo on its face after room service had been in and every next day room service stood it upright. It was an okay compromise.

Felicity had a nasty attack of flu when she first arrived at the Golden Bowl. Stomach cramps and weak limbs had made her more dependent upon the administrations of Nurse Dawn than she would have wished. When she recovered she found that silly little matters such as when breakfast would be brought to her room in the morning, when the valet service would collect and deliver, limitations on her time in the Library, expected attendance at the Ascension Room gatherings, had been arranged more to fit the Golden Bowl's convenience than her own. She had remarked on this to Dr Bronstein.

'It's very strange,' was Dr Bronstein's dark comment, later, 'how many people find themselves ill and helpless when they first arrive at the Golden Bowl.'

'It's hardly likely to be a conspiracy,' said Felicity. 'No-one's going to make us ill on purpose.'

'Aren't they?'

Felicity had taken morning coffee in the Ascension Room as soon as she was able. She felt the need of company. She'd joined Dr Bronstein and a Miss Clara Craft at their table. Both smiled agreeably at her, and put down their magazines. Miss Craft, who turned out to be a correspondent for *The Post* back in the thirties, and who had trouble with her sight, had been flicking through the latest copy of *Vogue*. She wore a good deal of make-up haphazardly applied, and her sparse hair was arranged in little plaits, which hung here and there from her scalp. Her back was noticeably bowed. Felicity concluded that like so many women who did not choose to thwart the natural processes, Clara took no hormone replacement therapy. Dr Bronstein was smartly presented and was reading *Harpers*, albeit with a magnifying glass. Nurse Dawn had lingered, hovered, and done her best to overhear.

Dr Bronstein's eyes were rheumy like a spaniel's. They dripped moisture, and made him seem in constant need of sympathy. Nurse Dawn resented this. Nor did she like the Doctor's choice of reading matter which to her was impenetrable but under the terms of residency was provided free. Magazines surely meant *Time* or *Newsweek*. *Vogue* was acceptable, though absurd in Clara Craft's case. Miss Felicity had taken on herself to read *Vanity Fair*, which was bad enough, the articles being so long, but at least, unlike *Harpers*, had a few pretty girls and advertisements to break up the text.

*   *   *

'Most of us will arrive here exhausted,' said Felicity, 'and in culture shock from the winding down of our days. Our immune systems are low. It's not surprising we get ill. Or perhaps it's suddenly eating three meals a day, of good natural food. I've been living out of packets for the past five years.'

She was well aware Nurse Dawn was listening, under the pretence of tidying up a bowl of flowers. She was stripping away yellowed leaves and faded blooms and putting them in a little bag for removal. She took her time.

'Natural?' asked Dr Bronstein. 'I hope I didn't hear you say natural. It's an illusion to believe that because something is natural, it's good for us. Nature doesn't care whether we live or die. Nature's only purpose is to get us to procreative age in one piece, by whatever slipshod manner she can contrive. Once we're past that she has no interest in us at all. We live by our ingenuity, not by her will. It behoves us oldsters to treat nature as enemy not friend.'
'Man's ingenuity!' interjected Clara Craft. 'I must tell you, Miss Felicity, I was present when the great airship Hindenburg caught fire as it landed. That was in 1937. One of the most spectacular tragedies of the decade. I was one of those little figures running away from the flames in the newsreel. How I escaped with my life I'll never know.'

Nurse Dawn, having heard all about the Hindenburg disaster too many times before, and finding herself bored even as an eavesdropper – to whom most things are fascinating by virtue of the secrecy attached – left the room. Miss Felicity – forget Clara's adventures, which were already being repeated, like a stuck record – found herself glad to be in the company of a man who used the word *behove* in ordinary speech. Such words had certainly not been in Joy's vocabulary. Felicity could see her horizons expanding. Once you could lose the sense that age was the most important thing about the old: that the passage of years wiped out individuality and that you were old yourself, just like everyone else around, all was not gloomy. Clara fell suddenly asleep. *Vogue* dropped to the ground and lay there. Dr Bronstein told her that he was eighty-nine: that until his enforced retirement he had been a biochemist, and, he was happy to admit to Felicity, had been a conspiracy theorist all his life. He was in good health, though he believed his two new titanium knees and one plastic and one steel hip (implanted of necessity over four decades of medical care – he had played baseball for his college team, and squash thereafter, and there is nothing like sport for damaging the joints, but who in the vigour of their youth is ever prepared to believe it) set up some kind of electrical discharge which interfered with his mental processes. He kept up an animated flow if not exactly conversation – he was too deaf for that – but at any rate talk.

That night when Nurse Dawn came by to turn off Felicity's light – Felicity had told her not to bother, she could turn off her own light perfectly well, but Nurse Dawn had seemed hurt so she'd consented – Nurse Dawn said: 'A friendly warning. Don't take too much notice of our Dr Bronstein. He has a problem with authority. Give him a chance and he'll feel free to buttonhole you for the rest of your life.'

Which Felicity realized with a shock might well be spent as a Golden Bowler. She refrained after all from asking Nurse Dawn if she could have Fat Free Choco Lite for her good-night drink, and decided to go along with whatever Nurse Dawn thought was best. As with the matter of the family photograph, it was of minor importance: she would save her energies for some greater battle which she had no doubt would soon enough come along. In the meantime she would lull Nurse Dawn into complacency. But wasn't this how one behaved with husbands? Putting off confrontation until a right time which never came? In the end, if only by default, you ended up living their life, not jours. But why not, here at the Golden Bowl?

The good-night drink provided by Nurse Dawn turned out to be semi-skimmed unpasteurized milk with a little acacia honey stirred into it, for, Nurse Dawn said, sweet dreams. As soon as the woman was gone Felicity got out of bed and poured the sickly stuff down the bathroom sink, keeping her eyes averted from the gilt-framed mirror.

*　　*　　*

On the day she had first moved in she'd thought she'd glimpsed the face of an elderly man looking out at her from the glass. The image had been brief but vivid. She'd told herself that she was overtired but hadn't quite convinced herself. Vision it had been. Well, these things happened from time to time in one's life and were overlooked in the name of sanity. She could only hope the vision was not prophetic: that she was looking at herself in ten years' time. It was sadly true that as one got older the distinction between a male face and a female one lessened, but hardly to so whiskery and rheumy a degree as this. Surely there would never come a time when she, Felicity, would cease to tweeze the hairs from her nose and chin? Or perhaps some kind of ghost looked back at her? Felicity had once owned a cat who continued to haunt the house for a few weeks after its death at the age of ten, under a car: just a flick of a tail out of the corner of the eye: the sound of purring where no purring should be, the feel of fur rubbing up affectionately against her shin: these things happened. She knew well enough that the Atlantic Suite had fallen vacant upon the death of the previous occupant: why else the new bed, the frantic redecoration? If the one she replaced now appeared to her, was it in welcome or in warning?

The apparition had appeared only briefly: she had looked away at once, in shock, and forcing herself to look again, had seen only herself. That of course was bad enough. You looked into a mirror as a young woman and your reflection looked out at you as one who was old. So what, honestly, was the big deal if the one looking out had changed sex as well? The shock of the stranger in the mirror was with you every time you looked into one. So why worry?

She didn't mention the matter to the management. As you grew older you had to be careful not to give anyone an inkling that you were not in your right mind. Incarcerated as she had once been, though briefly, during the course of a divorce, in a mental home, she had been much impressed by the difficulty of proving you were sane. If you wept because you were locked up and miserable, you were diagnosed as clinically depressed and unfit to leave. If you didn't weep someone else would decide you were sociopathic, and a danger to the public. Those who ran institutions tended to register criticism as ingratitude at best and insanity at worst, and though the Golden Bowl was not an institution in the locking-up sense, the mere fact of being old made you vulnerable to those who might decide you and your $5,000,000 needed to be protected for your own and its good.

Better to conclude that the unexpected face in the mirror was a projection of one's own fears rather than some occult phenomenon, and shut up about it. Miss Felicity lived in hope that death would be the final closing down of all experience: she wanted an end rather than a new beginning. All the same, throwing away Nurse Dawn's over-sweet milk, she tried not to look in the mirror. It was too late, she was tired, she had no appetite for either shock or speculation.

Once settled in, she was sleepless. She called her granddaughter Sophia in London. Midnight here meant sevenish there. Of course she had it the wrong way round.

Sophia answered from sleep, alert at once to her grandmother's voice. 'Felicity? Is everything okay?'
'Why are you always so sure something has gone wrong?'
'Because with most people when they call you at five in the morning it's some kind of emergency.' Sophia whispered, up to the satellite, bounce, and down over-sibilant on the other side of the Atlantic. 'Hang on a moment. I'm going to the other phone.'
'Why?' asked Felicity. 'Is there someone with you?'
'Don't be absurd,' said Sophia.
Krassner was there, of course, lank hair on the striped pillow, which coincidentally matched Felicity's pink and white décor. Holly had declined to come over to England to be with him. *Forever Tomorrow* had come and gone within a couple of months: had some critical acclaim, did well in the central cities though not so well out of town, and in general was expected to earn its keep. The film was to go sooner than hoped on to video and would no doubt make up any lost ground in the fireside medium. Krassner's reputation hadn't exactly soared but neither had it been knocked back. He was still in a position to pick and choose his next project.

He didn't like hotels: Sophia's apartment was within walking distance of most places he was expected to be. He loathed London taxis: they had no springs and you had to get out before you paid the driver, or they complained of back pain. Sophia found herself without the will to make any objection: his convenience had to be suited: he appreciated her, and was courteous and did not play emotional games. She knew he would not stay long. He was childishly and neatly domestic. He brought her aspirin if she had a headache, found her lost gloves, bought fruit and food from the Soho delicatessen and laid it before her; the sex was both peremptory and pleasant, though he always seemed to be thinking of something else. Her friends envied her. Harry Krassner the great director! She was between films. She was happy, poised between a current fantastic reality, and a new film fantasy to begin. Harry understood these things. He said he'd hang about until March, when she went back into the editing suite. Then he'd be going back to LA anyway. Holly was on location till then.

It was not so unusual, these days, thus to fit in the personal between the professional. Everyone she knew did it.

12

I took one of the duvets from the bed and crept into the living room the better to talk undisturbed. Harry, deprived of the extra weight, pulled the remaining cover around him more closely, but did not wake.

'It's time you did have someone with you,' said Felicity. 'I'm beginning to feel out on a limb. One grandchild is pathetic. There are people in this place with up to twenty descendants.'

'I don't think that's a very good reason for having children,' I replied. It occurred to me that if I set out to I could have a baby by Harry Krassner. I could simply steal one. And what with today's new DNA tests I could ensure that he supported it for ever. Did one dare? No. Forces too large for the likes of me to cope with would be involved. Ordinary mortals should not try it on with the gods down from Mount Olympus. Such a baby would be some large hairy thing, hardly a baby at all: it would spring fully formed into the world, with nothing in it of me whatsoever. The subject of offspring of the union had not been mentioned. It was assumed I was a sensible, rational, working adult in the business. Naturally I would be taking contraceptive precautions. As naturally I was.

'Mind you,' said Miss Felicity, 'I can see there's an argument for quality rather than quantity. The more offspring there are, the plainer and duller they get, generation by generation. Virtues get diluted: things like receding jaws get magnified. And I daresay it's as well if you don't have children, Sophia. Our family genes are not the best.'

*   *   *

Oh, thank you very much, Felicity! Schizophrenia may have a strong hereditary component: it may well run in the blood, though some deny it and I would certainly like to. I did not thank Felicity for reminding me. But nor did I want to risk having a child who hated me, as Angel had done Felicity. When the love/hate mode in a person switches as easily as central heating to air conditioning in a well-run hotel, it's disconcerting and distressing for those around. The more Felicity showed her love for Angel the more Angel resented and feared her. The daughter interpreted maternal concern as control, dinner-on-the-table as an attempt at poisoning. In Angel's eyes it was Felicity's fault that my father the artist left home, not the fact that Angel had decided that sex and art didn't mix, and when he failed to produce a canvas equal to a Picasso, a more or less ongoing state of affairs – how could it not be? – insisted on referring to him as Dinky. (His name was Rufus, which was bad enough.) No, in Angel's eyes, Felicity had *interfered*, paying for his canvases, buying oils, mending our roof, whatever. Felicity was a control freak. And so on. Even as a small child I detected the element of wilfulness in my mother Angel's insanities: to be mad is a great excuse for giving rein to hate and bad behaviour and bad jokes, while handing over to others responsibility for one's life. The net end is to cause others as much trouble and distress as possible, while remaining virtuous and a victim. Yet I admired my mother's style. In fact it hadn't been too bad for me; far worse for Felicity. The child tends to take mothers and their odd ways for granted: the mother is eternally anxious for the child. Angel's wrath and spite and mockery was seldom directed against me: only once when she decided I was 'difficult' and sent me off to boarding school did I get a taste of it. The night before I left for school Angel came into my bedroom saying I was the devil's spawn, sent by the Whore of Babylon to spy on her, and tried to smother me with the pillow. Scary stuff. But only on that one occasion and that was the worst of it. We'd managed okay till then, Angel and me and sometimes Rufus. Dinky.

When I was eight she decided in the face of all evidence that I had head lice and shaved my head with Dinky's blunt razor, and kept me away from school for three months. I hadn't minded that at all. I got books out of the library and lay on my bed all day and read them, and went to the cinema sometimes as many as nine times a week. Once a day on weekdays and twice on Saturday and Sundays. I'd wear a headscarf. Angel would often come with me to the cinema. It was what we did. The school said nothing. I daresay they were pleased not to have Angel turning up at the school gate to collect me. She could look strange and she did throw things. My hair, which had been straight and thin until cropped back to the scalp, thereafter grew rich, thick and crinkly in my mother's mode, and was what had drawn Krassner towards me. I was grateful. If Angel once decided she and I were to be street people on moral grounds what business was that of the social workers? That particular time I'd been taken away from Angel and our cardboard box under the King's Cross arches (we were North London people), and been put in a foster home for months, until she'd made it up with Rufus and was in a position to reclaim me. The cardboard box had been okay. It was summer: we'd go into the Ritz Hotel and use their washing facilities. Angel always dressed beautifully, stealing the clothes from stores if necessary. We'd eat in posh restaurants and run away. At the foster home they dressed me from the charity shop and fed me on chip sandwiches. And this time when I finally got home the head lice were real, not imaginary. And Rufus had gone again.

One day I'd come home from school to find Angel beating hell out of a pillow, claiming the devil was in it, and feathers floating through the air like the snowflakes in *The Snow Queen* – and had panicked and phoned Felicity in Savannah. The next day, by which time the feathers had melted and the devil had left, my grandmother swept into our semi-derelict house in a froth of scarves, lamenting and fussing about the place and bringing in psychiatrists and social workers. If I hadn't made the call I daresay my mother and I would have got by okay. She would have drifted in and out of psychotic episodes, making cakes and barricading the house against the landlord: taking petitions to Downing Street: going into smart restaurants and breaking plates in sympathy with veal calves long before animal rights became fashionable, and I'd have coped. Twenty years on, in fact, and Angel might still be alive, with new drugs keeping her in control, or at any rate more like other people. And I'd still have a mother.

The last lucid thing Angel had said to me when they declared her to be a danger to herself and others, and had jabbed her full of medication, and I was sitting next to her in the ambulance on the way to the psychiatric unit (from which she was to escape) was that it was all Felicity's fault. Felicity had destroyed her, and would destroy me too.

'Your grandmother is evil,' she said. I accepted then that Angel was indeed raving. Felicity was no worse or better than anyone else: she was better than the teachers at the various schools I'd gone to and not gone to: morally better than my father who'd walked out rather than have to do the dirty work of having his wife put away, and simply abandoned me, his child, to cope. She was less use to me than studying, or my passion for cinema, and certainly less use to me than my friends. I'd always had friends and mothers of friends who'd take me in, when times were bad. Children meet with great kindness. In fact Felicity did her best, I knew, within the boundaries of her own nature. But then everyone does. And a mother's last words are difficult to forget, if only traditionally. You know how it is.

Nor did I want Felicity, thirty years later, to be raising these painful matters at five in the morning. I would rather be lying beside Krassner, making the most of such time as I had with him: me, the person without past, without family, the one who just sometimes walked out of the editing suite and engaged in the real world.

I switched the conversation before I got angry and upset. I gave Felicity the information I was saving like the icing on the lemon drizzle cake my mother would buy in the early days, when we had a nice apartment like other people and my father was selling a painting or two and could pay the rent.

'I think I've found your Alison,' I said to Felicity. 'Your long-lost daughter.' For once it was quiet outside the window. Those of excessive habits had finally gone home to rest and recuperate. The tourists had not yet woken. Only the binmen still clattered along the edges of Berwick Street market, a few blocks away, clearing the detritus of fruit and vegetable. Krassner snored gently on the bed. It was the third successive night he had spent there. The insides of my thighs were agreeably sore. He was due to fly home on Friday. This was early Wednesday morning. When he was gone I would be able to get my clothes to the cleaners and have my hair trimmed and streaked, and do all the other small necessary things you don't seem to do when there's a man around because they seem so domestic and boring and not what the film stars do.

There was a long silence from Felicity's end. The lemon icing I so looked forward to was sometimes too tart and sour, I remembered that. When the silence was broken it was a slap sharp enough to dash the cake from my hand altogether.

'I didn't ask you to find her,' said Felicity. 'I just told you she existed. I should have known better than to mention it. I'm sorry I did.'

'I'm finding her for me as much as you,' I said feebly.

'Therapy babble,' said Felicity. 'For me! For me! What makes you so important in the scheme of things? What have you to do with this, something that happened to me seventy years ago and I've spent a lifetime trying to forget?'

'But what harm can it do? Another family member –'

You never knew what you'd get with another person, was Felicity's view, family member or not, and she let me know it. They'd come smiling over your threshold and stay to burn the place down. I was too young to know anything. As you grew older the soup of life – I beg your pardon? – got thicker and mushier and bits sank to the bottom and you'd better leave them there, not drag them up to the surface.

'Well, Gran,' I said, trying to keep it light, keep my voice from trembling, trying to remember the sheer unreasonableness of Angel's hostility, 'no wonder you like to live out of packets. One-minute minestrone with added vitamins. Just heat and serve and nothing in the murk.'

'What are you talking about?' Miss Felicity demanded. 'Don't change the subject. I can only hope you haven't set anything in motion you can't control.' I just felt tired and weak and in need of affection. I wanted my mother.

*   *   *

The door between Krassner and me had swung open. He stirred in his sleep. That was all going to go wrong too. I must be prepared for it. I was just a convenient bed, so he didn't have to take taxis to get to his meetings. I pushed the door shut with my feet. I have nice feet. Krassner admired them too; he'd gently pull the toes apart to admire the pink perfection between them, which, he claimed, when shadowed matched my hair. Men and women together can be so ridiculous: but it's such a wonderful vacation from real life, all this mutual grooming between lovers, or quasi-lovers, as we were. Just practising, or remembering, or passing time, holidaying with the wrong person, trying to forget the right one. Except I had never yet met the right person so what was I going on about? It was all right by me.

'You are two bloodlines and one generation distant from this person,' Felicity was saying. 'It is nothing to do with you. You are like all your generation: you know nothing and understood nothing. See a problem, sort it out! Most problems are unsolvable.'

I tried not to snivel, thus scolded. The attack was so unexpected. We had parted so amiably, and so recently, as if we were proper family, apart but supportive. But the old distresses still pushed their way up to the surface, excoriating. I was seven years old again, my parents rowing over my existence, my father angry, my mother at best dysfunctional (though the word hadn't been invented so it was a rather rarer condition than now), at worst raving. I was playing patience with sticky cards laid out on the carpet, willing the hand to solve itself and not end in stultification. It hits you when you are around this age that the pattern your life is making at this particular time will recur, 'til the end of your life, you being the person you are. It will take minimally different forms but essentially be the same. Pocket money will give way to earnings, parents to spouses, but nothing's really going to change, except the patterns of the carpet, and that's if you're lucky. What was Krassner but a game of patience played with sticky cards that wouldn't resolve itself? I was not beautiful enough, or rich enough, or interesting enough: mostly I was not brave enough, I didn't have the courage, the toughness, not to care what others think of me. Those who care least, win. That's why Holly does so well out of life.

*   *   *

'Now I suppose I've gone and upset you,' came Felicity's voice, softer now, and then, blessedly: 'Oh, go on then do what you like.' I heard muffled voices at the other end: remonstrations: and then my grandmother's voice again, to me.

'Sorry about that. It was Nurse Dawn, telling me not to have late-night telephone conversations. You remember Nurse Dawn?'

'Of course I do. And what business is it of hers?'

'She says talking to relatives is like eating cheese before going to bed; it leads to bad dreams.'

'Doesn't that depend on the conversation?'

'That's what I told her.'

'This one was a bad dream to begin with. How did she know you were on the phone?'

'There isn't a direct outside line. It goes through the operator. She must have told. I don't think this is a complex for the elderly at all. I think it's a CIA training ground for surveillance techniques and psychological warfare. I'd better go now.'

I quite liked being described by Felicity as a relative. It made me feel warmed and safe, and not so unlike other people after all. But I also quite liked the thought of this grandmother of mine feeling obliged to do what Nurse Dawn told her. Perhaps at the Golden Bowl I would find allies; people who would understand what it was like to have Angel for a mother and Felicity for a grandmother. Then I felt disloyal, and weak for wanting to *belong*, and sorry for Felicity, because her life was drawing to an end, and there was nothing she could do about it, not even a rewind button to press, no way of cutting the footage together differently: the picture was locked. No way now of editing out the boring bits. These had to be lived through in real time, with a body that was inexorably running down, and not all the efforts of the Golden Bowl could help her.

I would certainly not have a baby by Krassner, or anyone, ever. The smaller the family the better. One minute you resented them, or they were making you cry, the next you were feeling responsible for them, missing them.

All I could hear over the phone now was the wheeling of the stars, the singing of celestial spheres. She was gone. I listened a little on the open line to the chirrupings of the cosmos, before putting down the receiver. A group of tarts clip-clopped on brazen heels down the street below, back no doubt from some Arabian orgy in one of the big Park Lane hotels, calling one another a cheerful good night. People always manage to find areas of pleasure in their lives, whatever others may think of them. They get together and have a good time. It's that or death.

I slipped back into bed beside Krassner whose organ extended ramrod-like at the touch of my body against his, though he still did not wake. I did not interpret this as either love or lust: he was just a man of easy sexuality with quick, automatic and healthy responses. I felt shredded, raw, and cold of spirit, flesh and heart, and made no attempt to take advantage of so easy a prey. I was to be back in the editing suite sooner than I had thought, cutting a film called *Hope Against Hope*, a legal thriller, with a female director, Astra Barnes. When Krassner went back to Holly at least I would have something to do. I took the usual comfort from this. It wasn't good enough.

13

On 1 December, in the face of opposition from Nurse Dawn and even Dr Grepalli, who came tapping at her door to warn her against so doing, Felicity went to a funeral. The body of a man had been discovered in a beach hotel in Mystic and Felicity's name was in his address book, as living at 1006 Divine Road. Joy's brother-in-law had happily given the police her new address. The death was by natural causes: drunk, the man had choked on his own vomit. His name was Tommy Salzburger. He had been in the neighbourhood for only two days. The police had come up to the Golden Bowl to interview Felicity: fortunately they had telephoned first and Nurse Dawn had ensured they came not in a police car and not in uniform, so they could pass for insurance brokers or lawyers: the kind of professionals who do visit Golden Bowlers on occasion. To be on the safe side Nurse Dawn also persuaded them to park their car outside Felicity's French windows, to the side of the building, so their presence did not become a matter of curiosity for the other guests.

Tommy Salzburger was Felicity's stepson by her first marriage to Sergeant Jerry Salzburger of the United States Air Force, one time of Atlanta, long deceased. Miss Felicity freely admitted it. She had no idea why Tommy was in the neighbourhood, she had not seen him for fifteen years or so, but if his turning up in Mystic was anything to do with her, which she pointed out could be purely coincidental (maybe like her latest husband he was interested in naval history; appearances could deceive), he was probably after money. She had lent him sums in the past, never returned. He was a gambler and a drinker.

The police had called her the next day to say Tommy Salzburger had a girlfriend with two of his children living in the locality: he had turned up there but she had turned him away from her door: no doubt he died while attempting to drown his sorrows. Felicity surprised them by asking where the funeral was, and shocked Nurse Dawn by saying she was going.

'You will be upset,' said Nurse Dawn. 'You will catch cold and bring back germs into the building. It isn't fair to the other guests. No-one will expect you to go. Old people, like children, are excused from funerals.'

'But I want to go,' said Felicity. And when Joy called up asked if she'd come along to keep her company, and rather to her surprise Joy shouted that she would, since now she had a chauffeur, whose services she shared with Jack.

14

'We don't have to actually get out of the car when we get there, do we?' Joy pleaded.

A flesh-and-blood child was one thing but a vagrant stepchild from an unfortunate and short-lived marriage who wasn't even a blood relation hardly merited catching cold. Better to watch from the Mercedes window. She never liked burials, as this one was to be, the turning over of graveyard dirt. There had been plagues in the area, albeit long ago, and mass burials, everyone knew, and heaven knew what still lingered. There were bound to be germs about. Cremation was more hygienic.

'You're old enough to be excused,' Joy shouted into Felicity's shrinking ear. 'You could have got out of it, I don't see why you didn't.'

'He was a very nice little boy,' said Felicity, 'though he grew up to be a nuisance to everyone. I go to his burial in memory of the child he used to be, not the man he became. And if I don't go, who will?'

'We get the funerals we deserve,' cried Joy, to the world. Joy felt better able to assert herself now that she had Jack living next door. She felt protected. Jack was a sociable person; gusts of male energy swept through her house whenever he visited, which was every day. He did the sort of things men did. He had the Volvo taken to the garage and the dents got rid of. He had the low stone walls rebuilt. Somehow the drapes begun to hang less limply: the cushions seemed to plump themselves. There was a purpose to the place. When Jack said, as he often did, that she, Joy, reminded him of her deceased sister Francine, she did not sulk or feel hurt: she accepted the comparison gracefully, even as a compliment. With Jack in the house she had at last what was hers by rights. There was no special reason for thinking this, other than everything her sister Francine had ever had, Joy, being the older sister, felt was hers by rights.

If you just hung round long enough and kept cheerful things seemed to turn out okay. Francine had come along three years after Joy was born, and Francine had died three years before Joy, so Joy already had six years' more life than Francine, albeit a little deaf and a little short-sighted. That alone was a kind of victory: there might be more to come. Could you marry your deceased sister's husband? It was the kind of thing Felicity might well know: Joy had called Felicity at the Golden Bowl to find out, but instead of being able to discuss the matter had been roped in to accompany her friend to the funeral of some derelict she personally had never met and nobody seemed to like.

In honour of the funeral and her friend's presumed grief, Joy was dressed in suitable black, her hair was less blonde than usual, and her mascara kept to a minimum. She wore a bright yellow fluffy teddy-bear brooch to keep everyone's spirits up; its eyes were real diamonds balanced on emerald spikes, which spun when the wearer moved. Jack had bought them for her from a friend who imported jewellery. The shop price would have been in the region of $5,000 but Harry had acquired them for $500. He was like that.

Miss Felicity was still displeased with Sophia, and anxious for her too. To suddenly start searching for distant relatives was the kind of impetuous thing Angel would do, though real mental illness would surely have surfaced in her granddaughter by now. To worry about it, she assured herself, was a symptom of the free-floating anxiety a doctor had once told her she suffered from: lighting like a fly here or there without real cause or purpose. All you could do was wait for it to go away, which assuredly it would. In the meantime she could only hope that Sophia's search would lead nowhere, and that no news from her was good news.

*   *   *

The graveyard where Tommy was to be buried was next to a small clapboard church outside Mystic, prettily sited in a snowy landscape. Just a light sprinkling of the stuff: just enough to make everything seem fresh and clean, and cover up the layer of rotting autumnal leaves which at this time of year got everywhere, staining the landscape with the dankness of decay. The chauffeur turned out to be Charlie, the very same Charlie from New York who had collected Sophia for her Concorde flight, and whose looks had so alarmed Joy. He had left his card on the hall table, at Passmore, from whence it had inadvertently fallen to the floor. Jack, moving in, had come across the card and read in this event a sign from God. Joy was talking of employing a chauffeur and handyman as well as a housekeeper: let it be Charlie. She could well afford it: when Joy protested that she could not Jack said he'd made such a good deal on the house, thanks to her, he would be happy to pay something towards the cost of a chauffeur; he would only occasionally want to borrow him. (Of such sensible arrangements are future difficulties made.) Charlie had been summoned and interviewed: he was from the former Yugoslavia: he had arrived three years back as part of a refugee settlement programme. He was taken on in trust and hope.

He was to live in the guesthouse above Joy's garage block. Of course, his family could join him. Anything else would be inhumane. Everyone must do their bit to make the world a better place. Of course, Joy was to sign forms without reading them: of course the guesthouse would fill up with wives, children, sisters, sisters-in-law, young girls with soulful looks and permanent tears in their eyes, old ladies in headscarves. Two of the tearful girls would turn out to be pregnant: no-one liked to inquire too closely about the father, or fathers. Of course, thanks to Charlie's cleverness on the Internet and his familiarity with immigration law, relatives once scattered all over the world were to fly in to Boston and find themselves united in the Connecticut woods. A wife, a dark-eyed, bouncing, energetic, always pregnant young woman, was to replace Joy's mean-minded housekeeper. In time the family would clear some of the woodland which bordered on Joy's land, the ownership of which had never quite been established, and start to grow their own food. They were even eventually to keep a cow, which required massive amounts of feed to keep it nourished, since grazing in these wooded parts was not good, and for which Joy would in her kindness pay. But since the diamond eyes alone of Joy's new teddy-bear brooch, the gift from Jack that showed just how precious she was to him, would keep many a cow in comfort, what was the big deal? Charity begins at home. None of this was quite what Jack or Joy had intended, but in the end it is impossible for the softhearted to keep the teeming, seething rest of the world out, nor should they try too hard. Care for animals today, care for people tomorrow. It escalates.

In the meantime, on the first day of December, Miss Felicity and Joy drove to Tommy's funeral, driven by Charlie, who made an excellent, polite if melancholy and wild-eyed chauffeur. He wore a peaked cap, under which locks of black curly hair escaped. He owned a laptop. While sitting in the Mercedes waiting on his employers' bidding he would consult it on obscure points of immigration law. The life of the battery was only three hours. Charlie let it be known that he preferred not to be kept waiting longer than this, or if he was, at least to have access to a power point. Tommy's funeral, Felicity was able to reassure him, was unlikely to last more than half an hour.

The cemetery was forlorn: sea birds wheeled above, as if they mistook themselves for vultures. A few people clustered round an open grave, and stared openly as the Mercedes drew up a little distance away and the two expensive old ladies were handed out by Charlie. Otherwise all there was to look at was an open grave, a not very expensive coffin being lowered on ropes by impassive attendants, and a perfunctory parson.

Joy's feet were cold. She wished she had worn her fur-lined boots with the high heels, but though they kept her feet warm they tended to make her totter. She did not want Charlie to see her tottering: she wanted to seem in command of herself and her body. Now that Jack was next door and Charlie in the guesthouse, the relaxed and slovenly days were over: she had a male audience. She wished she were not here by a graveside: it depressed her unutterably. She wished she were not Felicity's friend, at the very least that she had been allowed to stay in the car. The elderly should keep away from funerals: it was not healthy to be reminded of mortality. Life was a long road uphill; you travelled in a vehicle driven by others; it was better to appreciate the scenery than to speculate about what was going to happen when you reached the top and looked down the other side.

One of Joy's grandsons played computer games: she'd seen how you could topple down over the edge into a brilliant white nothingness: it had really scared her. These days she saw her own life like this, something almost virtual, perched on the edge of an abyss. Jack would stretch out his hand but nothing could stop her falling through the brilliance, and swimming round in the white waves below would be Francine, dragging her under in death as she had in life, laughing her victory. Joy realized she was sleeping, dreaming almost, standing there by an open grave. You could topple in, if you weren't careful.

She paid attention. She counted. There were twelve mourners round the dismal hole in the ground, and some of those were probably from the church, brought in for the occasion. She wondered who had paid. Proper burials were expensive. The deceased had obviously been neither rich nor distinguished. Any normal person in Felicity's position would simply have sent a wreath. Nurse Dawn had actually come down the steps pleading with Miss Felicity to stay, prattling about chills and depression and breaking ankles in the snow and the need to focus on life, not death. Felicity had been right about the Golden Bowl. They were certainly determined to look after you.

And what was Felicity to this Tommy, or Tommy to Felicity? A stepson, Felicity claimed, by a long-past marriage. How was one to say what people's marital pasts really were? Everyone told lies, even Joy to herself, she'd been to a therapist: she knew all about that. Lovers became husbands in memory, husbands became lovers. After a certain age you were entitled to alter the facts to suit your comfort. And memory itself became patchy. You could remember the wedding venue, you could remember the canapés, you could remember what your new mother-in-law wore, and wishing she wouldn't, but did you remember the face of the man who turned to you and gave you the ring? Not necessarily.

Joy had been married four times; she had certificates to prove it: one doctor, one lawyer, two insurance men in that order: if you left a husband you went up in the world: if they left you, you tended to have to take what was on offer. Men changed on the day you married them: though they always claimed it was you that did: that you didn't bother any more. By which they meant you couldn't be relied upon not to fall asleep in the middle of what they were saying, having heard it so many times before. She should never have left the doctor: at least the patients kept changing and had different symptoms and sometimes even died: but one law case is much like another, and what fascinates an insurance man is hard to keep awake for. This was the kind of thing you could discuss with Miss Felicity: Joy had been glad enough to see her go but now she was gone Joy missed her. No more popping next door: now it was a drive to the Golden Bowl, and just as well she had Charlie: Jack didn't like her driving. Jack was beginning to behave like a husband, that is to say she was beginning to fall asleep while he was talking. He was in and out all the time: she didn't even have the benefit of his bank balance let alone his company in bed. Francine had had all that. But at least Francine hadn't lived to inherit. Well, everyone had their own experience. Felicity might be mean about passing on her own life experience but at least was interested in yours. Joy looked forward to the drive home in the back of the Mercedes. They could catch up with a thing or two.

She'd thought Felicity might have an ex-husband here today, which would explain her insistence on coming, but no. There was one rather good-looking elderly man, standing opposite them on the other side of the still open grave, with the coffin lying there uncovered while the preacher droned on and the wind howled and her feet froze, but he was not her type. Joy liked men more blond and bullish: grey-suited and thick-necked. Wealthy men got shinier and plumper as they got older: this one was too bony to be any kind of success, tall and lanky, more Felicity's style than hers, but at only around seventy was well out of Felicity's age range. His overcoat looked as if it was borrowed and his shoes were unpolished. Maybe Charlie would end up looking like this. Hook nose, alert eyes, one of those lucky heads of hair which didn't just fall out as time passed, and turned proper white, not even grey. She'd never felt at ease with a man with plentiful hair. There was something unnatural about it: they were cheating. Men were meant to go bald. It was God's punishment for their maleness. The man with the thick white hair was with a middle-aged woman in a cheap coat standing next to two dismal-looking teenage boys, presumably the deceased's family. Even while Joy watched he said something to the woman and she rounded up the two boys and walked away, overcome with what looked more like temper than grief. Joy wondered what that was about.

In went the token clods of dirt. A thin and miserable hymn. Joy opened and closed her mouth dutifully: what was the point of exhausting her vocal cords: the wind blew away the sound in any case. And now what was this? What was going on? Felicity and White Hair were exchanging glances, in that peculiar way people sometimes did when they were young and very aware of each other, first looking away, not quite meeting the other's eye, then catching it. It was absurd. She nudged Felicity to stop making a fool of herself but Felicity didn't even notice. She'd gone bright pink. Or perhaps it was just the cold wind. Whoever blushed when they were over eighty? Whoever was looking, to see whether you blushed or not? As you grew older you became more and more invisible. The eyes of the world slipped by you. Shop assistants went on talking as if you didn't exist. You vanished into a background of little old ladies. The only answer, Joy had found, was to wear bright colours or a good deal of gold jewellery. Then people took notice. If she'd worn her jewellery today, which she foolishly hadn't out of respect for the deceased, who clearly wasn't a candidate for a great deal of respect, why then the man with the white hair would have been trying to pick up Joy, not Felicity. Joy and he were much of an age, and Felicity was old, old, old. 'Do you know that man?' asked Joy.
'No,' said Felicity. 'Not so loud, please.'
'He's wearing a wig,' said Joy, hoping out of habit to nip any potential new unsuitable relationship in the bud. So much one had

to do for one's friends: so much she remembered of her youth. She might as well have saved her breath. During the singing of the hymn the man with the hair eased himself round the graveside and ended up standing next to Felicity. Felicity still had a pretty voice: at one dire time in her life – one of the few snippets she had disclosed to Joy – she had sung professionally. The voice was by now admittedly small, and a trifle quavery, but Felicity knew how to present it to advantage, trilling away under the stranger's ear. The pick-up line was of course simple: they had a corpse in common.

'A close relative?' Joy heard him ask Felicity, in sympathetic tones. What was he after? Money? Felicity looked expensive; she always did, though her entire wardrobe could have been bought for a tenth of the cost of Joy's teddy-bear brooch.

'My stepson,' said Felicity, and actually batted her eyes. They had aged well – large grey-green eyes with heavy lids which hadn't fallen too badly: she might even at one time have had them lifted. Joy followed Felicity's coy downward gaze: she seemed to be examining the stranger's rather peculiar shoes; heavy, boat-shaped, scuffed and battered things.

'That's a bit of a downer,' said the man, taken aback. 'I'm sorry. I'd no idea.' He had a soft voice: Joy thought maybe he'd come down for the occasion from Boston. Joy herself tended to speak out of the side of her mouth: she'd started life in New Jersey and wasn't ashamed of it.

'But only a stepson.' Felicity seemed to have decided on candour. 'Not a blood relative. I hadn't seen him for fifteen years, and I can't say he loomed large in my life. I lent him some money and that was the last I saw of him. You know what people are like. No good turns goes unpunished.'

'That's for sure,' he said, and laughed. 'Nevertheless, you came to his funeral. You have a good heart.'

'To stand about in the cold for half an hour,' she said, 'to honour what was good in someone, is no big deal. How else are we to encourage it?'

This sort of preachy stuff would be enough to put any sane man off, thought Joy. You had to admire the way Miss Felicity took risks. Joy's mother had told her never try to be too clever with a man: never say anything they wouldn't say themselves: nothing put them off quicker, and look how well she, Joy, had done for herself over the years. Felicity was prepared to risk all at a stroke. It looked as if she'd blown it, thank God. The conversation lapsed. Now they could get on back. Joy tugged the sleeve of Felicity's ethnically embroidered cream-and-green coat to remind her that she, Joy, existed. That was another thing. Felicity wore such peculiar clothes: Joy's mother thought a girl did best if she took care to look bright and healthy, and not too deep. Felicity always looked as if there was some secret going on, something held in reserve behind the gauzy scarves and the embroidery.

Joy could see she was wasting her time. Felicity and the man with the white hair were now looking into each other's eyes, across the grave. The afternoon had become enchanted. It's how Joy had met the lawyer, though already married to the doctor, eyes meeting across a crowded room. These things did happen. But Joy had been thirty then, when these things did hurtle at you out of the blue to hit you and change your life. But Felicity was over eighty, and this was no crowded room, it was a graveside, clumps of dirt fallen on to a cheap coffin and no-one had so much as thrown a flower. Two of Joy's husbands had been cremated. The more elaborate and expensive the coffin the easier it was to avoid the thought of the body inside; what had once shared your bed turned to something that felt like marble, but wouldn't last as well. After the coldness, corruption. Dead bodies had a kind of compacted solidity, as if they were more real than you were. None of it bore too much thinking about. This flirtation, for what else could you call it, might just be Felicity's way of *not* thinking about it. Joy felt overcome by too much thought and overwhelmingly sleepy. She would go back to the car by herself. Charlie would put a blanket over her knees. He still frightened her but Jack swore he was okay so she supposed he was.

15

'Do you have transport?' asked Miss Felicity of William Johnson, for that was his name.

'I don't, as it happens,' said William. 'It vanished along with my stepdaughter some ten minutes back.'

'Someone or other always behaves badly at a funeral,' observed Miss Felicity. 'Let me give you a lift to somewhere more convenient than this hillside.'

'I would like to get in to Mystic,' he said. 'It's where I temporarily reside. We don't get many limos at our door.'

'Life has its ups and downs,' Miss Felicity said. They walked back towards the Mercedes. He offered her minimal explanations. That Tommy had been his stepdaughter Margaret's partner, on and off for fifteen years, that Tommy drank too much and had never been a good provider. That he, William Johnson, had stepped in to help the family whenever he could.

'She didn't seem very grateful,' said Felicity.

'No good turn goes unpunished, the way you said.' And he laughed again. She tried to match her footsteps to his. He slowed his to achieve the same. The sun came out and the snow sparkled. What had been dank and dismal obligingly changed its nature and became crisp and romantic. Joy's impatient face stared at them from the car.

They were in no hurry to reach it.

'But you came along to his funeral, all the same,' she said, admiration in her voice.

'I came along all the same,' said the man. 'And so did you.' He said he wasn't prepared to attribute all blame to Tommy: Tommy wasn't all bad. He let it be known that his wife had died four years back.

'How strange,' said Felicity, and let it be known that she was widowed, and for the same length of time that he had been a widower. To the very month, as it turned out. Another bond. She had, she said, only just given up living alone, and moved into the Golden Bowl. It was okay.

'It ought to be at that price,' he said. He'd read their brochure. He couldn't afford anything like that: he had given the marital home to Margaret and lived off various pensions. The best deal he'd found in the area was a place called the Rosemount: a dump but a pleasant dump.

He lit up a cigarette before he got in the car, and kept everyone waiting.

'That's the first in five months,' he said. 'Funerals are upsetting.' He stubbed it out after two minutes and ground it into the snow. 'Now you know the worst about me,' he said.

'It would have to get a lot worse than that,' she said. 'I haven't led an easy life.'

Joy raised her pencilled eyebrows at the prospect of giving this addicted stranger a lift. That his name was William Johnson did nothing to reassure her. He was a confidence trickster. The name was too plain and plentiful among the population to be for real. Felicity and William both climbed into the back seat beside her. Rather than be squashed she was obliged to clamber out and clamber in again and sit in the front, next to Charlie. A gentleman would have suggested he was the one to do that. What was the point of driving round in a limo if you couldn't keep undesirables out? That was the whole point of them. She hadn't felt as raw and flustered as this since she'd been at high school, and her best friends had started dating and leaving her out in the cold. Did nothing in life ever get better? She could see she had replaced the one bad sister, Francine, with another, Felicity, and how could she discuss this with Felicity if Felicity paid her no attention at all? Her first husband had been trained in Freudian psychoanalysis: he would marvel at her insights. 'A woman's intuition,' he would say, lovingly. 'It certainly can't be brain!' He had been eighteen years older than she. She had left him for a Jungian. You entered into a certain world when you first married and tended to stay in it, if only because the men you met were so often your husband's colleagues. She'd always envied Francine, who had married a car dealer and stayed married, though she thought Jack had affairs. Anything for a laugh. Just getting a smile out of Francine was a problem.

Joy heard Felicity tell the alleged William Johnson that she had first come to the States as a GI bride, married to Tommy's father. The plantation home in Atlanta she had been told about, and shown photographs of, turned out to be a shack with hens, Rhode Island Reds, running around. When she had charged her husband with deceiving her he had replied, 'I wanted it to be true.'

Lies, thought Joy. This was the first she'd ever heard of such a story. 'This must be an upsetting kind of day for you, then,' said William. 'Some things are better not remembered.'

'I've known worse,' Felicity said. A GI bride? Joy was shocked. One of the bad girls of Europe, fortune hunters, who'd pounced upon American servicemen overseas and robbed the girls back home of husbands? Could it be true? Joy had an uneasy feeling that it might be. Serve Felicity right if she fell in with a confidence trickster. They would be much of a muchness. Joy would do nothing to save her.

'How old are you, William?' she heard Felicity ask. So up front, how did she get away with it?

'Seventy-two,' he replied.

'A mere chicken,' she said, 'compared to me. I'm eighty-one.' More lies!

'Women age better than men,' he said. 'I'd have thought you were younger than me. Anyone would.'

Joy raised eyes to heaven, and turned her head – with some difficulty: she was having trouble with arthritis in the neck – and said William had better give directions as to where exactly it was he wanted to go.

'The Rosemount Retirement Home,' he said. 'Mystic. Not too far out of your way.'

'Not out of Miss Felicity's way,' observed Joy, 'if it were her car. But it is some way out of mine.'

'I am very sorry about that,' he said, courteously enough, and she felt mean at once and said he was welcome.

William Johnson directed Charlie through the narrow back streets of Mystic, where no-one of any interest lived. The Mercedes pulled up outside a large, shabby wooden house: a few old folk, well-wrapped up in rugs, sat nodding on the verandah. A clothesline was visible at the side of the house, from which male under-garments hung, neatly pinned. Joy clicked disapproval. A sign outside read:

The Rosemount Retirement Home.
Peace of Mind for Those who Deserve it.

'Calm, quiet and comfortable, and I get a sea view, which is more than I deserve,' said William, by way of explanation. He got out and indicated his thanks. He smiled at Joy in a friendly and forgiving fashion, which infuriated her. He nodded to Charlie. He pressed Felicity's ringed fingers against his withering cheek.
'This is revolting,' thought Joy. He turned and went up the path; the gate was rusty and hung loose. Felicity looked after him fondly as Charlie drove off.
'I forgot to take his telephone number,' said Felicity. 'But you know how it is with men. If they're really interested in you, they'll find you. He knows where I live.' A kind of snort came from the front: it was Charlie, but he managed to make the sound of mirth turn into a sneeze.

16

A private eye agency called Aardvark Detectives had done excellent work for the studio in relation to the Olivia/Leo fiasco. Aardvark. I kid you not. It seems that most detective agencies are chosen through the Yellow Pages, and although the A. A. this, and the A. I. that enjoy priority of initial, the more solid words are easier to read, and Aardvark I suppose did have a kind of relevance: it being an ant-eater, a creature which searches after scraps of scuttling nourishment with a long, busy, snuffling nose. By virtue of its name Aardvark Detectives picks up no end of passing trade, first-time inquiries – follow that husband, check out that home-buyer – and flourish accordingly. It had found me Alison within weeks, in a briefer time than I had needed to find the courage to contact them.

Wendy made the initial contact. She was one of the founding Aardvark partners, a comfy, inquisitive matron dressed in a neat navy suit and costume jewellery (though nothing that clanked or glittered too much, and attracted attention). The Aardvark agency had well-paid runners in all the big national enterprises: social security, national health, vehicle registration, tax offices, credit agencies and so forth, and within hours could provide any client with a broad picture of any other citizen, one not quite legally acquired, so long as in Aardvark's view that client was comparatively law-abiding. Amazing how by simply looking at credit-card expenditure you can acquire a snapshot of a life as represented by a pattern of purchase, or indeed in some cases, as Wendy told me, charity giving. Someone who spends a lot in expensive restaurants and pays vet bills and gives to animal charities is going to be a very different person from the one who spends in the supermarket, pays bookmakers, and gives to children. Some people manage to run undercover lives, of course, have credit cards in numerous names, false passports, and deal in cash – not necessarily from criminal motives, sometimes from a distaste of so much easy overlooking by the State – but even this lot, Wendy tells me, usually end up visiting a doctor or hospital and cover is blown. Personally, I don't mind who knows what about me, and having spent vacations in India, when you're lucky if your existence is noticed at all, and dead bodies lie round for days to be walked over, see some virtue in a society which at least has you on its computers.

Files on adoption are in a peculiar state. I know, having once worked on a film called *Babyroot*, and had to excise a five-minute sequence at the last moment, the researchers having failed to realize that the law had changed since the writing of the novel on which the book was based. Five minutes is a lot of footage and in the end the film quite frankly didn't make sense. But I like to think those who watched it were crying so hard they failed to notice.

Secret records were kept until the mid-seventies, when mothers could give their babies away secure in the knowledge that that was the end of it. But then, after the screening of *Roots*, together with the Insurance Companies' growing desire to know the genetic destiny of their clients – 'parents unknown' is doom to their ears: how can they make profits if expected to take risks – it was decided that everyone had a right to know their origins and would be miserable and unhealthy if they didn't; that given-away children, once they got to eighteen, should have the right to trace and find their natural mothers. The right of the mother to find the child was not asserted – the spirit of retribution still hung around, though undefined. The new world saw it as unnatural and callous for a woman to give away a child; the old world, living as it did without State benefits, and knowing that the orphanage was the normal destiny of most of those born out of wedlock, was well aware that early adoption, no matter how painful for the mother, was in the child's best interests. An unmarried mother could struggle on for a year or so with her child: in the end, since female wages were so low, unless she was lucky enough to find a man to give shelter to her and the child in return for whatever services he insisted upon, she would be defeated.

In the eighties and nineties, organizations sprang up to link the mothers of the old world with the children of the new; reunions were tactfully organized, bitter pills of truth buffered by soft-toned counsellors in the same way that aspirin is coated against stomach pain. Let us all know our origins: this way surely contentment lay. A myriad of disowned young turned up to claim their backdated right to natural mother-love, and as often as not to retreat disappointed and reproachful. A mere six per cent of all those reunited go on to deeper acquaintance. But I didn't know that at the time. *Babyroot* presented a very different picture.

Material comforts were not enough, the abandoned asserted: they wanted all this and mother-love too, their inalienable right. They could not understand, these children of the therapy age, that there once were more important things than the avoidance of stressful emotion. They had no notion of a world without safety nets, where people starved, or if they jumped in the Thames with the newborn baby in their arms, would be fished out and hung by the neck until they were dead. I know that from a film I cut called *Watery Grave*.

Many a girl, around the age of eight, looks at her parents and decides they can't possibly be hers: they're far too dull and ordinary: she must have been switched at birth. How much more so does the child who's told she's adopted – 'but we *chose* you, darling' – fantasize about the royal palace which surely must be hers by right of birth, if only the terrible mistake had not intervened. Alas, on discovery the birth parent turns out to be not the princess, but just another kitchen maid. An older, wiser generation of social workers contrived to be obstructive in reuniting a child with its parent: the new, younger lot ploughed ruthlessly on, destroying lives and families in the name of genetic truth.

Why then, you might ask, knowing all this as I did if only from the film *Mother Trouble* – I had an affair with that director too: his name was Tom Humble and we nearly got married but I didn't want to be called Sophia Humble, not after all that – why then was I determined to find Alison for Felicity? I do not know. Why does one do stupid things?

Revenge? Not as strong as that. I loved Felicity: that was my justification. I wanted a family: she could put up with it. Perhaps I wanted something of hers for mine: I never felt she gave me enough. Stupid, sloppy, therapy reasons. In the real world reason takes second place to what one just finds oneself doing. Reasons are for police courts and soap operas. *Why, why, why*, only happens when things have gone wrong. *Because, because, because*, is for settling the minds of the onlookers. *This happens because of that* is for science, not for human beings. I just did.

And okay, because of Harry Krassner, my own personal Hare Krishna, sometimes in my bed, sometimes out of it, making me weak and needy for permanence. Settled, now?

Wendy's favourite spy in the registered charity *Mother Unknown* was young Melissa, aged twenty-four and just out of college, who didn't see why mothers over eighty shouldn't get in touch with daughters of seventy, and fought her way through piles of actual dusty hospital files – no computers way back then – charred by blitz fire and stained by the water used to put the fires out, in the basement of St Martin's-on-Thames in Kingston, whence they had been moved to safety and forgotten, to discover that a bastard baby was born to Felicity Moore, aged fifteen, spinster of this parish, on 6 October, 1930. (Father unknown.) Further consultations of adoption records, in rather better state, showed three babies named Alison passed to new parents in the middle of November; the Registrar of Births, Deaths and Marriages showed that two of these children had later died – one at the age of three (of poliomyelitis), one at fourteen (killed in an air-raid), and the other one, an Alison Moore, had married at twenty-two a Mark Dowson, student. There was a one-in-three chance that Mrs Dowson was Felicity's daughter. Personally, I had no doubt of it. If you deal with fiction enough, your own life begins to be fictional. The narrative had me in its grip.

17

Felicity returned from the funeral in high good spirits, which Nurse Dawn found a little strange. Inappropriate emotions could indicate the onset of dementia. She mentioned her worry to Dr Grepalli, who waylaid his newest and favourite guest as she made her way down the long polished corridor, with the non-slip rugs and the double-glazed windows, towards the Atlantic Suite. He fell into step beside her.

She pulled off her gloves as she walked; he noticed she had left off all but one of her rings for the outing. Golden Bowlers, if they insisted on unescorted outings, were encouraged to leave their jewellery behind, for fear of provoking attack. It seemed to Dr Grepalli that the single ring was a compromise: she half-acknowledged the dangers of the outside world: half-defied the wisdom of the Golden Bowl. Soon she would give in and be happy. She looked at her fingers as if seeing them for the first time. The skin of her hands was creased, crumpled and liver-spotted, but the fingers were still elegant, long and lively. She stretched them, as if testing them, warning arthritis away.

'A funeral, Felicity!' he said. 'How brave and in such weather. You must be upset. Do drop by my rooms if you feel like it, and we can have a little talk.'

'I am not in the least upset,' said Felicity. 'I have been to many funerals in my life and survived them without your help, Dr Grepalli.'

He caught her arm in an excess of concern.

'God gives us feelings he means us to express, Felicity. Otherwise he exacts a revenge. Denial isn't good for us. A reluctance to face our emotions leads to chronic headache and exacerbates arthritic pain.'

'Personally I attribute arthritis to damp rather than denial. The heating in my room is inadequate now the wind is in the east. Perhaps you will see to it.' She smiled at him so charmingly he failed to take offence, and walked on. Baffled, he fell back. Nurse Dawn gave it ten minutes and then made tapping movements outside Felicity's door without actually touching it and went in. Felicity was sitting at her table throwing coins in the air and making notations when they fell.

'That looks fascinating,' said Nurse Dawn. 'Is it a game?'

'Kind of,' said Felicity. 'I didn't hear you knock.'

'I knocked really loudly,' said Nurse Dawn. 'We must expect our hearing to fail as we advance in years. Some of our guests choose to have a warning light above the door rather than rely on their ears.'

'I'm not that bad yet,' said Felicity. 'What are you trying to do, demoralize me?'

'Better to face than to deny,' said Nurse Dawn. 'The game seems really absorbing. Maybe you could teach it to the rest of us? It would be a good way of getting to know everyone.'

'Bloody hell,' said Felicity. 'I've thrown twenty-seven and not a single changing line.

'The Marrying Maiden.

Nothing that would further.'

'Shit.'

'There's a Reconciliation and Tranquillity session starting any minute in the Library, Miss Felicity,' said Nurse Dawn, at a loss to know what else to say. 'It might be a good idea if you joined us.'

'Please call me Miss Moore,' said Felicity. 'I am Felicity only to friends and family. I think I have told you this before.'

'Informality frees us up,' said Nurse Dawn. 'Research shows that friendly intimacy with others is what keeps us young in body and mind. And I like to think I am your friend, and counsellor too.'

'You are self-appointed in these roles,' said Felicity. 'I wish the Golden Bowl could simply provide me with my creature comforts and leave my soul alone.'

'You may be becoming a little confused in your memory,' said Nurse Dawn. 'We have you on our guest list as Mrs Felicity Bax. Now all of a sudden you are Miss Moore.'

'Don't worry about it,' said Felicity. 'Mrs Bax will still sign the cheques.'

And she rose to her feet and ushered Nurse Dawn out of the door and closed it quite firmly behind her. It was as if she had come back from the funeral ten years younger than she had set out, and thirty years more delinquent. Nurse Dawn wished she had stuck by her original plan and accepted the Pulitzer Prize winner, smoker or not.

Nurse Dawn joined Dr Grepalli in the Library for the R and T session. At least ten Golden Bowlers had come along. That was good. Attendance was in no way compulsory – how could it be? If your heart wasn't in it what was the point? But sherry was available – a moderate amount of alcohol kept old arteries flowing free, and invitations to local events were announced: to the Aquarium – there was always some new fish to see – or the new Indian Museum, or some theatre or dance event.

Trips to the Foxwoods Indian Casino were not encouraged: gambling was not within the Golden Bowl ethos: the elderly could get all too easily hooked on the slots: go into a trance and throw their money away. Not for the old the wildness and skill of craps, let alone blackjack or roulette, just the mindlessness of feeding in quarters, and waiting to see what happened next. Which was nothing, and then nothing, and then all of a sudden something. But never enough nothing to make up for the something, as any rational person could see, or how would the Casino live, despite the background beat and the dimmed lights and the rushing chinking of coins, and the wafting smell of barbecue sauce and junk food, and the row upon row, rank upon rank, of blue-haired widows and matrons not even playing a system, content to succumb to fate. Very blue-collar. Not Golden Bowl.

If there was one thing the Golden Bowl could do for the relatives, it was keep Golden Bowlers away from the slots: what price inheritance then? And were not Native Americans, on whose reser-

vation land normal anti-gambling state edicts did not apply –
therefore Foxwoods – and who didn't have to pay tax on their
vast profits, and who were scarcely pure-blooded anyway, having
mingled so freely in the past with African-Americans, playing the
victim card too ruthlessly? One way and another no-one who
slipped out of the Golden Bowl for a day's outing to Foxwoods
cared to admit where they had been. Entertainment on a higher
plane, that is to say self-improvement, was always available at
home in the Golden Bowl. Yes, home. The Golden Bowl was
home.

This evening Dr Grepalli sat in a deep armchair, backed by rows
of leather-bound books. Cruel white light from the snowy land
reflected through mullioned windows on to withered faces and
carefully combed hair. Eighty, ninety, for some even a hundred
winters had passed: still they did their best.
'*Is the glass half-empty or the glass half-full?* Altogether now!'
boomed Dr Grepalli.
'Half-full, Dr Grepalli,' came the quavery, stalwart answer.

> '*Every breath we take,*
> *Every move we make,*
> *What do Golden Bowlers do?*'

'We live life to the full!' came the answer.

As she listened, Nurse Dawn's ruffled feathers were soothed and
smoothed. She felt proprietorial towards Dr Grepalli, who today
was looking so patricianly handsome and benign. Hers, all hers!
As for Felicity, sooner or later something would happen to bring
her to her senses and a proper sense of gratitude. A hip or a knee
that needed replacing, arthritis in the hands, a disabling loss of
memory, and she would cease to be independent: she would
become like everyone else in the twilight of their days, and not
think herself so special. Time was on Nurse Dawn's side: the great
advantage the young have over the old.

18

Felicity was on the telephone, discovering the number of the Rose-mount Retirement Home. She would not call William Johnson first. She would wait for him to call her. But she wrote the number down on the pad beside the bed in case she changed her mind. The age gap was not so great: she was twelve years William's senior, but as he himself had observed, men age faster than women. And women live longer by a good seven years: if you were reckoning in terms of marriage and who would have to live without the other longest, William could be predicted to have to live only four years without her. It was not such a bad deal. Though a glance over a grave hardly added up to a marriage proposal, she could see that.

She threw the coins again and this time got fifty-four, *Kuei Mei*, changing to fifty-five, *Feng*. That was better. The *Marrying Maiden* turning to *Abundance*. How could you get proper results with Nurse Dawn in the room? The *I Ching* would be bound to present life in a static state, gruesomely fixed. The minute the woman was gone the atmosphere lifted: breezes of energy began to flow, pushing the coins as they fell – throw three heads and there was nowhere they could go but to two heads and a tail, or two tails and a head, and the readings changed and every step of the way there was something to be said. Life proceeded in a wave motion: as soon as everything seemed as bad as could be, and stuck like that, it began to change: life began to get good again. Took only two lines – the second and third throws – to turn from two heads and a tail to three tails, and the bleak *nothing that would further* turned into

Abundance has success.

Be not sad.

Be like the sun at midday,

by way of quite pertinent observations, such as

The perseverance of a solitary man furthers.

And what was William Johnson but a solitary man? Unless of course the oracle was suggesting he would be well advised to stay solitary? Surely not.

She was going too far too fast, of course she was. Whenever had she done anything different? Meet someone in the least possible, and her mind was off at once, nest-building in her mind in the face of all likelihood, casting coins like a silly girl, trying to predict her own future; cheating, even, until the coins threw up what she wanted to hear. Were all women as idiotic? She thought maybe she was not unusual in her own generation: born helpless, obliged to live off men, having no way of earning for themselves, their minds darted for ever into hope and a vague kind of mysticism. She didn't suppose Sophia thought in the same way: Sophia was the centre of her universe, she could afford to be. Sophia would be the one to do the picking and choosing, the men the ones to dream. Sad in its way: out of so much plenty struggled such a little shrivelled, shivering root of female trust, so much disinclination to engage in the future.

As for lust, it was not the prerogative of the young: as you got older desire presented itself in a different form, that was all: as a restless sense of dissatisfaction, which out of sheer habit you had the feeling only physical sex would cure. It was generated in the head, not the loins, the latter these days admittedly a little dried up, and liable to chafing rather than the general luscious over-flowing which had characterized their prime. Felicity had lived on her own at Passmore after Exon's death with only the briefest sexual fling, and that with a man who'd come to buy some antique furniture, whom she was pretty sure was simply trying to get a good price from her – she was not gullible. But she did miss being in love: the mantra of *I love you, I love you*, running beneath the surface of everything said or thought, being so much preferable to the Golden Bowlers' fall-back position, *we live life to the full*. How could they possibly do such a thing? No amount of self-hypnosis would make it true. Stuck as they were in those ridiculously deep armchairs, so difficult to get out of. The state of love – though she was not sure of this – didn't demand physical fulfilment: men were past it after a couple of active decades anyway – after which they took to litigation or melancholy. What she'd been missing, she decided, was the consciousness of some secret level of the self where things more important than the rational mind would ever know took place, to do with the wheeling galaxies and the purposes of the life force, reduced to the whisper out of the soul, the foolish, pleading, murmuring, subtext to everyday female life: *I love you, I love you*.

She found she was singing of all things an Elvis Presley song. She couldn't remember the words. *Dum 'de-dum, dum 'de-dum, de de de de dum*. That was the secret of it. Always there from the start, just not yet come along. No wonder generations refused to believe in his death, saw Elvis walking the earth everywhere, fat hopeless ruin of a man that he was. He'd put his finger on the truth. There was someone for everyone in the end, who had been there since the beginning. Mid-eighties was pushing it: she could be mad, this could be senility, the beginning of the end: she didn't care. She'd had a minor stroke, she was self-deluded, what did it matter? This elation was enough. Invulgar parlance, Mr Right had come along; and she was at one with every girl who'd ever hoped against hope he ever would.

When Felicity had the Rosemount's telephone number, she called through to Jack, Joy's brother-in-law. She asked him if she could borrow the limo on occasion. She would pay him for its use, of course. She'd gathered from Joy that Charlie was left unemployed quite a lot of the time. Such an arrangement might suit everyone. Jack agreed, as Felicity had known he would. He'd cheated her out of $200,000 at least over the house deal. Felicity had allowed it to happen. She knew how useful it was to have other people in your moral debt. You had to be careful, of course: some people who'd wronged you bad-mouthed you for the rest of their lives, but mostly, if you were on their conscience, they would make amends when they could.

William called her the next day, as the second hand moved to midday. She was watching the clock. She invited him to tea. He said he'd be delighted. She said she'd organized Charlie to collect him from and return him to the Rosemount. He said wasn't she taking rather a lot for granted. She said no, she just didn't have time for the waiting game. She was twelve years older than he was. He said she was twelve times richer than he was: she had the upper hand here. She said no; it just about balanced out. He said he'd stayed awake most of the night wondering if he had the nerve to call her. She said if he hadn't she'd have waited three days and then called him. Then both fell silent.

'It's easy on the telephone, isn't it,' she said, eventually. 'We just got three weeks' worth of games out of the way. It's in the flesh the trouble starts.'

'We could keep it to the telephone,' he said. 'If you'd rather. It might be kinder on both of us.'

'Hold your nose and jump,' she said. 'It's always been my motto.'
He said he'd be round that afternoon.

'Try not to let anyone see you,' she said. 'They're bound to make trouble.'

'We're free agents,' he said.

'Don't be so sure,' she said. 'I'm older than you are. I know more about the world than you.'

19

This is the account Wendy gave me of her visit to Alison Dowson, née Moore, adopted Wallace, at the address Aardvark Detectives had decided was in all likelihood hers. It was a good address, Wendy reported, on Eel Pie Island, a couple of miles short of where the Thames has decided to stop being tidal and runs clear and bright and wide towards the sea, unless a particularly high tide fights the prevailing current back. Pleasant turn-of-the-century houses stand prudently back from the riverbanks, all the same: well-cared-for lawns slope down towards the water, though this being November a general mossy sogginess abounded. (I had the feeling Wendy cared for nothing either watery or rural.) Boats were cocooned or else, neglected and with moorings grown slack, bumped up against the jetties and boathouses with the wake of every passing pleasure steamer. These, being mostly floating bars, cared nothing for season or view, let alone the spirit of Edwardian England so evident in these pleasant gardens; the sense of happy childhoods and plentiful cousins, of cheerful adventures without the help of drugs, and high teas with scones and cream and jam, before anyone feared fat and sugar.

Houses here were much sought after: rock singers and stars of stage and screen bought properties to re-create a sense of tranquillity for their children, the illusion of privacy and timelessness that the river brings. *Sweet Thames run softly while I end my song.* Wendy, awed, would have given me a rundown of comparative property prices in the area but I stopped her. Alison's house, numberless but registered at the Post Office as Happiness, would have changed hands for around a million pounds sterling if only because it was shabby and very little had been done to it in the last fifty years. Typical of the homes of a million comfortably-off elderly women, said Wendy, just before they decide they're too old to cope alone and go to live with family or into a nursing home, and someone buys them up cheap and does them over.

The porched front door was opened to her by a woman in her late thirties: the intellectual type, said Wendy: that is to say she had a thin pale face and large short-sighted eyes, into which unkempt hair would fall, and a chin which wanted to meet her flat chest, that being the best position for poring over books, and had that general air of abstraction which comes from living too much in the head and not enough in the world. I suffer from the syndrome a little myself: though it is not my own thoughts which keep me out of the world, just the inventions of others invading my head. I like to think that at least between gigs I can hold up a kempt head with the best; wave manicured nails and this season's shoes at the right places, and pass for any party girl. Not that Krassner seemed to notice either way. Maybe he was never in the real world at all. In his mind I was just an extra standing there on set until needed.

Be that as it may, here I was in pursuit of family, and here seemed to be a putative, well, what? Cousin? An aunt's daughter would be a full cousin; a half-aunt's daughter could only be a second cousin. Not close enough to be able to look for family likenesses, or to demand a Christmas dinner of right, but at least something. Alison had had children and here was one of them. How eagerly I listened to Wendy's account.

The young woman was not unfriendly, but cautious, when Wendy explained her errand. She identified herself as Alison's daughter Lorna, said she had an elder brother, Guy, and acknowledged that there was some hazy mystery in her mother's background.

The Aardvark agency had got it right. A mossy and mouldy wooden sign on the porch, Wendy was pleased to note, had

Happiness burnt into it as if by a red-hot poker. Her mother Mrs Alison Dowson, said Miss Dowson, had recently moved to a nursing home. Wendy, looking over Lorna's shoulder, saw a pleasant, shabby hall, a lot of books and papers, and beyond that a long room with large windows looking over the lawn and down to the river. She had the impression there were no children around. Lorna did not ask Wendy in. She made her stand on the step. She would consult with her brother Guy, she said, before deciding whether or not to pursue the matter. Lorna said she would call Wendy, and took her card, but did not give her own telephone number. Not that that would bother the Aardvark agency, to whom the e-mail, fax, phone numbers, credit card expiry dates, holiday details, overdraft facilities were an open book. You name it, they could find it out.

As Wendy was leaving Lorna said, 'I thought under the 1974 Children's Act children were allowed to get in touch with parents. I didn't think parents could approach children,' to which Wendy replied, quick as a flash, that the law didn't specify anything about grandchildren. She had the feeling, all the same, that Lorna would go at once and look the matter up in a reference book. That she did not have a trusting nature.

Given the names Lorna and Guy Dowson, Wendy was able to make short work of the siblings' personal histories. Guy was forty-six, divorced, not so far as anyone knew gay, and a lecturer in international law at the London School of Economics. Lorna was thirty-eight, unmarried and a professor of crystallography at Imperial College, where both her parents had once been students. There was no history of lesbian relationships: just a long presumably dispassionate relationship with a fellow academic – no sudden leaps in her John Lewis account in the lingerie department: these things usually betrayed themselves financially, one way or another – which had come to an end a year ago. (This latter was deduced from a sudden drop in Lorna's minicab bills.) She had sold her own apartment in West Hampstead and moved back into her childhood home to live with and look after her mother. That had been three years back. What she had done with the proceeds of the sale would require further costly investigation – bank records are the most expensive to crack. I told Wendy not to bother. It hardly mattered. What did matter was the reason Alison had moved to a nursing home two months ago, on finally becoming incontinent. She was an Alzheimer's victim. Medical and social security reports spoke well of Lorna: she had been efficient and competent in the care of her aged mother, but having injured her back could no longer cope with nursing her.

'Her back seemed perfectly okay to me,' said Wendy, 'but so what? This case is not about insurance fraud.'

The written Aardvark agency report went into more detail: it told me that Mark Dowson had been Alison's one and only husband, and father of the two children Guy and Lorna. Mark, a palaeontologist, had worked in the back rooms of the Natural History Museum in London for most of his life: he had died of lung cancer at fifty-three. Not then a non-smoking environment, I suggested to Wendy – but she, a smoker herself, said that people who worked with old bones and the dust of past ages had a lower life expectancy than average. It was not necessarily anything to do with smoking, or with curses for that matter. Those involved with the opening of Tutankhamen's tomb had all died young – but it was the dust that did it, not the curse. Both Guy and Lorna had done well academically, though neither could be described as outgoing or fun-loving. I had by this time seen something of Lorna, and could say so with some confidence.

Guy had moved in with his sister soon after his mother had gone into her nursing home. Lorna had apparently lived a blameless life but there had been some difficulty with Guy's credit ratings, and he had a couple of drink-driving offences to his name. These, mind you, had been around the time of his divorce, and Wendy was disinclined to read too much into it. The wife, Edna, had ended up with the child (good news: a second cousin for me!), the house, alimony, and the new lover installed. Edna was now making trouble about access (bad news: the second cousin no sooner found than snatched away!). The divorced couple had been back to argue in front of the courts five times within the year. There might well be money difficulties, Wendy said: lawyers would be taking most of Mark's money: Lorna wouldn't be making much as an academic, these days among the poorest in our society. Alison's care would have to be paid for: if the State was providing it would insist on her house being sold to meet a proportion of the cost. There might of course be trust funds somewhere, but they hadn't showed up. Wendy offered to run further bank and credit checks but I felt I had more than enough to digest as it was and said no.

The Dowsons seemed a respectable, aspiring, even rather dull family within the changing framework offered by the times: if this were a film, everyone would live happily ever after. Guy would meet someone new and now Lorna was to all intents and purposes without a mother she could spread her wings and fly. Though as Wendy described her, I was not quite sure that such was her temperament. One must not read oneself into other people. But maybe I had just come across the Dowsons at a low point in their lives. I, the cousin *ex machina*, would be the one to descend from the heavens to make all things well.

Lorna called Wendy who called me, and said that Guy had agreed to meet me for lunch. We were to go to Rules in Maiden Lane, halfway between the LSE, where he worked, and Soho, where I did, but rather nearer his end, I thought. It was his choice of restaurant, all rib of beef and Yorkshire pudding and treacle tart and a dress code. Comfort food. I was excited, and yet terrified: it was as if for once I was directing a film, not just editing it. And strange to meet someone about whose life you knew a lot, while they knew nothing about you: it gave one agreeable if unreasonable power.

I had a little trouble at the door gaining admittance: I had walked from Soho and so worn my sneakers. This did not conform to the dress code. I threatened to solve the problem by taking them off and going in with stockinged soles, so they quickly relented. Guy was already waiting there at the table. He rose to his feet politely. I had no sense of family from meeting, but why would I? The bloodline was running thin: we shared only a sixth of our DNA. Guy was broad-set, almost pudgy, with a born-old look, but with bright, quick, knowing eyes. He was already balding and had a long jaw, which gave him a mournful look, but might only have been the weight of the jaw dragging down the corners of the mouth. I reminded myself I was trying to gain a family, not a prospective lover. One was not meant to find family attractive. It was inappropriate. I found myself trying to please him, nevertheless. I did not get the feeling that he liked me very much: he ordered the roast beef and I ordered a Caesar salad without the croutons which he seemed to think peculiar of me and apologized to the waiter. I said I hoped he did not find me trendy and hysterical, and he smiled politely and said no of course not, but not very convincingly. When I talked about my job he looked puzzled, and couldn't really work out what I did or why I would want to do it. I almost liked that. It was refreshing to meet someone outside the business. One's life narrows down with the years: there is so much to say and so little time to say it in – one sticks to the patois of the profession, which can put others off. He had not heard of Harry Krassner, whose name I brought into the conversation. (I can't help doing this, I notice.) He, Guy, told me he had no real interest in meeting Felicity – Rhode Island was a long way away: she was very old and living in a home: his own mother was more than enough to cope with. His work seldom took him to the States; he lectured in Europe. He could understand that his mother Alison might well have liked to meet her real mother, but Felicity had left it rather late. His mother was now past wanting to do anything except be comfortable in her bed. I tried not to show, in the draining of my espresso – he had filter – that I thought he was a real wet blanket. When the bill came he suggested I pay it, since my interests were served by the meeting, not his. Startled, I paid. He said politely he had enjoyed the meeting, and it was pleasant to meet a cousin once removed, which put me in my place. Humiliated and hating him, I left him at the door of the restaurant.

I called Wendy and told her the meeting was something of a washout, and Wendy said she was sorry after all that, but it was pretty much par for the course. People were not very adventurous after the age of thirty: they did not want anything new to happen. It took them all their energy to deal with what was in front of their noses. I was an exception. I prepared myself to cope with disappointment. But then the next day Alison's other child, Lorna, called me in the cutting room and said I must come over to tea sometime. She was busy with students at the moment but as soon as a window opened she'd be in touch. I was unreasonably blissful. I danced round my apartment naked that evening and Krassner, back in town, asked what on earth had got into me? Delighted though he was to see me like this, who usually crawled into bed with him too exhausted to undress at all.

'Scones and jam and sandwiches and family snaps!' I cried. 'Family at last!'

He was puzzled and intrigued. I have the feeling that Americans use their large country to advantage, simply to get away from family, paying it lip service at Thanksgiving. They do not like to cluster together as we do, our little family units our defence against the world. They are braver and tougher than we are. His parents had started out in Buffalo: his father now lived in Texas, his mother in Sacramento: both had remarried, and started their lives over. He reminded them both of what both would rather forget, their time together. His father said how like his mother he was. His mother said how like his father he was. Both claimed to be proud of him and both wanted money from him. At night, lying next to me, he would sometimes sigh heavily in his sleep, and I would feel my heart almost break for him, but there is no healing the world's grief, of which he had no more than his share. I really cannot understand why we are born with such a capacity for it. But there is always cinema, to take us out of ourselves.

20

Felicity and William met almost daily over a period of six weeks
without attracting the attention of Nurse Dawn. Between two
o'clock and five o'clock in the afternoon, activities at the Golden
Bowl ceased: guests were expected to retire to their suites to rest
and meditate. Videos were provided: a supply of black-and-white
movies out of Hollywood second to none, as the brochure put it,
plus a whole range of self-help extravaganzas: *Breathe Your Way
to Tranquillity*, *The Art of Happy Memory*, *Meet Yourself As You
Really Are* and so on. Most Golden Bowlers, having seen the old
movies the first time round, and exhausted emotionally by the
daily effort of self-improvement and self-revelation, simply slept.
Nurse Dawn slipped upstairs to be with Dr Grepalli, and the other
staff relaxed in her absence. The place dreamed.

In the West Wing, the long, low building which Sophia had noticed
from Dr Grepalli's office, morning or afternoon made little difference. Life-support systems hummed and buzzed; heart and blood-
pressure monitors called for constant help. Benign old eyes gazed
dreamily ceilingwards, all passion spent, drifting in the good
dreams that today's hypnotic drugs induce. It was here in the West
Wing that those Golden Bowlers who were finally lost to senility
or incontinence were cared for. This was where, from time to
time, priests came to administer last rites – mostly to keep the
staff happy (many in the caring professions are of Irish or Catholic
extraction): the departing guests themselves beyond worrying
about the afterlife, or the punishment or rewards ahead. This was

where the undertakers called with their discreet vans, to transfer the husks of the once living out the back gates. Golden Bowlers knew well enough when the back gates were opened: staff talked, and the gates creaked mightily, in spite of any amount of oiling. Dr Rosebloom had been one of the few to succumb in the main house: it happened sometimes, but rarely. Nurse Dawn had an eye for an impending sudden death: the sharp pain in the big toe, which, though considered innocent enough by the one who complained about it, could be the precursor of an infarction; sometimes a sudden pallor, an abstraction, as the soul, almost as if told in advance, prepared to quit the body. Then a sedative in the three-times-daily vitamin drink, and a discreet transfer to the West Wing, and a return to the main house in a couple of days if happily the crisis passed. However, Dr Rosebloom had just sneakily and suddenly deceased, almost, Nurse Dawn felt, to spite her: a wrong note: how the discordance jarred. Nurse Dawn played the Golden Bowl as if she were a piano player and the organization was her instrument; she hated fumbles and jumbles. At the moment, she felt in her fingertips, all was running along well, smoothly, almost merrily, with no false notes, Pianola style. She could go up to Dr Grepalli's suite and relax, or at any rate help him to, with corsets and stiletto heels and a neat little horse whip, without concern.

The arrangement between Felicity and Jack was that Charlie would drop William off at the Atlantic Suite at two-thirty every weekday and pick him up at four. Joy took a nap every afternoon: there seemed no reason to agitate her by letting her know how Charlie was occupied. If he were not around she would assume that Jack next door had some use for him.

Seeing a Mercedes and driver, the security man at the gates of the Golden Bowl opened them without question to let the vehicle through. Charlie, instead of driving up to the big front door, which everyone refrained from calling the Golden Gates, drew up outside the French windows of the Atlantic Suite and there dropped William off, before casually driving away. Charlie knew where his bread and butter lay, and how to be discreet. Even in his native land such a budding relationship would have aroused comment and disapproval. Only in the United States, he thought, would the old have health and energy enough thus to complicate their lives. It gave him a sense of future. He might even give up smoking the better to fit in.

Felicity, on the first visit, obliged to unhinge her vision – a whole day in the making – of William Johnson from the reality, was relieved to see coming towards her a lean well-set-up man wearing jeans and an open-necked shirt. He did not hobble, or dribble, or shuffle, things she might have chosen to forget. From a distance he could even have been in his forties. Close to, yes, the grey-green eyes were rheumy, the mouth thinned, all that. What did it matter? So he was seventy-two, she was eighty-something. That was the way the world went, these days. What was age, for a woman? Mostly the absence of oestrogen. She had taken one little yellow tablet a day from the age of forty-seven: she had not even known when the menopause started, if indeed it had ever come. She had looked in the mirror twenty minutes back and for once had been satisfied with what she saw. It was a magic mirror, she decided: it threw back your soul to you, and not your looks. *Mirror mirror on the wall, who deserves love most of all?* Me, me, me. Just one last time. Please.

For the first two weeks the couple sat opposite each other across the table, studying one another, not touching.
'What happened?' she asked. 'Why have you ended up in the Rose-mount? Don't you have a pension, insurance, entitlements, like other people?' He was vague. He was looking for the right place. He had for many years been a teacher of English literature in a school in the Bronx, head of a department in the days when to be a teacher was a noble thing, suggested a life of dedication to the common cause, bringing a dream to the nation's children. It wasn't like that now, of course. Teachers were nobodies. They had no status. He'd been offered promotion many a time, could have been principal, joined the School Board, that kind of thing, but he loved actual teaching too much. His task, his vocation, his skill. And there'd been problems with taxes after his ex-wife's death. A lot had been paid out that shouldn't have been. Then lawyers had taken more than he had got back. Besides, he liked the Rosemount.

*   *   *

'I like company,' he said. 'Living alone has its compensations. I've tried it. But spend days without hearing a human voice and when you finally do you can't understand what it's saying.'

Sometimes she felt he was not telling her the whole truth. He was not necessarily lying, just missing something out. She was not sure she wanted to know what it was. You trusted or you didn't. She trusted.

'And after families, I suppose strangers could be a relief,' she said, and he agreed, but he was not forthcoming about his family. She asked what life was like at the Rosemount.
'They try to give you happy pills,' he said. 'So long as you never swallow them you're okay.'
'It was never happiness one wanted,' said Felicity.
'If you hurt,' agreed William, 'you know you're alive.'

That was on the first meeting, which set the pattern for the ones to come. They talked, but didn't touch. Maybe that was all he wanted, just someone to talk to? Maybe there was no sexual component in his interest in her. She was a woman in her eighties. It didn't feel like it, emotionally: apparently you learned nothing when it came to affairs of the heart. You started afresh in folly every time. Look in the mirror, and you always saw something different; sometimes you saw the spirit of yourself, perfectly fresh and youthful: sometimes you saw corrupted flesh. Once or twice again lately she'd even caught a glimpse of something shadowy, a flicker of a reproachful Dr Rosebloom: get as old as this, he was saying, and male or female, what's the difference? She didn't want to risk humiliation by insisting on the distinction. She'd met younger men in her time who, just as girls will do with older men, took pleasure in inferring a sexual interest only to draw back in shock-horror when brought to the test. *But what are you doing! You're old enough to be my mother! I thought we were just friends!* That started at forty. Foolish she might be, but not as foolish as to risk this particular hurt. Though the quality of William's candid stare, the steady grey-green eyes regarding hers, reassured her. He wasn't the kind to play games. Yet they had a glint, an urgency she'd seen in soldiers, excited by the adventure of killing. She wanted part of it.

'It's good to have someone to talk to,' he said, on the third visit. 'You could talk to people at the Rosemount,' she said. 'Why come all the way out here to do it?'

'At Rosemount talk is for the exchange of information, not ideas,' he said. She could see she did rather better at the Golden Bowl, where the other guests were hand-picked for intelligence and lifetime achievements, mostly in the sciences, if only because Nurse Dawn was convinced that those with active minds outlived those without. With the exception of Dr Bronstein, whose ideas, though so interesting the first time you heard them, seemed to be on a loop, and were beginning to be repeated, the great majority of Golden Bowlers were not chatterers. If they had great thoughts, they kept them to themselves. Scientists were never ones to share their homework answers, at the best of times. Sometimes she missed Joy, and the easy, noisy flow of nonsense and self-regard, which kept the demons out.

'Then why don't you apply to come here?'

'Let them eat cake,' he said, and laughed.

On the fourth visit he confided more, by way of explanation. A late and painful divorce had put paid to his savings. He had given his house, not far from here, on the edge of the Great Swamp, to his stepdaughter. That had been in the days of his comparative prosperity: now she would not let him back in. He felt King Learish about it all, he said, lightly.

'Why did she take against you? What did you do?' she asked.

'Existed,' he said, briefly, 'as the person I was.'

Felicity wanted to make things up to him. She wanted to be kinder than his wife, better than his stepdaughter. But what would he accept from her? She had no idea. Just because she had an erotic impulse to him did not mean he felt the same about her – perhaps he came every day simply because Charlie turned up and cost him nothing, and there was vodka and pretzels at the end of the journey. And because he could talk about himself, somewhere comfortable, away from the washing hanging on the line and the littered front yard. Perhaps he saw her as a mother.

She'd never had a son: for once she was glad, she would be in no danger of treating him like one, since she had no idea how to go about it.

Nothing changed; whenever had falling in love not been like this? Except now there were no girlfriends to brush up against, to give you a view of what was going to happen next, help you with the confusion between what seemed to be happening and what was really going on: *He loves me, he loves me not.* The only person who might understand was Sophia in London. But Sophia was impetuous: if Felicity said anything she might take it into her head to come over and inspect William. The idea made Felicity uneasy: maybe Sophia would drive William away, or William might fall for her – that was absurd, she could not possibly be jealous of her own granddaughter – still it was not safe. She hardly thought she could confide in Joy, who would shriek and tell her that William was a confidence trickster after her money. Which of course, and here was another thing, and one she really didn't want to think about, he could be. What he said about himself didn't quite add up.

'Is that a Utrillo?' he asked, on the eighth day.
'Only a copy,' she said. He got up and studied it. Houses, a bit of tree, a street, a sky. Realer than real. She loved it.
'I wouldn't be so sure about that. It's a very good painting. White period, too.'
'If it were real,' she said, 'I'd get a couple of million for it.'
She had told him the truth and yet not the truth. It was a Utrillo all right, with papers of provenance to prove it, part of her settlement from old Buckley, in Savannah, her rescuer and persecutor. Old Buckley, she called him, out of habit. When he died, she realized, he had been twenty years younger than she was now.

Every day William Johnson came, and every day they talked, and while they talked she had no doubts. Except she didn't touch him and the table kept the space between them, the no-man's land between desire and fear of consequences.

Every time he left he said, 'Shall I come again tomorrow?' and every time she said, 'Of course.' And he'd look over his shoulder with such an expression of marvel and pleasure it was impossible to doubt his interest. Only when Nurse Dawn came bustling in for her five-fifteen look-in as she called it, checking up that Felicity was alive and well, and hoping she'd come along to the Library for an Affirmation Session before supper, or whatever the day of the week provided, did Felicity feel old and useless again, and slightly dotty, since that was how Nurse Dawn saw her.

She sent off by post for cosmetics and face creams and even pretty underwear. Not that she thought the former would do any good, or the latter be seen. It was part of the habit of youth, of what you did when you fell in love. She had married men on grounds of common sense: this one was kind and prosperous and would look after her: that one because he could take her into high society; the next as a safe haven, and though God knows that was dull, she had not complained. She kept her side of the bargain. She did not exploit them. She did not offer love, but affection and services. It was a trade-off and they knew it, and were prepared to settle for it, to have at their command her charming smile, her slender body, the diversion of her conversation and the creature comforts she offered, if not her total attention. As for love, in Miss Felicity's comprehension that was a wildness reserved for outside marriage: something which would obviously collapse if you attempted to confine it within the boundaries of domestic responsibilities. Within marriage, love turned into habit: yet without permanence it faded away. But while it lasted, how magic was the exhilaration, the exultation, the sense of being properly alive. Just one more time, and this time let me get it right. True love. Could it be that if you just hung round for long enough, your faith intact, it happened? When you least expected it, there it was at last.

21

More riches! Aardvark Detectives had discovered another relative: a half-sister for Felicity herself, younger than she by seven years. Mrs Lucy Forgrass, née Moore, still alive and in full possession of her faculties, and living in some style in Highgate in North London: by some style Wendy meant that the Forgrass home was a large beautifully maintained house in the £1–£1,500,000 bracket and there was a heated outdoor swimming pool at the end of the garden, in a country which rarely indulged in such luxuries, and why should it, its skies being mostly grey. Now as well as cousins I had a half great-aunt. But she could wait. I had not yet met Lorna, I had not yet visited Alison. I had told Miss Felicity nothing yet of my successes. I did not want to risk her censure again.

'Go slowly with all of this,' said Wendy. I found it difficult. Real life is so slow, film with all the *longueurs* left in, the move from chair to door, the folding of linen, the waiting for the taxi. 'Cut, cut, cut,' one longs to cry. 'Go slowly!' forsooth. But I did.

The Aardvark agency had consulted documents held at Somerset House and now knew the history of Felicity's birth family. The child had been born Felicity Moore, on 6 October, 1915. Her father, Arthur Moore, was described as a novelist and journalist: her mother Sylvia, as a concert pianist. Sylvia, poor thing, had died of influenza in 1921, in one of the great epidemics that swept Europe after the Great War and took a greater death toll than that conflict itself. Felicity would have been six at the time. Her father had married again within the year – to a Lois Wasserman, from Vienna. There had been one child of this union, Lucy, born in 1922. She would have been eight when Alison was born. Arthur had died in 1925, when Lucy was three, leaving Felicity orphaned and in the care of her stepmother. In his will Arthur left everything to Lois and Lucy: Felicity was ignored, for reasons unknown. And yes, Lucy was still alive, thrice widowed, and living in Highgate.

Thrice widowed! I had once worked on a horror film, a rip-off of *Basic Instinct*, about a serial marriage killer who successively used an ice axe on her husbands. I should never have taken on such a film, and never did again. Too much blood and gore and dismemberment viewed over and over and over, is upsetting. Some editors get hardened to it, I never have.

I still did not doubt the wisdom of stirring up the past. I had found an aunt in Alison, albeit one with Alzheimer's, a half great-aunt in Lucy with a swimming pool in Highgate, some cousins in Guy and Lorna, and a cousin once removed in Guy's question-of-custody little boy. My Christmas list would soon be full: I could join the rest of the world in wrapping up parcels and complaining about it over the festive season. It was enough for me.

Krassner had gone home to Holly, not for Christmas – she was Jewish, but then so was he, through his mother – but because she wanted to adopt a child, and required him to sign a form declaring something called 'dedicated fatherhood'. This he had to do in person: fax or e-mail would not suffice. Adoption is the motherhood-of-choice in Hollywood: pregnancy can interfere with a film career, or spoil a perfect body. Suppose the chance of a lifetime turned up at a day's notice and you were just going into labour! An adopted baby may arrive suddenly but will do so ready-formed and can be left with the staff almost at once.

Krassner had seemed surprised when I said but what about the genes? Doesn't Holly want her own child? What is the point of a baby who is someone else's? Krassner said we Europeans were hung up on heredity. In the US rearing was what counted – babies burst bright and beautiful into the world: it was up to whoever adopted them to keep them that way. Holly would have checked the birth parents out for health, looks and sanity. I persisted that I didn't see how you could really love someone else's baby as your own. Krassner said of course you could and it was irrelevant anyway since I'd decided to have none. Perhaps in the US love isn't so passionate and painful a thing as it is in Europe: Krassner flew off easily enough, with an absent-minded peck goodbye, already in his head halfway to Hollywood.

I was to be out of the cutting room for the three holiday weeks over Christmas and the New Year. I had proceeded apace with *Hope Against Hope* and left great swathes of it on the floor. Three hours' meandering mishmash was now a sleek piece of work premiering in February. I had reason to believe that Astra Barnes, whose tedious director's cut had been understandably ruled out of order on commercial grounds, was badmouthing me all over London but that was to be expected. My association with Krassner, now more or less public knowledge, did nothing to damage my professional reputation. On the contrary. If he did not contribute to our living expenses while he was with me no doubt he bore this in mind: that every day he spent with me put up my earning potential. These are the rewards of fame.

Now Krassner was gone, leaving me with my jealousy, an emotion entirely new to me, and all I had to take my mind off the worm gnawing at my vitals were my finer feelings, my friends, and my acquisition of new family. For once work had failed me. The Aardvark agency closed on 21 December and didn't reopen until 8 January. I felt abandoned. Wendy was like a tight-laced know-it-all mother, bustling about, the kind you will grow up to leave behind, such are your superior sensitivities and their lack of them. It doesn't mean you don't miss them when they go away and leave you.

I called Felicity at the Golden Bowl. The operator told me it was afternoon rest time and she should not be disturbed. I decided it was probably for the best. Supposing she really hated it there and wanted me to come and rescue her? I sent her a Christmas card instead. I would wait until I had her family sorted out and then surprise her thoroughly: I would visit her properly with names and addresses and telephone numbers and photographs and life would be so rich.

22

For three weeks Felicity faced William Johnson across the table. They debriefed one another: her politics, his (which in him amounted to nothing specific, just a state of perpetual indignation): her musical taste, his (they differed on Wagner, but that tended to be a normal gender divide, or at least they so persuaded themselves): how in her youth she'd fled England for the new world of America, to reinvent herself; America, the promised land. He in his thirties going back to England, hoping to uninvent himself in Shakespeare's land, and failing: meeting there the woman who was to be his wife, Meryl, bringing her back. He'd wanted children, she hadn't. She'd had a daughter already, by an earlier marriage, yes, the one at the funeral, Margaret, the one who had Tommy's boys. He looked forward to the Judgement Day, to the great debriefing, in which all things would be made clear: whether or not he had been unkind to Meryl, unfair to Margaret, who killed Kennedy, what happened to the *Marie Celeste*, and so forth.
'Do you mean a literal Judgement Day?' she asked, alarmed, alerted. All this, and he might turn out to be a Born-again Christian.
'Wishful thinking,' he said. 'It would be great to think someone, somewhere was in charge. The great gambler, the great dice roller in the sky.'

The metaphor was unusual but she thought no more of it. Every day brought new confidence, greater expectation: layer after layer of agreement or at least acceptance; getting closer, feeling safer, she giving an account of her life starting from the present and working backwards, since her life had got better as she got older: he, for whom it had been the other way around, starting at the beginning and working forwards, this for both of them being safest. Both, it seemed to her, putting off the day when they would have to face the problem of being no longer young. Bad enough at twenty to work out how to proceed from physical distance to physical intimacy: how to move from the chair to the sofa, from the sofa to the bed: fifty, sixty years on and the problem was back again. About some things she still remained silent. It would not surprise her if he did too. He was no fool, like her old enough to know that some information had better come after sex and not before or there might be no sex at all. Conversation between them grew difficult: they'd fall into silences. She became restless, almost irritable.

Charlie would tap on the window to remind them when time was up. She would be the one to hear it, not William. She realized that he was quite deaf: perhaps his silences were to do with that, nothing more significant. He just hadn't heard what she'd said. The secrecy she had insisted on began to seem silly. It was ridiculous that Charlie had to be back before Joy woke from her afternoon nap: that William had to be gone before Nurse Dawn put in her appearance, bustling everyone up for their next assault on the day. She put it to William that he could stay longer if he wanted. But William said he needed to be back at the Rosemount because he minded Maria's baby while she went off to collect her older children from school. Maria? Just one of the domestic helpers at the Rosemount.

'She's thirty-one, I'm seventy-two,' he said. 'All I'm good for is baby-sitting.' And Felicity hadn't even asked. He could read her mind by now. She didn't like it.

'But what did you do all day before I came along?' she asked. 'You are a mystery to me.'

'This and that,' he replied. 'What did you do?'

'The same,' she said. 'But it suits women to be like that, it doesn't suit men.'

He looked at her seriously for a moment or two as if debating with himself and then said, 'Why do I always sit opposite you. Couldn't I sit next to you, on the sofa?'

He didn't wait for her answer but pushed the sofa round so the table was in front of them and now they could lean into each other when they talked. She felt a charge of electricity when she touched him, as if she'd laid her finger on the metal of a bell push, first one in to the office in the morning. If the carpets were nylon and the wall paint acrylic, the charge could throw you back across the corridor if you were unlucky. She'd worked in such an office once. She'd complained and lost her job; or perhaps it had been because the boss wanted to sleep with her and for once she wouldn't. The electric charge was quickly gone, anyway, some waiting energy finally released. Maybe he felt it too. If so, he didn't show it. Still nothing was said. She could be wrong about it: he could be teasing her, manipulating cruelly. She could be making a fool of herself. Maybe all this was in her head? Eighty-three! But now they leaned into one another, came nearer to one another's imperfections and still, it seemed, he did not shrink. His hands, like hers, were wrinkled and liver-spotted. Though she thought the new creams she had been using had rather diminished the discolouring on hers. That encouraged her. She held them up boldly for his inspection. She took a risk.

'Such old hands,' she said. 'Can you bear the reality of them? Or do we just go on talking for ever?'

'It may be all you'll allow,' he said. 'How am I meant to know?'

'We could just lie together on the bed,' she said. 'I'm so old that sitting up straight for so long quite tires me out. We have to think about these things.'

He didn't reply at once. *I've blown it*, she thought. *All my life I've blown it. Gone too fast. Had too much faith. Now I'll have to die knowing I never got it right, that how you begin you are doomed to go on.*

He stood up abruptly. 'You don't know how anxious I am,' he said. 'I'm an old man. I'll only disappoint you. I think I'd better go now.'

Go then, she would have said in her youth, hurt and angry, sexually rejected. *Go and I never want to see you again*. But now was now and when it came to it William was younger than she was: what did he know what was good for him?

131

'Oh sit down and shut up,' she said. 'You're such a chicken compared to me.'

'My wife left me because I was too old and inadequate.'

'Confession time,' said Felicity. 'And anyway I don't believe you. It's too easy.'

He stood at the French windows. It was touch and go. Then he sat down on the bed. 'Charlie isn't here yet with the car,' he said. 'I'm in no position to walk out. So if your back is tired we'd better just lie on the bed together.'

He stretched out on the bed. She lay down beside him. He was five inches taller than she was. Female hip fitted neatly into male waist: she'd known it would.

'Did you love your wife?' she asked. It was easier to ask this not looking at him.

'Meryl? I was married to her for nearly twenty years. You become like one person: it isn't necessarily the person you were born to be.' Not quite a straight reply.

'After twenty years most women would stay. They wouldn't up and divorce you for nothing. What had you done?'

'Nothing I did. Perhaps what I was. Maybe she was like me, maybe she felt she wasn't the person she was born to be either. Perhaps she wanted to find out who she was before it was too late. People get desperate.'

'But you didn't want the marriage to end.'

'Of course not.'

That hurt her. She'd forgotten how such stupid things could hurt, a man loving his wife.

'I had grown into her, for good or bad,' he said. 'I didn't have the heart for divorce lawyers. She did. She'd joined a women's group. They egged her on, I guess. What she didn't take I gave to her, and after she died Margaret had it. Now I live at the Rosemount. I read a lot. I watch the sea and the sky changing, and think about living somewhere else, doing something with my life. It's okay: if you take it day by day. So the world thinks I'm a loser, so what do I care? But I never thought this was how it would end. An old man at the ocean's edge.'

'And I'm the old woman of the woods,' she said, but she was shaken.

*   *   *

132

Joy would think he was a madman. In Joy's world you looked after yourself, and William Johnson had spectacularly failed to do so. Joy did not understand the gestures which made living with the self bearable. A lame duck, Joy would say. A sponger. Why are you lying here on a bed with this loser? Felicity wanted to cry: she wanted to be home again in England, where failure was a more honourable state. 'Except now I've met you life doesn't seem to have ended,' he said. 'I can see there just might be a rebirth.'

For once in my life. No-one can take this away from me. Why has it had to take so long? Doubts fled as quickly and suddenly as they had come. There they were, lying on a bed, flesh touching, albeit the other side of fabric. The denim of his jeans, the silk of her skirt: her legs still long and shapely, the skin no longer taut, blotchy; a blue network of veins beneath the ankles. How much did it matter? What had love ever been about? The spirit or the flesh?

'I haven't told you everything about me,' she said, on impulse. 'Only the things I wanted you to know.'
'I guessed as much,' he said. 'Speak to me.'
But Charlie was tapping at the window.
'Saved by the bell,' she said. And she stayed lying on the bed, bold as brass, not minding that Charlie was there to see, watching William Johnson gather his coat and leave, saying he would be back tomorrow. It was true, it was all true: she was eighty-three and felt the exhilaration of true love once again and no-one could take this away from her.

Miss Felicity consented to go to the evening's Reconciliation Class, and was charming to Nurse Dawn.

> *'What do Golden Bowlers do?*
> *We live life to the full,'*

she chanted with the best of them.

Did you have to tell people the truth? She could see the wisdom of it when you were twenty. Secrets were likely to emerge when least convenient and upset the applecart. Social disgrace, madness in the family, illegitimate babies, a spell as a whore – whatever it was, was best faced up to at the beginning. But at this end of life the past was so far away, and seemed to have so little relevance to the present. Past states, past sins, drifted into forgetfulness. Better perhaps to let the past be. She'd told Sophia on the satellite link that she was old enough now to speak the truth. Brave words, and ones that might have been true even a couple of months ago but were not true now. Acquaintance with William Johnson had sent her spinning back into insecurity as to what she should or shouldn't say for the best, like an adolescent. But she was grown up now and if she still wasn't equipped to make judgements about the world, when would she ever be? Except when had she ever thought differently? At fifteen, an assignation, stepping into a snowy garden while the full moon looked down. *I know what I'm doing*. Some fifteen years later, stepping across the gang-plank at Southampton which would lead her to the new land – the seductive upwards tilt of the heavy damp dark wood, ridged to stop you slipping; the smell of salt sea and engine oil, the noise of engines and seagulls. *I know what I'm doing*.

'Is our cup half-empty or our cup half-full?' inquired Dr Grepalli. 'Half-full!' returned the happy chorus. Only Dr Bronstein and Clara Craft seemed unwilling to join in the general enthusiasm. It occurred to Felicity that Dr Grepalli was setting his sights too low. Her own cup was pretty much full to overflowing.

23

It was remarkable how friends thinned out over Christmas: gays retreated either singly to the maternal bosom to discuss gender relations, or to the paternal one to torment it: or in pairs the better to dissect the subtleties of the reaction they had had to endure over the season: the significance of the offering of the single bed (rejection) or the double one (acceptance). Single women went home to their county families to hole themselves up and protest the fullness of their city lives; lone mothers might ask you round to Christmas dinner, but what with the childcare absent, the ritual thawing of the turkey serving only to mark the thinness of the living, and the desperate smoking of joints behind the children's backs an embarrassment, made me disinclined to accept invitations from this source. Two-income professional childless couples offered the best and most lavish entertainment, with their minimalist Christmas trees and their elaborate, fashion-conscious meals, but the drug of choice, cocaine, made everyone jumpy and even evil: I would limp home to my lair exhausted.

I thought I would have to spend Christmas Day on my own: disappointingly, Guy and Lorna didn't seem anxious to extend an invitation. Though since my first encounter with them they had become quite friendly and I had been to visit them on several occasions, their hospitality was never lavish.
'We don't really keep Christmas,' said Lorna. 'Such a hypocritical time: commerce lurking under the guise of religion.'
Well, everyone knows that: they just choose to ignore it, or better

still, make a meal of it and enjoy it. I hoped Lorna would relent: the house on Eel Pie Island seemed so perfect for Christmas. I would put up the decorations, streamers and so on, if they were too self-conscious to do so. I wasn't afraid of stepladders, as Lorna might be. I would even pay for all the baubles, if the thought of what they cost was Guy's problem. Did they have no feeling at all for tradition? Had this house not been their childhood home? But even as children, I could see, such were their natures they might not have entered much into the Christmas spirit. Lorna would have found fault with any toy she was given: Guy would have worried himself sick in case her gifts were more expensive than his. Both seemed to have been born with *a wicked waste of money* on their lips. Yet I did not feel Alison had been like that: the house was too pretty, the lamp-fittings needlessly expensive, the dish cloths proper Irish linen. And the name on the lintel was Happiness, though her children had let creepers grow over it, and woodlice scuttled around in the damp, flaky wood of the board.

I was, it was beginning to be evident, rather disappointed in my new cousins. I looked for lightness in the dullness. Perhaps Guy and Lorna, brother and sister, were having an affair? But the fact that I had edited a documentary film on sibling incest, *Family Bond*, which suggested that among the intellectual classes such deviancy was common, did not make it true. There was nothing Byronic about Guy: though something of Dorothy Wordsworth about Lorna.

At first Lorna showed no more interest in Felicity's existence than did Guy. She actively disliked films; her enthusiasms were reserved for the crystalline structures with which she worked, the subject on which she lectured. Crystals are no doubt beautiful and extra-ordinary, but at the other end of the spectrum from the flashing, changing life of celluloid, and to the non-scientist, once you have applied an adjective or two, a difficult subject for conversation. When they discovered that Felicity owned a Utrillo, brother and sister became rather more interested in their new relative. *I suppose, when you come to think about it, she's our actual grand-mother*. I think both had associated *widowhood* and *living in a retirement home* with poverty. That she owned a major piece of art intrigued them, though Lorna's eyes glazed when I began to tell them the story of how Felicity had acquired it. Long ago and far away, and how things come to be as they are, held no interest for them.

Both brother and sister had reddish hair and the same long, broad, rather grim jaws, though Lorna's drooped to meet her chin and Guy's tilted aggressively upwards. Lorna's hair was the exact same orangey shade as Angel's and mine, but straight and thin, not crinkly and thick. Glints in what remained of Guy's hair suggested the same shade. Clearly the overweening colour gene had come through from Felicity, but those corresponding to texture and plenty had been diffused over a couple of generations. Photographs of their father the palaeontologist showed the same jaw, but set in a pleasanter expression than either of theirs. He looked, in fact, a rather nice quiet studious person of integrity. A photograph of Alison as a young woman showed her with straight dark hair, mine and Angel's pale skin, Felicity's widely spaced, rather hooded eyes, and a lively expression.

It seemed Alison's adoptive parents, the Wallaces, had played little part in her children's lives.
'I think they were shopkeepers,' Lorna said. 'Rather ordinary. They ran a chain of corner stores, but in the seventies the big supermarkets opened and they lost their money: they retired somewhere dreadful, like the South Coast. Mother didn't speak of them much.'

I heard the story of the Dowson parents' meeting. Both had been studying geology at the Imperial College in South Kensington. He was twenty-four, she was twenty-two. They'd married within three or four months, and both sets of parents had disapproved. Guy and Lorna, from the look on their faces, seemed to disapprove too, although they owed their existence to the union. Alison had ended up a stay-at-home mother of the cooking, cleaning variety as was typical of her generation, when learning was, for women, for learning's sake. Mark had become a palaeontologist, a man of note, the one they could proudly acknowledge as parent. Lorna found a tattered photograph in a drawer of Mark receiving an honorary degree of Cambridge – and another one of him showing the young Prince Charles around a hillside in which something remarkable out of pre-history had been found. If they'd been photos of me I would have had them framed and in pride of place on the wall: even if only in the lavatory to show I took none of it seriously: not so the Dowsons. They had a nervy diffidence about their place in the world. They wouldn't have gone so far as to throw the photographs away: the bottom of a drawer getting scuffed under other things should have been no surprise.

Mark's background was county English: both his parents had died recently: the expected inheritance having been swallowed up by nursing home fees, as so often happens these days. The aged live longer, though no more steady on their pins than heretofore. The Dowson grandfather had been a Harley Street physician: the grandmother had edited a natural history magazine. Their snobbery would have been of a vague and throwaway kind, to do with intellect and education rather than wealth: Mark had married below him, Alison being out of nowhere and presumably pregnant with Guy when they married, but at least she had a brain. From her photographs she had been no great beauty, this throwaway child of Felicity's, though her eyes were good, like her mother's, and her smile shy and sweet. The young Alison stood stooped and awkward, as Lorna did.

In the fifties abstention was still the favoured method of birth control. Abortion was difficult, surgical and for medical reasons only. If a man got a girl pregnant he was expected to marry her and that was that. Otherwise he was a heel and a cad. Contraception was the man's responsibility: coitus interruptus the next best thing to no sex at all. If the man failed in self-control, if he got the wrong girl pregnant, too bad: if lifelong unhappiness for both ensued, too bad as well. Sex was meant to happen after marriage, not before: in theory girls stayed virgins until their wedding night: if they didn't they deserved what they got. Wedding guests stared at the hang of the bride's dress and speculated. Young couples would go away for a few months after the wedding and return with a baby and be vague about the date of the birth.

*　　*　　*

For the Dowsons the church wedding would have been an embarrassment: the social gulf between the groom's side of the church and the bride's noticeable. The Wallaces were shopkeepers. That Alison was herself the adopted child of an unmarried mother would not have helped. Like mother, everyone must have thought, like daughter. Product as she was of two disgraced generations, perhaps Lorna's life problem was that she was trying too hard not to be a bad girl. Parental-in-law disdain might well have extended to Alison's children, and account for the way the pair of them were so socially ill at ease. Proper social responses, in other words, did not come naturally to them. If you required someone else to pay for your lunch you did not then choose the most expensive dish on the menu. If someone crossed London to come to tea you served more than digestive biscuits: you offered sandwiches as well. It would occur to you that your guest might be hungry. Socially secure people, from whatever class, as Miss Felicity would have put it, *knew how to behave*. If someone like Wendy pulled a packet of sweets from her Crimplene pocket she would take care to offer you one: Lorna took out a packet of cigarettes, looked inside, said, 'Sorry, only one left,' and smoked it without thinking this was in any way odd. But then, most people have quirks of one kind or another, and I daresay I have myself. Habits and actions that seem normal to me but strange to other people, and that no-one has pointed out to me.

When I told Guy and Lorna that I had found them a half-great-aunt Lucy, younger half-aunt to their mother Alison, or rather that she'd found me, they seemed unmoved. What to them was a newly discovered half great-aunt? Widow of a manufacturer of exercise machinery? A person without PhDs or publications? Who cared? And still they did not suggest I visited Alison.

'If you're visiting your mother on Christmas Day,' I hinted broadly, 'maybe I could come with you?'
'There's no point,' said Guy. 'She can't tell one day from another.'
I did not see that the world stopped just because the inside of one's head stopped. If Alison didn't know it was Christmas Day they could always tell her, even if she forgot almost at once. The rituals of civilization – even if hardly based in religion any

more – must be observed, or what was the point of being civilized?

And she was my half-aunt as well as their mother; I was family too. I resolved to visit Alison on Christmas Day, no matter what her children did or didn't do. In the meantime I would call on Lucy, if only to get the back story of the film now building in my head, inch by inch, reel by reel, into the totality of its narrative. That Miss Felicity's life wasn't finished yet did not occur to me. One tends to write off women in their mid-eighties as simply hanging around until death carries them away. One is wrong.

24

Also, of course, women in their seventies have a continuing life and a will of their own. Lucy, Felicity's younger half-sister, turned up at my door. She had been alerted by Wendy that I was making inquiries into her past life. I was quite shocked, as if I'd been turning over earth with my spade, as was my legitimate right, and all of a sudden a small furry creature had leapt out of its underground lair and bitten me on the nose, slapped me round the ears with great strong mole-like hands. This investigation was not quite the one-way street I had imagined. I stopped digging, but what I unearthed had a life of its own.

She was still slender and elegant, straight-backed like Felicity, and unlike Felicity, of the kind who has managed to live a life without untoward alarms, within accepted conventional boundaries. I could tell from her controlled courtesy, by the way she looked in polite puzzlement around my flat, as if wondering where the three-piece suite could be, why the curtains hung from loops of fabric and were not properly fitted, why the freezer was in the living room, and who had painted it with scenes from Disney's *Fantasia*. She was well dressed in taupes and beiges, though one felt that the instinctive preference for poster blue, demonstrated by those who grow old without ever quite growing up, was only just held at bay. She had just such a blue ribbon woven into carefully curled, still thick, perfectly white hair. On the left hand she wore a broad gold wedding ring, and on the right a diamond ring of the kind it is unwise to flash around in Soho. They might not quite cut off the finger to get it but the finger could get dislocated in the tug. I had known it happen.

Wide, helpless blue eyes looked with apparent trust from a face grown old around them: I say 'apparent' because in some women of an older generation this way survival lies. If you're helpless and pretty enough, some man is bound to come along to change the tyre, marry you and fetch your handbag for the rest of his life, which will probably be shorter than yours, and what is more he will leave you the money so you can enjoy your widowhood in peace. When Lucy told me she had been recently widowed and that her husband had manufactured exercise bicycles, I was not surprised. If the only way respectability can be acquired is at the expense of deep seriousness, so be it. I can earn my own living. I was born four decades later than Lucy. I have a skill, a talent and a training. Other women are not so lucky.

Lucy had telephoned before she arrived to check that I was in, and when I warned her that there were lots of stairs but no light, told me that she was not bothered by stairs but liked to have a handrail. I had to think before I replied that yes, there was one. The young, I suppose, just run up and down stairs with confidence, taking two at a time if they're in a hurry: the old go more carefully: perhaps from a shakier sense of balance or simply because experience has taught them that falls are nasty things. They like a good rail. Even as I put the phone down I knew I should have told her there wasn't one and put her off. Her timing was terrible.

It was a Saturday afternoon: Harry Krassner was flying in the next day: the soap opera of my own life demanded my attention. Holly had decided to keep the baby: she disapproved of abortion. Harry had let me know this in the same breath as he asked if he could stay over at my place. I'd said for him to call when he arrived, to see if it was convenient. I had hoped to make a late appointment at Harvey Nichols or somewhere to have my legs waxed. (Me, Sophia King, exerting myself thus over a man? It hardly bore thinking about. If God gave a woman hairy legs surely it was man's duty to put up with them? Wasn't there some Country Music song, 'Did I shave my legs for this?'.) Perhaps Lucy's unexpected arrival was both a warning from on high and a salvation. If Harry Krassner took off because my legs were not up to Hollywood standards of silky smooth, I was well rid of him. And anyway once you give a subplot legs and start it running that's it – interweave itself it will, following its own rules, as intricate as the ribbon winding through Lucy's white hair. (It might have been a wig, but I didn't think so: I think the Good Hair Fairy was there at her birth, as it had been at mine.)

I finally understood the baffling question that writers get asked – *Once you have invented your characters do they take off in their own direction?* Most writers reply sensibly, if disappointingly, *No, they may try but I'm the one in charge round here,* but here was Lucy, whom I had relegated to the past, making her appearance in the present, taken off indeed, climbing my steep stairs, declining to be passive, and quite capable of distorting by virtue of truth and actuality the elegant pre-credit sequence of the film forming in my head. That film, of course, being the biopic of Felicity's life.

Lucy sat rather pointedly with her back to the *Fantasia* fridge – I realized she was right: it had seemed a good idea once, in the days of comparative poverty when there was time and energy to spare, and now there was none, whenever was it to be remedied? – and took command of the meeting. Her little-girl voice carried well. The cat slunk off under the cooker. It was the old-fashioned kind with legs. No time for that either. I was astonished that Harry from Hollywood put up with me at all. Lucy said in tones of childish formality that she was pleased to hear that Felicity was alive and well but that so far as she was concerned the past was better left alone. For her it was not so pleasant a place. She did not want private detectives snooping around in her life. She did not want to be in touch with Felicity: what could they have in common after so long? Her astrologer had advised against it, as had her doctor. Her solicitor had warned her that there might be endless trouble over wills and so forth. On the other hand, if Felicity wanted to find her long-lost baby, she, Lucy, did not want to stand in the way. She would give me one interview, here and now, tell me all she knew, and that would be that.

*   *   *

I am not a writer, I am an editor. I can speculate but not invent. I suppose I could have worked it out for myself, but the truth turned out to be even more dramatic than I would have dared suppose, and being reported by a seventy-five-year-old out of the memory of the child she once was, had already been conveniently turned into a shaped narrative: a tragedy, as it happened. I could see why Lucy did not want her view of the past upset after all this time: a happy ending for Felicity was not within the scheme of her universe.

Lucy had the characters well defined: her father, Arthur, was the wronged hero, Felicity the tragic juvenile lead whom the villain, Uncle Anton, had wronged and ruined, and Lois her mother was the wicked witch. It was pre-sound cinema, black-and-white film with piano accompaniment. Felicity was Clara Bow, wide-eyed and trembling, shrinking back against a wall while the landlord threatens her mother with eviction unless she surrenders to him. She was Alma Taylor, orphaned, wronged, thrown out into the snow. If she had ended up a gauzy creation who shopped at Bergdorf Goodman and owned a Utrillo, Lucy really didn't want to know.

If it had been me in Felicity's shoes, all those years ago, I would have curled up and died then and there. Or I would have lined up with the other ruined girls to jump off Waterloo Bridge. But perhaps these days we just know too much about trauma, both emotional and physical, to believe we can survive and this is why we don't. If there is no language for the bad things that happen they are not so firmly sealed into our consciousness, our memory. They can drift off and be lost in the next experience. We're talking about a time when the word cancer was never spoken aloud, when insanity in the family was kept secret, when if a girl was raped she kept quiet because otherwise she was not just damaged but disgraced and unmarriageable, and how could a girl live other than by marriage or the goodwill of men? Even a couple of decades into the century only a very exceptional woman could earn a living wage, other than on her back. For all their frills and affectations and fashions, their shingled hair, their pretty pleats and flattened bosoms, women were, as ever, into the basic matter of survival.

*　　*　　*

The Fates have a way of doling out the same hand of cards to a woman, over and over. The cackling sisters had decided that Felicity was to get some pretty nice cards sprinkled with a few really nasty ones bound to mess the others up. They sent along a Fairy Godmother to the christening to give looks, charm, energy, courage, wit – then took away her parents, gave her Lucy's mother Lois for a wicked stepmother, brought Lois's brother Anton into the household, obliged her to give away her perfect baby and just when she'd managed to cope with all that, gave her the double whammy of Angel. It's true that if there wasn't Angel there wouldn't have been me, but what use am I to my grandmother? A cynical, distant, unmarried, unmaternal young woman who's never going to give her great-grandchildren, who's going to bring her branch of the family tree to a distinct and sudden stop.

Because not me, I'm not going to chance it. What, leave the baby which comes out to the cackling sisters? They're too mean, they have a rotten sense of humour, everyone knows. I'd rather trust a genetic scientist and that's not saying much. Pick the sexiest dad in the world and the baby could still be a throwback. It's like picking your lead player with a pin from the telephone directory instead of going to central casting and getting a star. You have no control over what starts growing inside. Even if it was okay to begin with you could take a drink too many or passively inhale and from what everyone says you could turn it into a serial killer or the Hunchback of Notre Dame. You could find yourself lumbered by, and like as not bonded to, the wholly unlovable.

Lucy had had two children by her second husband, an importer of exercise bicycle parts. One, the girl, was a specialist in aboriginal art in Western Australia and the boy was a banker in Hong Kong. She did not seem to miss them. Perhaps they had left the country not to escape from over-possessive maternal love but so as not to be reminded of the lack of it. No, neither had any children. They were '*too busy enjoying themselves*'. I decided I wouldn't chase this pair up. My great-grandfather was their grandfather, true: but the generations were too askew and sheer distance and airfares seem to thin the bloodline no end. And Lucy too was destined to be another shrivelling, dropping branch of the family tree. Poor

Mother Nature: I who so mistrust her could almost feel sorry for her – so many dead ends these days, or so many experiments taken over by the subjects, crying, '*Enough, enough.*'

After Lucy had told me the story of Alison's birth I made a half-hearted attempt to persuade her to change her mind and get in touch with Felicity.

'No,' she said, firmly. 'It would shift the ground on which I stand, and my legs are too old to cope, for all I cycle every day.'

And all of a sudden she was like Miss Felicity and I caught a vision of family, and of the continuation of mirth, that most precious of nature's creations, running through the generations and was charmed, and sorry that it was to stop, but not sorry enough. The gift had bypassed Guy and Lorna: it explained their literal plod, plod, plod through life. I hoped it wasn't more that that. There was something in them that seemed slightly worse: a banality. Why did people talk about the banality of evil? But because evil is banal, does not mean that all things banal are evil. Coal is black, but not all things black are coal. Forget it.

She rose to go. I helped her down the stairs. The phone rang as we were halfway down. It was not switched to answerphone. I let it ring itself into silence. I had a feeling it was Harry. I did not call back to find out. Perhaps I would not have him in my home again. Why should I be made miserable by a man whose only interest in me was that I saved him a taxi fare to work?

I know I haven't yet handed over Lucy's account of Felicity's early years but some things take more time to assimilate than others. Like making the key scene in the movie: you often keep it to last.

25

The grandfather I did not share with Guy and Lorna was from Vienna: he came to London to look for his missing sister Lois in 1928, or that is the reason he gave. He may have been what is now called an economic refugee: his name was Anton Wasserman. He is not by all accounts a person anyone would much want to have in their bloodline. You can tell I do not like the Wassermans. My loyalty is to Felicity and to Felicity's birth mother, poor Sylvia.

Lois Wasserman, Anton's younger sister, was a child prodigy who came to London in 1913 when she was twelve to study the piano at the Royal College of Music. She boarded with a family in Gower Street, within walking distance of the Royal College in Marylebone Road. Within months of her arrival in London the young Serb loyalist Princip had taken it into his head to shoot the Archduke Franz Ferdinand at Sarajevo: within months of that event World War I had begun. Princip was a lad of seventeen, who, fired with nationalistic fervour, took a pot shot at the Duke's carriage as it proceeded down the main drag of the city and missed. He put his gun in his pocket and went round the corner to have a cup of coffee. As one does. The ducal coachman, dashing for safety, lost his way and ended up asking directions at the very same café where Princip sat. *If you don't at first succeed, try, try, try again.* Princip went outside and shot dead the Archduke and the Arch-duchess too for good measure. Had he not done so Felicity would no doubt still be living in London and Lucy and Guy and Lorna and Alison would not exist. But you can drive yourself mad thinking this way. *What if*s can only be endured if they belong to the very recent past; before lunch is about as far as you can go.

With the outbreak of war anyone with a German name still living in England was harried, hounded and taken to be a spy. Little Miss Wasserman found her studies discontinued, her host family no longer prepared to board her and with no means of travelling home. Her parents in Vienna were unable to help, or not willing to. Thus Lois was left at the age of twelve to fend for herself. My great-grandmother Sylvia, herself a pianist, in her kindness took the child into her home. Here, in the Moore household, Lois grew up. (I'd been to see where the family house once stood on the lower slopes of Hampstead Hill. It was demolished in the sixties. Public housing tower blocks now stand where once these dramas took place. So all our personal histories are swept away: the bricks which once sopped up the passions of the past are ground to dust, and perhaps as well.) Lois was already part of the household when Arthur was sent off to war as correspondent for *The Times*. She was there on his return, and when Felicity was born to Sylvia: she was there when poor Sylvia died of the flu. Within six months Lois, cuckoo in the kindly nest, had married Arthur: Lucy was born two months later.

'Died from the flu!' Perhaps Lois was like Margaret Lockwood, the mistress in *The Man in Grey* (1943) who murders the wife as she lies ill with a fever, by throwing open the windows to let the storm blow in and giving her pneumonia. Perhaps, having got the husband from the wife, Lois then conspired with the lover to get rid of the husband? Barbara Stanwyck was forever doing it in all those fifties films, bumping off husbands to get hold of the insurance money. All that melodrama would not have been confined to film. Film mirrors reality, and vice versa. It could have happened.

Employees of the Aardvark agency sit in Somerset House, or wherever the national archive is currently kept, and by finding addresses and studying dates detect such dramas. Whatever changes? I don't suppose poor Sylvia much cared to stay alive. You don't not notice that a twenty-year-old girl is pregnant; Lois did not seem the kind to protect her benefactor from the news. *I'm pregnant and your husband is the father*. It's each for themselves, isn't it, then as now. I never knew a girl to actually mean: *Oh I don't go with married men,* though it trips off the tongue well enough – and these days: *Oh, he's not actually married, just living with her* makes a good excuse. In Lois and Sylvia's day there was even more at stake: not just sex and a relationship, but marriage and all that went with it: home, comfort, children and money – survival itself. It was worth the mistresses' gamble. Get pregnant by a man, enchant him with sexual services, make the wife upset and angry enough, and chances are he'll end up marrying you.

According to Lucy once Lois had got rid of Sylvia and trapped Arthur, she lost interest in him. She had memories of Arthur trying to hug and kiss Lois and Lois shaking him off. He was always gloomy and staring into space and she was always in a bad temper. (But then children tend to see the worst side of the parents' relationship. They don't get into the bedroom to see how the day relates to the night.) There was trouble over Felicity. Lois had wanted her sent off to boarding school. Arthur was against it.

Poor Felicity, now with an archetypal wicked stepmother, set on cleansing the dead woman's brood to make room for her own. (cf. *Babes in the Wood, Snow White. Mirror, mirror, on the wall* et al.) *Get lost! Off to the forest with you! Into the gingerbread house there to be eaten up; Daddy can't save you now.* Indeed, Daddy can hardly remember who you are, according to the social Darwinists. The new wife is younger and stronger and does better by his genes than the one who died. In other words a doting new husband would prefer not to notice what was going on in his own household.

'It might have been better for Felicity,' said Lucy, 'if she had been sent away. There was always something. She hadn't made her bed properly or left a tap dripping, and she'd be shut in her room, sometimes with her hands tied to stop her getting into more mischief. Or locked in the cupboard. She never cried. I remember trying to stuff bread and jam under her bedroom door, and getting caught and being made to lick up the jam from the floor. My

mother was a horrid woman. Why did my father never notice?'
'That's men for you,' I said.

After Arthur's death things got even worse for Felicity. She'd be
sent downstairs to live with the servants when punishment was
required, which pretty soon was more or less permanently. She'd
sleep in the attic and eat in the kitchen, while Lois and Lucy ate
in the dining room. (Shirley Temple in *Poor Little Rich Girl* came
to mind.) Lucy was told to call her May, not Felicity, the latter
being too fancy a name for an orphaned girl with no family, who
would have to make her own way in the world. (Some overtones
of *Jane Eyre* crept in at this point, the one with James Mason as
Rochester.)
'I think Felicity quite liked the drama,' said Lucy. 'She was always
such a little actress. She said there were worse things than peeling
potatoes and it was more fun with the servants anyway. One day
she thumbed her nose at Mama and then she really did get sent
off to boarding school.'
'Like the one in *Jane Eyre*,' I said. 'Or was it Dickens's Dotheboys
Hall?'

She looked at me blankly. I was beginning to feel uncertain as to
how reliable a witness Lucy was turning out to be. She recounted
Felicity's early life in a narrative in which myth and archetype
mingled and mixed. I did the same, of course, only I use film as
my reference. Lucy used the Arthur Mee's *Fairy Books* on which
she had been reared. Each to their own. Lucy saw her mother as
her enemy and because her mother hated Felicity, allowed her
enemy's enemy to become her friend, and so let the narrative
follow where it led, without shame.
'How did your father die?' I asked, allowing her time to calm
down. Her father, my great-grandfather, Arthur, who had had the
misfortune or the weakness to fall for the wrong woman in his
middle age and so destroy the happiness of generations. Married
to Sylvia, he had impregnated Lois. In these practical and unmelo-
dramatic days the word 'husband' has become unfashionable.
Even women with marriage certificates sometimes prefer to call
the men they sleep with 'partners' so as not to be out of tune with
the times. Alas, partner has no in-built drama, contains no sense

of coercion, no in-built *Thanatos,* no tragedy. It is not the stuff of major film. Okay for a subplot but you can't hang a film on it, let alone risk a generation of real human beings, as once you could. Something lost, and something gained, as we industriously smooth away our capacity for personal pain, by taking good care not to run into it. Lucy was one of the early aficionados.

'I don't know how he died,' Lucy said. 'We were told he was ill, and he'd been in bed for a month, with the doctor coming and going. No-one told children much in those days. My mother came out of the front bedroom one morning and told us he was dead, that's all.'

Lucy could not or would not be more informative, though I pressed her. But I could envisage the scene. Lois coming out on to the landing, in one of those straight long flat-chested dresses with pleats, looking down at the upturned faces of the two girls, Felicity at ten, Lucy at three. Victorious. *Your father is dead.* And nothing being the same afterwards: that sudden extraordinary line drawn between the past and the present. It was said to me too. *Your father is dead.*

'We were neither of us allowed to grieve, I do remember that,' said Lucy. 'She couldn't bear us crying at the best of times. We got slapped if we did. We were told it was for the best. Felicity wasn't allowed to go to the funeral. She dressed up for it and then Lois told her she couldn't go, it wasn't appropriate, Arthur wasn't her real father. There was a terrible scene. Felicity hit and scratched and Lois just laughed and said she was the coalman's daughter. Sylvia had been a slut. But we'd seen the coalman, he was hideous so we knew it wasn't true. One way or another I got to the funeral but Felicity stayed locked in her room.'

'You don't think Lois was unbalanced enough to have poisoned your father?' I asked, half as a joke, but Lucy was serious enough when she said that it wouldn't surprise her. Lois wasn't in the least unbalanced, reported her daughter, just cruel and evil. And Arthur had made a will just before he died leaving everything away from Felicity, to Lois.

'What used to worry me most of all, even back then,' said Lucy, 'is that after father died he fell into a pool of silence. No-one talked about him: it was as if he'd been some kind of nuisance wasp they'd batted out of the way. Mama kept a photograph of him in the living room, I suppose in case visitors came and she had to play the grieving widow, not the merry one, but there were hardly any visitors anyway. I don't know why she bothered. I thought there must be something wrong with Felicity, something bad, to get her treated the way she was. When Felicity told me she'd had a mother who'd once slept in my father and mother's bed I didn't believe her. Surely this woman would have left some trace behind, but there was nothing, nothing. Not a hairnet, not a cup or saucer, not a book. Then when my father died it was the same thing. All his personal things went, vanished. She missed his slippers for a whole year, but only because I hid them. I'd sleep with one of them under my pillow, and I once caught Felicity doing the same.'

I said it was all long ago and over, and she had the grace to say, 'But nothing's ever over.'

Snapshots: metaphorical: a scene in which Sylvia is dying of flu in the bedroom, and Lois is allegedly nursing her, but doing as bad a job of it as she can without anyone noticing, and Arthur coming home from his day at *The Times*, and being waylaid by Lois who says Sylvia is sleeping soundly (she's not: she's too weak to move but she overhears) and takes him to her bedroom as she has a dozen times before and gets herself pregnant. If Arthur has done it once he's almost obliged to do it again. Once a man is compromised in this kind of domestic situation he has to go on. He has to keep the other woman happy otherwise she'll tell his wife. Because once the wife knows, that's the end, so you might as well have a good time while you can, while it lasts. Round and round.

Lucy was not inclined to put any blame on Arthur: no, he was Lois's victim and that was that, and she herself was the product of the union so how could she disapprove of both parents without wishing herself out of existence? How much easier for all of us if humans hatched out of eggs, anonymously, so our problems began when we cracked the shell with our infant beak, and not before. No such luck. Lucy only lived in comfort because Sylvia had once died. All our cheerful todays depend upon someone else's fairly terrible yesterdays. I'm glad they pulled down my ancestral home: there's so much misery embedded in the walls.

But we have no information about that: it's all speculation, what went into the good-night Ovaltine and what didn't. Did the dying Sylvia shiver for little Felicity, wondering how she'd survive without her mother, left to Lois's mercies? No doubt she did. And still there was nothing she could do. The waters washed over her.

Real life is unsatisfactory, there is no resolving anything properly: you can go on for ever simply not knowing: murder doesn't always out: the only 'end' is death. Films at least offer resolutions, and answers, and solutions, the boring bits edited out. We who have lived through the cinema age have been blessed. It is not surprising we take to mind-altering substances: they being the next best thing. Like being at the cinema in our own body, looking inwards.

Within a month of Arthur dying, in 1925, Lois's brother Anton had moved into the house. Back to the Barbara Stanwyck wife/lover scenario, plus incest. If it was Hollywood, the lover couldn't be the brother too. You'd have to go to a French film for that, or a German, or indeed one of the few out of Austria, shadowy, dark and dramatic.

'Life got better when he moved in,' said Lucy. 'Mother cheered up. We were glad he was there. He'd make jokes and we'd sing round the piano. The food got better.' Felicity was allowed home for the holidays, and soon was taken out of school altogether and permitted to join the others in the dining room. Anton organized ballet lessons for both girls, for which only Felicity had the talent. 'I was always Miss Clumsy,' Lucy said. 'Anton didn't take any more notice of me than Father did. It was always Felicity this and Felicity that.'

'But Lois let her go to classes?'

'My mother always did what Anton told her,' said Lucy. 'I wonder now what went on between them. At the time it didn't occur to me. You think I'm exaggerating about my mother, don't you,' she added, eyeing me suddenly quite sharply, and my silence told her she was right.

'You're so protected, you young things,' she said. 'You've no idea what the world can be like, what people get away with if they think no-one's watching. In the days before social workers all kinds of things went on, and nobody thought the worse of you. Nowadays it's gone the other way. You can't do a thing without being spied on.'

She would not be patronized: she would take the initiative and come to me before I went to her. She would see me off. She was still Lois's daughter, for all she would rather not be. It's dangerous to hate your mother: you are obliged to hate yourself as well, and that can make you vicious. I was glad not to be a motherless, fatherless child in Lois's care. I would have fared as badly as did Felicity, I daresay, under the incestuous Lois Wasserman, onetime child prodigy, presently stepmother and maybe murderess. Lucy took out a scrapbook from her smart Italian leather shoulder bag. Photographs. We looked at them together.

Snapshots: literally, from Lucy's scrapbook. A yellowed newspaper cutting dated 1913: a photo of Lois at twelve, the caption – *Arrival of the child prodigy from Vienna.* On thin paper, much folded and refolded, and now cracking along the creases, an article about the nature of the child prodigy. Poor Lois, harking back no doubt to what might have been, had Princip not taken the opportunity offered a second time by fate, and World War I not started. What a sour offering by the Gods of Chance, which was to end so many million young male lives, and embitter so many women. The child Lois stared out of the faded picture, sullen, sensuous and plain, slightly pop-eyed, the family jaw stuck out in defiance. Poor Lois, as well as everyone else? What had she ever seen of family love?

Come to think of it, what did I know about it either? At least I tried not to go round doing other people damage. But if Holly linked up with Harry in any definite kind of way and then she died and I moved in with him how would I behave to his child? Any better than Lois? Would I too deal in humiliations and emotional torture? I'd have to be more subtle about it, of course, because these days, Lucy is right, people notice. I'd probably just do what was socially acceptable and send it off to summer camp while I got on with my work, and I don't suppose Harry would notice what was going on any more than Arthur had. Already I refer to this mythical child as 'it'. Already I am hating and resenting it. Easier to take the position Lucy had arrived at, with the wisdom of the decades, which I was prepared to acknowledge, that her mother Lois was born evil and stayed evil and forget it.

A *studio portrait* of the family: Arthur and Sylvia, loving husband and wife with little Felicity clinging on to her mother's hand, aged about three, and Lois leaning just a little into Arthur, managing to command the group. It was she whom the eye went to first. She had a nice figure, one could see that, shapely legs and pretty ankles below a knee-length, sporty, pleated skirt, and glowing with youth, and with her hair short and marcelled into rigorous waves, her jaw could easily be overlooked. Sylvia looked strained and pretty and faded and brave, and older than Arthur, who smiled happily and innocently at the camera, his head inclined ever so slightly away from his wife and towards Lois.

A *snapshot* of a family picnic: Lois and Arthur leaning into each other on the grass, little plain Lucy sitting with her legs stuck out in front of her: Felicity a little way away from the group, making a daisy chain. Angel had taught me how to do that; pick the daisy with as long a stem as you can, make a slit towards the bottom of the stem with the thumbnail, thread the next daisy through, make another slit, and so on. I supposed Felicity had shown Angel. No doubt Sylvia had found time to teach Felicity before she died. Daisy chains didn't seem Lois's cup of tea, somehow.

Another press cutting. Felicity at perhaps thirteen, little girl in a ballet dancer's tutu, thin graceful arms stretched high: a shy yet confident smile. Caption: *Local girl wins scholarship to Royal Ballet Company.*

'She never took it up,' says Lucy. 'She wasn't allowed. Mama said dancing was bad for the back and gave you big leg muscles. But I had to go on with lessons: my legs weren't worth bothering about.'

A *snapshot* of Lois and Anton on the steps of the National Gallery, posing for a street photographer. In their early thirties. Anton with his dull long face, his heavy Wasserman jaw: Lois a female version, like Guy and Lorna. They held each other's hand. They did not look like brother and sister, more like husband and wife. 'I found this one in my mother's pin cushion,' said Lucy, 'after she died, when I had to pack up the house.'

'Pin cushion?' I asked.

'One of those silk puffy padded things you fold over. You kept pins in it in the days when women made their own clothes. You'd keep your precious, private things in there too, soft and snug. Once Anton came to live with us, it was me who was sent off to boarding school too. He went into art dealing.'

Snapshots: metaphorical: Scenes from Felicity's life, for inclusion in the film narrative in my head. *Night-time.* Lucy unable to sleep, aged seven, wrapped in a blanket, sitting on her window seat looking out at the long back garden. A full moon. Bare trees, rimmed with snow and frost, bending over the stone walls. A summer house, an octagon with verandah and glass windows. A cat stalking across the lawn. The glow of a cigarette. Uncle Anton leaning against the old mulberry tree which is, they say, three hundred years old. He's wearing a raccoon coat, fashionable at the time. The back door of the house opening, Felicity slipping out. She's fourteen and thinks she knows everything and is in love with Uncle Anton. Lucy has teased her about it and Felicity has denied it, blushing. He says he's going to take her away from all this: he's going to Australia and she's coming too. He has a job lined up at the National Art Gallery: she can join the Sydney Dance Company. Felicity is sleek and brown: she has borrowed Lois's beaver coat. Beneath it her body is scarcely formed, kept skinny from all those ballet exercises. She has bare feet: she dances from foot to foot to keep her toes from freezing. Her red curls toss and glow in the moonlight. Lucy hears the murmur of voices. Does she hear *I love you, I love you* from Felicity? The audience does: it's what it always wants to hear and fears to hear. Anton's hand moves over the small breasts, the muscled girlish behind. She shivers. She has never felt anything like this before, of such mysterious importance. (Actually, we can do without Lucy's point of view. Hers was just our way in to the scene. Scrub Lucy.) We watch Anton with Felicity: we follow them. At first he kisses her and she draws back. But he is the ultimate authority: he has the power of life over her. Leave Anton out of it and Lois and Lois's unchancy behaviour are all she has in the world. Without Lois's consent she is penniless and homeless, orphaned. And Anton has authority over even Lois. He kisses her. This time she lets him. His tongue goes into her mouth. She doesn't like that. It is far too personal. She draws back. He pulls her closer. His hands are pushing up her clothes; there is something hard pressing into her stomach: she has no idea what it is. He push-pulls her into the summerhouse. He shifts her on to the wicker chaise longue that winters there. Now she is on her back and he is on top of her, his knee forcing hers apart. She cries out in alarm. That makes him angry. 'Little bitch,' he says. 'You led me on. You know what you were doing, all right.' His hand goes over her mouth: she bites the hand. Now there's no stopping him, he will have his revenge. *Cut away to long shot.* You know the dismal rest.

Back to Lucy. Lucy hears moans and cries from the summerhouse, and half knows half doesn't know, what's going on. What can she do anyway? Fetch her mother?
That would makes things even worse, she knows that without knowing why. Now she sees Felicity run from the summerhouse, without the fur coat, white nightdress caught up in her hand, bloodstained. Soon it's Anton's turn to come out. He lights a cigarette and leans against the tree and smokes it, snug in the warmth of his raccoon coat.
'That was the worst thing,' said Lucy, nearly seven decades later. 'That he was so casual. That he smoked a cigarette and enjoyed the moonlight, as if all pleasures were equal, and Felicity just another one.'

At breakfast the next morning Felicity avoids Anton's eye. He comes in cheerful and whistling, and devours liver and bacon and sausages, and urges Felicity to do the same. Then Anton adds, oh and by the way he's decided not to go to Sydney after all. 'My mother looked so happy when he said that,' said Lucy. 'But Felicity just fainted away. The doctor was called and said it was nothing, she was hysterical. Anton went back to treating her like a child. She was sent back to boarding school.'

*　　*　　*

Four months later Felicity felt ill and was growing fat and had no idea why. Lois, noticing her changing shape, beat her with her fists and told her the brutal facts of life, that is to say how sex and procreation were linked. Felicity was a moral imbecile, Lois claimed, dirty, disgusting and lewd.

'If what you say is true,' said Felicity, 'then Anton is the father.'

Then there was indeed uproar. Anton denied responsibility, and seemed entertained by the situation. Felicity was no better than she should be: he had seen her creeping out of the house at night, in Lois's beaver coat. God alone knew what company she kept. She'd been with the servants too much and now behaved like them. She'd got herself into trouble and was lying to get herself out of it. Devious, sluttish and sly.

There is no way Felicity is going to be believed. Lois throws her forcibly out of the house, push-pulling her, driving her with the force of her rage. She is driven by cab to the Society for the Care of Unmarried Mothers, or SCUM, in Coram Street in Bloomsbury, and there left upon the doorstep, as if she were an abandoned baby and not an abandoned mother. There being nowhere else to go Felicity sits down upon the steps to consider her lot in life, and by the end of the day is delivered to the care of nuns who run a sanctuary for the mothers of illegitimate children. She will work for her keep. Here Felicity stays through her pregnancy, expected to remain inside the grounds to avoid embarrassment to others, praying three times a day for God's forgiveness, fed meagrely, coldly housed, and locked in at night. The sanctuary is attached to a Convent: Felicity's job is to scrub the long tiled corridors, along which the clean and virtuous feet of the exalted and the celibate so softly tread. She accepts the world's version of her. This is what she is fit for. Sometimes she thinks Anton will come and rescue her, but mostly she doesn't. She keeps the company of girls and women from twelve to forty, all of whom, though pregnant, have failed to find a husband. Some are simply bewildered, some traumatized by rape: some are street girls whose abortions have failed. Some have been thrown out by their families, some never had them in the first place.

*   *   *

Felicity is one of those stunned by fate. She is in a state of shock, and the boring, steady rhythms of the days, the requirements of penitence, the orderly growing of the baby within her, give her time to recover from all kinds of things from which she did not know she needed to recover. The death of first mother, then father, the arrival of the cruel stepmother in between; the sudden, shocking jolts of cruelty and spite into a life once protected and serene, the understanding that God is not good – all these things she was able to assimilate and come to terms with, in a short five months. She cried a lot at first, and was expected to. Otherwise nothing much happened. (How to express the importance of *nothing happening*! A challenge to any filmmaker.) She did learn a thing or two.

She saw that she might live among the helpless scrapings of humanity, but that nature hadn't given up on them, not one bit, or their bellies and breasts wouldn't be swelling so; only society had, so society was an ass. She learned the more elaborate facts of life, and how she was hard done by: she was taught how to make a living from selling sex. She discovered she was perceived by the other girls as beautiful, stylish, witty and a cut above the rest of them. This surprised but gratified her. They placed great hope in her. They sent her in to deal with the nuns over the matter of no Sunday supper, and won. It was easy. No one was as bad as Lois. Felicity was almost glad to be where she was.

She knew she would be obliged to hand the baby over for adoption. It called out to her from the womb for approval and concern and she hardened her heart. She had no choice. She thought perhaps she could see a lawyer: perhaps she could make some claim on her father's house, but how could she afford a lawyer? She had seen the will in which everything had been left to Lois and Lucy, Arthur having come across love letters to Sylvia which proved that Felicity was not his child. How did you refute that?

Little Lucy contrived to find out where Felicity was and got to see her, just the once. The news from home, if you could call it home, gave Felicity no reason to hope for any sudden change of heart from Lois, any regret, any self-reproach, any admittance of moral responsibility. The police had turned up to take Anton away: there was a fraud charge outstanding back home in Vienna. He had represented himself as an art dealer in connection with the theft of a painting by Klimpt: the police had finally caught up with him. 'What did Felicity say when you told her that?' I asked Lucy, all these decades after the event.

'Just that he should have gone to Australia while he could.'

'And that was all? She didn't seem to hate him?'

'Why should she? She shouldn't have gone into the garden with him that night. She didn't have the instincts of a good girl: she was born bad, my mother was right about that. Innocence is no excuse. After Felicity went away Anton left as well; my mother was half-mad. It was probably she who betrayed him to the police.'

I said that even if you looked at Felicity as fifteen-year-old jailbait she was only doing to Lois what Lois had done to Sylvia, and serve her right. But surely she agreed Felicity was very harshly punished?

'I expect it made things easier for Felicity,' was all Lucy said, 'when it came to giving the baby away. Knowing the father was a criminal.' She didn't ask me about Alison's fate and I didn't tell her. Talk of Alzheimer's in the presence of the old is always tactless.

'And a rapist,' I said. She looked blank, but as if the other side of blankness she didn't like me very much at all.

'Adoption was the best thing,' said Lucy, firmly. She stood up to leave. The interview was ended. If I were Phyllis Calvert in *The Man in Grey* she would certainly throw the windows wide and let the storm get me.

It was at this point that I asked her to reconsider her decision not to be in touch with Felicity and she refused, but with a sudden surfacing of the charm and wit which left me liking her. She too had had a lot to put up with. Who hasn't?

26

At three o'clock on the afternoon of 3 January Jack had a telephone call from his sister-in-law, Joy. She was distraught. On three occasions recently she had called Charlie on his mobile phone and found it switched off. She had on each occasion put on her snowshoes and gone over to the Guest House, the door of which had been opened by yet another new female face who did not seem to understand what Joy was talking about when she asked where Charlie was. English-speaking reinforcements were called for from within the ranks of Charlie's ever-growing family. Obviously, Joy protested to Jack, contracts of employment meant nothing to these newcomers: the female shrug when finally the question was translated had suggested men did what they wanted when they wanted and it was no use complaining. Worse, said Joy, the Mercedes was not in the garage. Hadn't their agreement been that Jack would give her warning when he used Charlie's services?

Jack decided at that moment, as Joy's voice shrieked over the snowy fields, and he was able to hear her both over the telephone and from her house as well, that it was no use trying to replace Francine. He wished he had never shifted house to here: he was bored, he was lonely, he was being punished for having cheated Felicity out of $200,000.

He was taking Prozac. He was at his best in the barbecue season, and this was not it. This was a lonely and stand-offish neck of the woods: the local women-alone had been in to look him over as a potential man in their lives, but since he did not suit them, too noisy and brash, perhaps, for the quiet, genteel landscape, the even tenor of their lives, they'd left him alone and failed to ask him over. Sociability alone was not enough. Former friends, the couples he and Francine had one way or another acquired, came to visit once or twice to see if he was okay, said how splendid to be living next to family, and disappeared from his life. He had compounded the misfortune of bereavement – who wanted to be reminded that eventually it would happen to them – by the sin of *moving away*, always seen as a form of disloyalty. He was doomed to wither into old age with Joy tormenting him and only Charlie and his growing household to interest him. He envied the lot of the toothless old men of the Balkans, so frequently seen on CNN, lumped together with the women and children while the young men went off to have fun with guns, but at least included as *family*, and still battling it out with the old women as to who was in charge. He could have talked about this to Francine but Joy did not even have CNN, she wasn't sufficiently interested in the out-side world. Joy seemed as lonely and isolated as he was, but she didn't notice, she had the gift of making a lot of noise, perhaps this was why. He did his best to infuse her lonely house with noise and energy, but he could not keep it up for long, single-handed. Felicity had been wise to move the few miles into Rhode Island: life seemed livelier there. The nearer the ocean the better perhaps: more happened. Who knew what ships, enemy or friend, might not appear any moment, over the horizon. The flash of a sail, the drift of a smoke stack. You had to keep your eyes skinned, what-ever century you lived in.

'I thought you had a rest every afternoon,' he said.
'I used to,' Joy snapped. 'Not any more. Someone told me that it was because of my afternoon nap that I sleep so badly at night. When you get to our age it's important to change the pattern of your days. I thought I might drive over to visit Miss Felicity. Now this! No chauffeur! What else does one keep a chauffeur for, but to be spontaneous?'
Prozac, or something, or the need for event, had made Jack over-confident. He told Joy that every afternoon Charlie drove William Johnson to the Golden Bowl to see Felicity.

'They're courting,' he said. 'Aren't you glad for your friend?'

There was a short silence from the other end, and then: 'Not that con artist she met at the funeral?'

'That's him,' said Jack. 'Charlie says he seems okay.'

'Charlie would say that,' said Joy. 'He's a con artist too. Look how the devil exploits us! For all I know he's running a whore-house from above my garage. William Johnson! Obviously a false name: it's too ordinary not to be. He's decades younger than she is: he's just after her money. You should see the dump he lives in.'

'She seems to like him,' said Jack.

'If you mean what I think you mean,' said Joy, 'that is revolting. People of that age have no business having sex. It's too upsetting for those around. If Felicity has a toy boy then she's being taken for a ride. It's shaming, embarrassing and humiliating. Next thing is he'll marry her and run off with all her money.'

'I guess seventy-two seems quite old to be a toy boy,' said Jack mildly. 'And we have no idea if they're having sex.'

'It's Felicity so of course she's having sex. Exon hadn't been dead a month but she was having it off with some antique dealer who came to the door. He must have been some kind of pervert or else half-blind. He went off with the oak dresser, and to all accounts she got a good price for it so he must have been halfwitted as well. Whose side are you on anyway?' yelled Joy, and Jack watched a deer which had come cautiously to where woods met the fields, but now took sudden flight and was gone. Joy said she was calling the Golden Bowl and would not have her limo, *her* limo, dammit, used for assignations with unsuitable men by an old lady who had lost her marbles.

'What do we say when they find out?' asked Felicity. She lay naked in the bed with William. They touched, her left flank of familiar flesh stretched up against his right unfamiliar flank, but becoming more accustomed by the day, looking up at the ceiling, occasion-ally at each other. They missed the anonymity of the night, both agreed. Day was all very well until the fourth decade, then the dimmer the light the better. Close the curtains as you wished, daylight was cunning and seeped in round the edges of the window frame. To lie together in the dark, in the actual night, as other people did, was what both wanted. But that meant commitment, and declaration to the outside world, and neither was quite ready for that, though neither was quite sure why. And so far they simply lay in the bed, because that made talking easier. His hand sometimes strayed to her breast, to find out more about it, and for once she wished she had her former body back: it was as if now the power of her will was obliged to sustain her physical existence and keep proving it: whereas once the body had run off so boldly with the self, taking over: the firm bosom, the bouncy flesh, flying ahead of the will, having to be restrained.

It was pleasurable, it was companionable, it was even exciting: the nerves still ran from the nipple to everywhere, but that excitement was not what this was about. It might, she thought, be about true love, something she had heard speak of, and pretended to experience, but perhaps never had. Something to undo the time she preferred not to think about, the first rough hands ever on her reluctant, obedient, unknowing breast. Contemporary wisdom, which to someone of Felicity's age and experience seemed mere folly, maintained that you could never recover sexually or emotionally from such a beginning as hers. But far worse things had happened after, and indeed before – how could you compare the death of first mother, then father – the father who had betrayed you twice, first by bringing the likes of Lois into the house, next by failing to stay alive and abandoning you to her cruelties altogether – than that gross hour on a moonlight night in a summerhouse in the garden. Anton, with his questing, searching, bullying member, tearing into your surprised self. The voice used to groom and entice, soft lies going ahead, seductive messengers of the evil that followed. The baby, tearing its way out of your equally surprised self, sheets a mass of blood to the annoyance of nuns. But you recovered. You forgot. You took good care to forget: you forgot everything you could. You got on with what was left of your life, made something of it, just to show your defiance. You would not be defeated.
'Is something the matter?' he asked.
'I was remembering things it's better to forget,' she said.
'We all have those,' he said. Her hand, in return for his on her

164

breast, strayed delicately down to his penis. It lay confidently, and as if about to swell into life, but not quite yet.

'I can see I'll have to tell you the truth,' he apologized. 'Or it's never going to work. Mostly with women it thrives on lies. Not this time.' She liked being called *a woman*, even though it suggested a past rich in sexual event. They were both too old, surely, to resent what went before. Anything pursued with energy seemed in retrospect to be enviable and desirable.

'Tomorrow we're going out with Charlie,' he said. 'I want to show you something.' He wouldn't say what. It was a surprise. It might turn her off him for ever, but it might not. But she had to know. Someone else would tell her if he didn't. Whatever it was he didn't seem to be taking it altogether seriously. He leaned over her, his old eyes looking into her yet older ones, into a mirror which threw back only pleasant sights, livened by the unexpected.

What, what? He wouldn't say. She drummed impatiently with her heels upon the bed but got a sharp pain in her thigh so had to stop. What was there to know about people that would put you off them but wasn't immediately apparent? She knew where he lived. Perhaps there was another woman? But she didn't think so. Something so fundamental he would have told her, or she would have sensed. She didn't of course know what he did when he wasn't with her, and he had all the morning to do it in, and evenings too. She had assumed that like her, being retired, he did nothing: that is to say he pottered about, while the few things there were to do expanded to take up the time available to do them in, and the effort of doing them became more and more oppressive. If he did something, whatever it was didn't make him any money: so much was apparent.

'Confessionals!' she said. 'I suppose you want mine.'

She'd let it out little by little, or at any rate what she chose to remember. The girl she'd once been was no longer her, in any case. She'd shed too many skins, grown too many new nerve endings since she began. She didn't feel she was cheating. She'd begun with the marriage to Jerry, Tommy's father, the man who'd neglected to tell her about his wife, but had at least got her across the Atlantic, a new life, and a US passport for herself and her unborn daughter Angel.

*   *   *

She'd spoken of her time in Savannah thereafter, when the marriage had collapsed. An entertainer, was how she'd put it. Singer, dancer and occasional good-time girl on the finest riverboat ever, *fin-de-siècle* style. The slow, shiny water beneath the hull, timeless, the smell of hot oil, the private cabins, red plush and gold fitments: whatever changed through the decades? Well, some things did. She'd had the best of it, she thought: not much fun now the whisky had turned into sparkling water and even cabins dedicated to vice were non-smoking. But then it was cigarettes and whisky and wild, wild women and she was one of the women. *They drive you crazy, they drive you insane.* No-one minds a woman with a past so long as that past was wild for wildness' sake, and not for money. If now she became vague on certain points, who cared any more? Mostly as women got older what they regretted was what they'd never done, not what they did. She told William Johnson, fairly and squarely, of the circumstances in which she'd married one of her patrons, clients, customers, call them what you like, who adored her English accent. He wanted his domestic affairs taken care of. He had an airline to build. For a year he'd taken her to his grand house with the portraits of his forebears on the walls, outside that fringed, damp and mossy town, Savannah, and to his four-poster bed, and just have her lie there while he listened to her speak. He proposed to her one day as they walked in the town, a hot sun slanting down between pale cooling fringes of Spanish moss. How she had been too tired to say no. *Yes* is easy, *no* takes energy: and it was so hot. How she'd married him in romantic white, to whispers behind elegant fingers, male and female, how she'd hosted his expensive parties, and run his elegant house, and helped him buy paintings – she had always had an eye for art – Edward Hoppers and Mary Cassatts. How the marriage had not been consummated. How for a while she had been glad of that, pleased to have her body to herself for a while. But then she began to chafe and feel trapped and full of complaints. You think you can sell yourself and you can for a while, a day or a night or a week is nothing, but years? Comfort and security are less important the more you have of them. He was gay, of course, nothing unusual in this closet city of gay, pallid, beautiful men, whispering and conspiring as did their wives – but she'd more or less known that from the beginning. At least he'd tried, as did so many of his generation. If the expression of homosexual love, if doing what the desires of your body dictated, was a criminal act, of course you would try to be heterosexual, and marry, and if that failed, secretly seek out the company of others like you, and in the end relish the secrecy: it would be what turned you on. How could she resent it? Five years on she asked him for a divorce and he sighed and gave her one.

'Five years without sex?' asked William, horrified.

'Of course not,' she said, but did not elaborate other than to say: 'I never stole other women's husbands, or not if I could help it. Most grand Savannah marriages were shams, anyway. At parties you'd see the men gathering together, whispering, smiling, making assignations, while the women made bright Southern conversation, all charm and trills, and honey this and honey that, but to no purpose whatsoever.'

In the end she'd left. You wait and wait for something to happen, but in the end you have to stir yourself to make it happen, or nothing ever does.

'I guess that's where the Utrillo came from,' said William. 'Part of a divorce deal.' Sometimes she thought he was overly interested in the Utrillo, but she could see it would bother people not accustomed to it, just sitting on the wall, using up $2,000,000 or so to no apparent purpose. She'd told them at the Golden Bowl it was a print. They didn't have the knowledge or interest to look at it closely, or know what they were looking for if they did.

But what activity of William Johnson's was it of which she might not approve?

Something that couldn't be talked about but had to be seen? Perhaps he helped out at a funeral parlour? Laid out corpses? She could think of nothing else. She might ask Dr Bronstein over supper if he had any ideas, only it would mean shouting, and was too elaborate a matter to be imparted briefly. And Nurse Dawn would turn up before she was halfway through. Nurse Dawn need not worry: Felicity's relationship with Dr Brontstein was circumscribed by his deafness. He spoke and Felicity listened, perforce. This seemed to suit him well enough. He could have switched on what he called his ear machine, but never did, even though it was one of the more

167

expensive kind and probably worked. His deafness had become a metaphor for an ongoing state of affairs – all his life he had used women as witness to the life, not a true participant in that life – and was the sort of aural fix – in the same way as TV ads have visual fixes – which happened when you got old and began to lose your marbles, and used your incapacity to finally get your way without argument. If a man could not hear you, you could hardly demand that he listened to what you had to say. She wondered what kind of life Mrs Bronstein had lived, what troubles she had had to put up with, and if she, Felicity, could ever end up lying naked next to the good Doctor, and decided, no, that was impossible. It was a particular man she wanted: this man, William Johnson, and whatever he did she could not imagine that it would cloud their relationship. 'You're drifting off,' he said. 'You're thinking of another man, I can tell.' She laughed and said she was beyond that, she was thinking about what she would wear tomorrow.

There came a tapping on the door. It was Nurse Dawn, an hour early with her sweet, stern call.

'Miss Felicity, Miss Felicity!' Felicity was agitated when anyone called her that. You could never quite trust the motives of the one who used it. It sounded good in the mouths of friends, derisory in the mouths of enemies. Today Nurse Dawn sounded smarmy and hoping to please. When Sophia called her Miss Felicity it was at least with a certain irony, albeit with that faint air of disdain with which the young treated the old: affectionate but distancing. When Joy did it, it was to keep her in her place, to mock her Southern past and suggest that she was unduly pernickety and had to be humoured, but it was done mostly with affection. When Dr Grepalli used it, it was an attempt to infantilize her. Nurse Dawn's *Miss Felicity* suggested plot, and outrage, and machinations to beware of. If Nurse Dawn had her way Felicity would be sent off to the West Wing as an incompetent. William lay quiet under the bedclothes. They were like schoolchildren, discovered.

'What is it, Nurse Dawn? I'm resting.' How easily lies came, after a lifetime's practice. How convincing they sounded.

'Could I come in? The workmen report a leak in the roof. I need to take a look.'

'It will have to wait, Nurse Dawn,' said Felicity, but Nurse Dawn had used her passkey and was already in the room. Felicity drew the sheets to her chin, but William's clothes were folded over the back of the chair and his shoes were on the carpet.

'Whose shoes are those?' asked Nurse Dawn. 'They can only fit a man's foot.'

William flung back the bedclothes and sat up. Nurse Dawn gave a little shriek but did not flee.

'Miss Moore is free, white and over twenty-one,' he said, 'and that's not a racist remark.'

'Be so good as to cover yourself up,' said Nurse Dawn sourly. 'You haven't checked in as a guest of Miss Moore, you are trespassing on institution property for the purpose of harassing one of our residents and I must ask you to leave. We can talk about this later when we're calmer.' Her strong face, usually pallidly opaque, as if the effort of self-righteousness both drained it and toughened it, was flushed and hot.

'I am perfectly calm,' said Felicity, whose colour had changed not at all. 'And this is dreadfully vulgar. I am not a child to be told what I can and cannot do.'

'There is not so much difference,' said Nurse Dawn. 'Once you're in your second childhood you have to be looked after for your own good.'

'If you'd just go,' said William, 'I could get dressed.' Felicity quite admired his physique: the hairs on his chest were white and wiry, and the ribs showed through pale, thin skin, but his shoulders were broad and still well muscled. She could see she might be biased in his favour, from the distaste with which Nurse Dawn regarded him. 'I am a trained nurse,' said Nurse Dawn, 'and used to old men in the nude. I doubt you could show me much that could shock me.'

But she left the room, all the same. William dressed. They heard Charlie's limo arrive outside.

'That's a really poisonous woman,' said William.

'She didn't seem to like you much,' agreed Felicity.

'We'll have to get married,' said William. 'If we're going to go on meeting. Otherwise there'll be endless trouble. What do you say?'

Miss Felicity, who had no years to waste, let alone days, opened her mouth to say yes, of course, but he put his finger on her lips, and told her to think about it and say nothing until the next evening, by which time she might want to change her mind. 'You have so much to offer and I have so little,' he said, and she was inordinately flattered, but then a memory came to her out of nowhere, of the particular wheedling note in a particular voice. *Please, please, darling, let me. You promised.* Whoever said that? Yes, out in the garden under the moon in the snow. The soft brown warmth of her coat, Lois's coat. Anton so shaggy and heavy in his raccoon, once he had abandoned talking.

27

Nurse Dawn went straight to Dr Grepalli.

'She had a man in her bed.'

'I often have a woman in mine,' he said. 'But not this afternoon.'

'That's because I had a very distressing phone call from her friend,' said Nurse Dawn. 'She is very concerned. Our Miss Felicity is being taken advantage of by a known criminal, a con man and a gambler. This can be very dangerous for the Golden Bowl's reputation.'

It was true enough: one of the unspoken promises to the relatives of those interred in the Golden Bowl was that old men would be saved from the machinations of pretty young nurses who were after their fortunes, and old women likewise from gigolos. Those who, indecently enamoured, marry late in life, tend to remake their wills so that the money ends up outside the family that has cared for them so long, and sacrificed so much time and energy on their behalf. It is the revenge of the grateful. As William Johnson once remarked to Felicity, attributing the words to that other, eighteenth-century, Johnson, the learned doctor and great wit. 'No good deed but goes unpunished.'

'Oh dear,' said Dr Grepalli. 'Oh dear, oh dear, oh dear. So Miss Felicity is still an attractive woman, in spite of her age, or indeed because of it. I suppose the relationship couldn't be genuine?'

'Don't be absurd,' said Nurse Dawn, and gave up, at least for the time being. Dr Grepalli was not going to take her seriously. In her experience, the relationship between men and women was seldom genuine. It was, for the most part, a form of trade. Your body for my money: you fill my bed, I'll take you to the party: you make the will, I'll cook for you, clean for you, go to your funeral: I'll act like your father, if you'll be a better mother, whatever. Very little was freely, genuinely offered at the best of times.

Some men, she knew, were genuinely attracted to old women, just as some were genuinely attracted to children, but both were equal perversity, other than that there was less time available for those abused in their later years to suffer as a result. Strange how you could sleep with men and be so intimate with them and still know so little about them: how you tended to believe that their interest in you was the outer limits of their desire. The wives and lovers of paedophiles and rapists often have no idea what goes on behind their backs.

It wouldn't do, Nurse Dawn warned herself, to think that old people's homes were like children's homes, and too often attracted as staff those whose interest in the inmates was unhealthy, being either sadistic or erotic, or both. But if something gave pleasure, did the motives of those who gave it matter? If a bomb falls on you, does it make any difference whether it was dispatched in the genuine interests of world peace or of terrorism? She, Nurse Dawn, placed her stiletto heel in the small of Dr Grepalli's back in the interests of promotion, and an easy life, not because she was genuinely thrilled by so doing, but who was to say that the happiness of the greatest number was not thereby better served? His smile within the Golden Bowl kept everyone cheerful, and out of the West Wing, whatever it was that made Dr Grepalli's eyes glitter and the corners of his mouth stretch. But what was the point of talking about these things? Dr Grepalli dismissed her fears because he didn't want trouble: if he didn't look the problem would go away. Nurse Dawn knew that it would not. There was trouble ahead.

'I'm losing my touch,' was all she said, dropping the subject. 'I made a mistake accepting the woman, and have to accept it. I should have taken the Pulitzer Prize winner, even if she did smoke.

The fact is, even leaving aside the lover, Felicity Moore has trouble growing old gracefully. She has too many visitors: she brings in the outside world.'

'We're not a closed community,' said Dr Grepalli, gently reproachful. He was locking the door. Nurse Dawn took off her jacket and then her blouse.

'She stirs up the other guests. Now Dr Bronstein has someone to listen to him he gets overexcited and that makes him incontinent. I don't want the leather chairs in the Library soaked. It might be time to get him into the West Wing. Old Clara Craft has taken to eavesdropping. She hides behind columns and acts like a madwoman.'

'Wasn't she a journalist?' asked Dr Grepalli. 'The outer and visible form of an inward and spiritual state, more apparent as the inhibitions are loosened with age.'

'That's as may be,' said Nurse Dawn, now in suspender belt, black stockings and scarlet high heels. 'All I'm saying is that if Felicity Moore could be persuaded to leave the Golden Bowl it would be to everyone's advantage.'

'Except to our overall statistics,' said Dr Grepalli, 'and it would upset the Board. They would see it as a failure. Look at it like this. You and I have our pleasures; the old so seldom do. Why grudge them to others? Be generous with them as you are with me.'

He lay naked on the sofa: she bent her head over him and he stroked her soft, dull hair. She took away his power, for which he was grateful. Responsibility weighed heavily upon him. She felt her power over him, and that released her, if only temporarily, from the nagging sense of her lack of it.

That evening Miss Felicity called her granddaughter Sophia in London's Soho. 'It's two in the morning, Gran,' complained Sophia. 'I wish you'd work it out.'

'It's the only time you're ever home. How are you ever going to get married if you have no time for love?'

'There's always sex beneath the editing desk,' said Sophia, who was working for Harry Krassner again. Clive had been brought in as executive producer on *Hope Against Hope,* which was still giving trouble. Astra Barnes was suing the studio: to satisfy the lawyers a known director had to be brought in to redo the work already satisfactorily accomplished by Sophia. Clive had brought Harry over from LA, and he was now in Sophia's bed again.

'It's fate,' Harry Krassner had said.

'No it's not,' said Sophia. 'It's Clive. It's in case I start suing as well. He thinks you'll keep me busy.'

'Or make you happy,' said Harry Krassner. 'You English are so cynical. You have no soul.'

'I expect Holly has more,' said Sophia, irked. 'Why don't you go back to her.' Then she went to the hairdresser and had six inches of hair cut off, to punish herself for the remark. She could see she was getting possessive. She made a scene at the salon, too, seeing her beautiful hair on the ground, bursting into tears and snarling at the stylist and saying he'd taken off too much. It was completely out of character. And then having to apologize. After all that Harry Krassner didn't even notice that she'd had it cut.

'I thought I'd better tell you,' said Felicity, 'I'm in love.'

'Is it reciprocated?' asked Sophia cautiously, trying to get the measure of the statement.

'I think so,' said Felicity. 'He's asked me to marry him.'

There was an expensive silence from Sophia's end. Then: 'I can come over at the end of the week,' she said. She would miss five precious days of Krassner in her bed, but it would have to be done. She would not alter her behaviour, abandon her family duty, for any mere man. That way madness lay. She could do it for a film, but not for herself.

28

'Just think!' I said to Guy and Lorna, who had asked me over to Happiness for Sunday lunch, 'our grandmother has received a proposal of marriage.'

They looked at me cautiously. Guy was slicing a rather pulpy half-leg of GM lamb, so lean as to be singularly dry, while Lorna doled out a few potatoes boiled with their skins on, and some spinach which stayed in the shape of the package, having been slightly under-microwaved, so it was still crisply frozen in the middle. I could have been eating linguini in Dean Street at Zilli's with Harry and Clive, but this afternoon we were going to visit Alison. I had decided to act with Harry as if I was not particularly anxious for his company. I have never before in all my life played games with men – which just might be, as Felicity once pointed out, the reason I did not have one to call my own. But I seemed to have begun to learn how, prompted by Harry's upfrontedness: he was so little a gamesman when it came to matters of the heart, it behoved me to be a gameswoman. Holly would call from the States and I would hand the mobile over with a smile and say, 'It's Holly,' and not, 'that bitch again'.

The adoption had fallen through. The mother turned out to have sold her baby to four different parents at $200,000 or more a throw, and though prepared to actually hand it over to Holly and Harry (such integrity) for an additional $100,000, they had decided that the baby might inherit the genes of dishonesty. I did not even murmur to Harry that 'dishonesty' was socially defined, and you would have to know a great deal more before disqualifying a baby on those particular grounds. You could as well claim the baby would inherit the genes of sensible self-interest and a sense of humour. I even had a sudden desire to fly over to LA at once, and take the baby for myself, but that was absurd. I did not want a baby. I wondered to what an extent competition between women, in the old days, had led them into repeated pregnancies. But no, it was probably just the absence of contraception; in the face of male sexual drive once you were married pregnancy would just happen. Krassner quite wore me out. He could not fall asleep, he said, in the absence of sex. He was half-joking. He was in fact a considerate and emotional lover, who wanted me to say such simple things as, 'I love you,' which I found difficult. Like most Americans, he talked a lot during lovemaking. The English tend to be silent, in a world minus language and so the more intense.

Holly would not have sex with Harry while she was filming – it made her puffy around the eyes in the morning – so I took care never to appear reluctant, no matter how tired I was. And though by day my body cried out to be close to him, and I believe he felt the same need to lean into me as I did to him, here I was at Guy's and Lorna's and not at Zilli's, parting with knife and fork bits of gristle and a strange glutinous fibre which the lamb had grown in place of fat, not olive oil, glistening agilely around my fork. Lorna did not even know their house was called Happiness, she said she might once have known but was at pains to forget, though Guy acknowledged that as a child he had been sufficiently inquisitive to pull aside the creepers and find out. Both were more interested in the inside of books than in the real world. They ate to sustain life, and asked me over out of vestigial politeness, rather than enthusiasm.

The matter of Felicity's proposal did stir a certain interest.

'Someone after her money, I suppose,' said Lorna. 'The same thing happened to poor Mother. That's really why we had to have her put away.'

Put away sounded rather unfortunate. Even Guy noticed.

'She's not exactly put away, Lorna,' said Guy. 'You couldn't go on nursing her. Your back was bad. She is very happy where she is, well looked after and safe.'

'She'd start wandering,' said Lorna. 'Dangerous so near the river. It got very bad last summer. She'd begun to give money away. I took away her chequebook, but she was very cunning. She'd go round to the bank and get another. He coerced it out of her, of course.'

'He', on close questioning, turned out to be a semi-naked, glistening young thug working in the boatyard, casual labour, rough trade: Alison had asked him home, the police had been called; rough trade had a police record. And Alison was not yet seventy: think what could happen when a woman was eighty-five.

'Eighty-three,' I said. For some reason the two years seemed to make a difference. And Alison was sixty-eight, not yet seventy. Were older women not to be allowed their excursions into unreason? I supposed, when money was involved, not. They must be locked up, before they gave it all away.

Lorna and Guy ate glumly on. I longed for the noise and good cheer of Zilli's. There was a singularly pretty waitress there: long legs and an intelligent face. Perhaps Harry, bereft of my company, and spiteful, would offer her a part in his next film. Not that spite seemed in his nature. He might I suppose do it in the spirit of sheer exuberance. If I wasn't under his nose he would forget about me. He lived in the present, not the past, or the future. Holly summonsed him, he went; but to make her go away. Easier to do as she said, so long as work permitted, than work out what she meant to him. How could I hope to disturb such a solid relationship?

I told Lorna and Guy that I was flying over to Rhode Island to see Felicity, to find out more about her romance, and they could see the necessity, though obviously thinking it a wicked waste of money and Guy wrote down the number of a bucket shop where I could find the cheapest flight available.

'You'll have to nip it in the bud,' Guy said. 'Or some con artist will end up with the Utrillo on his wall, not you.' They were coming round to the idea that their grandmother was quite well off.

I said my walls were singularly unsuited to a Utrillo, which was the last of my concerns, and this seemed to shock them. There was apple pie for dessert, which Lorna had made herself. Lots of thick heavy pastry and a thin sliver of apple squeezed between, but never mind. I was touched that she'd tried. I said Lorna and Guy could have the Utrillo, if and when Felicity died, it was only fair: it would look right on their walls, which were the right shape for framed paintings.

I regretted having said it as soon as the words were out of my mouth. Guy went out to make coffee and Lorna took out the dessert plates and I could hear them murmuring in the kitchen. I saw a kind of gleam in their eyes when they came back which I hadn't seen before, and I remembered that Lois's blood ran in their veins, as well as Anton's. Perhaps Felicity had known what she was doing when she gave Alison away, and with the baby, that baby's progeny. But too late now.

29

The Glentyre Nursing Home was much as these places are in this country. The same satellite TV goes unwatched: chairs, though they may begin informally grouped, end up with their backs to the wall, where the occupants insist that they be. Even a slight touch of paranoia is enough to make you want to keep an eye on what the others in the room are doing. Safer not to have your back to anyone. The same smell seeped into the very fabric of the walls, of urine and disinfectant and old-fashioned face powder. The same staff: a few cheerful and kind, most sullen and under-paid. The same sense of waiting, of bemusement that life has come to this. Communal (that is to say, lowest common denominator) taste when it comes to the colour of walls and drapes. The food provides nothing that anyone is likely to object to, a consideration which more than anything leaves the flavour of sadness in the mouth. What we value all our life, what fires us and sparks us, the sense of our individuality, dampened down, crushed, deprived of oxygen. No outrage allowed.

The three of us trooped in to see Alison, who was bed-bound: they had not warned me of that. She sat against pillows in a small single room. She stared into space. She looked wilfully old, as if she were pretending. She had my hair, but it was white and crinkly: it spread in a witch's fuzz around her face. She had Felicity's eyes and Anton's heavy jaw, around which old flesh drooped, and when she turned those still beautiful eyes towards us they were sulky and dull. I know one should not say it of those who are past improvement, but I did not like her. Pulses of noise came and went: the roar of young male voices rising and falling in unison: the sports stadium was all but next door: Sunday afternoon's fixture at Twickenham was under way: but what was it to her?

'Who are you?' she asked. 'Did Lorna send you? She never comes herself.'

'I'm here, Mummy,' said Lorna.

'Lorna had me drugged and locked up in here,' Alison confided in me. 'I was all right until they started giving me pills. Now my legs don't work.'

'Your legs don't work because you had a stroke, Mummy,' said Lorna.

'Guy was always in love with me,' Alison told me. 'Even when his father was alive. But then he had me walled up in this prison.'

'Now why would I do a thing like that, Mummy?' asked Guy. Sunday lunch, however meagre, had given him a well-fed bursting look, or it might just be that his blood pressure was already mounting, and we'd been only two minutes in the room. 'I was running off with a nice young man and my son couldn't stand it,' explained Alison. 'He thought I might change my will. He didn't know I'd changed it already.'

'I don't think there's any point in we two staying,' said Guy. 'We thought you ought to see for yourself. We'll go and wait in the car while you try and get through to Mother.'

Getting through to Mother was clearly a phrase frequently used: it had a familial, helpless kind of feel about it.

'That got rid of them,' said Alison, once they'd gone. 'They come here sometimes and pretend to be my family but they're not. I was adopted, so they're no blood relatives of mine.' I sat on a wicker chair and once I was settled she directed me to another, from which I first had to remove a rubber hot water bottle and a variety of woollen garments. No sooner was I sitting down when she asked me for some water. Then she told me not to sit in the chair I had just cleared because it was where she kept her hot water bottle. I could see she would have been the sort of mother who never gave her children a moment's peace. The minute they'd sat down she'd think of something for them to get up and do, and if they were busy and on their feet she'd suggest they sat down: their ceaseless activities were making her feel tired. I understood

Guy's and Lorna's liking for what I saw as dullness but which they saw as peace and quiet. To the end of their days, they would appreciate just moving from one side of a room to another without being told what to do: and if it was the room where they had spent so much of their childhood, so much the better.

She asked me if I were the cleaning girl and I said no, I was her half-niece, and that I was glad she had brought up the subject of adoption because I had news of her real mother. She peered at me suspiciously and pushed her hair back from her head with a hand that was uncannily like Felicity's. She felt around for her purse and pushed it under her pillow, pointedly.

'They send people in to steal from me,' she complained. 'They even stole me once, when I was a baby.'

I tried to explain that she was given away, perforce, by her birth mother, not stolen by her adoptive parents, but she would have none of it. She had been dropped in Woolworths and not handed in. Anyone honest would have spoken to the Manager about it. I could not make up my mind whether she was teasing me or not. I could see the resemblance to Felicity and liked her rather more. Alison took a plastic beaker out of her locker, into which was wodged a rather nasty lump of tissue paper. She removed the paper and showed me a collection of blue and green capsules, pink flat pills and large white tablets.

'I saved these,' she said. 'They're trying to poison me. The sooner I'm dead the more money they inherit.'

'Who're they?' I asked, though I knew the answer.

'Guy and Lorna. They don't even come and visit me.'

'They were in this room just a minute ago.'

'No. Guy and Lorna are little children. They take after their father. A very dull man.' This last was said with a Felicity-ish sigh. 'I should never have been born, you know. It was a great mistake. But I always liked the river. It should have been called Mother Thames, not Father Thames. *Old Mother Thames keeps rolling along, down to the mighty sea.*'

She sang this last in a high-pitched, quavery voice. A member of staff came in with a cup of tea.

'Singing again, dear,' she said. 'That's nice.'

When she'd gone Alison poured her cup of tea into a pot plant with a shaky hand. It was a miniature palm, much overwatered. Not a single leaf but was tipped with brown.

'Your real mother,' I began again, 'is alive and well and living in Rhode Island.'

Alison looked at me as if trying to decipher what I was saying. I think she managed because she seemed to give the matter some thought and then said quite sharply: 'That's all very well, but finders keepers. Tell that to them in Woolworths. If you want to keep your purse don't drop it. Good layers, though, Rhode Island Reds.' She closed her eyes and the interview was over, and with it my hope of enriching my grandmother's life. What a lot of money I had spent and to how little purpose. I joined Guy and Lorna in the car. Lorna tried not to look too reproachfully at her watch. They liked to be in and out of the Glentyre Nursing Home like a shot, and who could blame them?

'Now we'll be caught up in the rugby crowd,' she complained.

We were, too, but after the Glentyre the thronging of thoughtless young male flesh, the sound of drunken revelry, the very air fetid with testosterone, was a relief. When I finally got back home the waitress from Zilli's was not there in my place, of course she was not. Harry was, waiting.

30

Once we were in bed again – and under the duvets, not on top of them – Krassner said: 'I had a call from home, while you were out.'

It was a cold night, and a great wind got up and found branches and leaves to fling against our window even here in the very heart of London; and the street signs swung around and creaked atrociously; and the sound of breaking glass had more to do with the weather than the recreational violence so common in these parts as the nation prepares itself for its Monday morning best-foot-forward, but Harry and I were snug and warm. I remember lying in my narrow bed as a child and wondering what the future held: would I ever lie next to a man as of right: would I have a wide bed forever rumpled, or with children crawling around it and over me: would there be maids to bring orange juice and toast, and a silver tray for the post? Knowing even then that things turned out never as good as you hoped, never as bad as you feared.

Perhaps the bed would be forever narrow, and clean, and quiet, as Angel's was? She was such a still, cool sleeper: as if all her energy was taken up by her mind, roaming and plotting and scheming even while her body slept. I was all over the place, tossing and turning and murmuring in my dreams: she'd complain of it. 'Like your father,' she'd say, which to the child of the single parent is condemnation, less for the girl than the boy, but there all the same. I have broad plain hands, not like Felicity's or Lucy's, not like Angel's, like my father's, Angel said, and I vaguely remembered. And what crimes had they not, in my mother's mind at least, committed? I will tell you more about my father presently.

Right now here I am happy with Harry in my bed, my leg pushed between his, his arm over my shoulder. Nevertheless ice gripped my heart again, when he said he'd had a call from home. It is terrible to be a woman in love, if only because such images come to mind. Ice gripping the heart! I suppose you could do it in special effects but it would look pretty silly. I remembered Kay, Gerda's childhood sweetheart in the Hans Christian Andersen story. Just a sliver of ice in the heart from the Snow Queen and he wandered the world as her servant, forgetting Gerda back home. Harry was the real Kay, Holly was the Snow Queen, and I was Gerda. Such a plain, dull name, and such a silly good girl. She got him back in the end, though.

I thought the phone call could only be Holly summoning Harry back. She would want to go into therapy with him, to recover from the shock of losing the baby (it would seem to her like the most drastic miscarriage, no doubt), something, anything, to have him by her side and not have to come after him herself, swell her ankles at 30,000 feet. What would she think of me, if she knew about me? She wouldn't mind much, I didn't imagine. I was only the hired help, one of the production team. Not one of the principals, the ones who counted. I wasn't seen with Harry Krassner in publicity photos outside smart nightclubs, or entwined by someone's pool or in the gossip columns, any of those things that so upset the great and famous: I didn't think she'd much mind Harry's habit of sleeping entwined with me, to the detriment of my back (it always ached in the mornings) or the calm domesticity of how we got along. Him putting up shelves: me sweeping outside my front door with dustpan and brush, singing: doing, as Harry put it, my Doris Day impersonation. Not Holly's style. Terrible to think of one ending up as the girl next door.

I had a feeling that maybe bed didn't count in Holly's scheme of things: what counted was how you stretched and roamed in your silk wrap first thing in the morning, and sat sipping your orange juice in your vast kitchen which overlooked the ocean, with Harry Krassner, hairy-legged and white dressing gowned, facing you, saying the kind of things film stars say to their director-lovers, binding them closer and closer, delivering charm, demanding guilt, while the paparazzi duck and dart beneath the windowsills. But the call wasn't from Hollywood: it was from farther north and to the west, where the winter days are short and cold and people still fall in love, not into relationships.

'I think it was a friend of your grandmother's,' said Harry. 'It was hard to tell, she shouted so loud. I kept saying I wasn't you, but she didn't believe me.'
'That would be Joy,' I said. 'I hope everything's okay.'
'I could tell from the pitch of her voice that it wasn't,' said Harry. 'I said you'd call back.'
I reached across him for the phone, disturbing his tranquillity.
'God,' he said. 'You really worry about your family.' Men never like it if you pay too much instant attention to anyone other than them. 'For someone who has so little of it, it's truly wondrous.'

I got through to Joy. I begged her to put in her hearing aid and once she had the vibrations of her voice became differentiated and it was possible to tell what she was saying. She had been on to the Golden Bowl and warned them that a fortune hunter was after Felicity. She had hired a private investigator to check him out: I was going to get the bill: after all I was family, she was only a friend. I said perhaps she should have waited until I came over, and could judge the situation for myself. Joy thought otherwise, said I was selfish and ungrateful and took after my mother, and put the phone down. So much for transatlantic calls. I re-entwined myself with Harry but he was asleep; real life drama did not impinge on him; presumably it wasn't focused, drifted along, needed editing. Outside the wind banged and crashed. I lay awake and listened to the radio, which told me what I already knew, that force seven winds were sweeping London.
The phone went again: I leaned across Harry and still he did not stir, though my elbow went into his hairy chest. This time it was Jack, apologizing for Joy.
'She's upset for your grandmother,' he said, 'I guess you've got to excuse her. She isn't as young as once she was.'
'Are you over in Joy's house?' I asked. I like to envisage where

people are when they speak, that's all, but the question seemed to make him defensive.

'I just came over for a game of cards,' he said. There was the sound of a struggle as Joy took charge of the telephone.

'Jack says I was hard on you,' she said. 'It's just such a worry. I shouldn't have to go through this kind of thing at my age.'

I agreed, no, she shouldn't. I am the great placator; the picker-up of unconsidered pieces: the scavenger of the good deeds of the universe, the fitter-together of snippets to make as narrative. I like to create a cheerful viewing, a good read. I should have said, 'If you can't stand the heat get out of the kitchen,' but I didn't. I should have said, 'Call off your dogs,' but I didn't.

And while I was busy reassuring myself, Guy and Lorna, I could see in retrospect, sat up late and wondered how they could get their hands on the Utrillo, sooner rather than later, for the fees Alison was paying to the Glentyre Nursing Home were excessive, and Happiness would have to be sold to pay for them, and they had remembered how much they loved the house, and what happy childhoods they had enjoyed, and wanted to live on the banks of the sweet Thames for ever and ever, to the end of their lives, which is much the same thing, in Happiness.

So Lois must have felt, waiting for Sylvia to die, so she could marry Arthur and move in, and oust Felicity who was not her own blood, or joined to her by semen as a husband is, making the pair more one flesh than otherwise. Lois worked by atavistic instinct, to plant her own family in this good soil, to look after her own, and not the stranger's. The cuckoo in the nest, easing out the contender's genes. No, that was just some film starring Joan Crawford or was it Bette Davis? Or had Felicity not been an innocent victim at all: perhaps she'd set out to seduce Anton to pay Lois out? Perhaps Arthur had seduced an innocent Lois? All we knew of Lois, really, was what her child, who was not a reliable witness, had said: and how two of her grandchildren had turned out. Could one work backwards? No, because others could choose to conclude that because I was taking Harry from poor lost and bewildered Holly, in all probability Felicity was a bad lot too. Far-fetched to see Felicity not as victim but as perpetrator.

But it was there in my head, the archetypal scene, waiting to be born: *Fatal Attraction* or *The Mistress's Revenge*. Of course we do not do this kind of thing these days, not in sophisticated circles: I was able to contemplate Holly's existence easily enough: I was not moved to murderous rage. I hoped the same could be said of her, in relation to me.

Harry stirred and put his arms around me, and beseeched me to stop thinking: he could feel it through my skin. I did too much of it.

'Do you have a grandmother?' I asked him, refraining from entering into a debate as to whether he ever felt Holly thinking through hers. He laughed and said he barely had a mother. He'd left her long ago in Sacramento. Americans don't seem to have elderly relatives in the way we do. It's as if they spring fully fledged into the world, and the old keep going playing golf and singing in choirs until one day they just drop down dead or retire gracefully into places like the Golden Bowl, where visitors are discouraged. The weak die young from drink, drugs and rock'n'roll: those who survive are strong, fit and wealthy. I know it can't really be so: I daresay the old creep and shuffle in the States as anywhere: all I know of the nation, like most Europeans, is from out the window of cabs in Boston, New York, Washington, San Francisco, Los Angeles and the odd dash up to Seattle: wherever films open or are edited and occasionally I get sent. And my little scraps of family visiting into Connecticut, and the land of the Rhode Island Reds, the best laying hens in all the world. And the whole history of film, of course, and Harry in my bed; focusing all America, my new-found land, my love. See what I mean? As bad as turned to ice: the leap to cliché, to what e'er was felt, and ne'er so well expressed. E'er being ever, and ne'er being never, those Victorians being so punctilious about rhyme. What's on the late-night film, what old black-and-white love story? Turn the sound softly. Krassner sleeps again. Outside the wind drops. A stillness descends. Everything stops in the face of love, freezes, for just one second before entropy wins again. I sense it. To hold back time itself, to halt the inexorable descent into the darkness of death mid-flight, what power is this? It's not as if new life were going to come out of this union.

31

Felicity was waiting at the French windows of the Atlantic Suite for her day's mystery outing by ten on Monday morning. She had dressed leisurely and carefully, in the full pleasure of expectation, addressing every spot and blemish. So she remembered similar outings in her youth, when her skin had been firmer and the line of her jaw cleaner. She did not care. Only one woman in the whole world could look in the mirror and be told 'You are the fairest of them all', so what did degrees of failure matter? And if that was what the mirror did ever tell you, everyone hated you: you became wicked witch to Snow White. And besides, it didn't last: good looks were all anxiety and disappointment: she had given up worrying years ago. She caught a flicker of Dr Rosebloom in the mirror today: she thought he approved.

She would miss a lecture on *How the Past Feeds the Present* by a Gloria Fensterwick PhD and Monday's Light Lunch, which would be ham quiche, arugala and boiled potatoes. She had recently ordered a book called *Salad, the Silent Killer* from a publisher whose list specialized in healthy living and thinking, and left it prominently in the dining room, to have it slammed back in her room by Nurse Dawn. The lecture and the lunch would be no great loss.

A spectacular red Saab coupé, driven by William, swept past the French windows and round the corner to the formal Atrium entrance of the Golden Bowl, and parked in the appropriate place.

The days of secrecy were over. William Johnson stepped out, dapper for once in a blue and white striped shirt, red and yellow tie, navy suit, and ordinary well-polished loafers, which might or might not have been Gucci.

Felicity, dressed more seriously than usual, without the usual swathing of scarves, in taupe and stone and other neutral colours, did not wait to be summoned but left her room and went to the front desk where William was waiting for her. Nurse Dawn appeared as if by magic, to protest that Felicity had not cancelled lunch in proper time, and she could not countenance a trip out in such weather. Mr Johnson was irresponsible in suggesting such a thing.

'Good heavens,' said Felicity, 'it's a perfectly fine day. Mr Johnson and I are going out on a date, and I don't suppose we'll even notice the weather.'

Nurse Dawn said that was a pity: she'd hoped Miss Felicity would be there this morning to help Dr Bronstein stay in the land of the sane.

'What can you mean?' asked Felicity, alarmed, stopped in her tracks as she swept out on William's arm.

'Poor Dr Bronstein,' said Nurse Dawn, 'is getting quite confused. What we used to call senile in the old days, before we knew so much. He so enjoys his chats with you: they keep his mind alert. His appointment's after lunch; I don't want him to let himself down.'

'What appointment?'

'With the psychiatrist. His family think it's time he was declared fiscally incompetent and moved on to the West Wing for fuller nursing care. And Dr Grepalli agrees he's beginning to quite disturb the other guests with his ramblings. We can't have that. Poor Dr Bronstein. You know the kind of questions they ask, to see if you know where you are and who you are. What year is it, who's the President, where's Kosovo, that sort of thing.'

Felicity leaned against one of the Roman pillars. She seemed to feel suddenly weak. William held her arm in support.

'Oh dear,' said Nurse Dawn. 'I hope I haven't upset you. I'm sure Dr Bronstein will do just fine. It's just we'd all really miss him if he had to move on to the West Wing, especially you, Miss Felicity. You two are such friends. Don't worry about it: I'll speak up for him: my recommendation counts for a lot.'

'Once you pay the Danegeld,' said Felicity, enigmatically, recovering, 'you never get rid of the Dane. I will keep to my plans, but thank you for mentioning it,' and she smiled at William and they went out.

'You have a nice time now,' Nurse Dawn called after them.

'I didn't know you could look so smart,' said Felicity.

'I had a good week last week,' said William, looking for some wood to touch.

'If I'm not mistaken,' said Felicity, 'those clothes are all new.'

'I went into Hartford,' said William, 'I couldn't let you down.'

'And the car?'

'Do you like it?'

'I love it.'

'All for you,' he said. 'All because of you.'

William took Route 95 North to Exit 92, then Route 2 West: they travelled through roads where sometimes the woods crowded in to the very edges of the tarmac, sometimes kept aloof so you could see the shapes of the hills: the eye became accustomed to muted browns and greens. It was a bright day: the world seemed young and cheerful. It felt natural for Felicity to be sitting there beside him: as if she had been doing it all her life. There was a rightness about it. He drove fast and competently, like a man twenty years younger, at the height of his power to impress the world, eager to be getting where he was going. Men always drove more slowly coming home. She buried anxiety about Dr Bronstein: Nurse Dawn was being both absurd and malicious. Even if the good Doctor too was due for a psychiatric examination that afternoon, which was not necessarily the case, it wasn't likely that a conversation over lunch would make much difference to the Doctor's mental state. He talked and she listened; it was not exactly sparkling dialogue. She could of course have checked that he knew the year and the President's name, and they could have looked up Kosovo together – she dismissed the thought. This was her day and Nurse Dawn was not to be allowed to spoil it. Felicity didn't take up the matter with William. He was not going to be impressed with her concern for another man: Dr Bronstein relegated to the West Wing would suit William well enough, and even, for all she knew, Dr Bronstein himself. Just because she, Felicity, feared the West Wing, and the chancy kindness of nursing staff as over the years you were stupefied by tranquillizers, rendered paranoïac by pain-killers, confined to your bed and became a source of profound irritation and trouble to others, did not mean the rest on the world shared her fears. Some might quite look forward to the rest, the absence of decision, the notion of *too late now*. Some cared what others thought of them scarcely at all: worried only about what they thought of others. In the West Wing Dr Bronstein could talk on to himself, without the bother of having a face opposite, sitting watching. She knew she was trying to convince herself. She should have done her duty by friendship and stayed. But when did a woman ever put a friend before a lover?

It was not too late. She would ask William to turn back. She opened her mouth to say so, and closed it again. So much you could do for others, no more. This was her day: hers and William's.

The Saab turned a bend in the road. There, gaudy, impossible and sudden, towering over the woods, stood an emerald-green Disney Castle, all spires, glass, turrets and towers.
'Foxwoods Casino,' said William, happily. 'My secret. Property of the Mashantucket Pequod Tribal Indians. This is reservation land. All profits free of tax, in due compensation for the injuries of the past.'
'This place can hardly be secret,' said Felicity, 'to anyone who comes along this road.'
'It is only a dream,' said William, 'which keeps coming true. It is happiness snatched away and rendered back to you. It is wealth beyond your wildest dreams yet always in them and beyond them. It is excitement and compulsion and infinite choice. It is the battle against the self. It is Eros in the face of Thanatos. It draws you back and back and yet it never happened. Outside you, this is my life. Last week I played the purple tables. Minimum bet $500; I chose orange chips only. That's $1,000 a throw. I cleared $50,000 and left before it was gone again. I had to, to get back to you.

That's your influence, Felicity. My luck has turned. I'm on a roll. Can't you sniff it in the air?'

He smiled as he drove, for her but no longer to her. There was a gleam in his eye, an alertness; she could feel the magnet pull as well. Others had the same idea. The road filled up: they were part of a pilgrimage. She felt jealous. She wanted to be his only preoccupation. This was no fly in the ointment: this was a great writhing caterpillar with staring eyes on stalks. She had not bargained for this.

'What a perfectly frightful building,' she said, as English as she could be. 'How quite extraordinary. Whoever gave them permission for that!' She felt she spoke with Nurse Dawn's tongue but couldn't help it.

'They don't need permission,' William said. 'It's their land, not Uncle Sam's. You get used to it, you get even to like it. I come here most days, mornings only since I met you, and two or three evenings a week.'

'Gambling,' she said. 'A gambling man. That's why you have nothing left, why you live in the Rosemount. It's an addiction.'

'Good car, good shoes, good tie,' he said. 'They can't take this away from me.'

'No, but you can lose them again,' she said sharply. He looked sad, misunderstood. She put her hand on his knee: and he cheered up suspiciously quickly. He had been too sure of her. Perhaps she could cure him? She'd thought that once of someone – who was it had had the drink problem? – and of course been wrong. Those were in the Twelve Step days, but whoever got beyond six? *Hello, I am a reformed gambler, drug addict, alcoholic, loveaholic. How can I help you?*

William Johnson, gambling man, the opposite of contrite. Take his money from his bank, put it on a horse, or its casino equivalent, weep and grovel for a bit and then go back for more. Except he did not seem the grovelling type. She wanted to overlook it, tell herself it didn't matter, a man of seventy-two was allowed his entertainment, but what would Exon say? His stiff, kind face would have turned stiffer still in disapproval: even Buckley, back in Savannah, who played poker on mahogany tables in the houses of friends, would never have frequented a casino. 'That's why your family left,' she said. 'That's why you're all alone. They couldn't stand it.'

'Margaret's a po-faced bitch,' he said. 'She wanted the house. She got it.' He showed her a savagery he had not so far brought to her attention, but did today, almost carelessly. He was handing her reasons to break the relationship off, sink back into the safeness of the Golden Bowl, to spar with Nurse Dawn till the West Wing called. Anything was better than that, even the attentions of a gambling man, when he had time off from his obsession to think of you.

'So what do you want me to do?' he asked. 'Turn back? Is it too much for you? Too vulgar to endure?'

'Of course not,' she said.

'Praise the Lord,' he said, and put his foot on the accelerator in his eagerness. She could see that if he had delivered her back home again, he would simply have set out again for these shimmering topless towers of Ilium. Take me, take all of me.

The towers and turrets differentiated themselves as they approached: some turquoise, some silver; the magic diminished, the place looked more like a gigantic shopping mall than Mickey Mouse's fantasy of heaven. Still incomparably vulgar, hopelessly at war with nature, but kind of local all the same. The Pequod Indians changing their tune, subduing the natural world for a change, false God as it had turned out to be, for them. A toothless, hopeless God, when faced by an enemy with a flair for logistics. Commune with nature all you liked, meld and mystify, worship and magnify, placate and please, in the end it betrayed you. Nature had sided with the white man, trampling and crushing through undergrowth though he might, slaughtering animals, burning the prairie: nature admired him. Talk loud, act tough, win. The survival of the cunning, not the valiant. That's what nature respects.

William and Felicity parked underground in a vast dark concrete cavern, and rose by lift to glassy, noisy, much peopled levels. Here gathered were the blue-haired and the bald, the disabled, the quick – not many – and the lame, the fast – not many – and the slow; united in the wafting smell of junk food cooking, in the solidarity of a common enterprise, the warmth of companionship, of shared elation and despair, of instant empathy one for the other. If there was a common enemy it was the Casino and its profits, yet how they rushed to embrace it, how friendly they found the foe, how moody and attractive the wall of noise; the beating pulse of vaguely familiar music, the background susurrus of a thousand slot machines, tinkling their triumph and their sorrow, generously disgorging money. The soft smiles and greetings of management. Give us your money and all will be well. We will not let you come to harm. Trust us. Here was one vast family of choice: here was home, companionship, support, charged by the agreeable excitement of risk, the continuation of youth by other means. Challenge for the brave at the blackjack tables, at craps, brisk male voices acting father, censorious – *Surely for once you can get just this right: place your counter over the line, please, not on it: over I said, are you deaf?* – soft maternal female voices for roulette – *You're sure this is what you want to do, you're sure?* And on the slots in shadowed halls at last the friendly siblings you never had, legion upon legion of them, row upon row of sharers in delight, hypnotized in concert at the family prayer wheels: whirling sevens, bars, cherries, jackpots.

Booths everywhere: booths for change, booths for cash, booths for turning tokens into money, money into tokens: a temple given over wholly to moneychangers. Security cameras sweeping back and forth, back and forth, for your protection not your detection. Surely. Punters wandering, gawking and gaping, but knowing what to do, how to be, what the rules were. It was obvious to Felicity that she did not. And William walked ahead: she followed close behind. If she lost him she would be a time-traveller stranded in a future: she would never get back home. She saw that she had lived a long life on some other quiet planet, powered by the rising and the falling sun, but still unnatural. Here in this Casino was a wholly satisfactory alternate universe, the true one, as provided by a restless tribal nation obliged to settle down, created out of the male imagination for the delectation of women, and the furtherance of male power, the forces of nature quite undone.

William realized he was walking too fast, and slowed and took

Felicity's arm. He took her elbow: the floor was glittery with some unknown substance. She hoped her feet would stay comfortable: there were women of her age wearing trainers; she'd sworn never to do so: but you could always change your mind.

'This is nothing compared to Vegas,' said William proudly. 'Let alone Atlantic City. Good taste personified.'

A central glass giant, a well-muscled Indian, milky white, in the attitude of Rodin's *The Thinker*, towered above all else, directing the last battle. The white man was tricked, after all, and wandered lost in woods, and didn't even know it. This was where victory and prosperity had led him. He had come to these shores wanting gold, and freedom, and killing to get it: now what he wanted destroyed him. A Japanese car, today's prize, circled gracefully at his feet on an orange plinth.

William, however, seemed far from destroyed. Twenty years had dropped away from him as the lift rose.

'Much better than Vegas,' said William. 'I was five years in Vegas, two in Atlantic City. This Casino you get a better return on your money than anywhere else in the States.'

'You said you were a teacher in a New York high school,' she said, sadly. You told lies to men to get out of trouble, as you had to your father, yet expected them to be father, and not tell lies in return. Exon was the exception: he didn't tell lies: he had no imagination. His fancy never outran his caution. And though his loss still grieved her, there was no denying he was the most boring man in the world. The wicked make better company than the good. 'I was,' he said. 'But gambling paid better. For a time. Until I had a run of bad luck. Margaret went to law to get the house. It had been in my family since it was built: 1890. That didn't stop her. The courts don't look kindly on a gambling man. They don't appreciate the work that goes into it. Now Margaret lives there with Tommy's boys, and they let it fall down around them.'

'Why didn't you tell me this before?' It wasn't a reproach. She wanted to know.

She stood still in the crowd, which flowed gently by like a river, parting without aggression. Everything lacked definition: seen through a vision darkly, like Dr Rosebloom in the mirror. She remembered her mother's dressing table, when she was a child. Rodin's *The Thinker* in Lalique glass, milky blue, a Chinese ceramic powder bowl, a hairbrush and mirror set, silver-backed. Her father moved nothing after her death. A month later the brush still held a single red hair: the puff stayed in the powder bowl, as if one day her mother would just come back and continue. But how could she: she was dead. There was a little pile of hairnets behind the powder bowl, made of a delicate mesh of finest brown silk within an elasticized circle of ribbon. Women slept in hairnets in those days, so as not to muss their hair. Every time you washed your hair you removed the grease but left a fine film of soap behind. You put vinegar or lemon juice in the rinsing water but still you couldn't get it out, still it refused to shine, she remembered her mother lamenting. You could buy hairnets at Woolworths, her mother said, cheaper but just as good as anywhere else. Little Felicity would choose to stretch the nets between her hands and look at the world through them: a fine crisscross of brown between her and reality, distorting it but softening it.

'Careful,' her mother said, when she was alive. 'Don't break it. It's so delicate.'

Now why had she remembered this after so long? What was her mother's name? How could you forget your own mother's name? She'd died and gone away and left her child without protection, that was why. Sylvia, of course, that was her name. Then Lois had taken over and within a day the dressing table was cleared and there was a stepmother in her mother's bed. Felicity felt tears in her eyes. William sat her down on a fluorescent yellow bench. 'If it upsets you I'll take you home at once,' he said. 'I didn't tell you because I didn't want to put you off me.'

'It's not that,' she said, 'I understand that. It's nothing. I'm crying because my mother died.'

They went and sat down in a fast-food restaurant, without caring what it served. He told her about the death of his mother, when he was ten, in a car crash. His twin brother had died too: he himself had been thrown clear. Luck of the draw. They were all on the way back from hospital: William had trodden on a needle: it had gone right in, the doctor had to extract it with an electro-magnet. Yes, it felt like his fault, of course it did: if he hadn't trodden on a needle they'd all be alive today. And why them, not him? All that.

'Perhaps that's why we get on,' she said. 'Because our mothers died when we were small. We recognize each other.'

The waitress, in pert pleated blue shirt and red and white blouse, brought them coffee and bagels. Perhaps they'd ordered them, perhaps they hadn't. 'I never think about it,' he said, 'if I can help it.'

'They say we ought to,' she said. 'But it's so long ago, and no-one understands what it was like then. It doesn't fade: so you blot it out.'

'Perhaps you have to be strong enough,' he said. 'Perhaps we make each other strong.'

But soon he began to look restless: she lost his attention: he wanted to get to the tables: they filled up early and sometimes even when it got crowded management didn't open up all the available craps tables. Understandable, craps being least profitable from management's point of view – which meant it was best for the punters. He preferred craps anyway, said William. The sense of others in the game with you: he liked that. One for all and all for one. Blackjack was a loner's occupation. He'd won so much at blackjack last month they'd be keeping an eye on him. (He boasted: cock of the dung-heap.) No Casino liked its patrons to be too lucky, but this one was both the most relaxed about it and nearest to home. Why should the Casino worry? It didn't pay taxes. Death and tax, the two great certainties of the white man's life, halved at one stroke.

He wasn't stupid like some people: he kept money aside from his pension for the Rosemount: he never mortgaged that, never risked it. Of course his fortunes were up and down. At first you hoped to even out in a day, then a week, then a month, then a year. Last week he'd evened out about two years' worth of enjoyment. Felicity would bring him luck, he knew she would. She already had. The new shoes had an extra level on the heels, she noticed. He walked tall and proud: eyes followed him.

*   *   *

She hovered behind him at the crowded craps table. He tried to explain to her what was going on. She tried to focus, but it was like listening to traffic directions. You stopped to ask strangers the way, but when they spoke you didn't hear them. There were two croupiers, darting, stretching, raking. Each player waited his turn, rolled two dice directly down the centre of the table to hit the low wall at the other end. It bounced back and stopped. People sighed or rejoiced as their interests were affected. William explained that the player threw for the whole table. You could have sequence bets or roll bets. He lost her there. Could she have understood even in the old Savannah days? She doubted it.

'A six or an eight is most likely,' he said. 'A four or a ten least likely. But then the rewards are higher. The greater the risk, the higher the reward, that's the principle. Jesus, it's like life.'

There was some disagreeable confusion and delay at the table. Someone had declared that his winnings had not been paid out properly. Of course they had been: punters tried to cheat the Casino, not the Casino the punters. The Casino's confidence trick was so vast as to go unnoticed. Security men gathered: gently the offender was eased away. William occupied the interval instructing Felicity further. She appreciated his efficiency. He didn't like wasting time. Money, certainly: time, no. She had been trained for years in disapproval, she realized: she had never been a willing pupil, but some had rubbed off. She, the one-time hooker, had learned the pleasures of moral superiority: she didn't like it in herself; it chafed like a too-tight shoe.

She had never in her life thought of herself in those terms. A hooker. But that was long ago, so long it didn't count.

And now she was with William, wasn't she? This was what she'd always wanted, always trusted would happen: she'd never quite given up. She loved him. He wanted to marry her. This was his pre-nuptial confession. She had yet to make hers to him. So he was a gambling man: was that so terrible? It might be if you were a young woman with children dependent on a gambling man for your comforts. But now both were free, surely, to

198

entertain themselves as best they could? It was all there was left to do, at the close of life. And who cared about the money?

Felicity had a momentary twinge of guilt about Dr Bronstein. Of course he couldn't place Kosovo on the map. Who could? It's not as if it was a place where academics gather together. Reykjavik in Iceland he would know about, a great conference centre at least in the summer months, volcanoes for side shows, and he would even be able to spell it, but they wouldn't ask him about Reykjavik. It was one question suit all, just as cheap clothes came One Size Fits All. Kosovo was the upgrading on Kuwait. And Dr Bronstein might so hate Clinton as to refuse to name him, unaware of the dire consequences of so doing, of being declared incompetent, and all because she, Felicity, had failed to give him proper warning. He might very well get the year wrong: the young, for whom time passed slowly, never realized how easy it was to misremember the exact year you were in, in sheer amazement at the number since you began: and it was the brisk and sensible young who did the testing and sorting of those who could still manage, and those who couldn't.

'It's like climbing mountains,' William was saying. 'It's rolling with destiny.'

'Or casting the *I Ching*,' said Felicity, forgetting all about Dr Bronstein. 'Discovering the pattern of the times.'

'We'll make a gambler of you yet,' he said, and turned back to the table. The seas had closed over the complainant: the urgency of the game was picked up as if it had never been lost. William's hand was steady on the dice. He threw a double three. Everyone seemed to like that and cheered, and she could feel him glow and could not resent it.

Presently Felicity began to feel bored. Whether William was winning or losing she could not be sure. He flung tokens in the table one side of a line or another: croupiers raked them in. From time to time he fetched others in. If you didn't understand they barked at you, asked what you'd meant. She'd never been to school: presumably this was what it was like. Her father had wanted her educated at home, which meant she had educated herself. Though he'd allowed her to go to ballet lessons. White tutus and points.

She remembered her mother teaching her to read and write. After that there had been Lois, and Lois's baby – what was the baby's name? She couldn't remember even that. And through the haze of the brown silk net, more things to remember. Uncle something, with the heavy jaw, who had given her history lessons, and been all charm, like William, until one day he wasn't: everything held together, by the memory of once good times which yet might come again, so suddenly shattered. And after that, the baby, and a different life.

Why did she remember all this now? She had worked so hard at forgetting. She had told Sophia about the baby. She should not have done it. It stirred up too much stuff better forgotten. If you dwelt on the past it gave you no time to live in the present. And then there'd been Angel, who'd run away to Europe, got married, gone mad, produced Sophia, and died. Of course she didn't want to think of the past. Who would? Bury it with the noise of the present: that's why she had always got on with Joy, who understood the importance of moving in a cloud of shimmering sound waves, even if she couldn't hear the sound itself.

Stocky girls with plump bosoms, short skirts and massive thighs moved round the tables carrying trays of cold drinks. Challenging fate is a thirsty business. Their bare arms were bulky and sweaty: they could never stop: the trays were heavy: the drinks were long and free, and were exchanged for tips. William had gone to time and trouble saving five dollars on the way here, picking between gas stations; now he paid out an unnecessary ten. No Vegas showgirls these, with legs up to their navels, the pick of all America, albeit hard-drug skinny – these were local girls for local tastes. Once in Savannah she'd been just such a girl, supporting Tommy, though he was none of her own. You did what you could, sold what you had. She'd always been the girl behind the bar, never the one in the chorus line, high kicking; the one who got propositioned, not the one who got red roses. In those days she'd blamed her legs. Not long enough. Ballet lessons when small had overdeveloped her calf muscles, she'd always suspected. Buckley had called them English legs, and someone, before Buckley rescued her and turned her back into the lady she was born to be, had once told her fat legs meant good in bed, and that was why she was so popular. She thought it was more to do with the fact that she was nicely spoken and smiled a lot and handled the customers with tact and politeness, where most of the other girls were tough and brassy and looked as if they'd give you a social disease, if it were left up to them. Age had slimmed her legs down, of course: these days they were as skinny as you could wish. Practically stick-like. Some things, not many, got better with the passage of the years.

William's eyes didn't follow the girls; she was glad of that. They moved among men who had their minds on more subtle excitements than sex. She failed to attract his attention, shrugged, and went to play the slots. If others could work out what to do, so could she. She turned fifty dollars into quarters, found a vacant seat flanked by two women so large they overflowed their seats – which was why it was vacant, no doubt, but she didn't mind – and fed them into the slot. Feed, press the button, watch the next spin. Wait, feed again. She could make no sense of what was going on, but the machine knew when it had won and when it hadn't. When she won it disgorged coins, and her neighbours, alerted by the clatter, looked at her and smiled, happy for her. That was nice. When the machine hadn't won, it stayed silent. That was all. You could trust a machine to do something as simple as that. But quite what constituted winning was beyond her. You went into a trance; what brought you back to reality at intervals was a sense of triumph. Only eventually did she realize what everyone else around seemed to have been born knowing, that the lines which went through the middle, above or underneath the symbols when the drum stopped rolling represented success or failure. The payline. In the middle was best.

Gamblers believed money was for spending, not for saving; they were generous, not envious; they were the salt of the earth: thus they defied fate, bent it to their will. They shared common wisdom: she could feel it emanate down the row, even from her fleshy neighbours with their scanty hair, double chins and hopeless bodies. When she had over $150 back she stopped. So easy. She filled the bucket provided by the Casino to hold her winnings, changed it at a booth, and put $150.50 back in her purse. She went back to William.

'I won,' she said. 'Three hundred per cent profit. Beginner's luck.'

'Don't you believe it,' he said. 'From now on in you're a lucky person.'

He stopped too: $7,500 in profit. In counters.

'The art,' he said, 'is knowing when to stop.'

'It's now,' she said, so they both did.

32

Valerie Boheimer of Abbey Inquiries, Private Investigators, Hartford, equivalent of London's Aardvark Detectives, reported back to Joy at the end of the week. Joy had had to fork out $1,000 in advance, and further sums would be payable until the investigation of William Johnson was complete.

'What I do for my friends!' shrieked Joy to Jack. 'Do you think that English girl will pay?'
'Depends what this Valerie finds out,' said Jack. He was feeling more cheerful, and becoming accustomed to the noise Joy made. She had been remarkably good about Charlie: hadn't sacked him for running around behind her back, using her gas without a by-your-leave and inciting Felicity to madness and keeping it secret. Joy balked at making ten living creatures homeless, which would have happened had she let Charlie go: the ten including various women, four wide-eyed children, and what was more important, two dogs and one cat which had just had kittens. If the humans went Joy would have felt obliged to take in the animals. Francine would have fired Charlie on the spot and had the animals put down. No messing.

Yet Francine, Joy's deceased sister, Jack's deceased wife, still seemed to live among them, to trot to and fro between Windspit and Passmore as they did. If you listened you could almost hear her soft footsteps in the early morning mists. Francine had never liked animals; she had an asthmatic reaction to cats and an aversion to dog hairs on her clothes. She had been as quiet as her sister was noisy, padding cat-like about the house – maybe it was that she wanted no feline competition. It was not Joy's fault that Francine had developed cancer. Joy didn't believe the nonsense about it being the disease of unspoken grief: of faulty genes more like it, which Joy hoped to God she didn't share.

Jack had the builders in to Passmore, as Francine would have wanted. Francine liked everything to be state-of-the-art and spotless, and Jack, after forty years of top-of-the-range car dealership – Mercedes, BMW, Jaguar, Saab – could afford it. Indeed, he felt obliged to provide it, even though Francine was underground and not actually living in the house, or only in spirit. Joy, who had always been obliged to live more modestly than her sister, could never understand why Francine, who specialized in moral disapproval, and wouldn't let a man smoke or drink spirits or swear in the house, had ended up with wealthier husbands than she, Joy, had ever managed to acquire. There was a certain breed of moneymaking men around, it seemed, who needed their wives to look daggers and keep them on the straight and narrow. They didn't want fun. In the same way, she noticed, very good-looking men often had the plainest, dullest wives. But the very beautiful women often had fat and ugly husbands, so she supposed it kept the balance right. Except those man were usually wealthy, and the wives not. Perhaps the female capacity for moral disapproval served as an equivalent currency.

Be that as it may, Felicity, who had married Exon to be disapproved of, so far as Joy could see, had spent too much time looking in mirrors and buying clothes to have looked after Passmore properly, and now Jack was left to put up with the consequences. Felicity had simply not noticed that paint had chipped, that bathroom sealant had gone mouldy, that there were squirrels and worse under the roof, and rot under the floorboards. Or perhaps she had indeed noticed, and that was why she had been so anxious to so suddenly sell up and move into the Golden Bowl: nothing to do with falls and burns, just a disinclination to face facts, spend money, and put up with the annoyances of builders. All that would be left to the purchaser, and Felicity had taken no pains to point out to the buyer – even though that buyer was Jack, Joy's own brother-in-law – just how much would be needed to get the property back into good repair. Joy resented this on Jack's behalf. He had paid over the odds.

Felicity had kept the place crowded, English-style: ornaments on all surfaces, and no place mats, so French polish had been scratched to bits and no-one cared. The walls had been crowded with drawings and paintings, but when it came to packing up, Felicity had just thrown up her hands and sold the lot at a knock-down price. Charlie had organized a field sale for the small things and it was amazing how much you could get for rubbish, even reckoning that Charlie probably returned only fifty per cent of the cash he took. Selling Felicity up had proved a lot of hard work for everyone, and throughout the process Felicity had been at her most lordly, declaring herself bored with material possessions, happy to move into the hotel-like, bland, unadorned nothingness of the Golden Bowl, taking only a few personal belongings and the Utrillo with her. She had given Joy the first choice of her wardrobe, which Joy had declined – not her style – and after that had let Charlie and his family take their pick. The two little girls, Beck and Georgina, though their mouths were grubby, were seldom seen out without pieces of expensive fabric pinned here and there, peasant-style by way of Bergdorf Goodman.

Charlie's daughters would be a handful when they grew up: already they eyed even Jack as if he were natural game: the little boys, whether their cousins or their brothers, Joy was disinclined to find out, were tough, handsome and surly. Charlie had the matter of nationality in hand. Immigration officials turned up from time to time to ask questions but seemed satisfied with what Charlie had to say and went away.

Jack was beginning to feel more at home. Dramas and events did that, gave you memories, rooted you in a place. Having the builders in added tension. If living with Francine was like floating on a smooth sea, albeit one calmed by an oil spill – he did not know why the image came to mind – living with Joy was all choppy water, but at least things happened.

* * *

205

Valerie, the private investigator hired by Joy was blonde, brisk, tough and professionally indignant. She was not as young as she would like to be but neglected to flirt with Jack, as most of his older female employees had done in the past, however minimally. Jack felt his age and asked Joy anxiously if his neck was becoming shorter and Joy said, yes, it was. His head was sinking into rolls of flesh above his shoulders. That's what happened when you retired and stopped questing, sniffing out money, and relaxed. It had happened to all her husbands, she assured him. Golf did not help.

Valerie reported that the subject William Johnson had four traffic violations, one in 1958, one in 1974, two in 1994, but no criminal record. He had spent some time in Europe. He had cashed in various insurance policies over the previous ten years to the tune of $900,000. Currently he owed a total of $82,000 on eight credit cards. He had $208 in his current account. He had been born in Providence in 1927.

'Twelve years younger than she is!' said Joy, making rapid calculations. 'What do they call them? Toy boys?'

Valerie was really quite attractive, thought Jack. When Francine died it had opened the door again to legitimate adventures of a romantic kind, but here he was again, hemmed in this time by Joy. Women crowded you: they didn't want you to get away. He'd believed that age in a man didn't matter, only in women, but they'd got it wrong. Women these days looked through him and beyond him. But he was only sixty-nine.

Valerie continued. The subject came from a once wealthy textile family, originally from Massachusetts, who had come north to Rhode Island in the 1860s, been burned out in Narragansett in the great fire of 1900, lost all its money in the crash of 1929, and been finally blown out, uninsured, by the great storm of 1937. Subject's father had been an unsuccessful sculptor and painter. The mother was Italian-American, a Catholic, from Providence. There had been a twin brother, who had been killed in a car crash along with his mother, on Ocean Drive, just before World War II. There were no records of school attendance, but William had gone to college in Boston and studied English literature at Queen's,

New York, and qualified as a teacher. He had married three times. 'Unstable, I told you so,' said Joy. Jack murmured that Joy herself had been married four times, and so come to that had Felicity, but Joy said it was different for women, which baffled Jack. Valerie was anxious to get on.

Valerie's report went on to detail William Johnson's marriages. The first at twenty: Emily, twelve years his senior, who had seen him through college, and died of cancer eight years later. The second when he was thirty-six, to eighteen-year-old Sue-Anne, killed in a car crash when she was twenty-five.
'What a chapter of accidents,' said Joy, meaningfully. Jack pointed out that Joy had outlived all her husbands, and Joy snorted.

The subject William Johnson had been fifty-one when he married Meryl Mason, aged forty-one, a publisher's editor from New York, who had come to the marriage as mother of a daughter, Margaret. The Agency could find no record of a divorce, though this did not necessarily mean there had not been one. Valerie would be happy to find out, but it would me͛ ͙ngrading the basic packet of enquiry, and would cost a further͙ ͙ ͙ ͙trouble with these common names was that a great ͙ ͙ ͙ ͙ng was required. Give the Investigation Indust͙ ͙ ͙ ͙ould trim their costs accordingly, but ͙ ͙ ͙ ͙re than enough and the fee w͙ ͙ ͙ ͙
to get home to chan͙ ͙ ͙
with her husband.

'Just look at tho͙
had shown Va'
man murdere͙
up with a se͙
'I too am a͙
wife. And͙
It might ͙

Joy sul'
side: ͙
sleep

These days Jack would do this once or twice a week, the short cut through from Passmore to Windspit being barred by a stock-fence put up by Charlie to keep his two goats and the cow from getting out, and Jack having to use the long way round via Divine Road to get home. Sometimes at night it just seemed too far to go. Joy told Jack that she spoke perfectly quietly, it was other people who whispered. It was a long way from the road, and who was there to hear anyway?

'Charlie and his family,' said Jack. 'They might not be above blackmail.'

That didn't please Joy either. She liked to be the only one to think badly of the family in the guesthouse. The younger of the two women now in residence – both of whom claimed to be Charlie's wife, but maybe that was just a difficulty with the language – was now engaged to clean Joy's house, for which she was paid a considerable sum, and scrubbed the paint so hard it began to look scratched. Joy discovered that Esma, for that was her name, *Me Joy you Esma*, was using a saucepan scourer for the paint, silicone polish on the antiques, and glass cleaner on the floors. Esma had to be excused, Charlie told Joy, accustomed as she was to those rusty tins of scouring-powder – one powder cleans all – that in dimmer parts of the world, where there was no consumer choice, were all anyone had by way of cleaning agents.

Joy felt bad mentioning it. Esma spent unconscionable hours iron-ing, and weeping into Jack's shirts, which Joy had agreed to laun-der for him at Windspit. The kind of pick-up-and-deliver valet service Francine had been accustomed to seemed to be extravagant ...retired man who didn't even have an office to go to.

...ured about not having the control on the iron set to ...o doing crinkled up silks and left scorch marks ...Esma would weep and talk about massacres ...Joy couldn't bear. Otherwise Esma was ...very fast: she had arrived in the ...f clothing: now she wore dresses ...u could see the shape of her

and the two boys

belonged to the other wife, Amira, but could not be sure, again because of difficulties with the language. The two girls, around twelve, giggled and hid and peeked if you caught sight of them, but the boys, both about ten, Joy thought, swaggered about and had once got hold of the shotgun she kept in the garage, and fired at innocent songbirds, and brought their dead bodies into her kitchen for her to admire, just as a cat would. Francine would really have hated that. You could almost hear her ghost protesting. Charlie, summoned, had disarmed and shouted at the boys, but Joy dismissed that as just for show. She was not stupid. But for some reason unclear to herself she did not like Jack criticizing this unfortunate family. Jack was still a newcomer, living in what still felt like Felicity's house. Granted he had been instrumental in employing Charlie in the first place, Windspit was her (Joy's) property, her (Joy's) guest apartment, her (Joy's) limo. Jack should remember that. If Charlie's lapse was anyone's fault, it was Felicity's. Felicity took advantage of her (Joy's) goodness, ordering Joy's chauffeur around as if Charlie were her own.

Felicity went too far. If now Felicity had got herself into trouble, she had only herself to blame. What made Felicity think she was so special that at her age she could be loved for herself and herself alone, not for her income? Pride comes before a fall, and the fall would bruise and hurt her but had to happen. Felicity didn't of course deserve to *die*, and it was Joy's duty to warn her that William Johnson was at best a bigamist and at worst a serial wife killer.

Joy called the Golden Bowl to let them know she would be coming soon to visit Miss Felicity, and asked Esma to drop a copy of the Agency report in the post to the Director, Dr Grepalli. Esma said she would do it as soon as she had milked the cow and put the goats in the goat shed over at Passmore – once Felicity's garden studio – so the document did not get off that night. In the world of the stock keeper, bits of paper take second place.

33

My grandmother called me at midnight.

'So how's love?' I asked.

'Just fine,' she said. 'My dear, the irrationality! I'd forgotten. The sky brightens, the future beckons, you start again! William turns out to be a gambling man, I'm afraid to say, but I can put up with it.'

'You mean gambling Las Vegas-style?' I asked. 'Atlantic City? Crime, vice and pole dancers?'

'Foxwoods-style,' she replied. 'Reservation money, not Mafia. The Mashantucket Tribal Nation. Frankly, all rather on the muted side: you can hear the backwoods calling. But I was never one for the high life. Casinos are fantastic, Sophia. You hand them money and they hand it back with interest.'

'Sounds just like investing,' I said. 'Though I must warn you it's rumoured not to be as safe.'

'One can only go by one's own experience,' she said. 'I went in with $50 and came out with $150. I am naturally lucky, or so William tells me.'

'Beginner's luck,' I said.

'That is an irrational concept, Sophia. Why should a beginner be more lucky than anyone else? No, it's me. Since William and I got together he's been on a lucky roll.'

I envisaged an elderly man sitting at the slots, feeding in a quarter at the time. The pair of them, side by side, holding hands between rolls, as much interested in each other as what went on behind the windows. Why shouldn't they? Just two of many grey heads lined up on stools beneath bright lights, safety in numbers. You couldn't get into too much trouble, a quarter at a time. Cherries, red sevens, triple bars, whatever, whizzing away on command, the little orgasmic shudder when they stop, for good or bad. A sex substitute, according to a docudrama I once cut, though I wasn't quite convinced. Not all pleasures have to relate back to sex. But at eighty-odd you do what you can. You get fruit machines on rail stations all over Britain but the pleasure's furtive and solitary, the payout's disgraceful and the train pulls in to rescue you. 'In fact he's been able to afford a new car, a top-of-the-range Saab,' said Felicity. 'I don't have to borrow Joy's Mercedes any more.'

This didn't sound so good. If they were playing the slots, it was certainly not the quarter machines.

'He plays mostly craps,' she said, reassuringly. 'You get the best odds. Blackjack's most fun, but you can get overexcited. William's no fool. And he knows when to stop.'

'Oh yeah, yeah, yeah,' I said, and no more. This woman was in love, and who wanted to rub her nose in reality? I hadn't heard so much nonsense since my friend Evie fell in love with a drug dealer and told everyone he was going to go straight because of her. The odd thing was that he did.

Felicity sounded intolerably cheerful. Personally I'd had a hard day in the cutting room, and a row with Harry. He had been no help at all: he'd been too absorbed with himself to so much as remember there was an outside world, and I said so. He'd sat and stared into space or flicked through magazines and let me get on with it. I felt, since his presence was being paid for by the studio, he might just sometimes give the job in hand a little attention, if only for form's sake. He said that was absurd: I was an independent female perfectly capable of making my own decisions.

I said I'd been doing that all my life and was tired of it.

He said I was pre-menstrual and I thought I would kill him. There was no sharp weapon around, though, so I solved my problem by simply editing out a whole thirty seconds of Astra Barnes's filmic meanderings instead of wrestling it into shape.

'I bet you don't tell Holly she's pre-menstrual,' I observed casually when it was done without so much as a comment from him and

211

he was sitting still reading the paper and smoking. It was a tiny room, but what did he care?

'She doesn't have periods,' he said. 'She's too slim.'

He was behaving monstrously. He *was* a monster I had inadvertently let into my life. What was I doing with this alien being? I had to get rid of him somehow.

'In the US we know how to keep our bodies under control,' he added. 'We don't guzzle Danishes.'

The PA had brought in Danishes and coffee at lunchtime, without being asked. I'd eaten one. He'd eaten two, both the apricot, which I preferred. I made do with apple.

'Oh yes?' I asked. 'They all look pretty vast to me. I hear many American citizens have to be moved around with cranes, they're so heavy.'

'They're the other ones,' he said. 'Not the real Americans. In this country you don't even know how to get hot water out of a shower except in a dribble.'

'We don't like to waste hot water,' I said. 'The US uses up seventy per cent of the entire world's energy in its selfish obsession with its own comfort. North America is single-handedly destroying the planet.'

'We know how to live,' he said, 'and stand tall. The rest of the world just creeps around in its own shit.'

'Europe's as big as the US,' I said. 'You watch out.'

'Europe's primitive,' he said. 'Look what happened in the Balkans.'

'That's an anomaly,' I said. 'At least we don't still have chain-gangs, and schoolkids shooting up their own classmates.' This was ridiculous, but we couldn't stop.

'You don't even shave your armpits,' he said.

'At least I don't wear a wig like Holly,' I said. 'At least I have hair. Why don't you go back to her? You only live with me so you don't have to take a taxi to work.'

'That's about the level of it,' he said, icy.

'Personally, I take Buffalo's view of you,' I said. 'They got it just about right. Small town boy! So do me a favour, just shuffle off.'

What was upsetting Harry – and I would have been more sympathetic, he was quite right, if I hadn't been pre-menstrual, which I was, but who's going to admit to a thing like that –

212

was a stinking review of *Forever Tomorrow* in the local Buffalo newspaper. All over the rest of the States the film had met with critical approval, if not staggering commercial success. Just not in Buffalo, Harry's home town. Headed *Local Boy Makes Bad*, the piece dismissed the film as exploitative, sentimental, badly cast, badly acted and amateurishly filmed. The striving for effect was painful, the contents embarrassing. Harry Krassner had lost the plot and all Buffalo was disappointed. He might see himself as the Boy from Buffalo Made Good but Buffalo was quite happy to see the back of him, thank you very much. The journalist had even dug up a former schoolteacher to say Harry had been an arrogant child, too full of himself to get his homework assignments in on time. And so on and so forth. It was the kind of thing they say, in fact, when they really want to go for you, and there's something personal behind it. I asked. Yes, Harry knew the journalist. Irene Degusto. She'd been at school with him.

'You got out of Buffalo,' I said. 'Irene didn't. Of course she's going to be vile. You probably stood her up at Junior Prom or whatever you call your adolescent shindigs.'
'Whose side are you on?' Harry demanded, and that's how the row began, because of course I was on Harry's side. But women always make the mistake of trying to explain away misfortune, and to comfort and console, believing they will thus lessen the blow, when they would be better advised simply to join in male rage, despair and general ranting.

It was our first row. It had left both of us so exhausted and surprised that we crept home, and had the sweetest of languid sex, which took us both even more by surprise, it was so intense: it felt more like love than passion. I think even Harry was shaken. As ever, Felicity called when all I wanted was sleep. She had the knack of it. But she wanted to talk about her new love, as women do, at any age, regardless of who wants to listen, and she must do it *now, now, now*, not wait 'til I got over there. I'd booked the ticket. I was flying on Saturday. Today was Thursday. I said as much.
'So long as you don't marry him,' I said, 'and you don't start lending him money, and you don't mind being seen as a gambler's

moll, I suppose you can't get into any real trouble between now and then.'

'He has asked me to marry him,' she said. 'I'm taking my time replying. I wouldn't want to seem too eager.'

I was alarmed, but it would be imprudent to show it.

'A gambling moll is one thing, a gambler's wife is just plain dreary. It just isn't you, Felicity.'

'You've no idea what's me and what isn't,' she said. 'Things happened to me when I was very young that you don't know about.'

'I know quite a lot,' I said. And then because I was tired and wasn't thinking I said something stupid. 'I know about Lois and Anton. I know what a hard time you had. Poor Felicity.' There was silence. Then the phone went down. I called back, horrified. At least she picked it up.

'Look, I'm coming over in a couple of days,' I said. 'We'll talk properly then, shall we? It's difficult on the phone.'

'How dare you,' Felicity said to me. 'How dare you pry into my life. I wish I'd never had Angel, I wish she'd never had you. I don't want to see you, I don't want you to come over. I just want to be left alone to start over.'

It was a double whammy. I doubled up as if in pain.

'I'm coming to Rhode Island and that's that,' I said, and put the phone down and realized it was truly pain: my period had started and my whole body was protesting. I cried for a bit and then the phone went again.

'I'm sorry,' she said. 'I didn't mean that. Of course you must come. But just don't *interfere*.'

And Krassner slept on, as Krassners will. I think that what happens just before I have a period is that I turn atavistic and want to drive men away. Female cats do it to tom-cats, just before the females have kittens. Bite and snarl at them 'til they slink off. They say it's in case the male cat eats the kittens, which toms sometimes will, but who's to say what a female cat thinks? You can watch her behaviour and work out some Darwinist rationale to do with survival-friendly tactics, but I think it's just to do with the surge of impatience any female gets with the male when she's preoccupied. This great lolling creature with its impractical masculine attitudes. When you're pre-menstrual the sharp understanding and clear vision of the unconscious is nearer the surface, that's all, and it's probably the accurate one. The rest of the month is all self-deception and wishful thinking and unreasonable smiles.

34

I visited Guy and Lorna for Saturday lunch. They had few friends
– partners are easier to acquire than friends, for some people. Guy
had an ex-wife to moan about, which somehow occupied the space
most people reserve in their brain for friendships: and Lorna had
a dolefulness which could be mistaken for unsociability and would
put people off. They had each other for company, why should
they bother with the rest of the world? They liked me to come
over, though, to divert them with tales of ridiculous goings-on in
filmic places. Lorna had once had an affair, she confided to me
today, with a fellow academic which had droned on for years –
cinema, or a show, dinner, then bed, but as she pointed out to
me the films got worse over the years or seemed to, and the shows
more and more predictable, and in the end even habit was not
enough: she started making excuses, like the flu, for not turning
up: he'd have family in town, whatever, likewise. After a couple of
years the weekly intervals became two, then erratic, then stopped
altogether. She still worked with him occasionally – they were
setting up a museum space for a display of *latest ventures in the
wonderful world of crystallography* – there weren't any really,
only better ways of making the old ventures look pretty – but
could hardly imagine, let alone remember, what she had seen in
him. I'd had variations of just such desultory relationships over
the years: I supposed a lot of people got married on the strength
of them, in a might-as-well mood, in which case no wonder a lot
of people got divorced.

*   *   *

216

Lorna improved as you got to know her better, or so it seemed to me. She talked more easily. I was touched and pleased by her confidence about the lover. I told her a little about Harry. We laid the table for lunch in the conservatory at the back of the house. It was a bright day: there were little yellow crocuses sticking defiantly out of the lawn: the Thames was running full and furiously at the end of it. The boatmen were out, the pleasure steamers busy, megaphoning away. Lorna prepared a bleak salad with no dressing and found packets of ham in the back of the fridge. You can tell a person's temperament from the state of their icebox. Lorna had a frugal, saving, but ever hopeful disposition. Little saucers of congealing stew, a mug of juice from boiled carrots, a third of a sponge cake: a single old cold Brussels sprout – such a waste to throw leftovers away. I made a vinaigrette and she expressed delight at what it could do for a salad, and I taught her how to make it, but I didn't suppose she'd ever turn her hand to it when I was gone. She wouldn't want to indulge her senses. She was a brilliant crystallographer, I had no doubt; an appreciator of icy delights, not fleshly ones. She served frozen peas and carrots mixed, without salt or pepper or butter. But it was all right; I was not there for culinary delights. She was being generous with her confidences, and indeed her lunch, and it was a real effort for her and I appreciated it.

Harry had gone to have a shave and a haircut somewhere grand in Mayfair, and after that he was meeting a sound engineer in a pub in Wardour Street. I'd told him nobody went to pubs any more, only to clubs. He said how come in that case the pubs were so full? All those people spilling out on to the sidewalk didn't look like nobody to him. I said he knew what I meant and I needed a rest and was going to go visiting family out in the suburbs. At least now I had one to visit. I loved being able just to say it. Family at last.

'If ever I'm going to be out for a couple of hours,' he said, 'you make sure you're out for at least five. Why's that?'

'What am I meant to do?' I asked. 'Hang round counting the minutes 'til you come back? Is that what you want me to do? Is that what Holly does?'

'Why do you keep mentioning Holly?' He looked genuinely

puzzled, but men are good at that. 'What has she got to do with it?'

'I never mention Holly.'

'Yes you do. You talk about her all the time.'

'That is a complete lie,' I said. It was too, and we both knew it. Holly was on my mind, not his. He stomped off about his business and I stomped off about mine. We each called the other on our mobile phones within the half-hour, though having some difficulty getting through because of it, to make sure the other hadn't taken the tiff seriously. The existence of the mobile has caused a difficulty in plotting in the drama-adventure category of contemporary film: trees' and trees' worth of storyline once depended on people being out of contact with one another. Now, though at a physical distance, or in a remote spot, they can talk to one another nonstop. *Why didn't they just call the police?* has been replaced by *Why didn't he just call her on his mobile and explain?* But so it goes.

I sat and watched the Thames flow softly, while we sang our life songs. Once indeed the river had run softly, spreading itself where it chose: now so much of it had been confined inside embankments that it ran focused and strong, and had changed from wandering female into charging male. Guy, who had been in his room finishing a deposition to his lawyer, came down to join us. His ex-wife had accused him of sexual abuse of his little son, and he was understandably upset. His lawyer had been reassuring and said it was a common charge these days which most judges had the sense to ignore. To thus accuse the father saved the mother the bother of organizing access days, made her feel better about initiating divorce, and made an easier explanation to her child in later years. *Your father was a total bastard. The Court agreed. There was nothing I could do.*

'I'm sure that isn't true of most mothers,' I said piously. Guy always made me feel pious. But like Harry, he would have nothing of soothing palliation. I could see how distressing the accusation was, and how disturbing to the child even to be aware of it. So many of the bad TV films I had cut in my time – a couple of misspent years spent electronically editing tape – had involved some kind of dysfunctional family, in which the traumas of today were laid at the door of childhood abuse – wicked stepfathers or fathers. It was as if decades of subfusc TV drama was necessary to compensate for that one sharp fifties film, *Sybil*, when the damage was done by the mother, and the daughter took flight into multiple personality. Once that primal scene was disclosed, the personalities closed up again, and there Sybil was again, one charming person, healed! Though what was so good about being one person instead of a number was never made quite plain. I suppose in the fifties not to know where you had been the night before would be horrendous: nowadays, at least in the world of pubs and clubs, it wouldn't be anything out of order.

I tried to cheer my cousins up. There is no such thing as a free lunch and Lorna had trusted me with her confidence, so after Harry I repaid them with lurid tales of my mother Angel, my father Rufus the artist, and my and their grandmother, Felicity. I didn't tell them how Angel died. I did not tell them how Alison came to be born – they were not particularly interested and it was not an edifying tale, other than that it demonstrated, to me at least, just how heroic Felicity was. She was such a survivor, I said, catching piety from Guy. To which Lorna responded bleakly that she could never understand what that meant. Either you were a survivor or you were dead, you didn't have much choice. Sometimes I thought the inside of her head was rather like the inside of her fridge. Not given to wild statements or random promises. Mine is either totally empty or crammed with whole sides of smoked salmon and French cheeses and organic butter and slabs of chocolate. There seldom seems an in-between state: I don't know how it happens.

Lorna found sufficient curiosity in herself to ask about the person who had first turned up on her doorstep with news of my existence, and I explained Wendy from the Aardvark agency. We laughed a little about the name. Guy expressed himself shocked by the agency's methods of rooting out information, which in the light of the Data Protection Act were surely illegal. Lorna said no harm had been done: Guy said ends never justified means. They even had a sort of quarrel: their voices rose as if they were children. I almost expected Alison to come rushing in to tell them to stop it at once. How different life would have been, I thought, if I had

had brothers and sisters, a family home like theirs. I almost envied them.

I was still suffering from Felicity's sudden attack on me. To be wished out of existence by one's flesh and blood is not nice, even if Felicity had apologized. I felt accursed, unlucky. I was sorry for myself, still all grated up the wrong way and insecure. Harry had said perhaps now I understood why he had felt so bad about the attack from Buffalo, and I acknowledged the reproach. To be told to stay away, you're not wanted and never have been, is horrid.

And then again trauma is never done. People hand on the damage they've had done to them, these days we all know that. Felicity did what she could, as is God's purpose for us, to absorb and incorporate and de-barb her father's infidelity (how it all started, after all), her mother's death, Lois's cruelty, Anton's abominations, the random humiliations and shames she had encountered over the years as she did what she had to do, but seldom chose to do. But only a saint could absorb it all: that's why the world lurches little by little downhill, bouncing from one evil to the next. Little acts of bitchiness, little shreds of unreason which hurt others, which you didn't mean to do but just somehow find you did, grease the general human slither down into entropy. We are all alchemists, trying desperately to turn base metal to gold, which can never quite be done. Felicity managed brilliantly, skittering along the surface of her life, still at it after all these years. Personally I can't stand the heat and so stay out of the kitchen. Except Krassner seemed to be dragging me into it, by the scruff of my neck. I hurt, how I hurt! But quite where the hurt was coming from I could not make out. If your motives are good, surely nothing can go wrong?

35

Oh, the Grand Panjandrum said! I don't know where the phrase comes from; from which little section of my childhood; it becomes the kind of luminous chant there always in the back of the mind, an exhalation, a relief, the recurring echo of some past elation, which serves to set the present dancing, render it bearable.

Oh, the Grand Panjandrum said! What did he say? He said my mother was out of her mind, and therefore no-one around her is to be blamed, because how do you cope with the deranged; they bite the hand that feeds them, and so if you try to snatch your hand away, how can you help it? When brains are wired wrong, though the reasoning power's just fine: when the emotions are assembled in force but overwhelmed by the priorities of the frontal lobes where morality is seated (this is *right* and this is *wrong*: this is *good* and this is *bad*, and I'm the only one in step) all hell breaks loose. I always thought those lobotomy surgeons in the fifties who snipped away at random in the frontal lobes where conscience lies – I had to edit a trepanning in *Death of a Genius*; I could only do it Valiumed to my eyebrows, and demanded danger money – were on to something. If the patient didn't die at least they ended up happy, being morality-free. Amazing how *ought* always causes such trouble. Cocaine has the same effect: releasing people from their sense of duty to truth, to others, to everything. I bet one day they find the white stuff works on the frontal lobes, and they genetically engineer the coca plant to make sure it doesn't. I digress, naturally. This is hard stuff to face.

* * *

Oh, the Grand Panjandrum said! Felicity is not to be blamed. In 1945 Felicity, then an entertainer at an American airforce base in Norfolk, England, got pregnant by one Sergeant Jerry Salzburger of Atlanta, Georgia. He married her in a civil ceremony the day before he was posted back home and she was shipped out later to join him. That was the GI Bride scheme, in which after World War II the brides and acknowledged children of American servicemen from all over the world, in a generous if unexpected gesture, were gathered in. There was no-one to meet Felicity at the station; indeed, no news of her arrival had gone before, or else no-one had bothered to open official envelopes. But she had his address, and enough money for a taxi. The taxi driver propositioned her, pregnant as she was, but she said she was to start a new life. He was handsome and white and stubbly and amiable; this was white trash land. She said no. Begin as you mean to go on. She found Jerry Salzburger lying drunk on a broken bed under a filthy blanket in a shack in the middle of a chicken farm. A little boy of around six – Felicity could tell because his two front teeth were missing, who said his name was Tommy and his daddy was Jerry and his mummy had left home – was doing his best to look after fifty Rhode Island Reds. Excellent birds – superior reds of the old Mohawk line, with perfect head points, lustrous blood-red quills and beetle green tails, bought from a Mrs Donaldson of Decatur with Jerry's demob money, but already too distracted and distressed, moth-eaten and wormy, to think of laying eggs. Many were practically bald – birds eat their own feathers to offset nutritional deficiencies. Feather picking can lead to bleeding, sores, infections or even death. Thus deprived of our needs, we self-destruct. The smell was terrible.

Oh, the Grand Panjandrum said! Jerry Salzburger had described himself to Felicity as from an old Lutheran family settled in Georgia two hundred years back and so he might well have been. And he had described his home as like Scarlett's Tara in *Gone with the Wind*, and she had believed him, and perhaps it had been, a couple of generations back. Oh America, my new-found land, the land of dreams, nylons, chewing gum and good cheer. Well, why wouldn't he lie? Anton had lied. She was never to learn. He had married her to do her a favour, thinking he would never see her again.

She set to work. She threw a bucket of water over Jerry, who woke up to demand food. She found eggs and made an omelette but he threw it at her. 'Damn you to hell,' she said, and washed and fed the little boy. She watered and fed the chickens and moved the ones who couldn't stand up to a separate hen house, and cut feverfew and threw it in with them. Some died but some recovered. She shovelled chicken shit and mended the holes in the wire fence, to keep animal predators out. She didn't know what they would be, just that they were bound to exist. She found Jerry's shotgun and worked out how to use it. That would keep the human predators out. She was six months pregnant. It was hot and muggy. On the first night she made up a bed on the broken verandah and slept there. It had been a long journey.

In the morning he apologized and said he'd never believed the child was his, he'd married her as a favour, he was married already but as it happened his wife had left him; gone without taking the little boy. Felicity could stay if she liked. There was nowhere else to go so she stayed. There was one tap to keep humans and hens watered. Little Tommy helped; he was a valiant child. They got on well together. She moved into Jerry's bed. She had been happy enough there in the past, though she could see the taxi driver might be a better bet. Angel was born.

Felicity wrote a letter to Mrs Donaldson asking her how to keep hens, because Jerry sure as hell didn't know, he thought you just owned them and they laid eggs all by themselves. It hadn't occurred to him that they needed to be looked after. No wonder he had taken to drink. Mrs Donaldson replied in detail, advising her to breed for neck lacing in the females, because that was where the future lay, but to beware of it in the males: that would lead to a flock with slate in their neck undercolour; the worst sin in a red breeder.

The Salzburger family lived on nothing and the hens lived in splendour. The family ate fried eggs and baked eggs, scrambled eggs and poached eggs and the hens lived on scraps from the neighbours bulked up with scratch grains and though the shells were too thin the hens were content. They laid better if the cocks didn't run with them. Emotionally deprived hens console themselves laying eggs; every one a sense of achievement. Soon there was enough money to put in a proper water supply in the hen houses, and after that to mend the roof, replace the stove, and buy nappies instead of laying the baby on moss. Moss, like the mosquito, is always plentiful in a hot, damp land. And to pay for cigarettes and whisky and wild, wild women for Jerry, who never grew out of the habit, for all his Lutheran ancestry.

Oh, the Grand Panjandrum said! If only Felicity could have settled, but she couldn't. She wasn't born to this, but to London bohemian life, no matter what the events in between. She had learned to be grateful but not as grateful as this. She got the Rhode Island blues and left one day, when Angel was five and Tommy was twelve, and who could blame her? At least she took the children with her: many don't. She worked as a singer and dancer on an old-fashioned riverboat, with its burnished copper pistons, pumping up, pumping down, and the smell of hot oil everywhere. Up the Savannah every night, past the cotton warehouses, still in use, and back again, on the *Old Glory*'s Moonlight Cruise. When there were private parties she'd dance topless, or so my mother told me, but Angel's testimony is not to be relied upon: her brain was wired wrong.

It was at one of these parties that Felicity met Buckley, remembered that she wasn't legally married and set out to be his wife. Buckley had a good library and she wanted to give herself an education: she knew there wouldn't be much else to do, once she was rich, except read.

Buckley said he would take on the little girl, since she was so pretty, but not the boy, who did not appeal, so Tommy went back to Jerry, and grew up to be a wastrel and father William Johnson's stepdaughter Margaret's two boys out of wedlock.

Oh, the Grand Panjandrum said! That can't be laid at Felicity's door: it was in the genes, like the slate undercolour of the neck feathers in a Rhode Island Red if you get the breeding wrong. And she did go to the funeral.

Oh, the Grand Panjandrum said! Felicity shouldn't have told Angel on the eve of her eighteenth birthday, that what Jerry was accustomed to saying in a drunken rage and then apologizing for the next day was true: that he wasn't Angel's father. Angel's real father was a folk singer who played bad guitar and sang out of tune in a club in London's Soho. The news so upset Angel that something in the brain wiring that had been holding out gave up and snapped and thereafter there was mayhem in her head, off and on. To some people a drunken chicken-shit father that you know is better than one you don't know and is suddenly thrust upon you. And no-one can even remember his name, or isn't telling.

Oh, the Grand Panjandrum asks: Why did Felicity choose the eve of Angel's eighteenth birthday to speak the truth? Answer comes there none, other than that Felicity's sopping-up project was nowhere complete, and since there was still evil abounding to be passed on, that's what happened. A life spent toiling on a chicken farm is a better preparation for goodness than singing and dancing topless as a riverboat entertainer, which can make you kind of careless. And not even on the mighty Mississippi, but on the lesser Savannah, the latter being to the former in style and glamour as Foxwoods is to Las Vegas. Only later did Felicity learn more restraint. She reproached herself for ever afterwards, but that does not excuse her, and she was still calling me from the States to say the time had come for her to speak the truth: she would not acknowledge that she spoke it more than enough. Mind you, I daresay Angel rising eighteen was a handful: how do you keep a girl modest and good when your own past is what it is, and word tends to get about beneath the damp and ghostly fronds of Spanish moss which festoon the trees hereabouts. In Rhode Island everything is clear cut: the dogwood is bright and clean and white in early spring: but there are always humming birds to remind you of the South: shiny green above, white chest, green sides and the male with a ruby red throat. I expect someone, somewhere is breeding them to make the females as pretty as the males, though it would require ingenuity. If you can think of it, someone somewhere's doing it, that's my theory. More digressions.

Oh, the Grand Panjandrum said! That my mother, as mad as a hatter but nobody knew it then, went off to London on her eighteenth birthday. She was sent to Europe on vacation with friends but shipped out mid-National Gallery and never came back, leaving Felicity and Buckley and Jerry distraught: a thin, wild-eyed, talented, beautiful thing with pre-Raphaelite hair and a good education, who knew a lot of poetry by heart, from Whitman to Byron, and had pretensions as a painter. She went in search of her father. This was in 1964. She just went round the corner from the National Gallery in Trafalgar Square into Soho, not far from where I now live, to a club called the Mandrake. *'Catch with child a mandrake root,'* Felicity had once rashly said to Angel, *'and that's where I caught you.'* Angels don't forget.

The club was closed and up for sale, but there was an old caretaker there who remembered a man who could well have been her father. He played the guitar and sang folk songs: that was at the time when the V2s were falling in London, just before the end of the war, in the days when people drank whisky or beer, not wine. Artists and writers came to the club: they played chess. The showgirls from round about would come in to keep them company. No, he didn't remember one called Felicity: he reckoned he would have. Mostly they were called Vera or Anne or Fluffy St George. But he seemed to remember the folk singer was knifed to death in some incident outside a pub. The night after V-E night, Allied Victory in Europe night, 8 May, 1945. So much for my maternal grandfather.

Oh, the Grand Panjandrum sings: English folk songs crossed to America back in the eighteenth century: their natural home seemed to be in the Appalachian Mountains, and there they stayed in a purer form than happened back home, where for the most part they simply died out. Except for songs like *The Sweet Nightingale*, which they'd make us sing at school, and everyone hated but me.

My sweetheart come along.
Don't you hear the sweet song,
The sweet notes of the nightingale flow.
Pray sit your self down,
By me on the ground –

Oh yes, and we all know what happened next. Shut up singing, Grand Panjandrum, what did we know as children, what was to happen next in our life songs.

Oh, the Grand Panjandrum calms down to say my grandmother came to London to rescue her daughter, but Angel refused to go home: she was determined to go to the Camberwell School of Art. She would be fine on her own.

'Well,' said Felicity, 'I seem to remember I wanted to do ballet once,' and let Angel stay in a strange city with no friends. How you deal with your children depends on your own life-experience, I suppose. Or perhaps she didn't want Angel to find out about Buckley's closet gayness: the world could still be shocked, and Buckley was increasingly rash: be that as it may Felicity set Angel up in a small apartment in Soho and flew back to Atlanta as quick as she could.

Oh, the Grand Panjandrum is not surprised to note that Angel never turned up to art classes, nor did she phone home, and that the apartment soon filled up with winos and druggies she had asked back. The mentally ill frequently seek out the company of the dispossessed: they have a fellow feeling for them, an empathy. But victims are not necessarily nice people and soon Angel was locked out of her own place and sleeping on the floor of the art student who was to be my father. When I was one year old my crib was placed on the lid of the bath in the kitchen – this was how people lived in those days: if you wanted to own a bath the kitchen would be the only room in the house with plumbing, so the bath would have a wooden lid which doubled as a shelf. It was okay. When I was four my father Rufus had an exhibition at the Marlborough Gallery in Cork Street. He had fifty paintings on display. He sold twenty-five. When the time came for the remaining ones to be taken down Angel piled them against the wall outside, doused them with methylated spirit, and set fire to them. The public had had their chance to buy these works of genius and turned them down: they would not be given another chance. They were pigs without taste. Rufus wept. The police did not press charges but she was made to see a psychiatrist. She became increasingly violent. She threw the cat across the room. Its yellow eyes proved it was the devil. But she never harmed me, or only the once when she thought I was someone else and tried to smother me. As I grew older I became her companion in setting the world to rights. Sometimes we'd throw things: sometimes we'd go to the cinema together and she'd sit quiet and good. I loved that. Sometimes I went to school, sometimes I didn't. Felicity flew to and fro. It was as well that Buckley by now owned an airline. Whenever her mother came over Angel got worse. She wouldn't accept money. If anyone gave it to her she burned it. She didn't approve of it. Rufus came and went: he tried to stay but had to go, often at knifepoint. When the social workers turned up my mother was sweet as pie and always had reasons and excuses for bad behaviour. Sometimes they didn't work and they'd take her away: I remember her walking away from me down a long echoing corridor, hand in hand with a nurse whose keys jangled at her belt. Doors slammed, with an extraordinary solid clunk. When she finally ended her life, when I was ten, which I think she did to save me from her, she was in a good phase, remission, they called it, but both Rufus and Felicity were away and I had to cut down her body.

Oh, how sick I am of the Grand Panjandrum: he's no use at all, someone tell him to shut up.

36

The day after her outing to Foxwoods, Felicity rose late. She breakfasted in her room on yogurt, orange juice and caffeinated coffee. Love makes some women fat with contentment: it makes others thin from an all-purpose eagerness. Felicity was of the second kind. She would have to have her skirts taken in, or better still, buy new. She wondered how William would be with shopping, and decided not very good, he would be impatient and like everything she tried on, not seeing that it mattered very much. Exon had been an attentive escort, carrying shopping and summoning attendants, but his taste led to the dull and out of politeness to him she would end up with clothes too boring to wear.

After breakfast she spoke to William on the phone about this and other matters for at least half an hour. The more time two people spend together the more there is to say when they are apart. Trivia between intimates is as compelling as major world statements between strangers. Felicity had seen a rare green-throated indigo bunting outside her window: it had stayed where it was for at least five minutes, giving her time to find her bird book and identify it. She could swear that's what it was. Good things were coming to her door. William had a blister from his new shoes, and the question was did one burst the skin and let the fluid out, or slap a plaster on it so the fluid dispersed? And so on.

By the time Felicity wandered down to the Library to have a chat with Dr Bronstein and possibly Clara Craft, it was nearly midday.

If she found Clara there she would have to listen yet once again to the details of the Hindenburg disaster, which ran through Clara's mind like a film seen over and over, blocking out other thoughts. Just sometimes the footage seemed to leave her alone and then she would have a lot to say of interest. As it happened there was no Dr Bronstein seated among the leather armchairs: only Clara, whose skinny hand clutched Felicity's arm, Ancient Mariner fashion. Dr Bronstein had been taken away, Clara whispered, against his will, in full view of his relatives, to the West Wing. Something must have been put in his drink: he had seemed confused. Not his usual self.

'When was this?' asked Felicity.

'Just after the Reinforcement Session with Dr Grepalli,' said Clara. 'Yesterday afternoon. Everyone else had left the Library. I will never sing that half-full song again. Our cup is half-empty, I don't care what he says. You should have been here, Miss Felicity. You could have stopped them doing it.'

'I don't see how,' said Felicity.

'People take notice of you,' said Clara. 'They don't of me. You have a present. The rest of us only have pasts.' Which at a less distressing time would have flattered Felicity greatly.

'He didn't want to go,' said Clara. 'Nurse Dawn manhandled him. She told him he had to go: he had no choice: they'd taken out some legal order. As for family, I don't see what rights they could possibly have had, three generations down. But they don't play it by the book, they do what suits them. Poor Dr Bronstein, his great-great grandson and his girlfriend, not even married, too young to know anything!'

Miss Felicity had to manually loosen Clara's grip on her arm. The rheumatically bent fingers seemed to have gone into spasm. They were hurting. Clara didn't notice.

'Mind you,' said Clara, 'I never know how old young people are any more: they might only have been in their mid-twenties. She was trying to be kind: she said it was for his own good: if you didn't know the name of the President of the United States you weren't capable of looking after your own affairs. And she was the one who wasn't even a blood relation. They didn't know I was listening. I was snuggling down in my chair.'

*   *   *

More likely, thought Felicity, Clara hadn't been able to get out of it without help and Dr Bronstein had suddenly found himself in no position to give it. The chairs were low, deep and squashy and a perpetual challenge to the elderly.

Nurse Dawn entered the Library, smiling sweetly. She carried in her arms, cradled like a child, three long-stemmed white lilies of the kind people used to give on the occasion of a death. Both Felicity and Clara were of an age to know that cut white lilies are unlucky. Funeral flowers. Seeing Nurse Dawn and the lilies, Clara stopped talking and didn't have the sense to switch the conversation, as Felicity would have done.

'Something you don't want me to hear, Miss Craft?' inquired Nurse Dawn, consequently. 'Some terrible event to equal the loss of the Hindenburg?' She carefully laid down her lilies and went from chair to chair, testing their seats. She stopped at one, with disapproval.

'Damp!' she exclaimed. 'Dr Bronstein's favourite chair, of course. We can't be surprised, though we can be revolted. Only one thing for it, replacement, and you know the expense of these real leather chairs. We kept Dr Bronstein out of the West Wing longer than was wise. Well, as they say back home no good deed goes unpunished. This kind of thing is not pleasant for the other guests.'

'They don't say that back home,' said Miss Felicity, 'I say it, and I'm sure I've never set foot in your home state, Nurse Dawn. As for damp, that is not in the least damp.' She had braved herself to test the soft, leathery surface, and found it dry enough.

'As we get older,' said Nurse Dawn, 'our tactile senses get less acute. We smell and don't know it, repeat ourselves and don't realize it. And when we lose our judgement we have to be looked after by others for our own good. Sometimes we even smudge our lipstick and can't see it even in a magnifying mirror.'

She leaned forward and touched the edge of Felicity's lips with the edge of a tissue she took out of her pocket. It smelt of disinfectant. Felicity drew back in disdain. 'Which is what seems to have happened this morning, Miss Felicity,' Nurse Dawn continued, unabashed. 'We don't want to look like hen dressed as chicken. As we grow older we should use less make-up. At least then we keep our dignity.' And she shook a plump finger at Miss Clara, whose face was slashed across as ever with a line of scarlet lipstick, drawn regardless of the shape of the lips.

'If only Dr Bronstein had known where Kosovo was, Dr Grepalli might have been persuaded to let him stay,' went on Nurse Dawn. 'Pique might have led the good doctor to forget the name of the President, as I was at pains to point out to the family, but it is not a good sign when once intelligent old men forget geography that's been all over the papers and CNN. We tend to forget what we want to forget. Place names, unconnected as they are with emotion, are usually the last to go in the descent into senility. Not many people know that. But I hope you had a good outing yesterday, Miss Felicity.'

'I did,' said Felicity. 'I shall organize outings to Foxwoods from the Golden Bowl. There are special rates for those wise in years.'

'Wise in years,' jeered Nurse Dawn, sticking the lilies into a vase amid existing foliage, as if they were javelins. The tough stems pierced with ease through obstacles of leaf and stalk. 'If only women didn't get sillier as they got older. And what euphemisms these places use.'

'That's a big word,' said Felicity.

'In my days at the *Post*,' said Clara, who had taken all this time to get her courage back, 'we were never allowed to use a long word if a short one would do.'

'So you have observed a hundred times, Miss Craft,' said Nurse Dawn. 'I hope you know what year we're in. Dr Bronstein got that wrong too.'

'I do indeed,' said Clara, sensing danger, forgetting to be languid. 'And it's far beyond any I ever thought or hoped to see. When I was twenty I hoped to die by thirty, when I was sixty I found that quite astonishing, now I am ninety I wish I had died yesterday but haven't got the courage to do it.'

Nurse Dawn was now pushing her active fingers through the greenery in the great vases, which stood in the formal fireplace where no fire ever blazed, searching out withered leaves and faded flowers. She wore her bold white uniform today, with brass buttons on the shoulders, voluminous pockets, and little tarty red high heels which she had forgotten to change.

'You wouldn't want our visiting psychiatrist to think you were depressed,' said Nurse Dawn to Clara. 'In his book that's one of the worst geriatric disorders. We like everyone to be happy, our cups half-full not half-empty. I don't think too many of our guests will even notice Dr Bronstein's absence. So shall we not draw too much attention to his departure? I thought I caught a glimpse of you yesterday, Miss Craft, hiding in your chair, legs drawn up like a naughty little girl, trying not to be noticed.'

'It wasn't me,' said Clara. Her courage had been short-lived. Nurse Dawn smiled with her mouth and not her eyes, and left, taking with her a little bag which she kept in her uniform pocket, into which she stuffed the derelict leaves and flowers she had stripped from their stalks.

'Is visiting at some special time over in the West Wing?' Miss Felicity asked Clara.

'You wouldn't want to visit over there,' said Clara. 'It would be too distressing. Goodness knows who we would see, who we've forgotten. Did you know I was one of those people on the ground when the Hindenburg caught fire as it landed?'

37

Later that afternoon the Mercedes, Joy and Jack within it, arrived at the Golden Bowl. Charlie, as Joy bitterly observed, knew the way well. They were to visit Dr Grepalli. Valerie Boheimer's report had gone ahead of them. Joy wore a diamond and gold choker which lay not on the skin but on the polo-necked collar of her pink velour running suit. 'Just because a girl needs to be grand,' she said to Jack, 'doesn't mean she can't be comfortable.' Jack protested he didn't see the need to be grand, but Joy said it was important that Dr Grepalli took what they had to say seriously. Felicity's future welfare depended upon it.

Joy had lately taken to wearing her diamonds nearly every day. Francine had kept hers in the safe for years, claiming it was far too risky to wear expensive jewellery in public. If you wore a ring some drug-crazed villain might cut off your finger to get hold of it, if you wore a bracelet they might take off your whole arm. Francine had heard of it happening. Precious rings, beads and bracelets – her neck was too short for chokers, fortunately, Jack always thought, considering her fears – stayed in their velvet-lined boxes gathering dust under lock and key, until one day, a year before her death, her cancer still undiagnosed, she had without warning removed her valuables from the safe and sold the lot, giving the proceeds to, of all things, a dogs' home. She had not even liked dogs. Jack had been upset. They had, after all, been gifts from him, bought with the sweat of his brow: he had had a hard life: becoming a wealthy man takes drive, long hours, and concentration. All he had done to deserve this treatment, so far as he could see, was to try to persuade Francine to wear at least something – even if only diamond earrings – to the sixty-fifth birthday party her sister Joy had so kindly organized for her.

Joy had hoped that perhaps Jack would dress up a little for the visit to Dr Grepalli, but she was disappointed. Jack, now a member of the Country Club, would be playing golf later in the day: he declared he would wear only what was suitable for that. His days of dressing to please others were over. His pants were elasticized, his sweaters familiar and baggy.

When Dr Grepalli rose to his feet, a handsome, broad-shouldered, benign figure, he could be seen to be wearing a well-cut grey suit, with white shirt but no tie – a mixture of formality and casualness designed to put others at ease. None of Joy's husbands had ever achieved sartorial success, and she felt it. She herself preferred ease, a bit of show, a bright colour and a nice fabric, and couldn't help it, but had always hoped for more from the men she married. In vain.

'Mr and Mrs Epstein,' said Dr Grepalli. 'Welcome!'

Joy and Jack both started to explain together that they were not man and wife but man and deceased wife's sister, but both gave up. Jack because Joy drowned him out and Joy because she lost interest in denying it. She might as well be Mrs Epstein, the way they had begun to bicker. Francine's title, once too high an aspiration for Joy, no longer was. Thank God sex did not enter into it, the way it did with Felicity. She, Joy, had never liked sex much and increasing age spared her the necessity of pretending she did. In any case it was young men who required you to enjoy sex: as they got older they became almost relieved when you didn't show too much interest. Yes, to be Mrs Epstein would be all advantage, no disadvantage. It is better to be a wife than a widow. It would be an entirely suitable match.

Dr Grepalli did not pursue the matter of the couple's marital status. He was flicking through the Abbey Inquiries report. He looked up at them with calm brown eyes. Joy felt a certain frisson;

not sexual, certainly not, had she not decided she was beyond all that; but a kind of emotional spasm which lay just the other side of spiritual into the worldly. Merely a matter of possibilities, a suggestion of shared intimacy. But no doubt he looked like that at all the ladies.

'I appreciate your concern for your friend,' he said, 'and I know my executive assistant Nurse Dawn shares it. But old people are not paper parcels. They have free will, they have feelings, they have a right to love just like anyone else. They may even have a right under the Constitution not to be followed by private detectives but I'm not sure about that.'

'There you are you see, Joy,' said Jack. 'I told you so. You shouldn't have done it.'

'I had to do it,' shouted Joy. 'Felicity's my best friend. She's in her second childhood. What about her fortune?'

'She is entitled to dispose of it as she wants,' said Dr Grepalli. 'And as fortunes go it is not so very great. Many of our guests leave their money to philanthropic institutions, not to their families, and just as well for this nation that they do. Men tend to be showier with their wealth and dispose of it in their lifetime. Women tend to wait until they're dead –'

'– Or want to make a point,' interjected Jack, bitterly, thinking of his many gifts to Francine, love tokens all, gone to support stray dogs. Was this how she had thought of him? Or perhaps she just felt bad about her failure to love all God's creatures equally and wished to compensate.

'So I don't think you have a problem there,' the Doctor went on. 'Those who earn money are more free with it than those who receive it through the medium of others, which tends to be the case with most of our lady guests. Their husbands made the money: they stayed home.'

'But supposing she marries,' said Joy.

'Ah then,' said Dr Grepalli. 'We may have a problem. Any will and testament she may have already made becomes invalid. Until and unless she makes another one all property would automatically go to the new husband.'

'She has to be stopped,' yelled Joy. 'He's a con artist and a cheat, a younger man chasing an older woman for her money and that report proves it. You have to call the police.'

'Quieten down a bit, Joy,' said Jack. 'No need to get excited. Calling the cops may be way down the road here.'

Francine could be like this, Jack recalled, obsessive, when she got some notion into her head, though she was quiet about it and brooded rather than shouted. She'd always believed he was having an affair with Joy. Of course he hadn't been, in the true sense of the word. He was no saint, but he would never foul his own nest. *It'll happen*, Francine had even whispered to him once. *It will happen one day. Men have no taste*. The memory depressed him.

'It's not me being excited, it's you just letting things go,' Joy rounded on him. Francine would just have given him a look. As a consolation you never had the feeling that Joy was keeping things back, the better to pounce. She was looking a little strange today. The diamond choker over the shell suit, or whatever they called it, was all wrong. But at least she didn't keep the stuff in the safe. At least one day he wouldn't have to open it and find his gifts missing, sold, the past they symbolized evaporated, gone as if it had never happened. It was after that that he did begin to see Joy, he had to admit it, and thirty-five years too late, began to think he might have married the wrong sister. But too late now.

Dr Grepalli turned back to the report.
'Four traffic violations in a lifetime,' he said, 'doesn't seem too much to me.'
'It depends,' said Joy, having asked him to speak louder and repeat himself three times, 'what those violations are. DUI or DWI. Driving under the influence or driving while intoxicated.'
'Joy knows what the difference is,' said Jack. 'She had an incident once, and her alcohol levels were dead on point one five. First thing I did when I moved into the area was make her get a chauffeur. Not a side-view mirror left in the neighbourhood and the dents in the old Volvo had to be seen to be believed. Lucky she had me to trade it in for her.'
'Those dents,' said Joy, 'were animals running into my car at night.'
'Sometimes one's night vision isn't what it should be, as we approach the golden years,' said Dr Grepalli, absently. Old dears tended to bicker on. It should be seen as a demonstration of custom

and affection rather than antagonism. Grown children, listening to their parents, often made the mistake of believing they were unhappy, when what they were doing was keeping little ripples of response flowing from one to the other. 'At least he doesn't have a criminal record.'

'He goes under many names,' said Joy. 'Anyone called William Johnson is making it up. The commonest name in all America.'

'Dr Grepalli may not follow your logic, Joy,' said Jack. 'If it's common a whole lot of people will have it.'

'And just look at those age gaps,' Joy shouted. 'That's not love, that's calculation. He marries old women and then murders them for their money.'

But Dr Grepalli's eye had fallen on something in the report that worried him.

'Is that an actual Utrillo she brought with her?' he asked. 'I'd assumed it was a reproduction.'

'What, that old painting she fusses about? It could be for real. He did own an airline. But you never know what to believe.'

'If so, it has very serious implications,' said Dr Grepalli, 'in so far as our insurance is concerned. The thing should be in her bank: if there's a theft we could be sued. Miss Felicity has no business keeping it on our walls.' Dr Grepalli was upset beyond mere reason. Homer Grepalli, his father, had collected paintings. He had the best collection of schizophrenic art in the country on his walls, which had distressed Helen, Joseph's mother, very much. She complained she felt crowded in by such a bleak and tormented vision: nothing on these canvases was bright and cheerful: everything was twisted and inhuman, in black, grey, or if you were lucky, ochre, and at very best a smear of purple. Why did anyone collect lunatic art? Helen was convinced Homer spent good money on these paintings on purpose to annoy her, but as Homer had pointed out to Joseph, his mother was of a paranoiac turn of mind: indeed, she had once been one of Homer's patients.

Little Joseph had from an early age practised the art of thinking the best of everyone and everything. His father was not malicious. His mother was not insane. The artists represented on the wall did not paint like this all the time, only when they were in a psychotic state. In between episodes their minds would unfold, the tormented shapes curve and stretch into something healthy and whole: he would often look at the clawed arthritic hands of his Golden Bowlers, as they sang the half-full song, and wish for them that time would play backwards, so he could watch their hands unfold and be open, free and graceful once again. His telephone beeped a little tune: a Beatles number. Dr Grepalli excused himself and took the call.

'That was Miss Felicity's granddaughter, the English girl,' Dr Grepalli said. 'She too seems to be anxious about her grandmother's welfare. She's flown over with two other grandchildren and will be driving up from New York tomorrow.'

'But I thought Sophia was her only living relative,' said Joy. 'Miss Felicity is just not capable of speaking the simple truth.'

'It's amazing how family comes out of the woodwork,' said Dr Grepalli, 'when it's a matter of inheritance. Thank you for coming to see me, Mr and Mrs Epstein. I know none of us wants to get into any kind of zero sum game here. Nevertheless I will have a little talk with Miss Felicity, about this and that.'

38

After her disagreeable conversation with Nurse Dawn, Felicity, upset and panicky, called William at the Rosemount. She wanted his assurance that she was not to blame, that sooner or later Dr Bronstein would have ended up in the West Wing, and a little sooner made no difference. She wanted to be told that Nurse Dawn was not vindictive and dangerous, just stupid, tactless and a little nasty and doing her job as she saw it. That it was not her fate to be cast back into the convent again and again. That the Golden Bowl was not some kind of prison, where the mind kept the body in chains and the body did what it wanted, not what you wanted. No, rather it was that as you got older the sense that the spirit was incarcerated in the body became more intense: the temptation was to project it outwards. It was not the Golden Bowl which kept you in one place against your will, it was your body, now reluctant to run, jump and skip.

True enough that had she gone along with Dr Bronstein for his interview with the psychiatrist she could have pointed out that if powerful negative emotions were sufficient to block off recall of the President's name, why then the same thing would apply to Kosovo. It was not just a place on the map which anyone familiar with current events should know, but a terrible place of massacre and chaos in the heart. She could have explained that it was not an ageing brain which made you forgetful – it was the battering upon the doors of knowledge by the hammer of experience. If you suddenly sold your diamonds and gave the proceeds to a dogs' home it wasn't because you'd gone batty but because you'd come to the legitimate conclusion that dogs, creatures you despised, were worth more than people. The less able you were to act the more to the point your actions became, perforce. The old who spat out food showed what they thought of food, just as babies did, without inhibition. It didn't use up much energy.

Of all these things and more Felicity wanted to speak to William. So few people in a lifetime who understood what you were talking about. All those men in the *Old Glory* days, and earlier in London, who'd come and gone with hardly a word of talk. No exchange of ideas, just sometimes information. *They say the weather's getting better tomorrow* or *Chamberlain's back from Munich with a peace deal* or *I like your dress. How about getting it off.* She'd always thought herself that her mind made a more interesting offer than her body: and theirs too, of course, to her. More than the temporary loan of that piece of rampant flesh they seemed prepared to offer. If the body was used too much, and the whole person denied, the brain and the spirit would atrophy along with the sensibilities, which was why you could mostly tell a prostitute. It was the way the face muscles set when the attempt to ward off disgust had gone on for too long, the process of toughening up been too protracted. It was when you succeeded you were in trouble, when the spirit retreated, leaving the lineaments of all things tawdry behind. Not that she had ever been quite a prostitute, just a good-time girl who when offered payment would not refuse. She would have paid for sex, if she could afford it, if she hadn't been paid for it first.

William would reassure her, calm the panic: all she was feeling was the vestigial trace of what she had been through with Angel: the feeling you should do something, though you didn't know quite what, to stop disaster happening. A bad dream of secrets kept from you, the need to search for the little trap door which was the way out of the dark into sunlight once again. Except you knew there wasn't any trap door: the dark was permanent. With time your eyes got used to it, but that was all. What went on in Dr Bronstein's head was pretty much what went on in Angel's: that is to say it wasn't 'normal'. Little areas of the brain which lit up in 'normal' people when certain things happened did not light up in Angel's brain, or if Nurse Dawn was to be believed, in Dr Bronstein's. Not any more. However you defined *normal*: and what happened or failed to happen was to a different degree, of course, in Angel. Angel's disordered brain was housed in an active, flailing, young body, the lights lit up all over the place: Dr Bronstein's in a body too old to be much threat to anyone. Even thinking about it brought the feeling of panicky helplessness swirling in again out of her past: she was swept out to sea by a current she wasn't strong enough to fight, even had she known how, found anyone to tell her the secret. Love itself miscarried. Only perhaps you deceived yourself. Perhaps you'd had it aborted. The end of the world was your own doing.

She called the Rosemount. Maria answered. She said that Mr Johnson had left already for the Casino. 'Thank you,' said Felicity and put the phone down.

There had been two abortions. In the early days they were illegal, and no exceptions: they cost UK £200 or US $500 depending which side of the Atlantic you were, and the price seemed to stay the same for decades. Fathers, if they were decent, were expected to find the money for you. It was a cheaper option than marriage. If they weren't decent, or you didn't know why they were, or they'd given you a false name in the first place, you borrowed or stole or sold yourself before it began to show, before three months when they said the soul came in. And you could never be sure if you were really pregnant or not until ten weeks – anxiety wreaked havoc with the cycle – which gave you two weeks or less to find the money and the doctor.

There were three results: you lived and were safe, you did yourself damage and died, you lived and were found out and went to prison: they cost £200 or $500 depending and what did you have in return? That your body was not invaded by an alien growth. It was enough. Sex with strangers could be admirable: babies by strangers hardly could be. A mean initial trick by God to link the two, before humans intervened and separated them, distancing sex from babies so you could have the pleasure without the consequence. Except as Sophia had once pointed out, that was an oxymoron; the pleasures of sex were survival-friendly: the less reluctant a woman was to have sex the more babies she would have: left to itself the sex-hungry gene must in time dominate. Now necessity meant the size of women's families got smaller and smaller, babies turned into status symbols or were aborted as of right, we were going to end up in a world in which no-one liked sex any more. The process of enantiodromia, according to Exon: you go as far as the tramlines will let you, and then run back the other way. There's nowhere else to go, if you're a zealot. Rhode Island, the puritan state, ending up the Mafia playground: then back the pendulum swings again. The yearning for celibacy hadn't yet got to Sophia in London, thank God. It would be nice if Sophia had babies, but Felicity doubted that she ever would. If you loved instinctively and without reason, as Sophia had loved her mother, and that love was brought to such an end, with what amounted to a vicious attack – what else was hanging yourself so your child would find you – you would lack the resolution to carry on the generations. The love of the child for the mother, the love of the mother for the child, being so unconnected with that other love, sexual passion, which you sought out with a partner, turning the strange into the unstrange.

She wanted to be at Foxwoods. Yet William had gone without her. He hadn't even told her he was going. She wanted to be sitting at a slot machine in a stupor, all thoughts safely locked in her unconscious, on hold, maturing, the drum spinning, fate rewarding you or failing to reward you. Telling you its plans, the pattern of your destiny. And no harm done. She loved William. Lucky in love, lucky at cards, lucky, lucky, lucky.

She supposed so. Maria had answered the phone. William sometimes collected Maria's child from school. Perhaps he was the child's father? That had not occurred to her. He was surely of grandfather, even great-grandfather age. But strange things happened. In fact, she could see, she had let very little occur to her about William, considering how much they talked. Perhaps she was just determined to be lucky, the last forlorn hope of a desperate woman whose life had been a disappointment? How pathetic she must seem to the rest of the world.

*   *   *

Maria had called William 'Mr Johnson'. She wouldn't have called him that if they were on intimate terms. Or would she? Felicity thought she might very well cry. Why hadn't William told her he was going to Foxwoods when he spoke to her earlier? Was gambling so solitary a vice? He'd confessed his addiction, demonstrated it, expected her acquiescence, and now he was just going to leave her at home? He didn't want to share his life with her after all, only parts of it? Perhaps he'd changed his mind? Perhaps she had shown herself inadequate in some way? Perhaps he had expected her to hover behind him, constantly watching over his fortunes? Not to go off on her own, as she had, and gamble of her own accord. Not that playing the quarter slots was exactly gambling: you couldn't make or lose a fortune. Perhaps she was too dull, too cautious for William Johnson, gambling man?

She hadn't felt so insecure since she realized that Buckley was bisexual, and that she was the least of his interests, and was kept at home as a cover he scarcely needed since everyone *knew*; or felt so jealous since she'd realized he'd married her in order to have Angel in the house, the pale, beautiful elf-like child with the supple body, wild eyes and the red-gold, surprising, plentiful hair. His appreciation had been aesthetic rather than sexual, thank God – surely, since he preferred boys – but even so it had been enough to make her feel second best. Jealousy had nothing to do with sexual passion – she had been impervious to Buckley's charms, and he to hers – but to do with wanting someone's total attention. It was bad enough having girl children, all rivalry, all competition as they were, but you should at least be able to win for a time. But from the beginning Angel had been a creature of grace: all eyes turned to the child, not to the mother. She hadn't been accustomed to it.

Had she not gone to the funeral she would not have met William: she would be sitting in this room in mental and emotional comfort, bored out of her skull, but at least not subject to the panics and anxieties of being involved with a man.

Had she not gone to the funeral, Dr Bronstein would not be in the West Wing, and she not be torn by ambivalence; knowing she should go and visit him and frightened to do so for fear of what she would see. Perhaps Nurse Dawn was right, perhaps she, Felicity, was too old to tell a damp leather seat from a dry one. The future did not bear thinking about, although it was everyone's future. Perhaps falling in love with William – and they were right, it was an indignity and an absurdity – was compulsive, a strategy for postponing thoughts of death and the physical and mental decline that led up to it.

Thus thoroughly mortified and depressed, Felicity sat, as everyone from time to time must sit, young or old, until she was disturbed by a commotion from outside the French windows. It was the sound of the arrival of Joy and Jack, turning up as William was wont to do, but today had not. Joy's little white face appeared at the window, and the glitter of her jewels in a halo of misty pink velour. The thin fingers found the strength for tapping. The glass was no barrier to her voice.

'Miss Felicity, Miss Felicity, let us in!'

Jack, once burly, now thinning, good white teeth gleaming and smiling jovially in a square fleshy jaw, appeared beside his deceased wife's sister. His neck had shrunk. To Felicity it seemed his head sat squarely on his shoulders almost without any narrow bit in between.

The world won't leave you alone, it will always find you out, or your money, Felicity concluded. Dr Bronstein's great-great-grandson and his partner had found him out, to make sure he was looked after for his own good. This morning no doubt they would be preening themselves for the compassion they had shown. They had journeyed a long way to make sure the old man was properly looked after: the fact that they now controlled his money would go down well with the bank: would give them security to raise a mortgage or start some fine new business, and provide them with the life which was theirs by right of youthfulness.

Once she, Felicity, had been young and poor, had sung for her supper, and danced too, with or without clothes. There had been no-one to help her. There had been a house once, she remembered that. A rather fine house with a cook and a maid, and a mother

245

and father, and all had vanished away. Things did. And a garden and a full moon and a summerhouse in winter, and after that she had made her own life. But the generations had been dealt a savage blow, and had struggled on to produce Sophia, and that would be the end of it, this particular experiment in nature's passion for diversity, which caused human beings such pain. These girls with plentiful red hair, too bright and vulnerable for their own good.

Luck, mostly, that she had not become diseased or dissolute, or taken to drink or drugs; that the lineaments of disappointment had not written themselves on her face. Her share of bad luck had piled up in the first twenty years. Apart from the next blow in the form of Angel, which had well and truly struck home, she had dodged most of the others, eaten more good meals than most, slept in softer beds than most for the last fifty years at least. And worn prettier clothes than most. That was something.

'Miss Felicity, Miss Felicity, unlock the door! Are you deaf?'
'Fat chance,' thought Felicity, stirring herself to open the glass doors.
'My, you were in a dream,' said Joy. 'No William today? Well, I suppose there wouldn't be, since I'm using the Mercedes.'
'Don't be nasty, Joy,' said Felicity, oddly pleased to see her friend. 'William has his own transport now, but thank you for the use of it. Jack said it was okay. I had no idea it would upset you.'
'I'm not upset, Miss Felicity, just hopping mad. You went behind my back. You knew I wouldn't approve. One look at that man and I knew he was after your money.'
'Go a bit softly here, Joy,' said Jack. 'We have no proof of it.'
'Even if he was after my money,' said Felicity, 'I might not mind. I might think it was worth it.'
But her heart wasn't in it. She could hear her own voice, quavering for once, not ringing and defiant. He should have been home when she called.
'Once he gets his hands on your fortune it wouldn't be so pleasant,' said Joy. 'He'd beat you and abuse you, to help you on your way to the grave. You'd be glad to die. The papers are full of it.'
'Young women search out rich old men,' said Jack, 'and screw

them to death, and there's bugger all anyone can do about it. They make a business of it.'

'Language!' shrieked Joy.

'You're no different from your sister,' said Jack.

Joy fell silent, mutinous and sulky as a little girl.

'Only louder,' added Jack for good measure. Then he said to Felicity, 'I'd better meet this William of yours. See what I make of him.'

Felicity nearly said she didn't know what to make of him either, other than that he'd let her down, gone to the Casino without her, and was secretive about his past, but desisted. If Joy heard about Foxwoods there would be no end to it. She sat them down and prepared coffee. She did not want to stir up room service for fear of stirring up Nurse Dawn as well.

'So long as it's decaff,' said Joy.

'I'm a real coffee man myself,' said Jack.

'That's why you're so bad-tempered,' said Joy.

'What is the matter with you two?' asked Felicity. She had not heard them like this before. Neither was able to tell her.

'Perhaps it's the ghost of Francine,' said Felicity, joking, but they didn't think that was funny.

'I loved Francine very much,' said Jack.

'I loathed her,' said Joy, and they were both silent for a little. Some truth between them seemed to be emerging, the other side of irritation and resentment.

Nurse Dawn tapped on the door and entered without waiting for an invitation. She was in her white uniform. She had changed her shoes to trainers but Felicity could see the outline of a black corset bra beneath the white fabric. The uniform had been washed and rewashed until, though brilliantly white, it was soft and flimsy.

'Visitors again!' she said. 'I wish you'd ask them to come through the reception area and check in properly, not to use the French windows. I know Mr and Mrs Epstein of course, but it isn't safe, Miss Felicity. There are so many rough types around. Well, it is Rhode Island, isn't it?'

'Connecticut's much nicer,' said Joy. 'Much more classy. I always told you so.'

'The used car market's better in Rhode Island,' said Jack.
'That is exactly my point,' said Joy.

'If you can't observe these simple precautions, Miss Felicity,' said Nurse Dawn, ignoring the interruptions, 'we might have to move you to an upstairs room, for the safety of the other guests. You could always play Rapunzel, of course, but I don't think your prince will exactly be able to use your golden hair as a rope. This is such a dear room, with the view and all, it would be a real pity to have to move. Your granddaughter's turning up from London tomorrow. Such a competent young woman. I'll discuss the security problem with her, shall I? And Dr Grepalli will also be having a word with her about the painting.'
'What painting,' asked Felicity. 'Do you mean the Utrillo?'
'If it's worth as much as they say,' said Nurse Dawn, 'for such a little painting anyone could have done, it does leave all of us with yet another security problem.'

Nurse Dawn took leaflets out of her pocket. She waved them around to make sure everyone saw. Then she left them on the little polished table by the door.
'You might be interested in these, Miss Felicity. No Mr Johnson today? Stood you up? Well, that's the way it goes in the world of the love-lorn. I remember it well. I think Dr Grepalli had a word with him. Today's beau is tomorrow's history.'
She left, leaving Joy and Jack bemused. Jack examined the leaflets. They were issued by the American Gaming Association and offered free treatment for problem gamblers.

'Warning!' they declared. 'Gambling in moderation entertains millions and generates jobs. America has taken gambling to its heart – a 35 billion-dollar industry with a great future. But for the few for whom gambling is pathological, it can get to be a problem. Like any other addiction compulsive gambling can lead to lying, stealing, going broke, neglect of employment, and even suicide. If you are one of the unlucky few or know anyone with a gambling problem, contact the AGA helpline. Treatment is free. We're here to help.'

And so forth.

The phrase *Win the Wages of Life* appeared here and there, enclosed in a pink heart.

'Why did that woman leave you these?' asked Jack.
'I have no idea,' said Felicity. It was a lie and one she shouldn't have told. But she was weak, and undermined, as people are from time to time, by the accumulated misfortunes of the past, all the things that had gone wrong, all the disappointments and the hopes dashed, and for a moment lost faith. She did not want to hear Joy's roar when she was told that William was a gambling man. It is in such moments of untruth that the seeds of social disaster can be sown.

And suddenly at the French windows there William stood; silhouetted against the light, wearing his new suit and his lucky gambler's hat, bright-eyed and smiling, in good form, his bright new red Saab parked in full view. One of life's winners, not one of life's losers, and Felicity's faith was restored. She corrected herself.
'William is a gambling man,' she said. 'And Nurse Dawn is a poisonous bitch. Do come in, William. Joy you already know, and this is Jack her husband.'
'Deceased sister's husband,' both chorused.
'I'm so sorry,' said Felicity, 'I keep forgetting.'

39

Guy and Lorna did not make good travelling companions. They surprised me by deciding at the last minute to accompany me to Rhode Island. Guy got through to me in the editing suite on the Friday, and by claiming it was to do with Felicity and it was urgent actually got me to take the call. Not only did I lose focus but Harry slipped into my seat as I left it and took over at the console, which he had been dying to do. Men do so need to be in control. There was nothing wrong with Harry's editorial skills of course, I did not doubt them, but the same kind of thing happens at the board as when a friend borrows your car. It never quite handles the same thereafter.

But Harry mollified me by saying as he took my chair, 'This seat is wonderfully warm, what bliss!' For some reason this made me feel secure. So I wasn't just someone he slept with and someone he worked with, in separate compartments. I was someone he slept *and* worked with. The roles overlapped and melded. Holly had been very quiet lately, and if only by virtue of sheer distance, over oceans and landmass, had begun to seem in my mind a little bleached out and pallid. Or perhaps Harry just kept her messages from me. The last news he'd given me was a couple of weeks back, when he'd remarked that her latest plan was to have artificial insemination by donor, using someone else's egg, Harry's sperm (she had some on hand frozen – really it was revolting) and a hired womb, but she had to get it all together, and he thought it was beyond her. She had been more preoccupied, Harry said, with the possibility of getting a big part in a sci-fi special effects production, a film where the dresses were sheets of changing colour and very little else, so she was having to get a body-double to do her difficult parts, namely her back, which the producers had decided was over-muscled.

'You mean, she looks like Schwarzenegger,' I said.

'She's more like Demi Moore,' he said. Which put me in my place.

Perhaps involving a lover in the genetic make-up of a projected child was a normal Hollywood way of keeping a man? Who was to say? Would it work? Who was to say that either? It was on the cutting edge of the new genetic technology coming out of LA. Invented people as well as invented narrative. Holly was an increasingly unreal person but then films were unreal and Harry was a film person too. He effected reality: he made a really good stab at it: if this bouncing endomorph with the companionable testosterone-ridden flesh was in truth just a cartoon character, the big-time director out of Hollywood on the loose, you could have fooled me. I know there have been big advances lately in animation technology, but he was still amazingly detailed: his shoulders might be fantasy broad and unreasonably square, but one of his front teeth was whiter than the other, and his face was mobile way beyond the expectation of the ordinary viewer. Holly might be someone in one of the new special effects films coming out of Hollywood, but I told myself the longer Harry stayed out of that city the more actual, the less virtual, he became. And as for me, my obsession with films had lately been faltering. Offer me a choice between going to the cinema and going out to Twickenham for a dreary lunch with Guy and Lorna and oddly enough I'd choose the latter. And now I was abandoning Harry's company and flying off to see my grandmother when she wasn't even sick. Just in love and contemplating marriage.

What Guy had to say on the phone was that he and Lorna had decided on impulse that the time was ripe to meet their grand-mother Felicity. They'd be hard-put to find their way to her with-out me, so could they come with? I murmured objections to do with passports and bookings. You can't decide on the Friday that you want to travel distances on the Saturday, not if you're an ordinary person. I travel easily and without fuss, and like to put a difference between myself and those less well travelled, who ought to find journeys difficult. Crossing the globe is not like stepping on and off a bus, whatever people might say. The ankles swell, and paranoia with it, strange viruses circulate with the air, the body's time clock is shot to pieces: the short-term memory goes. You learn to ignore these things, just as you learn to ignore what goes into the water of the municipal swimming pool, but it doesn't mean it isn't there, that shit doesn't happen.

Guy was having none of it. He said surely I could put the studio's travel agent on to the problem of availability: I had often spoken of what marvels they could work. I had to agree that indeed they could. And yes, both brother and sister had their passports in working order. They holidayed in Barcelona in Spain every year: they'd told me this. So they had, though why I had forgotten. There was some good historical reason for it: as there is to most people's holiday habits. Perhaps Lorna once had a pen pal in Spain? I feel bad about forgetting. I called the travel agent, and they manoeuvred two extra seats in Club Class at economy prices. But we all had to go to New York not Boston. I of course was the one still travelling economy. That's the way it goes.

Would that it had. Lorna and Guy, in a flurry of self-sacrificing good nature, insisted on negotiating with the steward, once the flight had departed, to ease the two little Japanese newly-weds out of the seats next to me and into Club Class. Thus my cousins could sit next to me. This was remarkable behaviour and a better measure of their ignorance as travellers, I thought, than of their concern for me. They lifted the seat divisions and their solid bulk squashed up and pressed me in against the window. Guy was next to me and I thought he was unduly pleased to be so close, flank touching flank, but I overlooked it. He was family. Just sometimes I remembered his grandfather Anton and poor Felicity, whose pre-Raphaelite red-gold hair I shared, and what Lucy had told me of what happened next, and I shrank away. But all that was generations back and evil, like wealth, got swallowed up or dissipated with the generations. Forget it.

I had booked a suite in the Wyndham Hotel in West 68th Street so we could rest overnight before going on up to Rhode Island. I had called ahead to the Golden Bowl to tell them I would be arriving the next day, and mentioning the two extra grandchildren I'd bring with me. I left a message on Joy's answerphone to see if by any chance Charlie could come and pick us up in New York. I would not totally spring this new family upon Felicity, while yet not giving her too much time to react unfavourably to the notion of their existence. It would be a *fait accompli*, yet I could argue it was expected. Guy and Lorna, as I had, would have travelled a long way to see their elderly relative. She could hardly refuse them. And, I told myself, Felicity was of an accepting rather than a rejecting nature; she was never churlish. I was sure the meeting would go well.

But as I say, not a good flight. I should have expected it, I told myself. I cast the coins before we set out, and threw hexagram number three and not a changing line anywhere, the fates set fast and unswerving. *Difficulty at the Beginning works supreme success.* Described as *Chun*, in the *I Ching*. *K'an*, the abysmal, above: water, *Chên*; the arousing, below.

> *Thus the superior man*
> *Brings order out of confusion.*

In other words it was going to be all right in the end but fairly dreadful on the way. So it proved. Once the cousins were settled in – and it took a good half-hour into the journey before they were – Lorna kept pressing the button for attention and when the steward came asked any old thing: how the seat recliner worked – she could just as well have asked me, but it seemed she liked to get people to work for their living – or require him to adjust the airflow when she could just have reached up and done it herself or could have asked Guy to. And then she wanted to be brought water and when told she could get it for herself she was piqued. When Lorna finally subsided – I kindly put her behaviour down to nerves – it was Guy's turn to get going. He complained that his headphones didn't work – how his body had pressed into mine as he squirmed and searched for a plug point! – and demanded they be replaced. He complained loudly about the quality of the music. And then there was the matter of the missing free copy of the flight magazine, and how Lorna's food tray wasn't secure and could easily tip and spill boiling coffee on her, and so forth and so on. My cousins then contemplated asking the Japanese couple to return, so they could go forward, where they'd discovered the air was better: but I persuaded them otherwise. The turmoil would have been dreadful. One way or another I was unnerved. I couldn't pretend they weren't with me, because they so clearly were: they chafed and irritated loudly all the flight through.

Nine at the beginning, according to the *I Ching*, means:
> *Hesitation and hindrance.*
> *It furthers one to remain persevering,*
> *It furthers one to appoint helpers.*

Seasoned travellers know the only thing to do is not react to events, not to notice shortcomings, not to make objections: it is a waste of time and emotion. You go with the flow, pass out of full consciousness when you set foot into an airport and only go back into it when you step out of the other, the far side of immigration and customs. This was not Guy and Lorna's way. So circumspect and well-behaved at home, they were a far more obstreperous pair out of it. Perhaps Alison's maternal influence lay like a damp cloud over the house. Perhaps she was more like her Aunt Lois than she appeared: perhaps she too had been a tyrannical mother. Oddly enough, although I squirmed with embarrassment, I liked Lorna and Guy rather better for this outbreak of antisocial behaviour.

It is not a good idea to go on living in the childhood home: people should move out as soon as they can, and rejoice when the ancestral pile or suburban semi – both seem to rouse the same passions – *my train set, the walnut tree, the blue remembered hills: gone, all gone* – is sold up. Too many of my friends go into mourning when it happens. It's easy for me to say this, of course, never having had a proper childhood home, and so never having had one to move out of. I had just ended up living near where my mother had been conceived, round the corner from Mearde Street, Soho, which is little more than an alley linking Wardour with Dean Street, in the heart of London's film land. But I daresay that's just a coincidence, not the nearest I could get to home.

40

The day before we set out for New York I'd asked Wendy from Aardvark to see if she could come up with anything about my maternal grandfather, the folk singer.

'Tell me more about him,' she'd said.

'A man too inept to stop my grandmother from going to America, too inept to stop her naming another man as the father of his own child.' *Could have been anyone*, said Wendy's look. 'And too inept not to get himself killed in a street brawl the night after V-E night,' I added. 'Allied Victory in Europe night. The war in Asia with the Japanese was still going on.'

'That last is something to go on,' she said. 'At least there might be press reports.'

I said I would try to get more details out of Felicity when I saw her. I'd only ever had Angel's version of what went on anyway, and she was hardly a reliable witness. If Felicity was at last happy in love she might be more forthcoming about her life and times. She had never really been happy with Exon; she had been dutiful and well-behaved and half herself. Presumably that was the penalty you paid for being in a tranquil and suitable marriage. Heaven keep me from it.

My own ineptness had to come from somewhere, why not my so far nameless grandfather? Why was I content to be a film editor and not a director? Why be me when I could be Astra Barnes? Perhaps I needed to go to assertiveness classes? True, I was a very good film editor and she was a very bad film director, but I might be setting my sights too low. If I'd set my mind to it and done enough body building I could even have been a film star like the over-muscled Holly. I had the looks and better hair and certainly wouldn't need a body double for my back – but this was of course nonsense. I was a perfectly ordinary if good-looking woman: whereas Holly had the kind of personality and looks which made others excuse the sins of folly, perfidy and self-absorption. Stars, unlike the rest of us, are encouraged by the media to talk about themselves, ceaselessly, and can hardly be blamed if they begin to find themselves interesting. They fall for it themselves, forgetting that others are merely making money out of them. My main problem has always been that I am not a fool, and have very little capacity for self-deception. I would make a hopeless film star.

I was quite unlike my father, who would believe anything if it flattered him. Rufus believed that he was a great artist and that the mantle of the muse had descended upon him, and all he had to do was put paint on canvas and he would be hailed as a great painter. My mother Angel had believed it too, and to both of them, wrongly, that had seemed the part of her that wasn't mad. Rufus was all innocent inspiration; he had left the Camberwell School of Art after a couple of terms, quarrelling with his tutors and asking what need did Van Gogh ever have of tuition. He married a derelict American girl he met wandering the streets – my mother, that is to say – to confirm his bohemianism and further distance himself from his own Canadian parents. Europe was the home of art: centre of sensitivities denied to the rest of the world: London in the sixties the place to be; awash as it was with LSD, death to the brain cells.

I have two paintings of his on my walls; he favoured Fauve, swirls of heated orange and red. Harry quite likes them. After my father died, of lung cancer, my grandmother had the rest packed up into crates and put into storage. What else was to be done with these works of semi-art, semi-decoration? There were not enough friends with wall-space enough to hang them all – only the rich have wall-space, and my father's friends smoked too much marihuana ever to get going in the world and achieve such luxury. His parents had first disowned him – *Europe, drugs, permissiveness,*

257

art – and then died, one of those couples so close that if one goes, the other goes too. The children of lovers are orphans, as Tolstoy remarked. What a stick nature created for human beings with which to beat their own back, sharpened both ends. Too much love or too little of it, and all the world's to pieces.

Perhaps when after my father's first exhibition my mother made the bonfire of canvases in the street, she realized the eventual problem of disposal. Her rage with the gallery seemed irrational even for her: they had actually given Rufus an exhibition, which was more than anyone else had done, and made not a bad job in selling the paintings and might even have managed to establish him as a major artist, but after the bonfire they didn't have the nerve for it. They expected gratitude, not police, fire brigade and a madwoman. Word got round, of course, and suddenly no-one was eager to give Rufus so much as a show, in case his wife *did it again*, or something worse. She was famous all over town: beautiful but insane and dangerous with it.

Thereafter Rufus, with reason enough, blamed Angel for every rejection he ever had, for all the shakings of heads and the *not for me, I'm sorry* that was all he got from galleries everywhere – and since for the not-quite-good-enough painter the world is all rejection the marriage didn't have much chance, forget Angel's evident and increasing fits of insanity, the shaving of my head, the living in cardboard boxes and so on. My father found a nice plain normal girl in the end, a secretary called Angela who gave him bed and heart space on and off and kept him sane. I don't know what became of her. She took me in sometimes, in emergencies: she made rice pudding in the oven, and sprinkled it with nutmeg. She was nice enough, as was her rice pudding, but we all knew she didn't count. She wasn't a major player.

After my mother's death I lived with Rufus, on and off, but he was not a focused father: he spent most of his time in his studio, afraid to look at me in case I took after my mother and went mad. I was never afraid of this myself, oddly enough. I was the sanest one of all: I didn't paint or smoke dope or drink: I got on with my life, passed exams and went to the cinema. When my father died, which took him only two months from diagnosis to death, it was a relief to me, the end of a complication: now there was only me, with Felicity far away. Rufus had loved my mother and now he was with her. That must sound strange but the other side of her insanity, of her hatred, of her urge to destroy and self-destruct, lurked this most gentle and lovable person. I am too brisk to be like her in this respect, too rejecting of sentiment: I suppose I have had to learn to be. These days, though, since she won't come to me, I cross the ocean to visit Felicity, to put my toe in the water of complication. I am getting braver.

Difficulty at the Beginning. The *I Ching* again. Six (that's two heads and a tail) in the second place means:

> *Difficulties pile up,*
> *Horse and wagon part.*
> *He is not a robber;*
> *He wants to woo when the time comes.*
> *The maiden is chaste.*
> *She does not pledge herself.*
> *Ten years, then she pledges herself.*

But Felicity could not afford ten years before she pledged herself. The normal rules which apply to the rest of us – such as reading the *I Ching* when you're in love to see how things are going to turn out – do not apply at the extreme ends of life, in youth or age. But at least the *I Ching* seemed to have a good opinion of Mr Johnson. *He is not a robber.*

Difficulties pile up! I hadn't reckoned on company. I like to be alone on flights, I like the way life ceases to be, even as one's desire to keep it going is at its strongest. Had Angel flown above the clouds more she might not have killed herself: she would have been too practised in the fear of death.

41

As it happened, Felicity had earlier that day cast the coins to get her own reading from the *I Ching*. She threw *Difficulty in the Beginning*. This was no more than a coincidence. Do the *I Ching* five or six times a day and the odds against hitting on a particular one out of those available – there are sixty-four different combinations possible if you cast three coins six times – are not astronomical. It takes only sixteen people in the same room at a party for the odds of there being two people there with the same birthday to be greater than not. Felicity was glad to hear that William Johnson was no robber, for she too interpreted the oracle literally. The *I Ching* itself elaborates on the theme.

> *When in time of difficulty a hindrance is encountered from a*
> *source unrelated to us, we must be careful not to take upon*
> *ourselves any obligations entailed by such help, otherwise our*
> *freedom of decision is impaired. If we bide our time, things*
> *will quieten down again. And we shall attain what we have*
> *hoped for.*

Since the days when she wondered whether Exon was going to propose marriage or not, Felicity had scarcely opened the book, until the determination to sell Passmore and strike out into the world had been made. There had been so few decisions to reach in the quietness of widowhood. At any rate once the funeral had been arranged, and all that business, and then the shock of being alone accepted, together with the understanding that because of her age life was likely to remain like this. It wasn't too bad. You got to quite like being able to do your own thing and go your own way without comment, in your own time. Nothing much happened to widows of mature years.

Winters came and went, and summers too, and sometimes Sophia came to stay and more often she didn't.

Joy next door's deafness increased, and her determination not to wear an ear machine with it. Joy's sister Francine had died and Joy had been in extra noisy tumult for a time, torn between grief and relief.

Joy's driving licence had nearly been revoked: she had driven into someone else in a parking lot and driven away once too often, without so much as leaving a telephone number, but had escaped with a fine. That was almost an excitement.

A family of Northern Parulas – blue warblers with yellow throats and breasts – had established itself in a lilac tree in a swampy dip in the garden.

Otherwise what had happened? Just that tying the shoelaces became a little more difficult and getting out of the bath presented more of a problem than once it had. But on the whole she had been glad of the peace. Life took you up and shook you by the scruff of your neck and landed you somewhere almost without your own volition. Like being picked up by a tornado and dumped somewhere else and finding you were okay and it was rather better than the place you had left, just unfamiliar, though you were certainly bruised.

But the wounds of a lifetime healed, and here you were, and here was William, but now what about her freedom? Was she diplomat enough to manage marriage, living together, describing and accepting the other as *my. My* spouse, *my* partner. To go through the explaining and justifying of this one person to all the others – see how it already was with Nurse Dawn, with Joy, with Jack? Sharing a bed, trying not to snore: getting to the stage where you could not distinguish the self from the other and behaving accordingly: uttering reprimands which were really self-reproaches: a stream of consciousness which passed for conversation. At eighty-three, getting used to all that again? In return for what? Sex, which she now valued more as a token of esteem rather than a source of overwhelming physical pleasure? While she wasn't looking it had ceased to be an all-consuming need.

*   *   *

In this she could see she was in tune with the times: these days people went to clinics for liking sex too much. The pendulum swung, and swung too far: to be allowed your sexual pleasure, which had once been the passionate ambition of women, the very symbol of freedom, the end of bourgeois repression, no longer counted for much. For a woman to take her pleasures like a man was not an interesting aspiration: rather, men took pains to take theirs like women: all feeling and sensitivity, not brute power and enviable lust. Mind you, as men got older they had little choice. William had approached her nervously at first: had later gained confidence. But he too had caught the spirit of the times; he wanted to please her, he did not just wait to be pleased.

Companionship? Of course he offered that. Security? No, not that. You could win shooting craps, but you could also lose. But if she made sure he spent his money, and didn't let him touch hers, what did she have to worry about? Nothing.

She realized that the last line she'd thrown was actually a changing line – three heads, which being so totally yang could only turn to yin (it was nonsense, so much nonsense, of course it was). Any moment now the portrait of what was to come would turn to two heads and a tail. *Six at the top*. She knew before she read it that it wasn't going to be good.

Horse and wagon part.
Bloody tears flow.

No, not good at all. It could hardly be worse. She moved on to the hexagram that resulted from the changing line. Number four. *Holding Together*. Better. Much better.

Holding together brings good fortune.
Inquire of the oracle once again
Whether you possess sublimity, constancy and perseverance:
Then there is no blame.
Those who are uncertain gradually join.
Whoever comes too late
Meets with misfortune.

The trouble with the *I Ching* was that you read it and believed what you wanted to believe and ignored what you didn't. You

might as well wait for what was going to happen and then look back and know what it was. Why be in such a hurry? Because, dear God, she was eighty-three, and there was so little time left. She cast the coins again, and got *Youthful Folly*.
Number four.

> *The young fool seeks me,*
> *At the first oracle I inform him.*

Forget it.

42

If you fly Concorde transatlantic they wave you through immigration and customs. If you fly Club Class you get to the head of the line first and get through first. If you fly economy and at the back of the plane, as Guy, Lorna and I did, you get to the Immigration Hall only to find yourself in competition with another flight. It will be from some country everyone wants to leave, and immigration will be taking its time. As luck would have it an Air Pakistan flight landed as we did and Guy, Lorna and myself had to wait in line in the vast hall for nearly three hours. Over the sea of heads we caught sight of the Japanese couple going through the barriers within fifteen minutes of their arrival. Lorna worried loudly about possible infections: Guy fretted and fidgeted. I trundled meekly and silently forward, as was my wont, a step or two at a time, along the convoluted maze of pathways, which steered you near to the promised land of America and then doubled you back at an angle to the direction you had come. *So you think you're nearly there, we'll show you!* I felt responsible for Lorna and Guy's discomfiture, though indeed they were responsible for mine, my initial plan to travel to Boston having been changed for their convenience. But I did not say so.

Guy went into a particularly English mode: *My good man, look here, this is no way to treat guests to your country.* He told one of the black security guards what he thought of the system, and said that this kind of thing didn't happen in Heathrow. I intervened and said loudly that it most certainly did, if you were unfortunate to be labelled Other, and apologized for Guy's attitude, which of course I should not have done. It had been a long and uncomfortable flight, I said. We were all tired.

'What do you think we are, lady?' he inquired. He went away, eyes to heaven, but later I thought I saw him have a word with the officer in the booth. But perhaps it was about something quite different.

'Next time don't take it on yourself to speak for me,' snapped Guy.

'It isn't wise to piss off security anywhere in the world,' I said.

'Language!' said Lorna. 'We must all just try and be patient.'

When we finally got to the yellow line, shuffling our luggage in front of us, Guy stepped over it, and was asked to wait in the correct place by a courteous little Hispanic girl drowned in a navy uniform with gold buttons and a red sash. He shook off her small restraining hand with, 'How dare you touch me!' I had never accepted until this minute how timorous and law-abiding a person I was and quite how much I loathed scenes. Guy's eyes were dark and glazed and wild, and reminded me of my mother's, though I had never seen any resemblance to my side of the family before. But perhaps all insane people just look alike, and Guy was certainly, if only temporarily, quite insane. Flying does this to some people.

When he went up to the immigration officer and offered his passport they had a brief exchange of words, which we could not hear, but as a result of which security was called and Guy was taken away, physically struggling, to a cell. Lorna and I were not allowed to go with him but had to clear passports and customs first. We were taken off and body searched. I could hear Lorna in the next cubicle squeaking and protesting the indignity of it all and demanding to see the British Ambassador. They found nothing, nor had they expected to. We were being punished. I got a phone call through to the studio travel agency as soon as I could, and they sent someone over, Linda, to look after us. Linda managed to persuade the authorities to let Guy out into our care, though it hadn't been easy, she was at pains to tell us. 'These are not pretty people,' Linda said. 'Your friend was really pushing his luck. We're happy to be of assistance to you but in future please try and keep your friends in order. They are not studio employees, as you are.' She was annoyed: called out to Kennedy on a Saturday morning when she could have been shopping. She had the brittle thinness of a certain type of New York woman: good legs, lots of glossy hair and a narrow, attractive face. She thought she was too good for this job and probably was.

I wished I had never set eyes on Wendy from Aardvark, or Alison, or Lucy, or Guy, or Lorna. Guy was a little subdued by his brush with the slammer, but not much. He chafed and wriggled with indignation in the back of the yellow cab on the way into the city. He had been hustled, he maintained, manhandled, briefly handcuffed. What kind of country was this? I asked him what he'd said to provoke such a reaction.
'Whose side are you on?' he demanded. 'Theirs or mine? When that prat asked me the purpose of my visit I said to overthrow the government and take drugs. Don't they even have a sense of humour? It's enough to make your eyes weep blood.'
I said that in a lot of countries in the world he would have been shot. Lorna complained about the springing of the cab and the fact that the driver didn't speak English. She didn't even exclaim with wonder when she saw the old Trade Fair building or when the Manhattan skyline came into view, as do most new arrivals, and I was disappointed. I had wanted her to be impressed: it would have been my consolation.

They were too tired to complain much about the Wyndham, but did the next morning. The softness of the mattress, the shabbiness of the décor, the reluctance of the single lift to arrive. I explained that all this was designed to make the English feel at home: a large part of the Hemsley clientele was English. Americans would never put up with it. It occurred to me when Lorna referred to 'mattress' in the singular – there were twin beds in their room – that perhaps they only used one. But it was only a supposition. And even if they did share a bed, it might have been in the spirit of the little brother and sister they once had been, no more than that. It was none of my business, anyway. I was just cross with them and happy to believe anything scandalous. I went out to the deli for coffee and bagels with sour cream and smoked salmon and brought them back and all Lorna said was she hadn't come all

this way to drink out of paper cups. If this was how the Americans lived she didn't think much of it. All they seemed to be good at was raining down unsmart bombs on innocent children in faraway countries, in defence of their freedoms. Of course the siblings were having an illicit relationship. Of course. Guy was silent. I asked Lorna what the matter with him was. I cannot endure men sulking. 'He had a very traumatic time yesterday,' said Lorna. 'Poor Guy. And you've upset him by seeming to take their part.'
Screw that for a game of soldiers, I thought but did not say.

But Harry then called me from London and told me he missed me. 'Hi baby!' he said, and the usage did not make me squirm even a little, as it usually did. Why do men so want to relegate women to charming helplessness, and why do women put up with it? I was just pleased to hear his gravelly voice. Perhaps he called Holly too and said, 'Hi baby, how's the baby?' but I didn't think so.
I smiled at Lorna after the phone call and said, 'That was my boyfriend,' and Lorna said, 'Anyone who can make you look so happy must be okay,' and I felt really fond of her. Of course she wasn't having an affair with her brother Guy. They were just both of them very bad travellers.

43

When William appeared in the French windows, a ray of light streaming through to gloomy corners, Jack and Joy had made their excuses and left, as people will when presented without warning with the physical manifestation of their mistrust. Jack even managed a smile as he summoned Charlie on the mobile phone. But then he had put in a half-hearted defence of Felicity's suitor, and wasn't feeling as guilty as Joy.

'I didn't know you had guests,' William said, with a hint of reproach, when they were gone. 'You didn't tell me.'
'They were unexpected,' said Felicity, a little coldly. She was pleased that he was there, but he had still caused her grief. 'And I am still a free agent. We're not married yet.'
'So we're going to be?' he inquired. She did not reply. She stood with her eyes downcast, feeling mutinous, and remembered standing in just this way as a child. She looked at the floor: she felt dizzy. She was wearing little boots with brown laces; for some reason she had tied them in a double bow, which was unnecessary: a single one would have done, for the laces were not slippery, but of the old-fashioned kind, flat, not thin and rounded.

If she looked up now she would see another place, another country, another world. She would see a tall, square, white painted room with brown furniture and a lime tree pressed up against a barred window. In the summer the lime tree dropped sticky yellow substance on the pavement outside, and on the hats of anyone who stood too long at the front door. She could hear the rattle, rattle of a horse and cart passing by, the clip-clop of horses' hooves. She was how old? Four?

'Don't sulk, Fel,' she heard her mother say, 'there's nothing to sulk about.' She did not dare look up; she would see her mother's face. What did it look like? She did not know: she could not even remember knowing. You forget so soon, and there had been no photographs. Lois had burned them all: everything had gone. Even the tiny pink chiffon scarf that still held traces of her mother's warmth, her scent, left by mistake in the back of the coat cupboard in the hall, had one day just not been there any more. She asked Lois once what her mother had looked like, and Lois had replied, 'She's a skull by now, I daresay. *The worms crawl in, the worms crawl out – They go in slim and they come out stout.*' She didn't ask after that.

'What's the matter with Miss Felicity?' she heard a man's voice say. Her father.

'She can't tie her laces,' her mother said, still living, still with her own warm flesh and blood face. 'And she won't let me teach her. She thinks she can do it without.'

'Everyone has to be taught to tie laces, Fel,' said the father's voice. 'It doesn't happen by magic.' He was laughing; the voice was strong and kind, she believed it as she didn't necessarily believe her mother, but now she felt a spasm of rage so great she gasped. Where did it come from?

William had her arm, was sitting her down. She stretched out her feet and stared at her shoes. Flat brown old-fashioned laces, tied in a double bow: her father teaching her, her mother watching. *Right over left, tighten: catch the string between finger and thumb, loop over, under, out, pull.*

'My father was already seeing Lois,' she said to William. 'He must have been. Before my mother died.'

'Oh, the past,' said William. 'Is that all? It catches up from time to time, but only when you're strong enough. I must be good for you. Tell me more.' But Felicity couldn't find the words. She was an old woman or she was a child, and there was no space in between.

'You said you'd take me to Foxwoods today,' was all she said. 'I called, and Maria answered. At least I suppose it was Maria. What do I know about your life? What do you ever tell me? She said you'd already gone, without me.'

'My, we are insecure,' he said. 'I had a visit or so to make before I came along here. Stop sulking.'

'Where did you go?' She was childlike again, querulous, but now with the confidence of the child who knows however badly it behaves the sky won't fall in. Once she'd behaved badly, and it had fallen, but that was then and this was now. Once she'd said to her stepmother's brother that she'd be really nice to him if he took her to Sydney, but without knowing, of course, what being really nice meant. She was a child. Girls were, then, at fourteen. But that was not altogether true: you knew something by virtue of just being alive, more than enough. You knew why your father chose Lois, not your mother, and it was the worse part of him, and he knew it, and didn't care, and all things were sacrificed to male desire. Lois, the cruel voluptuary.

It had been winter and the lime tree was without leaves and pressed up against the window of the tall room, like bony skeleton fingers, grasping at you, and there was a fate indeed worse than death, that you didn't die, but lived with terror and evil for ever. That was what you fled from all your life, over oceans and continents, joining up with others, springing apart again because it was too dangerous, the hounds not of Heaven but of Hell pattering after you, because once you were complicit in the evil, and now they would never let you alone. If you stayed still too long you could feel their warm breath, hear the panting, smell the stench. She'd felt it, heard it, smelt it one day at Passmore: the creatures must have circled and circled for years before making their presence felt. They'd come for her. She tried to explain it to a doctor at the hospital, but he'd said it was a sensory disturbance caused by a minor stroke: it would pass. That was really why she'd left Passmore, sold up, come here, where there were good people, busy with their chanting, their determination to make the best of things. The hounds of Hell couldn't get at her here. They liked silence, and loneliness.

*   *   *

The old understood better than the young that the foundation of the earth was composed of good and evil, no matter how you struggled to see it in terms of money and sex and luck. The trouble was the old had no words, no language, no real remembrance; what afflicted the soul in the end afflicted the body. The old peered out of rheumy eyes, dimmed by too much exposure to the truth, deafened by a lifetime of lies, bent by the burden of guilt. They lost their wits like Dr Bronstein. Age itself was evil, and there was no escaping it: the young pity the old because once you know too much this awareness can only be perceived as paranoia. But what else can you do? How else express what you have learned of life, other than *beware, beware, bloody tears flow*?

'I went to see an art dealer I know to ask about the Utrillo, okay?' William said, but she scarcely took in what he was saying. 'He's retired and lives in Narragansett Pier, but he understands the art market.'

'Do you know who Nurse Dawn reminds me of?' Miss Felicity asked, not registering what he had said at all. 'Lois my stepmother. How strange to meet up with her again, after all this time.'

She smiled brightly at him and tried to focus on the here and now. On the pink striped wallpaper, which was pretty enough but dull: and outside the trees struggling to come into bud, and just a faint suspicion of spring in the air. Life was all renewal, as well as decay. She must hold on to that.

'I'm a bit upset today,' she said. 'I thought you'd let me down, gone off without me, and it triggered off all kinds of rubbish. Stuff so long ago I'm the only one alive to remember it.'

'You'll tell me when the time's ripe,' he said. 'It's talk of marriage does it. It's stirred up things for me as well. I thought I'd take you to the ancestral house in the woods, on the way to Foxwoods.'

'If it's in the woods,' she said, 'I'd better change my shoes.'

'But those are so pretty,' he said. 'The little boots with the laces. You were wearing them to the funeral. That was what I first saw of you. I was looking down at the grave, and my eye was caught by these little shoes. Not in the least sensible. In the face of death, I thought, someone's very much still in life. And I let my eyes travel upwards and there you were.'

271

'Double bows?' she asked, 'like today?' But how could he possibly remember a thing like that. Her father had said *And to be doubly sure, you can do a double bow, not a single one.* Be doubly sure. What had her father ever been doubly sure of? He had married a monster, from a family of monsters: a sister who knew how to trap a man and please a man, in unladylike ways in a ladylike time, when sex was in the dark and for procreation, and mouths never used except by whores: a brother who thought it was funny to seduce and debauch a child, first teach her the ways of whores, then make her pregnant and leave her to her fate. Her mother might look down from the heavens and grieve, but she doubted her father was by his wife's side. If you took another wife, that was that. He would have to peer up from Hell, along with Lois.

Which of her many partners, her many lovers, her nearest and dearest, would she find herself next to, met up again with after death, the way the spiritualists said? Were they all expected to get on? If you had more than one spouse, who qualified in the after-death stakes? If she went with Exon she'd be looking down, but it did not seem her natural place. If she went with William she'd be looking up. Hell was where the profligates, the sinners and the gamblers went. The fornicators and the loose-tongued. Him and her: that felt more like it. But perhaps they'd team her up with Sophia: she had earned Sophia, in return for Angel. Men came and went, family stayed.

On the way out with William, wearing flat shoes without laces, she asked, 'Why are you suddenly so interested in the Utrillo? Nurse Dawn was talking about it too. What's so remarkable about it?'
'Its value,' he said. 'It just isn't sensible having something worth three million dollars hanging there on a downstairs wall with no security. Word gets round about these things. You're on your own here. I worry for you.'
'As much as that?' she marvelled. 'I had no idea. Good for Buckley. At least he knew how to buy a painting. There's no problem. I have a call button by the bed. It's part of the Golden Bowl deal. And who round here can tell an original Utrillo from a print?

Except now possibly a retired art dealer in Narragansett Pier, who might well put the news about.'

She was back on form, here in the present, and it was good, and ongoing, and she loved him and would marry him. But she wouldn't tell him quite yet.

It wasn't until she was in bed that night that Felicity wondered how Nurse Dawn could possibly know the painting on the wall was an original. She'd told Joy once but Joy hadn't taken it in. Why did she always have the feeling that there were people around who were plotting against her? Age or truth, which bore in upon her more?
If you showed yourself to be paranoiac, like Dr Bronstein, you ended up in the West Wing. Just because you think there's a conspiracy against you, doesn't mean there isn't.

44

William took her not to Foxwoods, but to a house called Passchendale in the woods up by Hopkington, towards the Connecticut–Rhode Island State Line. They left Route 195 at Exit 3 and thereafter, sometimes uphill, sometimes down, followed a network of roads, tracks and lanes, deeper and deeper into woodland, narrowing with every corner they turned, every mile they travelled, until green rhododendrons, like the laurel thickets already showing new furled deep green buds for spring, brushed fingers up against the Saab windows, and then as suddenly gave way to more open hill and dale landscapes.

'I have to admit there's a shorter way,' he said. 'This is the scenic route. Too early for the blossom but at least you get the views. And we had to come here sooner or later. After Foxwoods, this is the other place that explains me.'

'Passchendale! What a peculiar name for a house,' she said, as lightly as she could. 'A battle in the First World War? A memorial to slaughter? Or perhaps it's just particularly muddy? In which case I'm glad I changed my shoes.'

He smiled at her. 'You've even heard of Passchendaele,' he said. 'You must be the only person left in all America who has and I'm the lucky guy who found you.'

'You're marrying me for my age,' she said. 'I was right to suspect it.'

There was hardly anyone about: they passed one group of walkers and one pack of crazy cyclists, and a single vehicle packed with screaming young people, far too early for the season's parties, William said, and that was all. Where the road ran for once a little straighter and wider, skirting the Green Falls pond, a deer sprang over a low stone wall to stand in front of the vehicle, stared at them briefly with brown eyes, and leapt away again into the woods. 'I always think that's lucky,' he said. 'See a deer and the dice roll right.'

'If it doesn't kill you first,' she said. She had cricked her neck as he slammed on the brakes. Who was it once told her their car had to be written off after a deer leapt straight over a hedge and landed on the bonnet? She couldn't remember. There was so much trivia she didn't remember: was heaven a place where you remembered everything, she wondered, or nothing? 'The thing about a deer is that it doesn't look before it leaps.'

'That's why they're lucky,' he said. She hoped they would get wherever it was soon: her knees were stiffening, she wanted to stretch them. William showed so few signs of decrepitude. She was older than he was: perhaps she ought to take the fact seriously. But really she could not. She put her hand on his knee as they drove. She'd had the nails manicured by the beauty therapist who came weekly to the Golden Bowl. Once so white, soft and delicate, now claws – but elegant claws. She had liked her hands through all their stages. She glowed in her own self-approval, and his, and forgot her knees.

The other side of pine and birch, ginkos and hickory, holly and young dogwood, where the forest held a rich undergrowth of huckleberry and pepperbush, the final narrowest track of all opened up into a grassed clearing, stone-walled, where stood a large tall shingle house, the wood panels stripped of colour where they were exposed, but holding the bleached remnants of green paint where each was protected by its fellow, so it seemed fashioned in a translucent, layered patchwork. Creepers crept over old windows. The place was beautiful but had seen better days. It even seemed to lean a little.

'If that house had knees,' said Felicity, 'they'd be very stiff.'

'It would need new ones,' said William. 'And I can't afford them. Ozymandius, king of kings, with hip and knee replacements. This summerhouse is all that's left of the family home: three centuries on and this is where the Johnsons from Massachusetts ended up. The poorer branch, that is. *Look on my works, ye Mighty, and despair.*'

'Shelley,' she said.

'You know everything,' he said. 'It's such a comfort.'

But he knew the names of all the trees, and could identify every one, and there was something erotic in that. Between them they brought together the interests and obsessions of two lifetimes, and she was older than he was, but still he knew more.

They circumnavigated the house. It was empty but only recently so. The birds had not yet finished the nuts in the feeder, which hung from the lower branches of the chestnut tree in the patch of level hillside to the back of the house, which looked over wooded valley and pond, and you could almost swear to the ocean itself. A brown thrasher, reddish brown above, brown streaks on white below, stood on the wooden edge on the feeder and sang a little until realizing it was overlooked, when it flew off. Its place was taken almost immediately by a mocking bird, a pattern of shiny greys, which set up the same song, completing the interrupted cadence, before flying off as well, leaving the feeder swinging. It seemed like an omen to Felicity, and a good one. A rebirth, a new chance, the finishing of what had begun. Hexagram Sixty Four in the *I Ching*. She could all but see the page before her.

> *Before completion. Success.*
> *But if the little fox, after nearly completing the crossing,*
> *Gets his tail in the water,*
> *There is nothing that would further.*

In other words, take care. You were not there yet. Things moved towards fruition but could still go wrong. Felicity had not yet told William about her weakness for the *I Ching*. She had the feeling he might object. It might seem to him to be her weakness, as gambling was his. The point where each could look at the other and decide *I have been deluded. This man, this woman, is not for me.* You could argue and argue that the *I Ching* came more out of Confucianism than superstition, that Carl Gustav Jung himself had written the Foreword and given it respectability, but it might be too like fortune-telling, altogether too vulgar, for William's peace of mind. And paradoxically, his own sense of the force called Luck being so strong, being almost religious in its intensity, the *I Ching* could seem too close a neighbour to his own beliefs for comfort. The most serious quarrels are between dogmas that are nearly identical, but not quite. He threw the dice, she threw the coins. It might be wiser not to mention it. Forsake the *I Ching* and go to church and thank God for her good fortune, and pray that he gave up gambling.

'This seems more than grand enough for a summerhouse,' she said, cautiously. 'If this is the poorer branch, what happened to the richer?'

They too had fallen on hard times, it seemed; peeled off at the turn of the century when the textile trade collapsed and gone to New York to be bankers, come back to build their great summer houses outside Providence, then lost everything in the great collapse of 1929. The houses themselves had been swept away by the hurricane of 1937. Only William's cousin Henry, who'd gone off to California in the forties to work on the new computer technology, could be said to be doing well and he had got to ninety without becoming Bill Gates.

'I guess the family just ran out of steam,' William said.

He had a key. They went inside. Nothing had been changed since the fifties. She recognized the crockery, the pans, the furniture of the mid-century. A wooden wireless stood on legs in a mahogany cabinet. A mass of small, high rooms, corridors with violet walls and faded rugs, half-stairs to unforeseen landings, everywhere paintings, on the walls or stacked up against them. Wood carvings: bronze castings; elegant, earthy, dark polished shapes, life-size, vaguely human, limbs and torsos folding in on one another. At the back of the house a vast studio with a good north light, two storeys high, once no doubt warm and dry, now cold and damp with a whiff of decay which she knew would soon spread to the rest of the house, if nobody did something soon. Everything tidy and organized: brushes still in turps which someone had replenished, a not quite finished painting on the easel as if the artist had stopped mid-stroke. A muted greenish grey landscape, in fitting with the quietness of everything around.

'My father's studio,' said William. 'He died seven years ago. My childhood home.'

A layer of dust covered everything; small nibbling creatures had made the place their own: spiders were happy here. 'When I can afford it,' he said, 'I get someone in to clean it up.'

Felicity remembered Rufus, Angel's husband: and the messy chaotic colours of his studio: the intensity and folly of his life. Artists were obsessional in different ways: but she'd never known one who in their bid for an elusive immortality wasn't parasitical on the vitality of their children. Artists taught the morality of aesthetics, not the politics of survival. William rolled dice: Sophia cut film. Neither were ever quite engaged in what went on around them; neither could quite fit into the energetic mainstream of life. At least the landlords had appeared after Rufus's death to claim their unpaid rent and take back the apartment and solved the problem of what to do with the paintings by burning as many as they could find, finishing the work Angel had begun. But what was to be done with these? Too good to throw away, hopeless in the art market: these days you can't create a reputation after death. They were part of the house.

'Why don't you live here?' she asked. 'It's so beautiful.'
'It's my father's place,' he said. 'I can't live in his shadow. I don't like solitude, and besides I don't own it any more. Now it belongs to Margaret. She doesn't even know I have a key.'
'Your stepdaughter owns it?'
'It's her revenge,' he said.

'Revenge for what?' asked Felicity, but he was disinclined to tell her. Wandered off explaining that the house had been built in 1919, a summerhouse, when his father came home from the war in Europe.
'But what was he doing there?' she asked.
'Refusing to fight the Hun,' said William. 'He was a Quaker, a conchy, an ambulance driver. For a year they made him pick bodies out of the mud at Passchendaele, one small town in Belgium. German bodies, Canadian bodies, British bodies: they took turns to be slaughtered. It was that or prison back home.'
'But that was our war,' said Felicity. 'A European war, European madness.'
The Great War, as it was called, the War to End All Wars, except

of course it didn't. The virus just lay low for a while, as it will, the body politic going into remission, before surfacing again. Bombs fly, blood flows, bodies are broken. War was a recurring madness, like Angel's manic depression. Nations were always building up to them or recovering from them. It was what nations did. She seemed to have seen so many. Ethiopia, the Spanish Civil War, World War II, Korea, Vietnam, the Cold War of Nuclear Terror, the Gulf War, Yugoslavia. Always the same excitement, the same terror by proxy, the same paroxysms of lies, exultant claims of glory. The virus changed its form of course, became more virulent. The casualties of war, once confined to the soldiery, were now ninety per cent civilian. With any luck she wouldn't see the next one.

'No it wasn't,' William said. 'It was America's war too. The Germans were inciting the Mexicans to invade. My father got drafted. He was furious. It interrupted his painting.' More furious still, William said, when he got home to find himself unpopular with one half of Rhode Island for having taken part in an unpopular war – isolationism resulted – and equally unpopular with the other half for being a coward and a conchy. He built the summerhouse, away from everyone, and called it Passchendale to remind himself of the folly of war. He grew still more furious when he married an Italian-American Catholic girl from Providence five years later, and no-one came to the wedding.

'A furious father,' said Felicity, 'probably isn't good.'

'He wasn't furious with me,' said William. 'Just the outside world. He refused to sell his paintings. There was no-one out there fit to appreciate them. My mother died when I was four: my twin brother too. I didn't often get to school. Do you know why I like Foxwoods?'

'The noise, the lights, the people,' she said. 'Forget the money. Better than silence and woods and the seasons, for orphans like us.'

'Now you know all about me.' It seemed to satisfy him.

'I most certainly don't,' she said. 'I may know why, but I still don't know what. You're so secretive.'

'You have your secrets too,' he said.

'Mine are just habitual: more important when I was young than now. Sex, and being a bad girl, and marrying for money, and

having a mad daughter. None of it's relevant to here and now.'
Here and now, with the strange green light coming in from the skylights, the only solid, continuing reality was that of the sculptures and paintings. William and she were the transients, fitful and unsubstantial by comparison. But she was welcome here: the mad old man didn't mind her at all. If he were alive he'd even let her buy a painting. Usually in places like this you felt driven out, a trespasser, unwelcome.

'I put all that together anyway,' William said.

'Take me to Foxwoods now,' she said. 'Get me to the slots, for God's sake. I can't stand the past. Just remember I don't have all the time in the world.'

But before they set off they made love on the bed in the room where William had been born. The bed was wire sprung and had lost its tautness with age and the mattress sagged in the middle: cobwebs hung from the ceiling and the quilt was soft and dusty. They both felt quite at home, with the bed, the place, and one another. He was anxious for her approval, she was happy to give it. Here in the woods there was no-one to judge. And sex for a woman, if she isn't crying rape, makes her go to the other extreme and feel trustful.

45

There are too many people in the world. You feel it at midday in the centre of Manhattan, when there's gridlock and the yellow cabs are hooting and howling, and those tall buildings bend over you from either side, threatening, like parents over an unwanted cradle. You feel it in London on a Saturday night in Soho, when the gay crowds are out en masse, making you feel clumsy and female and overburdened by bosom. These particular crowds know well enough there are too many people in the world: they have no intention of procreating. What would be the point of creating a further generation, since in their opinion the pinnacle of human wisdom has been reached? Since today's political correctness is the summit of moral aspiration, why bother about tomorrow?

Even the heterosexuals among us, myself, Guy, Lorna, there in New York that spring weekend, waiting for Charlie to turn up at the Wyndham and take us to Felicity, failed to see any real need to have children. Guy had a son, it is true, and argued in a desultory way about access, but I felt his heart wasn't in it.

First we went with Guy to FAO Schwartz. It was Saturday. I fell in love with a soft gold lion I thought Krassner might like (was I mad) and wanted to spend $200 on a thinking, talking robot in pink and green. But what was the point? The host of children I had thought to acquire through the Aardvark agency had failed to materialize: should I perhaps have one of my own? I trailed round after Guy and Lorna, feeling left out, as Guy rejected this marvellous and diverting toy on the ground of its ridiculous expense. He declared that he would spend no more than $10. If he showed himself lavish there would be no end to his little boy's demands, or indeed to the mother's, who would get it into her head that he earned more than he had declared to her lawyers. 'My ex-wife' had lately turned into 'the mother'. She was being asked to submit to tests before Guy would acknowledge paternity. He had begun to suspect he wasn't even the real father: the child looked so little like him, and on access days was difficult and sullen.

Come into my world, come into my world, droned the song from Mr Schwartz's revolving dome, over and over, mesmerically. It occurred to me that Felicity might have other secret children hidden away: it also occurred to me, for I was gaining in wisdom, that if she had decided to hide them away it might be the best thing to leave them hidden. *Come into my world and spend.* It didn't work with Guy. The place was crowded with the beautifully dressed of all ages. He was taking too long about not buying anything. Even Lorna was getting impatient with him, lamenting loudly the crude taste, the shock to the eye of everything on display. I thought it was all perfectly wonderful. But then I remembered how *Home Alone 2*, some of which was filmed in this store, was such a disappointment after *Home Alone* and I too began to feel tetchy. I overheard polite, persuasive mothers pretending not to be control freaks, saw weeping fathers on access leave, observed parents practising their false togetherness, heard the tantrums of their children and confirmed once again that motherhood was not for me. Let the world of the children's toy shop be lost to me for ever. Let Holly go to her Rodeo Drive equivalent, let Harry go too, with their odd misbegotten child, let him not surface in my mind all the time, wondering what he was doing *now, now, now* and who with. With whom. Four o'clock on a shopping afternoon in Fifth Avenue is nine o'clock at night in London, when compulsive courtship rituals are hotting up and the drive to sexual completion glitters in both male and female eye.

*   *   *

Guy was persuaded to buy a Ping-Pong set for $12.50. When he had finally done we went back to the Wyndham and there found Charlie and the Mercedes waiting. Jack had said we were welcome to use the car: though alas he had the builders in at Passmore, and Joy's guesthouse at Windspit was unavailable, so we would have to make our own arrangements as to where we were to stay during our visit to the Golden Bowl. But they would of course be delighted to see us.

In the few months since I had last seen him Charlie had turned into an American. His face seemed to have widened and flattened out: his glittering eyes to have become less wary. He no longer had the air of a mountain tribesman: he moved with a casual and athletic grace instead of the aggressive tautness of someone about to fire a Kalashnikov into the air for no particular reason, and which had so frightened and attracted Joy when she first encountered him. Charlie dwarfed Guy, it was apparent to both Lorna and me, and indeed to Guy, who disliked the look of him from the start. Guy, who normally seemed on a male enough scale, in Charlie's presence appeared puny, narrow-shouldered and unhealthy. Some men (Krassner among them) have the gift of doing this to other men. Charlie's teeth, once broken and blackened, now gleamed in a white, even, healthy row and spoke of health and vigour. Guy's by comparison were crowded, cramped, and yellow. He would not see fit to waste money on his teeth, and anyway had that European propensity to believe that because God burdened you with a flaw – such as a too large nose or a double chin – it was your moral duty to live out your life according to His Will rather than to your liking. That cosmetic dentistry, let alone plastic surgery, was somehow cheating. That you were dealt a hand at birth and it was your life task to make the most of it, not organize a re-deal.

I saw Lorna staring at Charlie, her mouth dropping open, as if taken by surprise. I saw that Lorna could actually be quite attractive: that she was younger than she dressed and felt. That when her face pinkened round the edges, as it was doing now, she actually looked rather sexy. That if she'd have her hair *done*, and not just sensibly dunked in a basin and washed, it would turn into

283

an asset rather than a celebration of dreariness. That if she'd wear clothes which didn't shroud her but actually suggested she had a body as well as a mind, she wouldn't have to put up with Guy. She could look outwards into the world and find a lover there. Forget being her mother's daughter, she was her grandmother's granddaughter as well.

'Hi, Charlie,' I said, as he tossed our cases into the trunk as if they weighed nothing. What all-American muscles. He had been working out.

'Hi, babe,' he said. 'Howya doing?'

'Just fine,' I said, 'just fine.' But I wasn't. I had loosed forces beyond my control.

'So am I,' he said, 'yes sirree I am!' He too would have seen *Father of the Bride* and looked in on a make-believe world in which people said *babe* and *howya* and *yes, sirree*, and contorted his life until it came true. We are all postmodernists now.

46

The drive to Rhode Island took three and a half hours. I sat next to Charlie. Lorna and Guy slept on and off in the back seat. They were jet-lagged and gave in to it. I knew how to fight against it and to put up with the way the world lurched into a muzzy cartoon and out again, without taking to sleep as a defence. Charlie's voice drifted in and out of my consciousness. He had lost the doffing subservience of the illegal alien, so suitable to the job of the chauffeur, and with it the reluctance to talk. He was a US citizen now. His mother and grandmother were on their way to it, he told me, as were two of his male cousins, but Amira and Esma, both his wives – he was a Muslim – were having problems. He would have to acknowledge one and deny the other, since under US law only one wife at a time was acceptable. Marriages over here had to be serial. But which one to choose? He did not wish to upset either. Amira had sons and Esma daughters so the latter perhaps needed him more. But unless he made a decision soon the women might find themselves and their children deported. Bosnia under the UN was not a place to which anyone would want to return. Sarajevo was still without light and heat much of the time. I suggested that he formally marry one under US law, and then quickly divorce her and so be free to marry the next one. We were only talking scraps of paper, as the German Ambassador reproached the British, when on Germany's invasion of Belgium in 1914 they insisted on taking a neutrality treaty seriously, and thus launched millions into mud and death, forget Princip the seventeen-year-old danger boy. *Over the Top* – a Harry Krassner film, 1995. I hadn't cut that one, but I saw it three times. And that was before I'd even met him.

Charlie told me that now the builders were in Jack Epstein spent so much time over at Windspit that he, Charlie, was going to suggest his own family moved into Passmore. They needed more space; they were sleeping three to a room in the guesthouse above the Windspit garage: there was nowhere to put the animal feed. Passmore's garage was full of used cars, which Jack, unable quite to retire, was hoping to sell. It was ridiculous. The builders were cheating Jack: his boys could do a better job of the woodwork. Summer was coming, of course, but the grazing was bad. The soil had to be tilled, and left, and fertilized, and tilled again. It would take a couple of years. No-one in the area knew how to look after land. Esma's sister Drusa was pregnant again: no not by Charlie, of course not, but by a US citizen, which might turn out to helpful in solving her immigrant status. Drusa had been working in an old persons' home in Mystic: one of the old men had put her in the family way. Charlie had thought she'd be safe enough, but no. American men of all ages turned out to be sex fiends, forever at addiction clinics.

I felt a chill up my spine. I asked Charlie to turn the heating up. He did. The chill didn't go away. I asked him what the name of the home was.

'The Rosemount,' he said. 'Not much of a place but a job's a job.' I didn't want to hear anything more, but he told me, once he'd negotiated the Mercedes through New Haven and on to Route 91. He'd been ferrying the old gentleman about, mostly to see my grandmother, but sometimes to the Foxwoods Casino, where Drusa had been working until her illegal status emerged and she was fired. Mr Johnson had obligingly put him in touch with Maria who ran the Rosemount, who'd found a place for Drusa. She got $8 an hour, which for an illegal wasn't bad.

'Are you trying to tell me that Miss Felicity's friend is the father?' I made myself ask. Best not to ask questions at all if the answer might not be to your liking. Which is of course why questions like, *Do you love me more than her?* or *Where were you last night?* are best avoided. Charlie glanced at me sideways and I caught a glimpse of the weathered mountain tribesman still there beneath the smooth American tan.

'For only a couple of thousand dollars,' he said, casually, avoiding the question, 'there are ways of getting Drusa citizenship which don't entail marriage. A shame to mess Miss Felicity about, when she's so happy. Quite the Miss Daisy, I thought, that first time I drove her to the funeral.'

Oh yes, *Miss Daisy*, the film held in common, the cultural resonance, the point of reference, all there in Charlie's head already, and no doubt in Amira's, and Esma's, and the mother and the two male cousins, and Drusa's new baby imbuing Hollywood by osmosis in the womb. And maybe the sheep and the goats and the cows on the grazing that needed improving would be acting like cartoon characters next. There'd be *Bambi*s abounding in Connecticut of course, but at least no *Dumbo*s because of the climate, and no *Babe*s either because of Islam. (Not a film which did well in the Middle East.) Foxwoods was peopled by the cast from *Pocahontas* and Charlie himself, ploughing up the land, was *Davy Crockett*.

'Mummy,' I'd said to Angel once, 'which is my back ear?'

> *Davy, Davy Crockett,*
> *King of the wild front ear.*

Or conversely *bloody tears flow*, as the *I Ching* put it and Guy had mimicked, as I suddenly realized, only this morning. *Enough to make your eyes weep blood*. Blackmail. Let 'em flow! Let 'em weep! Let 'em roll!

'In matters of paternity,' I said vaguely, 'truth is important. No-one should hide anything.' Charlie shrugged, as if it wasn't important. It had been a good try, and one he would have been ashamed to have neglected. We turned off at the Hartford Interchange.

Behind us Lorna woke with a little cry. Charlie looked over his shoulder and gave her a smile of glittering intimacy. If he found himself technically unmarried here, dual US/UK nationality might suit him. You can have more than one wife at a time if it's your religion and you're living in Britain. He could end up with three legitimate wives, I could see that. They'd all be living in

Twickenham, in Happiness, ploughing up the garden and a fishnet cast across the Thames. And the new Lorna might even take her mother Alison back to live at home: Amira and Drusa, from the sound of it, had better backs than Lorna. I needed a rest from the living nightmare which was worse than any I could encounter while asleep. I slept.

47

It was four in the afternoon before William and Felicity got to Foxwoods. The place had emptied out: colours seemed muted and the music quieter. Half the tables were closed. Such dealers as remained worked quietly, and made no jokes; strength was being conserved: the music was silenced. *Il faut reculer pour mieux sauter.* You could hear the determined slap, slap of cards. The revolving car on the pedestal was being changed for a newer, brighter model. The cocktail waitresses had time to lounge around: bosoms seemed to droop as if personal energy alone had ever kept them up. One girl, as Felicity watched, stooped to lay down her drinks tray on the floor and press a licked finger on a ladder in tights stretched over plump legs: an official in a blazer with brass buttons stopped to reproach her. Her upturned face seemed pale, tired, anxious and too young. *She's got a child back home*, thought Felicity; *she'll do anything not to lose this job. Once I was like that.* There were no bursts of laughter from the tables, no whoops or yells: and from the slots just an unexcited, murmuring rattle.

'It's the afternoon shift,' said William. 'The out-of-work crowd. It's serious business now. Eat or go hungry, and no credit for anyone. You've got to wait 'til ten o'clock before the big boys come in, for the fun and the laughter and the big winners.'

'And the big losers,' she said.

'Don't even think of it,' he said. 'Let alone mention it. I feel lucky today. Morphic resonance.'

'I didn't know that had anything to do with gambling,' she said.

She felt fidgety and cross: disappointed. 'I thought it was about cows knowing about cattle grids without being told.'

'Same thing. The way we all know everything, if we don't look at it direct. But my luck hasn't come in yet.' He seemed to be sniffing the air to get the feel of the wind. 'We'll wait a bit. We'll drink coffee.'

'Comes in like breast milk, does it?' she inquired. 'Just comes flooding in? You can feel it?'

'I like that you're tetchy,' he said. 'It means you're in tune. This place, when it's lying low, ticking over, the tide ebbing, waiting to come crashing back. Even affects the coffee machines. They get no strength into the cup. It'll be okay. Don't worry about it.'

A woman came up to him in the café and said, 'Can I just touch you?' and William smiled and nodded, and the woman, who had bleached hair and chipped purple nail polish touched his lapel and said, 'I really felt that. It jumped from me to you.' Then she added, apologetically, because Felicity was looking surprised, 'William's on a lucky streak. I watched him move from eight thousand down, to thirty up, just in a couple of hours.'

'Really?' asked Felicity, politely.

'Upped his league to purple and beyond. Way to go. I guess I just don't have the nerve.' She moved off and William said, 'Poor Kathleen. One of the natural born losers.'

'I wouldn't give my luck away like that,' said Felicity. She was feeling better. The tide goes out so far, then it has to come in again. Though William was right, the coffee was pale and thin.

'Sometimes you've got to take chances,' he said. 'You know you think like a gambler?'

'Always have been one, I guess,' she said. 'I just didn't know it.'

A Gamblers Anonymous poster on the wall behind them said *Winners Know When to Quit*. Felicity suggested that they move to the next table if he was waiting for his luck to come in. He said no, since the poster spoke of winners it had to be okay, so they stayed. Felicity said, 'While we wait for a following wind, tell me why your last wife divorced you. Was it gambling?'

'Of course,' he said. 'I didn't want to tell you 'til I was sure about you. Some people get peculiar about Casinos.'

'And the first two wives?'

'They both died. Luck of the draw. After that a guy feels like defying fate. The first one was cancer, the second just walked out into the road one day. She was a lot younger than I was. She was thinking of something else. She was on her way home from the doctor. He'd told her she was pregnant. If I'd gone with her it wouldn't have happened. But I was a teacher in those days. I was at work.'

'That's the terrible thing about employment,' she said. 'The way it interferes with real life.'

He was grateful for the lightness. He took her hand.

'I went for grief counselling,' he said. 'You know what I blame those people for? They never made me laugh. If someone had made me laugh I would have got better sooner. You make me laugh. You might even cure me of all this.' He nodded down towards the Casino. Another row of tables opened: an extra row of lights drew punters away from the quarter slots to the ten dollar.

'I might not want to,' she said. 'I might like it too.'

'Frankly, it's madness,' he said. 'Another world. But it gets familiar. You get to know the regulars. If people talk here they really talk: you're down to the basics. Other people's lives. Especially on the graveyard shift, that's just before dawn, when there's very little hope left. Last post for the drunks and the drugged and the desperate. I keep away from the tables then. You've got to be disciplined. No use thinking one last throw, one last deal, one more spin, and all will be well. You've got to set about these things with a bit of energy. You can get too tired to want to spend.'

He snapped his finger at a waitress with bright pink cheeks and a blonde plait of hair around her head and ordered a hamburger. It was out of mealtime, but Miss Felicity ordered one too. Back at the Golden Bowl there'd be salad and low-cholesterol quiche.

'We were talking about your wives,' she said. 'The last one, please.'

'I got to fifty on my own and then I married Meryl. I wasn't gambling then. I took her up to Passchendale: she loved it, her daughter Margaret didn't. Nothing to do. And I suppose I got bored and came back to this place and ran up a few debts. Nothing too bad.'

*   *   *

291

But then Meryl, egged on by Margaret, had joined a programme for the wives of gamblers, and they'd worked on her and soon she'd begin to get hysterical if he so much as left the house, let alone came back with the dawn, no matter how much he had in his pocket. She thought winning was somehow worse than losing. Finally Margaret had talked her mother into getting a divorce. The judge awarded Meryl and Margaret Passchendale. A bad day's play. And after that what was left of his family held the loss against him. Margaret had just let the place stand and rot, warts, sculptures, paintings and all.

'Funny thing,' he said, 'I've seen that Judge in here. You'd have thought he'd have known the pattern, that the debts were a temporary thing.' At the time Passchendale was all he had left, so Meryl got it, in Judge speak, before he could spend that too. Meryl had gone to live in California: Margaret owned the house now, but chose not to live in it, for all she cared it could just fall down. 'She told me as much at Tommy's funeral,' said William. 'She's a bitter wee soul.'

He'd gone into some other gear since the funeral, he told Felicity. His luck had turned. He had energy, and hope, and a sense of future. He found himself stopping while he was still ahead.

'Yes, but you're back the next day,' she observed.

'You're a hard woman,' he said. He shook tomato ketchup vigorously over the hamburger. The previous week, he boasted, he'd changed the pattern of play, paid attention, played crazy, and won big. Enough to pay off credit cards, the bank, and enough over to buy the car.

'How much?' she said.

'Three hundred thousand,' he said, almost shyly. 'You give me courage. I'd get shaky when the bets went up. At five hundred I'd be really scared, blinded. Money moves fast at that level. The night I won, I was up to ten times as much: five thousand. If you mean to win big you've got to spend big.'

'No wonder Kathleen wanted to touch you,' said Miss Felicity, primly. She was excited by the sum. Quarters in the slots were okay, but just a tickling of the surface of possibility. A way to keep your hand in, that was all. Otherwise forget it. The real life was when the orange chips, $1,000, were playing

292

fast: at the purple tables, minimum bet $500, while the lookers-over-shoulders crowded in, to watch the guys with the special chips, $1,000 plus, move in. This was when the tension of the place rose; the life beat quickened, the noise levels rose and fell with every drama, when the nerves stretched. Real man stuff. More, if you kept your nerve in a Casino a woman could be a man. When Dr Rosebloom's view of the universe came true: come on, you old whiskery thing, what are you, man, woman, mouse? This was what he'd been trying to say: why the shifting, mouthing glint behind the mirror glass. Time's short. Don't waste what's left.

'You should have bought back your father's house,' she said, 'not spread it about like that.'

'I thought about it,' he said, 'but some of those debts had got rather pressing. I cut up the cards when I paid them off: I had eight of them all up to their limit. I'm a strictly cash man from now on. I can't get into trouble. I got a hundred dollars to spend. If it goes, we leave. Why should I want trouble? I want you. You're not going to put up with this kind of shit, not if it gets serious.'

'Where are we going to live if we do get married?' she asked. 'We never got round to that. You wouldn't want to live in the Golden Bowl, and Nurse Dawn wouldn't like it. I don't think I'd want to live in the Rosemount. Not that I've ever been inside. You never asked me.'

'We can rent somewhere around here,' he said. 'You can get really nice places cheap. People are leaving all the time, without a forwarding address. Another problem while we're about it. There's a girl working at the Rosemount who's convinced I'm the father of her child.'

She was back again somewhere else, some other time. *We'd run off together but I've made this girl pregnant. I can't just abandon her.* Who was that? She couldn't remember the name, the face. Oh yes, Angel's father, that was it. He'd lulled her with folk songs.

> *Oh are you going to Strawberry Fair*
> *Where the days are merry and bright?*
> *Remember me to one who lives there,*
> *She was once a true love of mine.*

And then off they go to the other one, and you never see them again. For someone conceived in love, however one-sided, Angel had been very angry. Perhaps that was her, Felicity's, trouble. She'd spent so much of her life being brave she had forgotten to be angry. Angel had taken it all on herself.

'Felicity?' he was saying, this port in a storm, any port in a storm, this gambling man. 'Did you hear what I said?'

'I heard,' she said, drearily.

'Don't be like that, the girl's crazy,' he said, 'I haven't touched her. She just wants it to be true. I've been an okay guy to her. I got her the job in the first place. She's an illegal, but she still has to live. I once helped her peg out some sheets. She thinks I'm her father. Felicity, she's not my kind. She's young, she's pudgy, she's got bad teeth and she doesn't speak English. I like to talk to my women.'

She was almost convinced. At any rate she glimmered a smile at him.

'It's as I say,' said Felicity, 'no good deed goes unpunished.'

'She wanders round the place pointing at me, saying, *He father! He father!* I wish she wouldn't. It's the only English she seems to know. It's half a joke and half not. She seems to thinks it'll flatter me. But other people take it literally. It's getting awkward. Maria doesn't like it, Charlie neither. She's the sister of one of his wives. You know he has two? He says it's his religion. He threatened to beat me up last week. That's why I had to get my own car. That's why my luck turned. If you really need something, God provides.'

'You could have gone for a cheaper model. You could have bought that old house back for what you spent on that.'

'I had to have a decent vehicle, if I'm to take you out and about.'

'I'm not going to feel bad about it,' Miss Felicity said. 'If that's what you want.'

He looked hurt.

'How am I meant to win tonight,' he asked. 'If you keep putting a broom between my spokes?'

'If it's to do with Charlie it'll be a set-up,' she said. 'Quit worrying. Maybe she wants nationality, who's to say?'

'I hadn't thought of that,' he said. 'That begins to make more sense.'

'What worries me,' she said, 'if you're not going to use credit, what are you going to use for money tonight? Or is it going to be the quarter slots? What's the use of all this grand talk if that's where it ends up?'

'You've got to know when to quit,' he said. 'And you can do okay on the quarter slots: it's a kind of rest from risks. Build up slowly again.'

'I'd rather marry a rich man than a poor man,' she said. 'Forget it.'

She had Amex in her purse, and Visa. What were her spending limits? She had no idea. If you were a gambler of course you would. You wouldn't add stuff up, in case you found out what you didn't want to know, you wouldn't do too may sums in case the answers frightened you, but you'd know your credit limits. You'd have no sense in other words, you'd be the one after the conversion experience, lost to all doubt, proselytizing, giving up everything to the God of Luck. Yes, sorry, God. No Goddess, she. Not like the Muse, which governed the Arts, gracious, ladylike and dull. This was the God of Money; hard, glittering, erect. What you built up, compulsively you threw away. An expense of spirit in a waste of shame. Well, that might be true for the out-of-workers, for the blue-haired brigade, for the graveyard shift in the early morning, when only the desperate played on, when hope was at its lowest ebb. But it wasn't true for her. Already the buzz was rising: the new car down there on the plinth began to revolve, catching the extra light now shining on it, the music changing beat, the place was bright and noisy again, new crowds surging in, bent on pleasure not survival: the erotic undercurrent swirling again. The tide was full. Diamond tiepins, dangling earrings, natty suits and low-cut dresses, the cocktail waitresses on the run. William rose and stretched.

'Would they give me cash on my credit cards?' she asked.

'I swore I'd never ask you to do that,' he said.

'You didn't ask me,' she said, 'I offered.'

They went to the Main Cashier, a pink-faced young woman with orange curly hair rather like Joy's, but who seemed otherwise too young for such responsibility. Felicity put her MasterCard on the counter.

'Will you give her cash on this?' William asked,

'Not usually,' said the young woman, 'because she's a stranger.

But if she's friend of yours, Mr Johnson? You can vouch for her?'
'Oh she is,' he said. 'I can.'

'Make it ten thousand,' said Felicity. The cashier's eyebrows flew to her hairline, and she made sure Felicity saw that they did. She made Felicity identify herself on the phone to MasterCard's Customer Services, giving her date of birth and her mother's maiden name. They had Lois's name on record, that being the only one Felicity could remember. Or perhaps no-one had ever got round to telling her Sylvia's. Lois Wasserman. She repeated the name. Wasserman, surging up yet again from the past.

'You can run,' she said to William, puzzling him. 'But you can't hide.'

The transaction was allowed. The cashier carefully counted out the money in front of two witnesses.

'My lucky night too,' said Felicity to William. 'I know it. The wheel comes full circle. Fate takes away, but fate gives back. You've just got to hang around.'

She bought chips: four oranges, ten purple, the rest in black. She handed half to William.

'We're in competition,' she said. 'Bet you a thousand I do better than you.'

'Done,' he said, and went off laughing into the crowds. She had expected him maybe to show a little more gratitude, and linger a little longer, but he was a man and she was a woman, and the transaction between them was complex, and anyway the tables called. If you took up with a gambler, what did you expect? She changed her chips back into cash, bought ten rolls of quarters, paid the rest back into MasterCard, and went to the slots to enjoy herself.

48

Nurse Dawn took a trip to the West Wing to see how Dr Bronstein was settling in. The West Wing, unlike the Main House, which was redolent of fine wax polish and lavender, always smelt faintly of disinfectant and boiled vegetables: there was no disguising the fact that the rooms over here, though comfortable, pink and plump with furniture, were more like hospital cubicles than anything you would find in a hotel. Each room had piped oxygen on tap, plugs and leads for heart monitors, life-support systems and so on, leaving little room for bookshelves or mementos of the past. It was Dr Grepalli's belief that although intellectual and emotional stimulation helped prolong life and energy in those in the pre-West Wing stage, after a certain point of mental deterioration had been reached, the best thing you could do to lengthen life was to soothe, tranquillize and minimize all disturbance to the physical and mental equilibrium. If breathing became difficult the patient would find the air oxygen-enriched: if the heart fluttered or faltered, electrical impulses would take over: a steady diet of tranquillizers kept guests in a state of dozy bliss. Meals were regular, and lay as palely and as minimally spiced as could be contrived upon the plate; white fish, cauliflower and mashed potato the ideal: followed by perhaps apple dumplings. Recipes were taken from a cookery book, *Nursery Cooking for Healthy Minds and Bodies*, published in 1890, written by his great-grandfather, Dr Emilio Grepalli, and found by Joseph among his mother Helen's effects after her death. Just so, without spices, condiments or colours which might inflame and incite, had his own early diet been. The digestive system must be rested, given nothing to complain about, if nothing to rejoice about either. Breast milk being a case in point. And if this was true at the beginning of life how much more so at the end. Old age was indeed a second childhood: better to accept it than to fight it. Boredom, in fact, was what kept the very old going.

In the West Wing blood pressures were monitored twice daily: beta-blockers fed into tender veins in which the blood pulsed with too much determination. If cancers occurred – and they seldom did, inasmuch as Nurse Dawn had filtered out all those with a genetic propensity to the disease – they were usually slow growing (it is the young who are so suddenly, utterly and tragically consumed by cancer) and medical intervention unnecessary before natural death intervened.

Most guests in the West Wing were over ninety. Visitors were not encouraged: after a few visits in which their aged relatives made no response, but simply stared at them out of heavy, contented eyes, most stopped visiting and waited patiently for the years to pass, the Great Gates to creak open, and for the distribution of such wealth that remained after the Golden Bowl had subsumed what it would and what it must. People in their youth often claim they want quality of life, not quantity of life, but when it comes to it most want simply just to hang on in there, and medical science makes it possible. No-one these days can expect too much. It is not good for a society for the wealth of one generation to be handed down to the next. Is not this the point of our inheritance taxes? Occasionally the Golden Bowl was remembered in a will, but not often, and since it would have been drawn up in happier, pre-West Wing days, there could be no doubting the mental capacity of the one who made it. Who wanted trouble, or disagreeable questions, let alone litigation? Of all visitors, lawyers were the most discouraged in the West Wing.

Nurse Dawn was surprised to see Dr Bronstein out of his bed, sitting at his table, wearing not the appropriate dressing gown and slippers but an open-necked shirt and jeans and working on a laptop computer.

'Is that sensible, Dr Bronstein?' she asked. 'We wouldn't want you to tire your eyes.'

The old are not paper parcels, as she was fond of observing over in the main house, to be sent here and there without their consent, but once they are institutionalized it is not a good idea to encourage them in too much independence. You cannot legally lock them in or restrain their movements, but in their own best interests you can surely use psychological pressure. It looked to Nurse Dawn as if Dr Bronstein has detached his own drip and got out of bed. There was no law against it but it shouldn't happen.

'Those poor old eyes are already looking tired and sore,' she added. 'Remember the lace-makers of Bruges? How they all went blind from close work?'

'Rubbish,' he said. 'That was before electricity. For once in my life I have the time, the leisure, the peace, and still sufficient use of my senses to write my book on the moral duty of the scientist in the contemporary world.'

Nurse Dawn laughed merrily.

'Contemporary!' she cried. 'How long since you retired? Thirty years?'

'I've kept up with the reading,' said Dr Bronstein, but he was a little shaken. Had it really been as long as that? The active years are so vivid and full of event, they stay undimmed in the memory, and seem as much like only yesterday as do the college days of a woman who's spent the last thirty-five years a housewife.

'What a dear little laptop,' said Nurse Dawn, next. 'I haven't seen that before. I wonder where we got that?' Now that Dr Bronstein's great-great-grandson had power of attorney the doctor was no longer in a position to write his own cheques. But supposing such West Wing patients who could still read off the numbers from their credit cards took to shopping on the Web? It wouldn't do.

'Miss Felicity gave it to me,' said Dr Bronstein. 'She's been over to visit once or twice.'

'Oh has she,' said Nurse Dawn. Those in the Main House were not encouraged to visit the West Wing. It could be depressing.

'Well,' she said, 'I daresay Miss Felicity won't have to travel so far in future. She'll be joining you here in the West Wing soon enough.'

'Miss Felicity might not like it in here,' said Dr Bronstein. 'She doesn't have a book to write.'

'Miss Felicity may not have as much choice as she thinks,' said Nurse Dawn. 'Since considering her recent conduct no court in the world is going to believe she's capable of looking after her own affairs.'

She slammed the door as she went out, and told the Floor Nursing Officer to keep Dr Bronstein's lights low.

49

Dr Joseph Grepalli went down to the Atlantic Suite to have a word with Miss Felicity about the Utrillo. She should either have it moved to a bank vault, pay for its insurance herself, gift it away to a member of her family to avoid inheritance taxes, or simply sell the thing and put the money in the vault. She could not just simply leave it on her walls, pretend it was a print, and let the Golden Bowl be responsible for its safekeeping. That would be irresponsible.

He knocked on her door and was surprised to find there was no reply. It was unusual for guests not to be in their rooms during the Quiet Hour. He checked at the front desk and was told Miss Felicity had not showed up for Sona Harmony at eleven, and had neither eaten lunch in the Dining Hall or ordered Room Service.

'She might have slipped out by the side,' said the girl at the desk. 'She sometimes does.'

'You'd see the car,' said Dr Grepalli. 'Wouldn't you?'

'Not if Charlie parks round the side,' said the girl. She was new to the job, and spoke not very good English. She left her desk and stretched to close a window. She was pretty, thought Dr Grepalli: large soulful dark eyes in an agreeably sullen gypsyish face; tall and statuesque and quite commanding in her bearing, with long strong thighs and white high heels. He was surprised Nurse Dawn had hired her: female employees were for the most part on the slight, plain side. She told him her name was Amira.

301

She worked part time. She offered without being asked to show documents proving her right to work in the United States. He said that was not necessary and asked her where Miss Felicity was likely to be.

'At the Casino with her boyfriend,' said Amira.

Dr Grepalli felt like a child again, living in a world where everyone knew more than he did, where secrets were kept, and revelations made just when he was at his weakest. It was at the moment that you closed your eyes for sleep that family disharmony would erupt: when you were at home with measles that uncles crept out of bedrooms they had no business to be in, and all life shuddered and jolted into a different gear and your headache was worse than ever. Amira laid her hand on the doctor's arm. The pressure was quite urgent.

'He is also a very bad person,' said Amira. 'He has made my niece pregnant. You are a wise and good man. You are a doctor. Mr Director, I want you to tell this man to marry my sister. Or she will be sent home and then how will she live?'

Dr Grepalli changed his mind about suggesting that Amira came up to his office later so he could give her details about lessons in English available in the locality. Instead he told her he had no powers whatsoever to intervene in such personal matters, smiled thinly and discouragingly, and left.

He let himself into the Atlantic Suite; he found he did not need the key. The door had been left unlocked. He could see that this was evidence of yet more folly. Miss Felicity was childlike in her trust. He had been wrong to overrule Nurse Dawn. If Felicity was left to her own devices some scandal or other was bound to erupt. She was a loose cannon. The Golden Bowl lived by its reputation. He doubted that the receptionist could actually produce the documents she offered. But try and get her off the payroll and as a disgruntled employee she could do damage. She or the niece would call the local newspaper and complain. Then someone would recognize Miss Felicity going in to the Casino. What a gift to the local newspapers:

THE LOTHARIO OF FOXWOODS

**From Casino to Golden Bowl,
from twenty-three to eighty-three,
no woman is safe.**

Journalists would come nosing around. Who was to say but that some other staff might not be illegals? Institutions such as his own were always vulnerable to one kind of media attack or another.

What was the answer? Ask Felicity to leave? That was bad for business. Word got round. And who among the elderly wanted to sell up house and home, move into a residential institution only to be forwith asked to leave, for apparently insufficient reason? Because they were lucky enough to have a lover! When there was no law against gambling, only prejudice! No, the institution would be wide open to litigation, and if Miss Felicity was indeed in the hands of an unscrupulous villain a court case would be the perfectly likely consequence of upsetting her. So what was to be done? Have Miss Felicity declared incompetent to look after her own affairs? Moved to the West Wing? Kept sedated? It was tempting but it was even more dangerous. Dr Bronstein's transfer to the West Wing had been perhaps premature: if someone asked for a second opinion the competence of the visiting psychiatrist might be in question. Joseph personally was happy to accept Nurse Dawn's assessment of the situation: she took the wider view and was in a position to judge the mood and morale of the guests, which must at all costs be preserved. The few might have to go to the West Wing earlier, in order that the many could stay out longer. Occasionally the rights of an individual must take second place to the welfare of the group. Dr Bronstein's family, God knows, had been eager enough for the transfer, being the kind who liked to get in first to avoid trouble in the future. Some people just assumed that physical comfort was more important than emotional or intellectual enrichment, a view that found its apotheosis, alas, in the West Wing.

No, when it came to Miss Felicity, the answer could only be to take steps to break the relationship: Dr Grepalli was by virtue of his situation placed *in loco parentis*. The child might be twice his age, but with every year that passed he was increasingly a child in wisdom. Common sense, along with the body, peaked in performance, then slowly declined. What had to be done for the too young had to be done for the too old.

Dr Grepalli moved across the room to study the Utrillo. He noted wryly that knowing its value greatly increased his appreciation of its charm. The small French town dozed in sunlight. Not a human figure in sight, only masonry and a snatch of tree, which was a relief. Art had a capacity to make you feel bad: thank God there was nothing whatsoever inside this gold frame to disturb or affront. He supposed that to be the secret of its success, its value in world markets. His own father's posthumous Art of Madmen exhibition had not been a success. Only three of the grim canvases sold out of thirty, and those to relatives. Nevertheless he didn't think it would be a profound loss to society if this particular painting was kept in a bank vault and not on a wall. He caught sight of a small figure hunched in an armchair with high wings. It was Clara Craft, the Hindenburg person. He was glad to remember her name. He was not as cut off from his patients as Nurse Dawn claimed.

'Shouldn't you be in your room?' he asked, quite gently, because her eyes seemed so large and scared, and he could see the pulse in her skinny neck beating fast.
'Miss Felicity doesn't mind,' said Clara. 'When her boyfriend's not around. I used to visit Dr Rosebloom when this was his room; I like to be in here. But now he's dead and Dr Bronstein's in the West Wing there's nobody to talk to.'
'We can arrange for a therapist,' said Dr Grepalli. She shook her head.
'I might as well go off to the West Wing myself,' said Clara. 'I'd do myself in but I don't have the guts.' She began to talk about

the Hindenburg disaster but her voice slowed to a stop. She was gazing in to the door of the bathroom, which was ajar.

'There's someone in there,' she said.

Dr Grepalli went into the bathroom. No-one.

'Just a trick of the light,' he said. But he noticed that although he had asked for the mirror to be replaced, the original still hung there. He caught a glimpse of his reflection in the glass which didn't seem a particularly good resemblance to himself and looked hastily away. Nurse Dawn, saving money again! If you didn't spend you couldn't earn. Why was it so difficult for people to understand this? He felt angry with Nurse Dawn. The visiting psychiatrist was altogether too eager to do as she suggested. Was there some relationship there he did not know about, which might in the future be used against him? Some male Monica Lewinsky waiting there in the wings? He must ensure that in future Nurse Dawn did not sit in when patients were examined, prior to their transfer to the West Wing. A court might decide that her judgements were more personal than clinical. He might even have to discontinue his own relationship with her. He found himself reluctant, even afraid, to displease a subordinate member of his own staff, and that was ridiculous.

'It was the paint, not the helium,' Clara Craft was saying. 'They used explosive paint. On the R101 they impregnated the aluminium powder with cellulose nitrate – you might as well use gunpowder – so of course that went up: then the Graf Zeppelin went down in flames as well: they'd used cellulose acetate. On the Hindenburg they thought they had the problem licked and used cellulose acetate butyrate, less flammable but not conductive. They were wrong. Those poor people! Run, run, run, and still it wasn't enough. They died. It's time I joined them. What's been the point of everything in between?'

'Miss Craft,' said Dr Grepalli, 'what's the name of the President of the United States?'

'I knew yesterday but not today,' said Clara. 'Anyway what a boring question.' And she scuttled from the room, running as fast as her little stick legs would move, which wasn't very fast at all, as if pursued by a ball of flame: Dr Grepalli hoped she would not run straight into the arms of Nurse Dawn. It would be held against her.

50

I arrived at the Golden Bowl with Guy and Lorna at about five in the afternoon. The spring sun was low in the sky and the Roman pillars cast long elegant shadows over the lawn. In this sheltered spot the rhododendrons and laurel were just coming in to bloom, narrow splashes of pink against dark green, glossy foliage. The Golden Bowl was looking its best. Lorna was impressed.

'I must say,' she said, 'it's a whole lot better than where Mother is in Twickenham. Of course, Grandmother Felicity has more money. Those pillars are actually marble.' Guy said he thought they were made of some kind of compressed plastic aggregate. Lorna reminded him that this was America: no cheapskates here. The area was rich in metamorphic rocks. He replied, not to be outdone, that it was rich in Senators too. Although the smallest state in the US it sent two senators to Congress. Lorna said if they were Senators they probably went to the Senate. Charlie watched the pair of them from the car and by comparison he was 3-D colour wraparound digital Dolby Sound and they were European black-and-white, subtitled.

I could see the shape of a man standing in Felicity's open French windows, silhouetted by blowy curtains. Could this be the tricksy Mr William Johnson? But it soon became apparent that it was Dr Grepalli and there was no sign of Miss Felicity. It had simply not occurred to me that she might not be there. Eighty-three, one somehow assumed, was old enough to keep people more or less in one place. But no.

* * *

Dr Grepalli came forward to greet us with great affability. I intro-
duced Guy and Lorna as Felicity's grandchildren. I did not go into
more detail.

'It's too bad,' said Lorna. 'She knew we were coming. You'd
have thought she'd have waited in. Mother used to do things
like that. I was hurt at first but then it turned out to be Alzheimer's.'

'We don't use that word so much in this country any more,' said
Dr Grepalli. 'There being so many variations of the disorder.'

'Senile's senile,' said Guy, and Dr Grepalli smiled bravely, and
said he believed Felicity was out visiting a Casino with her friend,
but we were welcome to stay. He'd check us in with the front
desk. Room Service would bring us refreshments.

Guy looked astounded.

'A Casino? Gambling? A woman in her mid-eighties? And she's
allowed to? I don't think it would happen in Britain.' I squirmed.
Guy went over to the Utrillo and studied it, standing so close you
would think his breath might poison the surface.

Joseph Grepalli said mildly that he imagined human rights were
pretty much the same in both countries.

'People can and should be locked up for their own protection,'
said Guy, absently. He took a magnifying glass out of his pocket
and studied an inch or so of the painting yet more carefully.
'Especially old ladies who revert to adolescence and start keeping
bad company. I should know, it happened to my own mother.'

'You and my senior nurse would get on very well,' observed Dr
Grepalli.

'I must meet her,' said Guy. 'In any case my grandmother isn't
technically a US citizen. It seems she went through a marriage
ceremony with a GI back in the forties, but she was married
already. Only a couple of months previously, so she can hardly
claim to have forgotten. I imagine bigamy's bigamy, in this country
as well as ours, and all future marriages are invalidated. An interesting legal point.'

Dr Grepalli nodded politely, decided not to be involved, and left
the room.

'Oh, Guy,' squeaked Lorna, 'you promised you wouldn't say a
thing until I'd told Sophia.'

'Felicity is our mutual grandmother,' said Guy, 'and I'm sure I'm as entitled as Sophia is to find things out. Sophia doesn't own Aardvark. And God knows I paid Wendy enough.'

But Wendy was *mine*. I was the one who asked questions, fed out delicate strands of new knowledge as I saw fit, playing with fate like a fish on the end of a line. And here was Guy, who fished by simply throwing dynamite into the pond. How could Wendy have done this to me? Was there not some conflict of interest? But I supposed not, or none that she would see. We were all family: one grandchild was much like another. The worst I could say of Wendy was that she was disingenuous: but why should I expect anything else of her? If people slide and twine along the borders of legality, like a snake round a wrist, that's what they do. Why should there be an exception made for you just because you're *you*?

I'd asked Wendy to give me further details of my grandfather the folk singer, and provided her with the clues to trace him, but not the money to do it. I'd said wait until I got back from the States. I had given Guy and Lorna the same clues. It was information freely given and so could be freely used. And they had used it better than I had. I, in the creative arts, in the humanities, drew back instinctively if I thought I might find out something I didn't want to know. Guy and Lorna, professionally trained, he in law, she in academia, worried away at the facts however inconvenient the outcome.

'All Guy did was ask Aardvark to check the marriage registry around the time Felicity was pregnant,' said Lorna, rather too defensively. 'He wasn't to know they'd come up with bigamy.'

Guy rubbed the surface of the Utrillo gently with his fingertips.

'Well, well, well,' he said. 'Who'd have thought it. It's the real thing. White period. Worth about two million in the right auction house.'

'Dollars or pounds?' I asked.

'Pounds sterling,' he said, scathingly, 'or two and a half million Euros. And absolutely no security at all. We were able to walk straight in. I don't think our relative is strictly *compos mentis*.'

I didn't want Felicity to suddenly turn up and discover us like this, making free with her home, her things, uninvited. Okay for me, perhaps, but not for Guy and Lorna, though they would never understand why. I went to the French windows and called Charlie in.

Outside the sky was darkening: the rhododendrons glowed red against velvet. A moon was rising. It was all moving shadows out there. I felt quite frightened. Charlie had the interior light on, in the Mercedes. Presumably he was reading the law book he kept in the glove compartment. He never wasted a moment.

'Not bad for an alcoholic, I suppose,' said Guy, standing back from the painting and eyeing it up as if it were some kind of enemy. Such a gentle little painting, too. 'Though personally I could never see why anyone reckons them more than picture postcards. White period, fortunately. They fetch the most. Nineteen-eight to nineteen-fourteen. After the war started a bit more colour crept in. And no security here whatsoever. We walked straight in. She really should be locked up.'

I decided I simply loathed Guy, and always had. I'd dug him up from under rotting leaves. And I had led him here. What an innocent I was. I felt quite giddy and had to sit down and longed for Harry Krassner to be sitting beside me, looking out at the world with his quizzical overseeing eye. Once upon a time I had been like that, not now. I couldn't think of any film at all to relate to my current predicament, let alone solve it.

Charlie joined us and sat down on the end of Felicity's chaise longue, making himself at home, which was of course his great gift. Lorna moved up to make room for him. I can only describe her as dimpling at him. We really had to get out of here before Felicity came back.
'Guy knows such a lot about art!' said Lorna, admiringly. 'He deals in a small way, but the art market is so up and down, you can't rely upon it. I really can't understand how women can abandon their babies the way Felicity did poor Mother.'
'It was a long time ago,' I said. Where to begin? What was the point?

'So cruel and selfish!' said Lorna. 'Life's simply not fair, is it. When someone like Mother who gives up everything for others ends up in a dump like Twickenham and someone like Felicity ends up in this palace with major art works on the wall.'

I suggested to Charlie that since we had nowhere planned to stay the night, he should take Lorna and Guy into Mystic, or Wakefield, and find a hotel, leave the luggage and have a look at Narragansett Bay in the moonlight. I'd come over later by taxi when I'd seen Felicity. Charlie could get back home. They could visit the Golden Bowl tomorrow. Travelling is all logistics, and other people complicate them no end.

Why had I ever opened up the *Yellow Pages* and my eye lighted on the Aardvark agency? Why had I been so blind and frivolous as to find the name funny? Seedy is seedy and there's no getting away from it. From blighted seeds grow weedy plants.
And Guy wasn't having it. He wanted to be there when I talked to Felicity.
'Good idea,' he said. 'But you go with Charlie, Lorna. I'll wait for Felicity with Sophia. And I want a word with the front desk. Several, in fact.'

Thus it was that Lorna went off into the night with Charlie, and Guy vanished into the marble halls of the Golden Bowl.

Left alone, I used Felicity's phone and called through to the cutting room but there was no-one there. Of course not: I not being there to reproach them everyone would have gone home early. I called my apartment but there was no reply, and Harry had not switched on the answering machine. Faced by this blankness I panicked. I called through to Holly, in California. I'd stolen her number from Harry's address book and put it in mine, just in case, though in case of what I couldn't be sure. If you have people's numbers you own a little bit of them. He of course knew hers by heart. It had been his for long enough. Four years. I had never called her before. Her answering machine was switched on and the message went, in Harry's voice: *Hi, you've reached Harry Krassner and Holly Fern*. It meant nothing, of course. It probably just made Holly feel better to have Harry's voice on her tape, so she'd never wiped it off. But I was shaken. Of course I was. I lay down on my grandmother's bed and slept, and slept, and slept.

51

'Who's been sleeping in my bed?' said Felicity's voice, waking me up. For a moment I couldn't think where I was. The same voice had come to me over decades, with its lilt, its warmth, its determination to pass on energy. Waking from that dense, pleasurable, jet-lagged sleep I could have been any of the mes: the child I still felt I really was; or the adolescent with the pudgy face which hadn't yet found itself, its lineaments blurred by a mother's and a father's death; or the driven, ungracious young woman getting her degree in film studies, wearing a ring through her nose, and green nail varnish on her toes, thinking herself so proud and strong and *different*.

The best thing you can do with tragedy is turn it into difference, into narrative, and be proud of it. It's how Felicity dealt with it: so did I. She handed the art on to me, that familiar, chiding voice in my ears through all my years. *Take nothing seriously. It's all fairy tale. Who's been sleeping in my bed?* As if there was any choice: each family ends up in the same old bed no matter how it struggles. Like Felicity, like me. Sure she had once butted out when things really got tough: left me to find my swinging mother, but how was she to know that that would happen next? How was I any different? Joy had called me in London to say Felicity had suffered a stroke, she was in hospital, and what had I done? Thought up an excuse for not rushing to her side, and got on with my work. We can't all be strong all the time, I suppose, we can only take shifts at virtue. I forgave my grandmother there and then for her sins of omission and commission.

I launched myself across the room at her, thinking I was still the child with two living parents, and nearly knocked her off her feet. 'Where have you *been*, Miss Felicity?'

'At the Casino,' she said, recovering her balance, shaking off her shoes, massaging her feet. 'Thank God I changed my shoes. These are meant to be comfortable but still they're hell. What a day! We're both of us wiped out. It goes like that. But luck evens out, you know. Lose today, win tomorrow. It's all there in the *I Ching* and I must say life bears it out.' She was bright-eyed with adrenaline. William had dropped her off, she said, and gone home to the Rosemount. They were both exhausted.

Guy and Lorna. Where was Guy?

I confessed. I watched her face go grim with annoyance and then clear again. She looked at me with a fondness I did not deserve.

'For someone who thinks themselves so clever,' she said, 'you are remarkably stupid.' It didn't get any worse than that. I couldn't have borne it and she knew it.

'What you mean to tell me,' she said, 'is that Lois's grandchildren are after my Utrillo on the grounds that I'm not fit to look after it, and are prepared to go to law to have me put away, and William will be used as evidence against me.'

I said yes, more or less. She went to the phone and called William and told him to get over right away. She put her shoes on again as if she could see the necessity of sudden flight. I was relieved at that.

'People do get whisked off to the West Wing for less than this,' she said. 'I have seen it. *Weep tears of blood.* I wondered why the *I Ching* gave me that this morning. But we have time. The enemy is still gathering its forces. Thank the fates I came back when I did, that the Casino wiped us out so we came back early. *When the enemy is weak, attack.* Sun Sziu's *Art of War*.'

She then did an extraordinary thing. She took the quilt from her bed. She got me to help her take the Utrillo down from the wall. She was strong but her poor arms were quite thin and weak. The years take their toll on the body but not if you are lucky on the

313

mind. She wrapped the painting in the quilt. Together we carried it, in the moonlight, to the other side of the rhododendron bushes, where the gardeners had their shed. It had tools inside it, and deck chairs which would be brought out when the weather got warm. It was not locked. Gardeners, like Felicity, tend to have trusting natures, unless circumstances suggest otherwise. She leant the painting against the wall and put a folding table in front of it. Then we went back indoors, and got the pretty girl at the front desk who spoke so little English to bleep Nurse Dawn.

52

Nurse Dawn was showing Guy around the West Wing. The bright moon shone into darkened rooms, where the incontinent and the senile and the simply old drowsed their lives away; where there was no argument and none of the shrieks and howls that sometimes rent the air at the Glentyre back home in Twickenham. Guy said as much to Nurse Dawn. They were getting on famously.

'It seems a pity for Miss Felicity to be spending her own money on her keep,' said Guy. 'If she turns out to be a UK citizen the State back home will provide for her, and very comfortably, though not of course to this degree of comfort.'

'You are thinking of taking her home?' asked Nurse Dawn. She had not anticipated this.

'We'll see how things go,' said Guy. 'If she were in the Glentyre she could be back with her daughter again. Either way, she's certainly not up to handling her own affairs any more, we both know that. Bad enough having a batty old woman in charge of a major work of art, let alone her being in thrall to an unscrupulous gambler, twenty years younger than she is. I imagine the Golden Bowl could find itself sued if anything went wrong.'

'I don't think it can be as much as twenty,' said Nurse Dawn, playing for time. 'I'm quite an expert at ages: I'd say more like ten or eleven. What do you mean, go wrong?'

'If the painting was lost, or stolen, say: or if she was talked into parting with her money, and you had done nothing to prevent it.'

'I think the thing to do,' said Nurse Dawn, 'is for her to be declared incompetent by the visiting psychiatrist, and she can move into

315

the West Wing where we can keep an eye on her. After that the court will make no objection, I'm sure, to having you made her guardian. Sometimes the Golden Bowl takes on that role, but if relatives want the bother, so much the better.'

'I'd better take the Utrillo back to London for safekeeping,' said Guy. 'It's been in the family for a long time.'

'If you must,' said Nurse Dawn. 'We'd love to have it gracing our walls, but insurance costs over here are outrageous.'

They looked into a darkened room and there saw Dr Bronstein sleeping quietly.

'We're so proud of Dr Bronstein,' said Nurse Dawn. 'What a lovely old fellow! He once nearly won the Nobel Prize, you know. He and Miss Felicity are such good friends. She'll be happy to be near him.'

Guy looked at the tubes and leads attached to Dr Bronstein's body and could see that being near was about all that could happen. It seemed quite safe. What had to be avoided at all costs was marriage. Things might become complicated in the courts. Considering how temporary marriage was, these days, it always surprised him that the law took the act of trust so seriously.

The screensaver on the computer monitor on the table under the window flickered into colourful life. Birds fluttered across the screen. Nurse Dawn strode across and switched the thing off at the wall. 'No point in wasting electricity,' she said. 'Poor Dr Bronstein can't actually see it any more, let alone get out of bed. But we encourage our guests to have things they love around them.'

The room was suddenly bathed in light. Dr Bronstein's eyes jerked open.

'Joseph!' exclaimed Nurse Dawn. Dr Grepalli had been sitting in the dark unnoticed, at the far side of Dr Bronstein's bed. It was he who had turned on the light. 'What are you doing there? Praying?'

'That might not be such a bad idea,' said Dr Grepalli. 'I just popped in to have a chat with Dr Bronstein, but he does seem to have gone downhill rather fast. I looked at his medication chart, Nurse Dawn, and the stuff he's getting is remarkably strong.'

'I am the qualified person round here,' said Nurse Dawn, 'and I don't recommend you go round stirring up too many hornets' nests, Dr Grepalli. I don't know if the Board realizes you're a doctor of literature not of medicine, and perhaps it's time they were informed, and of a few other things that go on round here. Sexual harassment's only just a start.' She felt aggrieved. He had abused her and bullied her into bed, using his position of authority as a weapon. But she could see it might not be too easy to prove, the law always siding as it did with the powerful, and softened her position a little. 'We have too few trained staff here to meet State requirements; good hearts alone don't qualify. The fact of the matter is they could come in and close us down any time. Of course we'd fight it, but a lot of relatives might withdraw their loved ones in the meantime. We don't want Dr Bronstein agitated and distressed: I see to it that he isn't. Why do you think the West Wing is so peaceful? Well, you're the one in charge round here. You're not meant to think, you're meant to know. Now I suggest you leave Dr Bronstein to me.'

At the time of his divorce, Guy had once visited a dominatrix. He had heard that voice before. Dr Grepalli seemed to quail under it. At any rate he rose and left, though not quite willingly, as a person emerging from a hypnosis might still accomplish the entertainer's tricks. Guy stayed where he was and watched Nurse Dawn's little high red heels grind into the soft pink pile of the carpet as she prepared a new injection for the old man. Guy liked her more and more. Why couldn't Lorna be more like this?

Dr Bronstein's eyes were shut again – 'There, out of his misery once more,' said Nurse Dawn – and she and Guy made their way back to the main building, where Nurse Dawn left an urgent message for the Visiting Psychiatrist to call, that evening if possible. Amira, at the desk, was putting on her coat and preparing to leave.
'You can't leave now,' said Nurse Dawn. 'You have another hour to go before your shift it is over.'
'I go,' said Amira. 'Charlie wait. Charlie my husband.' And sure enough Charlie was waiting, big and bright and filling up more space than seemed possible, in the doorway.
'Amira's coming with me,' said Charlie. 'It isn't safe for her to walk home alone.'

'If Amira goes now,' said Nurse Dawn, 'that's the last pay cheque she'll get from me.'

'I wouldn't advise that,' said Charlie. 'Someone might find out you'd been employing illegals.' And Amira, happy and smiling, went with Charlie.

'Always best to stick to the letter of the law,' said Guy, sympathetically. 'But if Charlie's here, Lorna's back. Let's go and visit Miss Felicity, before my dear cousin Sophia stirs her up. Sophia is a sweet girl but very naïve and the naïve can be dangerous.'

What did they find? They found Miss Felicity flown, Sophia gone, a blank space on the wall where the Utrillo had been. The painting had not been up on the wall for long enough to mark the wallpaper: that is, to leave a square behind around which colour had faded and dust had gathered. Lorna sat disconsolately alone.

'Where has everyone gone?' she asked, querulously. 'As I came in Felicity and Sophia were leaving. All this way and I never even got a chance to meet my own grandmother. She just brushed past me.'

'Were they carrying a painting?' asked Guy.

'No,' said Lorna. 'Not that I could see. All she had with her was a purse.'

'Then there's no evidence they have it,' said Guy. 'Only supposition.'

'There was a bright red Saab coupé waiting for them,' Lorna went on. Excitement had made her garrulous. 'My boyfriend the crystallographer had one of those. I thought he was overcompensating for his dullness, you know what men are – long car, small dick – but perhaps he wasn't. Perhaps I misjudged him. That chauffeur is completely insane. He parked on the waterfront in the moonlight, made a pass at me, and then asked me to marry him and when I said of course I wouldn't he just reversed the Mercedes and took me straight back here and dumped me and the luggage. He must have thought I was desperate. Now what do we do?'

'What sort of pass?' asked Guy, red to his gills with mounting fury.

'It's nothing to do with you, Guy, nothing,' said Lorna. 'You're my brother, for God's sake. You don't own me.'

'Your brother should learn to control his temper,' said Nurse Dawn, 'or one day he'll pop.'

'Better to let it out than keep it in,' said Guy, losing interest in her, 'but you Americans will never learn that.'

Nurse Dawn put her head in her hands and sighed. One side of a border always chose to think ill of the people on the other, no matter who drew the line in the sand, it could be a square line that marked off a politician's map, like Rhode Island from the rest, or something more sensible like the path of a river or a mountain range. A whole ocean divided herself and this man, for whom she had felt the stirrings of interest. But no more. He could be a turkey cock as much as a man, a mere victim to his own testosterone. She marvelled at her own wisdom, and at how misunderstood she was. You worked so hard to get where you were: there was no appreciation and no gratitude. She had done her best for the Golden Bowl and its old folk. She had believed in Dr Grepalli for a time, and discounted his sexual proclivities. You had to do that with men, or where would you find anyone to admire? But like all the rest, he was hopelessly sentimental, a mixture of greed and the need to like himself. To con the old people he had first to con himself: that was the worst of it. Of course you had to keep the West Wingers drugged out of their minds or they'd swarm all over the place like incontinent flies. She was not going to stay on the coast. The weather was too fitful; too changeable; you never knew where you were. God lived over the plains, you felt His presence there, shimmery and dangerous in the hot air. Sometimes these days she felt He didn't hear her prayers: she was on the margins of His presence: if she wasn't careful she would wake one morning without His restraining hand and start increasing a dose here, a dose there, forget the Longevity Index: she would find herself doing Nature's work, not God's. She'd lost one job like that already. Dangerous to push deaths up beyond the statistical margins, though almost impossible to prove what had gone on in any but the most recent cases. Bodies were either already cremated or who wanted all that wretched business of disinterment? But she would not risk it, she would go back home where there was less money, and life was richer but shorter, and the old were grateful and left you money in their wills, and God was there to listen, and His wrath appeared in twister form, grey and writing over a flat landscape, and you could see it coming a mile off. She loved that. She would write a letter to the Board just before she went, concerning Dr Grepalli's maladministration of the Golden Bowl and the fudging of the Longevity Index.

53

'I want nothing,' said Felicity. 'I want to start again. I have my chequebook, my credit cards, my mobile and the clothes I stand up in. That should be enough for any woman leaving home. I have my Utrillo and its certificate of provenance. I don't need photographs, I don't need mementos, I don't want to live my life in the past, I want to live it *now*.'

'Way to go!' said William Johnson.

I am quite tall and the back seat of a coupé is not the most comfortable place to be, but the excitement of the flight made me forget my cramped circumstances. The painting was in the trunk, still wrapped in its Golden Bowl quilt. I hoped the Golden Bowl did not persecute her for theft of the latter. They would be capable of it. They would be hurt and angry at her flight. Institutions always punish people who run away, and beat them when they are returned, in order to make them like it better. Whack, whack, that'll teach you not to love us.

'So what do we do?' said William Johnson. 'I have to warn you no cheque of mine will be honoured and my credit cards are up to the limit. You could join me at the Rosemount, into whose account the proceeds of a life policy are paid directly, and which I can't touch. But I fully expect to be in a better position by the end of the week.'

'Of course you do, William,' said my grandmother Felicity, fondly. 'We can't get married this moment because the chapels are closed, and it always seems so unkind to wake up Judges to do it.' *I was familiar enough with that scenario, of course. Doris Day and Rock*

Hudson (or was it Gary Cooper?) back in the fifties, knocking up the Justice of the Peace in the early hours, marrying on impulse, repenting at leisure, but it all ends happily.

'First thing in the morning will do, and then if anyone is to be my executor and guardian it will be you, William.'

'Grandmother –' I started, but gave up.

'So what we'll do now is go and see your friend the art expert.' We drove to Narragansett Pier, where William's contact lived in a small wooden beach house. Charming it might be, but I hoped that major works of art would be safe inside: the elements had stripped the house of paint and there was seaweed on the front path. I stayed in the car while they took the painting inside. I called Harry Krassner on Felicity's mobile. I found him at home watching TV. It wasn't my phone, I told him. I was being brief. The contact was bad and getting worse. I told him relations between Guy and Lorna and me had broken down and I was coming back as soon as I could. Yes, I would have to pay extra but what did I care. Fancy him not out at the pub or the club or the sound studio but at home. *'We're actually watching TV,'* he said. *'Not even a video. Holly just loves your BBC.'* He said in response to some noise of mine, *'Yes, Holly's here with me, she's staying the night, I'll put her on.'* I went into that strange, dull emergency mode that wreaks havoc with your nerves later. Holly's strident yet seductive voice crackled over the Atlantic towards me. The signal was getting worse. 'Harry's told me so much about you,' she said. *Oh yes?* 'He said it was okay if I stayed the night. I'm like him, brother and sister, I just so hate hotels.' The voice came and went and I could hardly hear. Felicity and William were coming out of the house holding hands and without the Utrillo. I interpreted Holly as saying actually there were two of them staying, she was passing through London with her new Swedish girlfriend; there was a lesbian adoption programme in Stockholm for which she qualified. And lots of spare babies after Kosovo. Then the voice cut out altogether.

I asked Felicity what she had done with the painting.

'Sold it,' she said. 'To the man with a mighty chequebook. But he's not putting it into my bank 'til after we're married in case anyone tries freezing my account.'

'He's honest,' said William. 'He's a cousin.'

I said I didn't regard that as any kind of qualification. I asked William to drive around until I got a better signal. He did so. He seemed an obliging sort of person: the kind who might irritate a woman but not make her unhappy. Not the kind my family usually went for. I felt I ought to inquire about the rumour of him making the girl at the Rosemount pregnant – old he might be but he was an attractive man with a flash car: it was not beyond the bounds of possibility – and did. Boom or bust time.

It was Felicity who answered, not William.

'Darling,' she said, 'it's all in her imagination, and anyway it would have been before William met me. Don't worry about a thing.' We drove south down Ocean Drive and found a decent signal just before we got to the Towers, a great stone arch which spanned the road – all that was left, William told me, of a spectacular Casino which burnt to the ground in 1900. We stopped the car and I called through to Harry again. 'She's just left for the cinema with her friend,' he said. 'They hold hands all the time. There's a lesbian season on at the BFI. I thought you ought to speak to her. You can get paranoiac. I'm just the same, we've seen too many films, we know what can happen next: it's not a criticism.'

'People are bisexual,' I said.

'Not Holly,' he said. 'She never does things by halves. I reckon we've got a year of lesbian chic.'

It wasn't too bad. A year. One can't expect fate to deliver perfect packages. William drove us down to Galilee and Point Judith, where we left the car and went down the rocky path to the lighthouse and the wind whipped round our ears and the moon raced in and out of dark and yet darker clouds. William took Felicity's arm. I thought he truly loved her. I thought it would be one up to me if I had a baby before Holly did and then dismissed the thought as beneath me.

We went to call on Joy and Jack though at first William was against it. 'Why give yourself hassle when you don't have to?' But Felicity said Joy was her friend and had been good to her, Felicity, in hard times, and only occasionally bad. You couldn't expect more from people. Jack acquiesced.

*   *   *

323

We drove to Passmore and found the approach road blocked by a stock fence. In the security lights we could see activity outside: Charlie and his family were moving out of Windspit's guesthouse and into Passmore. The boys could help the builders. We went on to Windspit without investigating further. Joy and Jack between them must have owned sixteen rooms and eight bathrooms. It was more than enough for two people. Wealth is reckoned in some surveys by the number of taps in a household, and between them Passmore and Windspit would have a hundred, if you reckoned bathrooms, kitchens, utility rooms and the yard water supplies. Felicity had started out with a single tap. She said she could go back to that if she had to. William remarked that there were only two at Passchendale. He told me about the house. I said it sounded really nice, why didn't he and Felicity go and live there. They could more than afford it. Then I wondered if I had said the right thing. If you interfere with other people's lives they are your responsibility for ever. That is the wisdom of Buddhism. Felicity said she'd consult the *I Ching*. I said she'd left it behind at the Golden Bowl. She said she'd buy another.

We looked in the undraped window of Windspit and saw Joy and Jack sitting companionably together on the sofa. Felicity changed her mind. She left them undisturbed. Now she's got him, she doesn't need me, she said. The less she needs me, the more free I am.

I said she wasn't to bother about me. I didn't need her, I loved her. She can be very English and me saying this embarrassed her but I think she was pleased.

We drove to Passchendale. There were no lights. No electricity. Still only the fitful moon. I lay down on a sofa which I found in the dark, directed by William. My hands passed over strange smooth curved wooden surfaces as I felt my way. *Now go in between Eros and Civilization*, he said, *after that leave Motherhood to the right and The Fathers to the left*. Nonsense. Art works. Sculptures. I was grateful to be guided. I stretched out on the sofa. I heard them giggling and shuffling on the stairs like teenagers. I slept.

It rained in the night and in the morning the hillside was unbearably beautiful, and the house numinous. There was a butane stove with something left in it, and some old, old pitiful coffee which we drank. There were biscuits. We were all hungry. Felicity said she had taken my advice. William was going to buy the house back from Margaret. They were going to live here to the end of their days. She reckoned they had ten years left: they would just about outlast the house. They would all three fall to bits together. Felicity, William and Passchendale. I said surely she could afford to get the builders in, do it up, make the place strong and sound again. But they didn't want to do that. They liked its dereliction. It made them feel at home. If she divided the money from the Utrillo and what she already had into ten, that gave them $400,000 a year to see them out. This was the amount William lost annually, if you averaged out the winning and the losing years. They would spend their days gambling at Foxwoods; and if they lost there would be no sorrow, because they expected to, and if they won they could rejoice. They would aim to lose, and not win, and so could only be victorious. It was an entirely new strategy.

'But Felicity,' I started, and gave up. Why? I didn't want to inherit. I had my own future, forget the past. There would be nothing for Guy to quarrel over.

We drove into Boston: Felicity had to buy some clothes to get married in and a copy of the *I Ching*. William needed the where-withal to get Passchendale going. He said if he saw Jack about trading in the Saab for something more practical, one of the new station wagons, perhaps, Jack and Joy might decide to forgive him for existing.

I did not stay to watch the wedding ceremony. I took the first flight back to London, Business Class, full fare, happy to travel on my own. Harry actually came to Heathrow to meet me. I don't know why I was surprised, or even why I say *actually*. A kind of neurotic affectation, I think, rather than a real emotion, which I might learn to do without to everyone's advantage. I saw that I had extra decades to go, more than I thought. Life elongated before me. I saw it in my head as a kind of special effect, or SE (as the screenplay computer programs have it): paleish green and glowing and stretching into the distance, only slightly uphill: a path. Really there was no hurry to get everything right.

WICKED WOMEN

FAY WELDON

Brilliant stories from the hyper-real world of Weldonia, where self-deception rules; where a bully can believe he's a victim; a blackmailer see herself as a healer; and an artist's slave be sure she's free.

Travel in space and time: meet Miss Jacobs, the silent psychoanalyst, who receives the confessions of saints and sinners; discover the heart of a nuclear scientist, forcibly retired, who does his hopeless best to resist the wiles of a self-seeking, stalking, beautiful New Age journalist – in fact all human life is here, and still in amazingly good heart, considering.

'Weldon's stories pull no punches. There is always humour, and (good for fortysomethings to hear) the wry and life-hardened smiles of middle age are often set in contrast to the po-faced enthusiasms and idiocies of youth.'

Independent on Sunday

'Sparkling, sharply observing, insights delivered with a light touch that puts us in a good mood, however dark the comedy.'

Spectator

'Pure Weldonian. Brimming with mischief, heavy with hidden meaning and defiantly modern, they are a parable for our times and times to come.'

Irish Independent

'Weldon's writing is seductively readable.'

Times Literary Supplement

ISBN: 0 00 655018 5

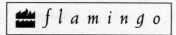

GROWING RICH

FAY WELDON

Bernard Bellamy has done a deal. He's sold out to the Devil, in all his forms. In return, he is promised that all his wishes will be granted, all his desires fulfilled. One of them, young Carmen Wedmore, is proving to be quite a challenge. Carmen lives in the new town of Fenedge, East Anglia, near her former schoolfriends Laura and Annie. The three girls dream of the day they'll escape their dullsville existence. Laura and Annie succeed, but Carmen stays in Fenedge under the powerful clasp of Sir Bernard and Driver, the Devil's agent. Disguised as a suave chauffeur, Driver cruises in his plush, sinister limo, stalking her every move. But Carmen becomes ever more determined to ride out the temptation laid in her path and not to sell her soul. Will she eventually succumb? Or will the Devil, for once, not have everything his own way.

'Glorious entertainment for the Nineties.'

Woman's Journal

'Catches its reader up in a gale of good spirits and devilment that keeps on blowing from beginning to end.'

Observer

'You can only marvel at her audacity, as in cat-burglar style she systematically plunders the treasures of myth and legend. Thoroughly entertaining.'

Scotsman

'A complex, ambitious and heretical book. *Growing Rich* is fecund, capricious, surprising and odd.'

New Statesman & Society

ISBN: 0 00 654495 9

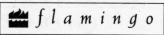

THE CLONING OF JOANNA MAY

FAY WELDON

Joanna May thought herself unique, indivisible – until one day, to her hideous shock, she discovered herself to be five: though childless she was a mother; though an only child she was surrounded by sisters young enough to be her daughters – Jane, Julie, Gina and Alice, the clones of Joanna May. How will they withstand the shock of first meeting? And what of the avenging Carl, Joanna's former husband and the clones' creator: will he take revenge for his wife's infidelity and destroy her sisters one by one?

'Chemistry, not biochemistry, is what Fay Weldon's style brings to mind: sodium fizzing its way across a watertank in the school laboratory – with occasional periods of smooth cruising before it crackles into energy again.'

New Statesman & Society

'Another totally original novel by the best woman writer in Britain. Sharp, funny, very modern.'

Woman

'Domestic and global concerns jostle along together: the manner is brisk, the plot wild, the content visionary. There is so much energy in this large, moral, angry book that it feels at times actively dangerous.'

Daily Telegraph

'Her fertility of invention transforms the incredible into the irresistible.'

Mail on Sunday

ISBN: 0 00 654593 9

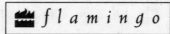

DARCY'S UTOPIA

FAY WELDON

Scandalous Eleanor Darcy, wild young wife of a world-famous economist, sketches her vision of Utopia to two journalists, Hugo Vansitart and Valerie Jones. In glorious detail, she describes an earthly paradise of peace, love and technological progress where sex is plentiful and money does not exist. Such is Eleanor's charisma that, to their own astonishment, Hugo and Valerie abandon their families and set up home together in a Holiday Inn.

'Weird, wild and wonderful reading.'

Best

'Fay Weldon provokes you to think. You'd expect no less of the social and sexual soothsayer of our literary times.'

Company

'Weaves a provocative view of modern society into a tale of explosive love and, perhaps, even, black magic. This is a dazzling tour de force from one of Britain's most inspiring and intelligent novelists today.'

Cosmopolitan

'A crash course in philosophy, religion, politics and idealism, with sexual passion, love and the nature of betrayal thrown in.'

Woman's Journal

'*Darcy's Utopia* is among the most frolicsome of her novels, but it still manages to display her quiet, grave insistence that we change our ways.'

Sunday Times

ISBN: 0 00 654592 0

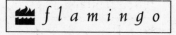

AFFLICTION

FAY WELDON

Annette and Spicer make a perfect pair: he thirty-nine, wide-shouldered, square-jawed, and often likened to Harrison Ford; she slight, fair, delicately featured, and sometimes likened to Meryl Streep. He with a son (Jason, eleven) from a previous marriage, she with a daughter (Susan, thirteen) from a ditto. He and she, after ten years, expecting their own baby. But on this, the first day of the rest of their blissful lives, Spicer fails to kiss Annette goodbye as he leaves for the office.

'Weldon writes as if she were Virginia Woolf and Roseanne Arnold joined at the hip. She is literary, well-read, totally in control, sharp as a needle and off the wall.'

Mirabella

'It has crackling dialogue, tremendous pace and a monstrous husband called Spicer.'

Daily Telegraph

'Her most passionate book.'

Guardian

'This ferocious novel moves at a pace you would hardly believe.'

Observer

'Weldon scythes her way like a flymo.'

Times Educational Supplement

ISBN: 0 00 654683 8

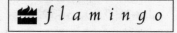